WHITE BLOOD

By the same author

The Temple of Optimism
Thomas Gage

WHITE BLOOD

James Fleming

JONATHAN CAPE
LONDON

Published by Jonathan Cape 2006

2 4 6 8 10 9 7 5 3 1

Copyright © James Fleming 2006

James Fleming has asserted his right under the Copyright, Designs
and Patents Act 1988 to be identified as the author of this work

First published in Great Britain in 2006 by
Jonathan Cape
Random House, 20 Vauxhall Bridge Road,
London SW1V 2SA

Random House Australia (Pty) Limited
20 Alfred Street, Milsons Point, Sydney,
New South Wales 2061, Australia

Random House New Zealand Limited
18 Poland Road, Glenfield,
Auckland 10, New Zealand

Random House (Pty) Limited
Isle of Houghton, Corner of Boundary Road & Carse O'Gowrie,
Houghton 2198, South Africa

The Random House Group Limited Reg. No. 954009
www.randomhouse.co.uk

A CIP catalogue record for this book
is available from the British Library

ISBN 0224077996
ISBN 9780224077996 (from January 2007)

Papers used by Random House are natural,
recyclable products made from wood grown in sustainable forests.
The manufacturing processes conform to the environmental
regulations of the country of origin

Typeset by Palimpsest Book Production Limited, Polmont, Stirlingshire
Printed and bound in Great Britain by Clays Ltd, St Ives plc

One

MY FATHER, George Doig, died of the plague. That was in 1903, when I was fourteen and he in the flower of his age. For many years he'd been the manager of their Moscow office for Hodge & Co., the big cotton-brokers. During this period he made himself attractive to Irina Rykov, and married her. She was the granddaughter of the Rykov who raised the loan that kept the Tsar's army going in 1812. In this way I was a direct descendant of the man who saved Russia from Napoleon.

Until recently, these were the principal facts in my life over which I've had no control. I must add a physical description of myself.

I can't remember having been small. Nanny Agafya sometimes sought to dominate me by saying that Mother had spat me out. 'Five heaves and there you were, all slimy and bawling, no bigger than a gherkin.' This has never been the sense I've had of my person. Some initial helplessness, suckling, infancy, these I concede, remarking that they belong to the period of the womb, which had nothing to do with me. It is from the age of my first complete memory, four years and two months, that I date myself.

It was the day that we moved into the fifth, the top, floor of an apartment building off the fashionable end of the Tverskaya. Moscow was entering its most capitalist phase. Accommodation was difficult to find, everything being half finished. It was a measure of Potter Hodge's satisfaction with my father that the firm was prepared to pay the premium on the Tverskaya.

To keep me quiet while the men were setting out our furniture, I was bribed with the gift of a troop of the 1st Sumsky

Hussar Regiment in a polished chestnut box: black horses, the soldiers in brick-red breeches and blue dolmans with yellow braid. The brilliance of their colours and the evocation of Russia's martial glories made me shudder with excitement. Things got out of control. It was not my fault that a subaltern spoke dishonouringly of his senior officer, or that satisfaction was demanded. But it was I who whispered encouragement to the captain, I who set the two chargers and their riders at each other across the new tan linoleum, and I who plotted the melee. Sabres rang. The horses reared as if boxing each other. They snickered with fear. Voluble advice came from the seconds, both of whom I represented. At the exact moment that the subaltern's shako'd head flew off, my father, made testy by a week of packing and argument, was passing the door.

'Why, you little devil, I'll have you know that I scoured the city for those. The best, none better in all of Moscow, and see what you've done to them. Already!'

'What do you mean, of course they could be better,' I countered. What were they for if not fighting? I threw the severed head at him. 'Look at that.'

For this I was walloped by Nanny Agafya with the back of a long-handled wooden clothes brush. It was my first meeting with physical force, mankind upon man, object on flesh. The scene has remained in my mind as an example to be followed. Pummel! Strap! Flog! It's the only way. The carrot is the solution of the dilettante. It's invariably construed as a sign of weakness. To offer it simply hedges the issue, defers everything.

From that day on I have been conscious only of being the Charlie Doig that I now am. Six foot two, strong in the shoulder and broad in the chest. Wide Russian face, straight dark hair, stubble. Eyes of blue: not the loony blue of the German philosopher but steadier, more brutal, with flecks of iron and schist. Powerful high-boned wrists. Mangling stride. A rugged obnoxious nose. And proper Russian balls that swing like the planets. Nothing of the gherkin down there.

My father left a sackful of debts, which of course made everything even more desperate for Mother. I loved them both. Not equally, that would have been too ideal. But Mother had an ample allocation, which she knew. We were happy together. It filled us with pleasure to be the family we were. There are no childhood grudges hanging in my mind like old meat.

Father's legacy to me was the unrequited portion of his ambition. Because he died so young this came to a sizable bequest, inferior in neither quantity nor zest. From the moment I got my hands on it I desired nothing less than complete success in everything that I did.

Top of my list was to honour the memory of my father, which I swore to do as I knelt praying for his soul.

Next: a mansion with a flagpole, sobbing fountains, a butler, footmen, cigars, concubines, racehorses, silken scarves and monogrammed underpants. A portrait of my woman done in crusty oils showing clearly her emerald rings and the richness of her bosom-salad, to be framed with the most glittering vulgarity my money could buy. This is for the front hall of the mansion, a knock-over to greet my visitors. I have wanted a blond birchwood desk in an office the size of a banqueting hall so that the butler bringing my coffee has to approach for sixty paces down a narrow red carpet. I have wanted a hothouse and its dusky perfumes, bushels of women's flesh and raw anchovies and French wines, to gorge myself on life, cramming everything in together, with both hands, as a man out of the desert goes at a swag of grapes.

Two

A SON MUST always tie up the accounting with his father. It's the final obligation.

George, my darling impetuous father, whose black curly hair like karakul lamb, his luminous eyes and tropical skin had won him the nickname Pushkin from his legion of Russian friends, had just been made up to junior partner in Hodge & Co. The gaffer, as my father referred to Potter Hodge, had collapsed and died during a municipal dinner in Manchester.

I remember so well his return with the news of his promotion. Surprise, triumph, beatitude, all were splashed like gallons of fresh paint across his face, which was bulging at every pore and resembled a brown paperbag stuffed with bulls' eyes. A partnership in Hodge & Co.! And cotton the thing! Wealth, solid dependable English wealth was at last within his reach. The barrel was rumbling towards him. He had only to whip the bung out and stick his hand inside.

A price was naturally payable to get my aristocratic mother to live in Britain, which she called a 'petity suffocating *island*', pronouncing the last word with the maximum derision that could be expressed by her tilted nose and a fading gesture with one plump white hand. Father, acting in full the character of the real Pushkin, gave her an IOU for his love in perpetuity and packed the two of us off to London to wait for him. He was going to undertake a last trip to the cotton fields around Tashkent. His spies had brought him early news that cotton-leaf worm was ravaging the crop. He was feeling his way to a spectacular coup that would wipe out his debts at one go. I know this, I know it as well as I know my name.

4

It was night. We were leaving Moscow for England, Mother and I. The giant bull-nosed locomotive at the head of the courier train's five, dark blue, twenty-metre coaches was smouldering its way up to the buffers, dribbling ankle-high wisps of steam. Father flung his arms round me. I pressed my face against his foxy newly-trimmed whiskers and hung on. He patted me, he moved my coat up and down my back like a separate skin, he hugged me closely – and held me off. 'Charlie Doig, I'm going to make us rich and when I've done it I'll show you how. Then we'll make some team, by God! Doig et fils, Moscow, Tashkent, the world!' We embraced, we kissed, the first bell went, and I entered the train in the footsteps of Boltikov, the sugar king, who'd barged into our farewell party at the station and smoked endless Northern Light cigarettes, holding them between his third and fourth fingers. (They came in a pink box with the manufacturer's name printed in Sargasso Sea blue on the papers. Their shape was oval, like Boltikov.)

So we parted, Mother and I into exile, Pushkin to his doom.

In the midst of his tour, which had hitherto been a lap of honour, he was bitten by a flea. This was not the common hopper *Pulex irritans*, the travelling companion of all Russians. I now know it to have been *Xenopsylla cheops*, a very different article whose host is the brown rat.

Father's swarthy epidermis was punctured without malice. He was perhaps recumbent on a divan, perhaps quaking with laughter, but probably moving restlessly in bed in a sticky Central Asian night, so attractively odoured that *cheops* thought to refresh himself – a beaker of the best. It sank its probe and thereby donated to Father the gift it had had from the rat, its host – the plague bacillus.

Within two days the buboes had formed and before the week was out my lovely father had died a gasping tossing bursting death.

We were in London when the news arrived. We had to engage an English lawyer. And Father, who had died swollen with putre-faction, in agony, with his glory stillborn, had his corpse stabbed and stabbed with the dagger of his debts by a pilchard-faced lawyer from Surbiton who at the end treated us to a sermon on thrift. Instead of asking, But did George Doig enjoy his stay among the living? this man did nothing but crab Papa for his 'exceedings'. I passed Mother a note during this session: 'May he take his seat upon the hot nail of hell,' which was a saying in our family. And when the lawyer took his leave I said smiling to him, *Poshol v pizdu*, which means 'disappear up your cunt'. Gravely he replied, 'Such a tragic business.'

This was a hard spell for Mother and myself, but especially for her. Then my great-uncle Igor, the head of the Rykovs, rallied round. The creditors were paid off and Mother was settled amongst artisans in a narrow red-brick house in Fulham, London, until I'd finished my schooling, for which Uncle Igor also footed the bill.

This was at Battle Hall, outside Hastings, on the cliffs looking towards France. Proprietor Capt. W. Slype, wedded to Muriel, who wore a built-up shoe. She dragged this foot, which was out-turned, and so could be heard approaching from a distance. Anyone caught mimicking her was taken off and caned by Slype. It was a brisk and biblical school that saw its purpose in supplying the Empire with irrigation engineers, bureaucrats and quellers of riots.

Mamasha, I wrote, they treat me like a Russian peasant. Why must the English always be so victorious? Let's go home, let's go back to Moscow. But she, having weathered the emotional catastrophe of exchanging Moscow for London and then having Papa die, was determined to stick it out. I think this was in the nature of a graveside vow, so to speak. Patience, she counselled.

And soon they had to stifle their scorn, these English school-boys.

The heat of my anger drove them back: that Father had died, that we were supported by the charity of relatives, that I was taunted for being a foreigner by a bunch of barbarians. I learned to punch first and punch hard. I carved out my territory with Russian fists and Russian balls. The day I arrived a boy called Morfet had me squeeze his testicles, I suppose to groom me for some sodomitical game. They were like a pair of boiled baby beetroots. I said to him, 'Don't worry, they'll fill up one day.' Later he became subservient to me. He was always short of cash – whereas I never was since Mother would go without to keep me in pocket money. Sometimes I'd get soaked when out birding on the cliffs. For threepence Morfet would sleep in my wet clothes and have them dry and clean by roll-call. So things got themselves advantageously sorted.

Three

THE NOTION grew within me that the best way to honour my father would be to avenge him. I'd become a naturalist. I'd capture a couple of *cheops* alive – only one specimen was known, in the Rothschild collection: dead. I'd force the brutes to breed for me. Put the lot in a cage with infected rats; milk them for serum; sell it and become rich on the old Rykov scale.

To do this I had to get my mind into all the right habits. I had to understand the structure of insects and their purpose.

My first collection was of moths and butterflies. I maintained a caterpillorum on a thicket of groundsel in the school's kitchen garden, hemming in my beauties with discarded panes from the vegetable frames. Fox moths and Drinkers were the worst for giving skin rashes. For a halfpenny each Morfet would let any untested caterpillar climb up his bare arm. The maximum incubation period seemed to be twelve hours.

The next stage was initiated by the discovery in the school library of Dr Erwin Zincke's *Insects of Europe*. It had a spine of the utmost black on which the title had been neatly painted in small white capitals. It made straight for my eye, begging to be opened. The raciness of his text and his sympathy for these unconsidered, often hated, creatures, which flowed through the book like a stream of luminous evening light, bowled me over.

I was fifteen, and in love for the first time.

The louse was my steady date. I was without prejudice. The ebony louse of Africa, the topaz louse of India, the ochre of the Japanese, the mushroom-brown of the Eskimos, and our own, the grey of our European skies, I loved them equally for their unrepentant hedonism. A louse feeds with less trouble than knocking a coconut off a tree. On the death of its host it has only to saunter across the blanket to obtain new lodging. Nothing too tiring, just a toddle in its bedroom slippers. As Zincke said, and how I adored him for it, the louse lives in a Shangri-La where nature has provided warmth, shelter, a constant spread of the finest food he can imagine, 'the odours he loves best, copses for love and secure undergrowth to nest in'. Could anyone resist such a description?

Vivid too was the scene that he painted of the death of Thomas Becket, when legions of lice fled the congealing body to be ground underheel by his killers, into the gore and the cathedral slabs. Perhaps this was a caprice of Zincke. Were the knights really so hygienic? Would they have acted so prettily after beheading an archbishop? Some reservations seemed to be in order. But I still loved the man for the succession of noises he presented: the rasp of swords leaving scabbards, the splintering hacked-about bones and at the last the oathy squelching of all these gorged episcopal lice. I loved him too for the danger I scented in the cathedral on that gaunt December afternoon.

But for the girl of my dreams I turned to the flea, my father's slayer, to which Zincke had devoted two intense chapters.

I was fascinated by the creature's techniques and by the grainy monochrome illustrations, hugely magnified, of its lethal weaponry. The maxillae that covertly parted Father's body hair, the mandibles that pierced him, and the labrum that sucked out his gambler's blood in exchange for the plague worm, over these I would linger time and again.

When I learned of his death I was certain that Father had gone down battling and cursing. But now that the mechanics were so clearly exposed by Zincke, I realised he hadn't a chance, from the moment *cheops* abandoned its host, a rat dying in a drain, and attached itself to a dog, then to a bazaar merchant, to a purchaser of that man's spices and finally to the mattress in the shabby Europa Hotel to which my exhausted father retired one night, his clothes speckled with cotton lint.

It's a still, dense summer's night in the land mass of Central Asia. The poplars hang their wilting leaves. Dogs bark sullenly. Lightning splits the huge indigo sky and thunder bombards the horizon, never closer. Papa sleeps fitfully and sweatily, eyelids trembling as in his shallow dream he pictures a foggy English apple orchard. *Cheops*, which has no eyes, inhales his human scent and emerges from its lair into the panting night, carrying – I thought like a fireman, upon its back – its cylinder of venom. Tick-tick-tick goes the pulse of life in that swollen vein in Papa's outflung arm. I see *cheops*'s mouth red with blood, and I hear my father check in his snoring. Perhaps, in what will be his only gesture of defiance, he rolls onto his side and scratches the spot where *cheops,* sated, is taking his ease.

Alone in the library I would sit with Zincke and his insects. How does ambition arise? From a desire for revenge. From dreaming, from necessity. I had all three.

Four

I AM SORRY now for that flamboyant beetle, a Green Tiger, that I dissected for the sole purpose of verifying that beetles had, as stated by Zincke, blood as yellow as the dandelion flower. There was no excuse. I should have taken his word. I destroyed its beauty in a frivolous cause, making me as evil as a cat. I was late returning to class on account of this experiment and was caned by Slype.

Regarding this as a dare to do something worse, and disgusted with myself over the Green Tiger, I forsook insects for a while and became a birder. Over the garden wall and down through the trees to the forbidden cliffs and a wilderness of gorse and salt-stunted oak and hawthorn scrub. It was an excellent location. In winter exotics from Africa and the Americas would pitch up on ocean-going freighters and hang around for a few days. Droughts or hard weather in Europe would bring all sorts of unfamiliar visitors. In one day I myself recorded two Little Buntings and a Sardinian Warbler.

I had no binoculars – Slype was the only person at school who could afford them. Therefore I learned field craft; patience, stealth and how to mimic birdsong. Most birds are natural conversationalists. They enjoy being spoken to. Watch them as they cock their heads and try to figure out your amateur notes.

Abolish the plumage trade! Extirpate all feral cats!

These became my mottoes as a birder. I would weep at the small heaps of feathers I found – pounced-upon victims of a cat's sadism. Eventually I got some snares through one of the gardeners and for the whole of a summer and half a winter did good work among the cat population. The corpses I would wedge into the fork of a suitable tree, jamming their heads tight into the cleft so that carrion-eating birds could get their fill and avenge the millions of their slaughtered brethren. In some cats the whiskery death rictus was the very picture of Muriel Slype, especially as regards the stained teeth.

An echo of this thought must have reached the Slypes.

As I was returning amid the embers of a magical dawn in April – a sky originally of blistering red whose temper had softened through every shade of pink, with some hues of lily-throat green, and settled at last on rose-grey clouds presaging rain from Ushant – I was collared by Slype. I came over the garden wall, hung the ladder on its hooks, and there he was, behind me in the doorway.

'Doig, I'm going to beat you for this. You could have been killed.'

I've had enough of you, I thought, and went to give him a low poke. If I was going to go down, I'd do it with colours flying.

But Slype, though having a cumbersome figure and not obviously quick on his feet, got there first. He darted inside my punch and belted me round the ribs, drove me right back, and ended by kneeing me in the meat of my Russian balls. I fell forward, choking, fearing he'd shoved them all the way up and blocked my larynx.

'That'll learn you, Johnny foreigner,' he said, pulling me up by my hair. He towed me inside through the French windows and there he and Muriel thrashed me in relays with his knottiest cane.

That Sunday afternoon I dressed in mufti, settled up with Morfet and walked out.

By chance it was Mother's name day. Her friends had just left the house in Fulham. She was a little flown on that sweet white wine that we Russians do love and greeted me as if I'd been no farther than to fetch the daily newspaper.

'My father's farm horses, we were speaking of them, you missed that part,' she started, even as we embraced.

'Because yesterday I read in the paper that a woman had left all her money to her parrot. What use is that? I said. Vasilisa Leonovna said, "The English have no real idea about love. It's all a pretence, even with their animals. From what they say you'd think they take them into their beds at night. But in fact that happens only in their books." And I said – but your hands are so cold, darling, put some more coal on the fire and sit close up to it – I said: My father always gave our horses a holiday on their patron saints' days. Florus and Laurus, such sweet names – the saints. The peasants took them down to the river in a double line and scrubbed them clean from top to toe. They stood shivering with pleasure and let themselves be washed every-where, even round their private places, even the stallions. Then the men tied different coloured ribbons to their manes and tails so they'd know they were loved, and turned them loose in the meadows for the rest of the day. The sunlight coming through the crooked alder trees always struck the water in flakes of gold. The men, who were naked of course, would ride one horse and lead two more. The horses never fought. They knew it was their holiday. The white of those men when they took their clothes off! Like snow! This is how it was with us at my home in Smolensk province, at the Pink House, Popovka. That's what we were chatting about, just a moment ago . . .'

The moment of tipsy rapture ceased as suddenly she looked at me afresh. I clearly saw the question spring into her eyes.

She sat down heavily on an upright chair. 'Dismissed?'

Not waiting for an answer, she poured herself another glass. 'Oh my heart, my poor Russian heart, how it's had to suffer.' Then she drained it.

I must explain. Her family name, Rykov, means only one thing to a Russian – money. It was actually her grandfather, the financier, and not Kutuzov who beat Napoleon in 1812. For what battles can a general win if he can't afford an army? A title, entry to Tsar Alexander's levee, and estates in Smolensk and the Crimea were awarded to our Founder by his grateful sovereign: wealth on a vast and barbaric scale. When he died he was the owner of eighteen thousand serfs.

Much good has this done us, the Smolensk Rykovs. For reasons now atomised in history, the Founder bequeathed all that was portable of his fortune to the Crimean branch – Uncle Igor's lot. The strongbox of deeds, the ropes of emeralds, the famous Rykov pearls, the cartloads of bullion, the carpets, the pictures, the furniture, all too easily I can see them trundling across the steppe to the Crimea on wagons flanked by troops of Cossack outriders. To my grandfather at Smolensk there was left the huge forest of Popovka and its untamable pigs, too many acres of poor ploughing ground, and a rambling wooden manor called by everyone the Pink House on account of the colour of the wooden columns that flanked a rose-covered verandah very suitable for invalid chairs and children's games. We often holidayed there, travelling down from Moscow. We'd be welcomed by the stationmaster, and then whisked away by my uncle Boris's coachman whose tall hat brushed against the leaves of the chestnut trees as we drove through the Popovka forest.

In the Pink House there lived my uncle and his three children: Viktor, Nicholas and Elizaveta, whom I always vaguely knew to be less than a normal cousin. In addition, in the honeycomb of the attics, there existed in a curious twilight all those whom Uncle Boris didn't have the heart to send packing – dotty old tutors, officers on half pay, friends down on their luck and a job lot of men and women calling themselves relatives when in fact their connection to the Rykovs was only by marriage. They were all of a certain age. Whist, bezique, canasta – those were their favourites to pass the time. On a Sunday they'd sometimes play one of the tempestuous Russian games like *terz* or *stoss*. The rumpus! But here's a sad thing. None had any money (it was why they were there). Yet it was vital to have some form of wagering in order to give vent to the force of life, to prove to each other what they might easily have been had fate been merciful. Listening at the door of their communal sitting room we heard the most outlandish bets being placed: 'I bet my oak wood at Semipensk,' or 'I bet Byron, the borzoi who killed a wolf by himself,' or 'my bureau with two secret drawers' or 'my dower house' or 'the smaller of my carriages', all of which were possessions they'd either frittered away or had invented for the pleasure to be had from describing them in meticulous and wistful detail. They boasted about their mythical estates, argued about the fabulosities of ancient Greece with a sacred, greasy, purple-bound copy of Herodotus as judge, got drunk when they could and lounged around with fingers crossed that their host's diminishing patrimony would last them out.

Except for the drink and funeral expenses, all costs were borne by my uncle Boris. It is true that he attempted to recoup some of these by charging for the laundry, which was done by his servants. But I think only token sums were involved.

Very Russian. I heard of nothing like it in England. Had my uncle thrown them out or charged them a rent he would have been ostracised from society. As a Rykov it was his duty to protect unfortunates.

From this household Mother was summoned by the bugle of love to become Mrs Doig. So she says, but I think my uncle gave her a good shove in the direction of the dark and energetic Scottish cotton-broker who was clearly on the way up. For it is as well known in Moscow as elsewhere that the Scots are destined to own the world.

In this way I was conceived and born, and in this way my parents and I entered the golden era that commenced with my father's elevation to a partnership and was punctured a few months later by the mandibles of *Xenopsylla cheops*. The entire story of our line of Rykovs from 1812 onwards was thus reduced to Mother sitting sorrowfully in a narrow house in London which had a toilet no closer than the end of the garden, and me, her son who'd just walked out of school.

'Where's your trunk?' she demanded, not really caring.

I was seventeen. Mother was tiddly. By the time I got her to bed she'd have relived three generations of her family history for my benefit. So much of disappointment and failure floundering in her bloodstream, and her eyes red with the pain of exile. Things were complicated. They needed to get easier for me.

Emphatically I sliced the air with the side of my hand. 'What's important is to keep everything simple, to have one idea at a time and think of nothing else until it's done.' She looked at me pityingly, knowing little of my dreams and my hours with Zincke. 'By the end of the week I'll have a job.'

'When necessity speaks, it demands,' she said, quoting our proverb.

Then she reverted to the pensioners living in the Pink House, describing how they'd come tumbling out of their rooms in dressing gowns and curling oriental slippers the moment carriage wheels sounded on the gravel. 'To inspect, to carry away a new painting in their minds, to hear the news shouted out by the coachman. The two-wheeled cart that we used to carry out the dead was pushed by hand and made a very different sound. For this someone would go to every room waking people up. They'd hang out of the upstairs windows, unwigged and unpomaded, hair all over the place like washerwomen. Who'd gone aloft? One of them or one of us? Or was it only a servant? They were like the doves that lived above the stables,' my mother continued fondly. 'When the grooms went round filling the mangers from their sacks of corn, they suddenly became bright-eyed and attentive.'

That evening, which as I've said was her name day, she went round the Pink House for me room by room, always in the past tense, knowing that for her the epoch had ended. I refused to open another bottle. She took to drinking tea in the Russian manner. Her nostalgia faded. I told her something of what I intended. The hours passed congenially.

In a pause I caught her looking at me tartly and soberly. 'My little son, *malenki,* go then into the world and be an honour to your father.' She rose and standing behind me put her palms on my shoulders and smoothed the cloth outwards with a soft, motherly movement. 'Honour, it's so important after a reverse,' she murmured as I reached up to grasp her hands. 'It makes everything level again, sometimes a bit more than level.'

Five

I APPLIED FOR a job at the British Museum. They were putting together a massive new catalogue of their bird collection. I didn't get it – my youth. However, instead of retiring downcast, I stood my ground and said to Mr Agg, a big boisterous man, 'But I can whistle a very good song thrush for you, sir.' I gave him a couplet:

> Kweeu quip qui chipiwi,
> Tiurru chirri quiu – qui qui.

They're hard to copy, song thrushes. Not one note is exactly the same as another. He looked interestedly at me.

'Again. More boldly this time, as if you were trying to attract a mate.'

I remembered the instructions for reciting poetry I'd had from my tutor in Moscow. 'Deep goes with melancholy, a light voice with high clouds, with daffodils and with anecdotes when drinking lemonade after tennis. Don't fall away at the end of a line.'

It came out even better the second time. I did five seconds for him.

'What's that in your accent?'

I told him, Russian.

'Useful. Go to the Darwin Club in Little Russell Street. A Mrs Mason will answer the door. Ask her if Goetz is back from Africa. Whether the answer is yes or no, in due course present yourself to him with my compliments. Good day to you, young Ivan.'

16

The Club is the building with the cracked stucco immediately to the right of the church. Every bird and butterfly collector, every dealer in these, every insect man, plantsman, big-game hunter, taxidermist and observer of the natural sciences, whether amateur or paid, whether from America, India or Europe, knows his way to the Darwin. It smells like a smuggler's den: pipe tobacco, gun oil, leather, westward ho. In the cramped hall are steamer trunks in tiers, each emblazoned with scarred P&O labels the colour of the azure seas: Shanghai, Valparaiso, Jesseltown, Addis Ababa via Aden and Djibouti. When the Indian butterfly season ends in April you have to turn sideways to get between the cliffs of baggage and thus approach the cubbyhole where Mrs Mason reigns and her husband has an underlordship as porter and handyman.

Thither I went hotfoot, having the picture in my mind of a rugged and misanthropic naturalist who took meals by himself and read as he ate. In this I was mainly correct.

Goetz, Hartwig Goetz, born in Berlin forty-three years before. What can I say about him that has not already been said in the Darwin Club, where he was loathed?

I have followed his obdurate, bat-like ears, his bobbing pith helmet and his mountainous calves, always encased in black elastic-topped stockings, for a very great distance. Round the Canary Islands for Agg and the Museum's bird collection we marched. Then came a gruelling two-year expedition to Cayenne after those startlingly blue butterflies, the morphos. Goetz had a collector, von Berlepsch. We had to find for him every one of the species, from *adonis* to *perseus* to *rhetenor*, in each of their biological states. It was hard going, mostly through jungle. The snakes were as thick as branches and the mosquitoes the size of moths. Leeches also were present. But you can tie them in knots and pop them, so they were fun to a young man.

In Burma they were smaller and darker and less amusing.

What I'm saying is that I've shared everything with Goetz, including a number of tropical diseases. I've eaten with the same knife and fork and I've drunk from the same metal beaker water that was humming with confervae. (In the better villages a trout or somesuch is maintained in the well to clean up the algae and insects.) I've shared the same lime green Skyproof campaign tent off and on for eight years. Lying sweatily alongside his hulk I've listened to his dreams and to his nightmares and also become acquainted with his most intimate disorders. I've known this man through good times and bad.

He was squat, powerful and taciturn in any language except that of science. Natural history was a holy cause to him. Collecting informs the public about our past, increases the general store of knowledge and provides a record of any species that may become extinct, that was his line whenever he could be prevailed upon to lecture. To take life in the interests of science was perfectly acceptable. The greatest moral crime a naturalist could commit was to make something appear to be other than it was: a little staining of a bird's plumage or some minor alteration to its anatomy, instances of cheating that both perverted the beauty bestowed on the creature by God and ruined it for science. He understood nothing of compromise. Truth was his gospel. He was welded to it from the navel to the forehead.

Truth is indeed the capital point in natural history. Someone like Goetz is necessary to root out the fakes. But a man's personality suffers when he becomes addicted to it, as was the case with Goetz. It shone from within his skull with a glow that was intolerably pious. He had a saying: that one can never be wounded by the truth, it's only lies that prick. I pointed to some difficulties judging which was which. But he would have none of that sort of talk. Truth, he said, puffing the ominous bundle of consonants at me with fierce sincerity, was as unmistakable as a fir tree on an iceberg.

Museum curators, who had only to deal with him from a great distance, venerated him. Mrs Mason had to store his correspondence in her desk when he was 'out' for it was far too much for his pigeonhole. But the Darwin couldn't stand his zealousness. The members regarded me with amazement that I continued to team up with him. The fact is that he was the finest naturalist in the world. I was happy to slave for him if I learnt thereby.

Six

'S NAKES'LL BE the worst of it,' said Norman Joiner, the
Chicago museum fellow who'd bought the duplicate morphos
from our Cayenne trip. 'So shake your boots out in the morning.'

'Ja, ja,' said Goetz sarcastically. We were having tea in the
safety of Norman's London hotel. Goetz was guzzling marmalade
cake.

'We'll pay you by time,' Norman went on. 'None of this so-
many-dollars-a-specimen stuff. That's old-fashioned, little
better than slavery. Ten dollars a day for top-notchers like you
two. Split it as you will. Portering and expenses on top. Huh,
boys?'

This was a neat commercial question. To capture a first or
some grand exotic was the dream of all of us who were interested in money. (Goetz was not, having this great regard for the
truth.) Taking a salary removed the risk of finding nothing. But
also the potential gain, for all that was caught belonged to the
sponsor.

I thought, Burma, not much worked over, eh? So I told Norman
he could pay Goetz a salary if that was what suited them both.
But for my part I'd take a chance and work by results. He offered
me the standard scale that pertains amongst the dealers. I looked
at him pityingly. I said, 'You want to have me expose my life and
health to the climate of Burma and pay me in pennies?' I rose in
my chair. We then agreed a scale of payments per species that
was more favourable to me, plus some additional clauses that
were new to him. Ours is a pretty passive profession when dealing
with these office types. The greatest aim of Darwin Club members
is to get into the field, add something to knowledge and revel

in nature's beauty. So after this negotiation Norman looked upon me with respect.

But he kept quiet about the rainfall in the mountains to the south of Manipur. I should have done my homework better and pushed up my prices.

To make the position clear: one inch of rain dispenses a weight equivalent to one hundred tons falling evenly over an acre. Multiply that by two hundred, which was the annual rainfall where we were working. Multiply it again by a squillion raindrops, imagine a good proportion of these hammering daily on your pith helmet and you'll marvel that we didn't go off our chumps. No stately English pitter-patter this. Those raindrops were as thick and long and grey as engine pistons. Down they came, day in and day out, flattening the slope of our helmets and slogging the wits out of our earholes. Stop! you bellow, because bellowing is the only way to assert your individuality amid the racket. Sun – dry land – send them before we drown! And suddenly you find it has stopped and you're shouting into a porridge of steamy silence and the porters are on the point of bolting, sahib having gone doolally.

No wonder Goetz knew suffering. They were not the conditions for an older man. Nor for a Russian brought up amidst snow and wolves. Listen, Yankee fellow: the snakes, the leeches, the wild porkers, the impenetrable barriers of bamboo, the bats, the mosquitoes, the slugging rain, we gave them all a chance to look kindly upon your servants. For that sort of money we were prepared to strive, and did so. But next time you send a team to Burma, hire some guys with fins or a gang of natives whose webbed toes will let them ascend the slithery mud trails without succumbing to the torments of Sisyphus. We tried, by God we did, for there was abundant and fascinating material to be had: Gould's thrushes, laughing thrushes, that funny tree-haunting family, the sibias, the little blue niltavas that are half robin and half flycatcher, dippers that built their nests in December – ten years would not have been enough if Norman had wanted a book. And had Goetz taken a white-headed form of the black bulbul, damnably shy and so rarissima, that he stalked for two weeks, he would have been the toast of the Field Museum.

But we were humans and our quarry had no sympathy for

the frailty of that species. They made no allowance for our powder getting damp or for our swollen cartridges refusing to fit in our guns. They didn't notice how our energy was sapped by the humidity. The water that our Sanitas tablets failed to purify didn't affect their guts one little bit. As blithely as ever they led their lives. We, however, declined.

A coffle of porters was at our disposal. Their headman was a small, dapper gentleman called Hpung.

'Mister not his chummy self today,' he said to me one noon when we'd stopped to brew tea. Despite everything, we'd been successful enough to satisfy Norman. But on reaching Nagaland, which had taken us nine months, we'd thrown in the towel, which had become sodden and slimy. Now we were heading back, through the mountainous jungle of the Chin country and the Yomas, the Chindwin river being to the east of our line of march.

'No by God he isn't,' I replied, having that morning put my leg through one of their woven rope bridges and skinned the flesh from my calf to the middle of my thigh. The insects were busy nibbling me. Every leech for miles around had scented the dish. They were standing upright on the leaves, on the tips of their tails, their bulbous sightless heads weaving as they took aim.

And Goetz, in addition to bouts of malaria, had sprung a hernia in his lower belly, a noisome area that he now had me feel, as we were drinking our tea, for my medical education. The swelling was like a young coconut, fibred with creeping black hair, but softer than I expected. I gave it a poke with a straight finger to see if he jumped; he was having me help him undress, which I disliked.

He was leaning back on his elbows, his shorts and disgusting underpants round his knees. He gave a great bellow. 'Be gentle, sod you.'

At which Hpung, fluttering over us in his clean, white, presidential style of dhoti, piped up, 'Mister's temper too near the surface. Mister no take his liver salts this morning. We make camp early. Misters put their feet up. Get rested.'

When we halted for the night – which in those parts drops with the speed of oblivion – I said to Goetz, 'At least we had sunshine in those other places. You know what I look forward to most? Going to bed in thick pyjamas.'

'Once a Russian, always a Russian.' He raised a leg for me to peel off his black elastic stockings, which was like skinning a dogfish. I chucked them to Hpung. Goetz waggled his toes and eyed his puffy, bitten feet, which after this period of continuous immersion had a bluish sheen like junket. 'For me roast pork with chitterlings and red cabbage. It's the rice that's caused my hernia. Made me strain. Weakened my stomach lining.'

We'd eaten, lit the mosquito coil, and were lounging beneath the flysheet, which we always extended to keep the leeches from dropping into our gruel. It took the edge off dinner having to scoop out their corpses, which floated around the billycans like rubbery croutons. We were belching and scratching and watching the fresh insect bites on our legs go bad. Our lower shins were ribboned with weeping sores. Everything was dank and mouldy. Our belts and all the leather strapping had turned chalky grey, as if powdered with cheap cigar ash. Our tempers also were crumbling.

About half an hour of daylight remained. Rain was falling, the same purposeful cylinders, each one about twice as thick as a knitting needle. They caused the bamboo thickets to tremble and rushed in cataracts down the grooves of their bowed, narrow leaves. Drapes of mist clung to the wooded slopes around us. The air was as thick as damp wool.

Clouds of the harmless fly they speak of as *ndangi* were swarming around the clearing. Their suckers hung beneath their bellies like nozzles. In separate groups, maybe on account of some prehistoric quarrel, mosquitoes were dancing jiggedly, up and down, left and right, to avoid having their puny torsos smashed to pulp by the rain. Goetz maintained they were pushed aside by the pillow of air preceding each raindrop. But to me this hopping about seemed deliberate. They'd see the raindrops coming over their shoulders, yes? They weren't idiots. But here Goetz held a high trump. For as we both knew, in a few minutes the jungle bats would flip crookedly through the dusk and pick the mosquitoes off in droves, six or seven to a mouthful. If the mosquitoes could see the raindrops coming, why couldn't they see the bats and jink out of the way?

I countered, 'Bats must have come earlier in God's scheme and so got the upper hand.'

'Of course. A mosquito, unless an idiot, should have learned to hide from bats by now. Therefore they are idiots, as I said.'

'But if bats flew in a straight line, like raindrops, they'd starve. The mosquitoes would quickly twig their game.'

'That's your silly English sense of fairness at work. That's the father in you speaking. How is any species to survive except by having better tricks than its competitors?'

Thus we fell to bickering. He was in bad shape, with the hernia, malaria, and our brandy having run out. I wasn't in what you'd call mint condition either. We couldn't get away from each other. It was hell being with him in our Skyproof tent. There were times I wanted to strangle his fat throat.

The porters were a stone's throw away on the far side of the clearing. With their jungle knives they'd knocked up a bamboo pavilion, the work of seconds. They were squatting on their heels round a cooking fire, arguing shrilly. A pipe was doing the rounds. Their swaggy loincloths bulged with contentment. So clean were they always, so damned clean, supple and enviable.

I said, 'I'm going to give them an earful. I can't stand watching them being so happy.'

Putting on my rotting boots, I padded towards them through the gloom and the hovering *ndangi*. Bats rent and vibrated the air above me.

Goetz called out, 'Don't kick them around. This isn't Russia.'

I said to Hpung, thinking to put him in the wrong with an impossible request, 'Got a woman for me?'

His eyes, dazed by the business with the pipe, were as big as moons as he looked up at me, six foot two, stained, bearded, warlike. 'Mister desire woman?'

Now that I'd thought about it, I had a very great need for a spill. 'Yes, Hpung, and not any old hag. A young widow would suit me.'

His next expression: was it politeness, interest, admiration or what in those brown, firelit eyes? There was no telling as he said evenly, 'Other mister also? Share lady fifty-fifty?'

'Christ no. Besides, he has a hernia.'

'Fetched to this place?'

'No.'

He rose with a wondrous elasticity of limb. 'Woman very good for mister. Makes him whole again. Takes all nasty feelings inside herself and buries them in the dark. Bad memoirs all gone into woman's secret place. Mister become chummy again. But no widow. Widows difficult in this land.'

'Fine, no widow. What now?'

There was a general chuckling as Hpung spoke rapidly to the porter we called Longman, a tall emaciated fellow whose ribs stood out like those of a sunken ship. He got to his feet, poured oil into a pannikin, stuck a lump of fat in the middle and lit it with a taper from the fire. Pointing at me, he said something to the circle of shadowed faces, at which there was more laughter.

'He say, three miles to village. Nice fat woman. Good jig-a-jig. Coming back will seem like five, mister being somewhat tired.'

I thought that wasn't what had been said, but the smiles and the sense of conspiracy belonged to the brotherhood of man and it didn't matter.

'Jig-a-jig how much?'

'Five rupees for travellers,' Hpung said quickly. I clapped the rascal on the back and galumphed over to the tent for money. Goetz told me not to wake him up when I got back. He wasn't a bit envious of me, just a sick man of middle age who was tired of jungle life.

'See if you can make something to help his hernia, to hold it in,' I said to Hpung. Then Longman came over. I followed his bobbing oil lamp out of the clearing – and as if by magic the rain ceased.

He led me along one darkened forest trail after another, always downhill, until dogs barked and I smelled water and curing fish. The tree canopy opened up, the night paled and I saw we were beside a lake of invisible extent. A line of posts – perhaps twelve or fifteen, not very many – stretched out from the bank. A small houseboat was tied to each, making a row of dumpy black beetles. Planks connected them. Longman indicated for me to take my boots off to get a better grip on the planks; that he'd stand watch over them until I returned; that my popsy was on the farthest boat.

I did as he said. Dogs sniffed at me and turned away. I thought, surely I can't smell any worse than the curing fish?

The planks had cross-members secured with hemp, which felt like hairy sandpaper beneath my soles. Whole families were sleeping on deck, upon thin quilts, robed according to age. The old people sat up, sheeted and spectral, and called after me mellifluous unalarmed greetings as I rocked their boats with my lustful tread.

The night was cooling. A rag of wind was on my cheek. The water slapped against the hulls and ran lisping up the beach to the curing shed. In place of a moon was a speck of lamplight on the farthest boat. From plank to plank, over the bodies of this weary tribe of fisherfolk, I bounded to the flame, my loins bubbling.

She was waiting on deck, cross-legged, smoking a pipe. I strode up the last plank, a foul and odorous boarding party, nine months of celibacy tapping at my belt buckle.

'Where? Here?'

Very calmly she put aside the pipe and pointed to my swollen feet. Her lamp was so feeble I couldn't make out her features. She rose and made to walk past me, hips undulating. Not tall, up to my top rib. Black buttered hair to below the shoulders, tinted by the little gleaming light. Bare feet, taking her noiselessly past me. 'Hey' – and catching her I bent and whipped her shift up to see what I'd got. Without emotion she delayed her pace to help me. The shift snagged on her chin or thereabouts. As I tugged at it I hefted the nearest breast to put an age on her. I got her naked. She became invisible against the dark of the night. 'For Christ's sake what is this, hide and seek?' I cried impatiently. She replied God knows what, but in such a lovely rustling voice, like the wind speeding through barley whiskers, that I was instantly penitent. In moments she was in front of me again with a glinting dipper of oil. She had me sit. Crouching, she began to anoint my feet, pulling at my toes, getting the oil right between them, freeing them up. Those were terrible times, she so composed and neatly breasted as she took my appalling feet into her naked lap and there kneaded them. It was too much. I had to stand up, to take some action. I towered above her. A whole teak tree was growing in my shorts, I was on the brink of Krakatoa. I grabbed her buttery hair and tried to pull her up. She clung to my ankles and made more magical sounds. 'Come on, you bitch, let me in.' But still she twittered, and I held off.

At last she finished with my feet. She lowered the plank overboard with a rope so as to prevent her neighbours' slumber being jarred, and led me by the hand down a few steps into a timbered stateroom that smelled of resin from its native woods. The latticework at the stern was wide open to the breeze.

She lit another lamp, set out more dippers. Whisperingly she unbuckled and unbuttoned me. She guided my Empire shorts to the floor. There I stood, as rampant as any man could be. *Any* man. I was in danger of bursting the membrane. But no, again she was murmuring. With perfumed palms she began to oil and polish my tool. I could take no more. I threw her down and on a mat I impaled her, this husky, practised, stupendous woman. I spiked her with my bad tempers. Goetz, the leeches, the beige flood from my bowels, the sheer waste in my life of this expedition, she inhumed them all, ungrudgingly, jutting her slick loins. As dawn struck the lake, marvellous clumps of pink on black, she engulfed me for the last time. Riding me beneath the wide stern window, the colour of her skin gradually abated to a light chestnut. Her face became clear for the first time and I saw that she was beautiful.

She made me a dish of bitter tea from a wild plant called *tookin* hereabouts. The hills also had been cleansed. The rain clouds had gone. Every leaf on every tree wore a sparkle as if dressed to go dancing. Canoes, two men to each, were setting off for the fishing grounds. Children were scuffling in the water. Bright women chattered as they washed their pots.

I gave her my money, all that I had, ten rupees in singles. She bowed, palms folded. She fished up the plank and I departed whistling, from one boat to the next, to where Longman was waiting with my boots.

I asked him the name of the lake. Mayanga. And of the girl? Phula, which is the small blue and yellow flower of the open hill in Burma, similar to heartsease.

Seven

LONGMAN DELIVERED me back to the camp with a certain grandeur. After I'd paid him he went and held court beside the pavilion. He raised his fist and opened it the full five.

'Wah!'

'You gave her too much,' Goetz grunted.

'Too much for what?' I said, and turned back to Longman who had allowed himself the teasing pause to which the sole possessor of interesting information is entitled. His companions shouted at him, begging for the full accounting. He eyed them from his great height. Then he raised his fist a second time. One by one, slowly and solemnly, he disclosed each long brown finger.

'Ten rupees! Wah!' Chattering among themselves and glancing at me, the men started to break camp.

This did my standing no harm. But Goetz was furious. Called me bumptious and said they'd think we were made of money. 'And on a woman at that,' he said more than once, as if a dog would have been better value. When we began the day's march he insisted on walking alone, behind the porters, which is no place for a naturalist.

Hpung said they'd tried and failed to make a truss out of bamboo splints. But, he continued, 'Biggest trouble this. Mister have good time at jig-a-jig. Too much good time, too much glory – yes?'

'Glory?'

Hpung stuck out one hand – flat, palm upward. 'Here is woman.' He slapped his other hand onto it, palm down and wriggled it around. 'Here is man. Woman have room for only

27

one man at a time. You that man, not him. He bit old, bit fat, bit ill – Mister Less-and-less. So woman give *you* all the glory, make you top fellow. You see now, Mister Doig?'

It was not sedition I saw in Hpung's smooth face but the certainty of somebody stating the obvious, that Goetz was no longer up to the job.

And two marches later, when we reached a fork in the track, it was to me that Hpung turned. Downward, to the east, in the valley of the Chindwin, was Kani. We'd passed through it on our outward journey. A queer, inferior township; two strips of wooden houses astride a single street, the whole outfit squeezed onto a narrow spur of gravel curving into the river. Was the resident population two hundred? Certainly no more. Yet it was the headquarters of the district commissioner. His name was Reynolds.

The rains had been at their heaviest when we arrived, and the river had flooded some of the lower houses. Reynolds had invited us to his bungalow for supper and billiards.

The water was up to the slate, which Reynolds, a bachelor, said was quite normal. We paddled ourselves round the table in coracles that he'd had made with this situation in mind. Bamboo wrack, chunks of timber, root curls and dead fish were floating in the brown floodwater. Rush lights swung from the rafters, casting a moth-infested glow on the proceedings. The baize was rippled by damp and pocked by insects. A strong wrist action was needed. Two house boys waded through the flotsam to hold our coracles when we had a shot. Afterwards they chalked our cues. A third acted as scorer. Reynolds, delighted to have company, put up a bottle of brandy as the stake. And Goetz had won it, spinning round the moat in a fever of excitement and urging the ball into the pocket with thunderous German exhortations.

This he now remembered, and the hilarity of those three nights, and the fact that a steamer of the Irrawaddy Flotilla Company called there.

'Down,' he pointed, 'down we shall go at last, Doig.'

Hpung, standing a couple of paces away, looked Goetz over with his muddy eyes and said without force, 'Not the boating period, mister. Too much water yet.'

'Who asked you? Look, Doig, I'm not a well man. Reynolds will have medicine. He'll know someone who can push back my hernia. There's bound to be a native trick to it. And we can have some decent food – tins straight from the Army & Navy. He had a case of jellied ham in his office, behind the door. Didn't you see it? Hiding it from us, I expect. You could do with a square meal. Both of us could. Down, I say.'

I looked at Goetz's burly jowls and glaring nostrils. And at that moment I knew that what I wanted was my own expedition, as number one and no dissent. Beauty. Money. Fame. And a dry climate. My temper rose and I can't say what might have happened had not Goetz made a sudden grab at Hpung and cried out, spittling at him, 'That's it, I can see by your creep-arse look that you and Doig have been plotting against me.'

Not even trying to get out of Goetz's grip, Hpung said, 'No boats at Kani for many whiles yet. Only one-eighty miles to Chaungwa. One eight zero. Much bigger place – post office, boat once per week, regular. Better you stay up here with us. Quicker by and by.'

I told Goetz I'd have a stretcher knocked up for him – and suddenly he surrendered. In a conversation lasting no more than forty-five seconds he handed over responsibility for everything, obliging me only to sign a chitty for the cash box and accepting it in scrawled pencil. That done he sat himself down beneath a wild fig tree and looked upon us softly, as if we were all his children, while a stretcher was rigged up out of bamboo poles and my spare clothing.

It was like a Visigoth chieftain that we conveyed him to Chaungwa, where the expedition disbanded and Hpung was murdered.

Eight

Tʜɪs ɪs what happened. We were to have had five days there
before the steamer arrived – the *Glorious Ina*. We started
by repacking our specimens, throwing out any that had been
damaged by rain or insects, and arranging our passage from
Rangoon to Calcutta and thus back to Britain. This we did
through Nicholson's, the shipping agents Norman had instructed
us to employ. They had an office and godowns at Edward's
Wharf. They owned pretty well all the waterfront.

The river was running high – level nine on the white marker
post on Ayub Island, a small wooded island that had once been
a leper colony. It was opposite Nicholson's main warehouse.

Everyone turned out to watch the *Glorious Ina* berth. The
Chindwin was rat grey in colour, voracious, heaving, licking
along. The week before the vessel had had to turn back.
Nicholson's men were keeping their fingers crossed.

We heard her whistle long before she came into sight. Then
we saw her smoke, black as ink above the jungle, and at last
she appeared, labouring round the long slow bend about half
a mile downstream and obviously trying to keep out of the main
force of the current. Her deck was stacked with freight. She lay
low in the water and skulked as close to the bank as the channel
would let her, at times being half hidden under the outspreading
branches. Her paddle wheels thrashed at the water with a mighty
clanking noise.

In order to make the angle into the quay she had to swing
out into the river. It was the moment everyone had been waiting
for. This was excitement at Chaungwa in the rainy season.

As she moved away from the bank and began to cut across

the current, we saw that a section of the boxing that protected the nearside paddle had been carried away, perhaps struck by a tree trunk travelling low in the water. Tall columns of water spouted from the paddle as the river struck at it. Rising they turned a pale shade of green in the dull sunlight, which was a curious optical effect.

As is always the case in this sort of accident, the damage had occurred on the exposed side of the *Ina* – upstream.

A native lookout, soaked and statuesque, stood on a packing case in the bow. Men with bamboo fenders were lined up and down the weather beam in case the river pushed the vessel askew against the quay. The captain himself had taken the helm: white shirt with rolled-up sleeves, belted white trousers, pipe gripped at the horizontal, his stripey red IFC cap almost touching the roof of the wheelhouse. We heard him ting-ting to the engine room.

One of Nicholson's foremen was standing next to me. 'He needs to get her a good bit upstream before he can afford to turn. Go on, man, more smoke, more smoke . . . don't let her fall away . . . Now! There you go, laddie, helm hard over.'

Water has a pleasant, mature disposition when being drunk or when it's considered in theory, as the necessary agent for all forms of life. But on the hoof its hostility is spectacular. For perhaps as long as two minutes, as the *Ina* turned across the current, it seemed that she'd lost steerage and was going to be swept broadside onto the reefs boiling at the head of Ayub Island. Ponderously, shuddering, throwing up curtains of spray, she got the better of it. The tilt of her deck decreased. The crew went round retying the loose lashings. We let out our breath and smiled at each other.

The boat entered quieter water. The captain relit his pipe and rang down to brake the paddles. The plumes and spindrift subsided. A crewman in a sopping dhoti went to join the lookout in the bow where they stood together on the packing case, gracefully swinging the coils of their light mooring ropes.

I was watching these lissome, muscular figures so I didn't see it the first time. But I heard the intake of breath around me.

'Good God Almighty,' said Goetz.

I looked at him and then the steamer. Its passengers had gathered below the wheelhouse and were shouting to their friends on shore. The paddles were revolving only slowly, enough to make headway and no more.

Nicholson's foreman gave his stevedores harsh, urgent instructions. 'Stand by to fend her off. You, run to the surgery and get Fothergill sahib. Quick now. Chop chop.'

'Good God,' Goetz said again. 'Did you see it that time? The poor wretch.'

Round the paddle feathered, so leisurely, so casually, and now I saw what was upsetting him: the naked corpse of Hpung spreadeagled upon the paddle's dripping shelf. He was held in place by the spikes left bare when the boxing had been torn away. By a fluke that bookmakers would have priced as impossible, the paddle had scooped up his body and dropped it against these spikes, which we could see had driven through him in three places and so pinioned him.

'I'm going to be sick,' Goetz said, surprisingly.

I said, 'He was already dead. No one swam down and nailed him to the paddle.'

Hpung's head was flopping around. The paddle descended, the head rolled over, and I now saw that he'd had his throat cut open from one ear to the other. Everything was visible. His windpipe had been severed. The stubs of it, which were corrugated like coupling hoses, had been cleansed and blanched by the river. Whether its force had stripped him naked as well, I couldn't say. Anyway, there he was, our headman, bolted to the paddle for all to see.

The foreman was going to knock up a bamboo platform out into the water to retrieve the body. It was the quickest way. 'Something tribal, do you think?'

'Money,' I replied. 'We paid him off three days ago. It can't be easy to hide a decent sum in the amount of clothing these people wear.'

At that moment Fothergill, the doctor, arrived with two native policemen.

This being murder, more senior ranks had to be summoned. The Indian mind is as intricate as the Russian's when it comes to legal twaddling. It revels in the fact that the law must be respected, the proper processes undertaken in a proper manner, and the slapdash eschewed.

A full-blown inspector arrived with his sergeant on the next boat from Pakokku. Those of our porters who were still in town were rounded up for questioning. Professional trackers called *puggies* were sent out to bring in those who'd already gone home. I don't think anyone actually cared: Hpung wasn't a local and no one's interests had been touched. But the procedures had to be satisfied. Goetz and I were requested to stay on as potential witnesses.

Nine

THE HUB of Chaungwa, and I daresay the British Empire's boldest curiosity east of Brighton, was the General Post Office. The construction of this vast, copper-domed, greenly radiant building in a Burmese town of a mere eight thousand people was said by Fothergill to have been an error by the India Office. The wrong plans had been put in the wrong envelope: it had been intended for the financial district of Bombay. 'Every time I see it, I'm cheered up,' said Fothergill. 'I too make mistakes. Anyway, it's been built and paid for. They can't move it now.' Indeed they could not, nor would the natives have allowed it for the post office was a fine dry place to have a chat and a smoke. (Only spitting was prohibited.) No one objected if a man took his goat with him while he did his business. Naked children played games in its dusty recesses. It was cool. Above all, it made the citizens of Chaungwa feel superior to the merchant capitalists of Bombay.

I went one midday to post a letter to Mother.

The overhead grass mats had just been wetted again. The boys pulling them – by twine looped around their feet – were seated dozing against the far wall. Sweat was coursing down the groove of my spine into the waistband of my shorts, which was black and soaking. The benches were alive with muttering conversations that would suddenly rise in volume as one of the parties went outside to spit. Sweepers were at work with besoms and pans. Leather sandals slapped across the floor, which was good quality teak planking. A clerk was languidly intoning the numbers of the tickets by which the order of approach to the counter was regulated.

I wasn't thinking about Hpung, about Goetz, or even about the date of arrival of the next boat, which was critical to Fothergill's diminishing supply of bottled Export. Impatience had run its course. I was exhausted by the heat and by doing nothing. Torpor was in full command. In just a few days I'd become the Oblomov of Upper Burma.

Wearily the clerk called a number.

An old man rose from the bench opposite me; toothless, a thin white beard clinging to the very point of his chin, a slight belly, lazy wrinkles at his waist.

He handed his counterpart ticket to the yawning clerk, who pointed officiously to his cheroot. Dutifully the old fellow slippered across the gritty floor to the line of wooden fire buckets besides the parcels counter. He inserted his cheroot about an inch into the sand. Straightening he said something to the clerk – 'Keep an eye on it for me,' I expect.

He lifted a corner of his lungi and rewrapped it. He squinted down at the ticket. Then something caught his eye on the wall. He leaned forward to make an inspection.

What was it?

I watched him. It always pays to see what strikes other people. He called the clerk over. They both leaned forward. The clerk removed his spectacles, cleaned them on his dhoti, replaced them, stared, drew his lips back over his teeth. They peered and consulted, heads almost touching.

Was something burrowing out of the woodwork? What other explanation could there be?

I jumped up. I ran over, shouting at them in Russian.

It came out of the timber at an unimaginable speed. I glimpsed a greenish flash against the clerk's white clothing as it whistled between the two startled men. I thought, Oh my God it'll head straight for a window, which of course had no glass, because that's what buprestid beetles do, they go instantly for where it's lightest. All the collectors' stories I'd heard at the Darwin came back to me in an instant, about the rarities that had escaped because the collector had fallen in a ditch or couldn't swim the river. 'Stop it!' I shouted. 'Kill it!' Already my blood was churning inside me. I'd seen the sheen of verdigris, the glow of its royal blue shoulders. It had to be a jewel. Which one? 'Kill it for God's sake,' I shouted

35

as the glittering bomblet flew straight as an arrow into the glass of the oil lamp on the parcels desk. I could see it, lying half stunned on the counter, showing off its greeny-bronze undercarriage, its stout legs bicycling vaguely. Even in that condition its instinct was to get flying. Where would it make for next?

'Block the window. Just stand in front of it, you idiots.' I was tearing at my shirt. By now the jewel's legs were waving furiously. In a second it'd be off. I flung my shirt at it.

The lamp slid to the floor, shattering the glass.

'Fire!' someone yelled. Casually the ticket clerk went and picked up a fire bucket.

But this I only saw in arrears. For I'd followed my shirt and gone over the counter on my belly seconds afterwards, flooring one of the parcel clerks. I flung him out of the way. The shirt was in front of me. Panting, I knelt over it, scrutinising the floor all around in case the jewel had somehow been squirted out. The post office was in pandemonium. It reached me as a loud humming noise. In the corner of my vision were bits of people leaning over the counter, heads and teeth and moustaches and spectacles all mixed up. I could see my jewel nowhere on the floor. So it hadn't escaped. Like a miser I lifted a corner of my shirt. My heart was going like a runaway horse. It was there. Undamaged, flexing its wing cases. Incredible eyes staring at me, eyes that took up half its head. I clamped down on the shirt. I bunched it together until there was only this one bubble containing my beetle. Then I said to the ticket clerk, who was generally keeping order, 'Have someone get my friend and tell him to *bring the bottle*.'

One could say such a thing in Chaungwa knowing that the person of Goetz would be understood immediately.

Breathing deeply, I stayed crouching over my shirt until he arrived with my pillbox and killing bottle.

We dealt with my jewel. I knew instinctively that it was a first. One develops a sense about these things in the same way as does anyone who studies beautiful things. It is the manner in which the individual parts are contrived, and then the impression that is left by the whole that sets bells ringing.

Goetz was very quiet. That was another good sign.

I went to stand up but found that my legs were too weak. My head was spinning. I just squatted there on the parcels floor holding the killing bottle between my hands, smiling foolishly at Goetz. There were tears in my eyes. I wished my father were with me. Fame was within my grasp, and the wealth that he'd always yearned for. I waved Goetz away. I wanted to have this moment without him spying on my emotions.

The parcels clerk was telling me I must move. 'How are we to do our work? There is a lady who is trying to give me three packages for her brother in Rangoon.'

And the ticket clerk was telling me I must move or his manager would scold him.

I asked if he had a safe-deposit box. Smiling, he said they had five hundred. I said I'd buy one. He looked puzzled. 'Rent it, I mean,' I said. My head was floating amidst clouds of bougainvillea, my limbs were weightless. I expect I still had the same stupid grin on my face. I looked up into his nice brown worried eyes.

'But first you must remove yourself from this particular place of business,' he said. He lifted the hinged counter and stood over me. He put his hand out, maybe for the money. I took it, hauled myself up.

I'd felt nothing while I was on the floor. I'd been in la-la land. My mind – imagination, subconscious, however it's termed – had been more powerful than my body. It was only when I stood up that I realised. Disbelieve me if you will.

The clerk lowered his gaze. 'Oh mister, this is a public place. We must get you into seclusion.'

He handed me my shirt, which I tied appropriately round my waist. I saw him put the pillbox on deposit: I pocketed the key. Then I went outside into the hot street and almost immediately bumped into Fothergill. He'd been coming to look for me. Goetz had told him I'd had a bit of luck in the post office.

I untied my shirt and showed him. 'Where are the women here?' My expression and the extraordinariness of the situation – the phenomenon, medically and psychologically speaking – stopped him laughing. He showed me the alley. He could vouch for nothing: it was only what he'd heard. I ran down it. There was no door, only beads. I brushed through them.

The three girls were playing mah-jong. In their first bored glance I saw, 'What is this whitey doing here?' The tiles clacked. One began complaining in a nasty whine. I untied my shirt with a flourish. This got their attention. They saw they weren't going to have to waste time arousing me. I undid my fly-buttons – popped it out and showed it to each of them in turn. I remember thinking it important that we all knew it was a fair deal: that perhaps they hadn't had a white man before.

I was still in the grip of my discovery. It touched upon eternity. How many thousands of years had the jewel existed without any person knowing of it? Excepting this chance, for how long might that state of affairs have continued? Until time ended? Where did I fit in?

My emotions were more concentrated than ever. I was suffused with the energy that I'd drawn into myself from the sky and from the earth, from the primaeval secret of nature that I'd just penetrated. There was an uncontainable head of pressure inside me, which I had to release before it exploded and spattered me over the walls and ceiling. I was like a caveman, grimacing and trembling. To get inside a woman and ram her to hell was all that could save me. I'd smash if I didn't. The girls saw this necessity and stopped giggling. We went through into a doing room of some size. The bed was a charpoy, a plain wooden frame with woven rope, no reciprocation in it at all. Besides it was for a Burmese and I was Russian and six foot two. I told them quite plainly it wasn't up to scratch. As they seemed to be at a loss, I stripped off my shorts and grabbed one of them, whereupon the other two immediately lifted her by the buttocks and offered her parted thighs to my tool. She wove her arms round my neck. Neatly, professionally, salaciously, they bobbed her up and down and left and right, just grazing my knob. I saw it was going to be an eight-hander, which was fine by me. But I had to have an immediate spill so that I could think straight. What I'm trying to say is that the experience of having been the first person since the age of slime to have cast eyes on this dazzling, bronzey, blue-shouldered buprestid beetle had turned my mind inside out. It was as if I'd smoked a pound of bhang. Since slime – since chaos – since man discarded his last set of gills. Billions of people – like grains of sand – had died in ignorance of my jewel.

But hey, who happened along . . . So let it be named after me! Let my fame resound forever!

My cock was swollen with vanity. 'Doigii!' I shouted, 'the

beetle of Charlie Doig,' and I jerked the girl down so that my gross length was inside her. Feeling this imperative, which at first made her squeak, the lady obliged me in double-quick time. Or rather the three of them together, fingers prying everywhere.

But nothing was diminished thereby. I was still roaring like a bull and my face, I knew, was as red as the sunset. Should I call it a trance, a phase of tantrism, of Buddhist other-worldliness? I was experiencing visions of beetles, the jewels in particular, interspersed with the graphic fucking of women – parting the hairy purse and pounding into Jerusalem. They could have entered no one else's head. Later I tried to describe to both Goetz and Fothergill what I'd been through, but they merely guffawed.

At any rate there was more to come, that much was obvious.

The girls were wetting up, starting to squabble over me. One bent over and waved her backside around. On inspecting it and finding it pocked like Reynolds's billiard table, I refused her. We settled for a combined operation and made preparations for everyone to be involved. My white and pink skin was a novelty to them, and they were still at an age to be experimental.

I don't know exactly how this next sequence came about. Of course we were making certain noises. Perhaps that's what brought the madam in. Perhaps she'd been on the premises all the time, flogging tickets to the back-room spyholes. All of Chaungwa might have been watching us – or preparing to, formed up in chattering queues.

It had been shown to me that the rope weave of the charpoy did, after all, have some elasticity, being made from one particularly blessed fibre. We were on it in a greasy mound, a knot of brown and white. I was doing one girl (a different one) with the assistance of the other two – one on my back and the other below the charpoy, fingering the girl I was doing and at the same time oiling my big Russian balls: milking them with a lightly closed fist.

I became aware of a lessening in the various rhythms of my partners. I said, 'What's going on around here?' Turning my head, I found the madam bent down to my level. I was snugged right into my girl – jammed there, up to the maker's name. It was a curious sensation to find this crone had been observing me from a distance of no more than a foot.

'*Kalati*, mister? Four rupees. Only four.' She showed me the fingers.

My girl shifted under me. I said, 'Too much?' not referring to the price. Then: 'Sweetheart, what are *kalati*?'

How was I to know what her reply meant? Raising my voice I said to madam, 'Where are they then, woman? *Kalati* – oh yes, oh yes, bring them on.'

Next there was a sort of curved wooden pipette or funnel thing. I described it as well as I could to Fothergill, having had no more than a glimpse of it. It went up my arse very smoothly. Then madam came back with a brass jug, which she twizzled around beneath my nose. The water was as dark as pitch. Things were swirling in it. I could see nothing clearly. The girl under the charpoy came out, giggling. '*Kalati* – make mister's blood go on fire.' She smacked her palms together, a signal for me to clench, which I did. I heard a watery swishing noise and braced, envisioning my jewel beetle. Down the funnel madam ladled them, into the hole they went, down the mineshaft – wrigglers, writhers, jiggledy-jig. Baby eels – poor bastards, thought I. But then – I closed my eyes. I could feel the silence all round me. The girls were waiting for a sign. I opened one eye – and winked at them. I don't know what exactly the little fellows were doing inside me or where they'd got to, but I recommend it.

My toenails tingled. My eyeballs shot out of my skull. My cock began to hum like a tuning fork as the elvers twanged the cords – or whatever, I'm not an anatomist. Energy was pouring through me like an electric current. Was it the past my beetle had shown me or the future? Was it the pull of the moon that gripped me? Or the mystery of the Orient – or what? I wasn't bothered to work it out. What was certain was that there was a girl beneath me and another beneath her and they had forty fingers between them and a basin of hungry little eels were nibbling my navel from the inside and the last girl was shrieking on top of me, sitting on my back with her dripping thighs clamped round my ears, pulling at my hair with one hand, frigging herself with the other, riding me and bucking – my mahout.

Afterwards I slept for two hours, like a dead man, naked on a mat in that brothel. I knew the key to the safe-deposit box would

40

be safe in my shorts. Madam would already have been up to ask the clerk. Just a beetle, he'd have said, not worth the trouble.

I was purified by the sleep. The only comparison is the obvious one, to do with drink.

Then I got my beetle from the post office and had two Exports with Fothergill. He'd heard many stories about the brothel. The Forestry Department survey team had drunk all his beer one night and talked of nothing but tantrism and the sexual act. I returned to our rooms. I unpacked the case and started to mount my jewel: nothing splashy, but I wanted Norman to be impressed when they opened it in Chicago. I had it striding up a bank of cotton wool, antennae curling and its chocolate eyes at their hugest.

Goetz desired to help me but I showed him my teeth. The moment he touched it he could have a claim. Glory isn't the same when you have to share it. Coleoptera label 113 was mine, one hundred per cent. No smudging of the rules, no confusion. And when Norman's naming committee met in the museum, I wanted my name in there somewhere. Doigii, same as I told the girls, to bring renown to the dearest father to have existed and to advance myself.

Next morning I returned to the post office and bought from the parcels clerk one of those small wooden boxes used for sending sample goods of less than eight ounces. I took care that the clerk placed the stamps where a cancelling impress could do no harm if wielded too forcefully. 'Put them at the corner – there.'

His tongue, mauve with ink, dabbled over the backside of King George. His dark eyes regarded me with humour. Layering the stamps neatly below the horn of my fingernail, he said: 'Mister become famous! Maybe world's number one beetle!' He tied a doubled length of sisal round the box and applied a red wax seal to the knot. 'All finished up! Beetle going safe and sound to Chicago in captain's hold.'

I said a prayer. 'Thank you, Hpung, for giving up your life and thereby causing this delay. Please, God, send calm seas between Rangoon and America.' Opening my eyes I fixed on the clerk, who'd been trying to stare into my soul, and made him say Amen with me.

Ten

SOME MONTHS later, after our return, I heard from Norman that my beetle had been named, for the benefit of all the human sort, *Chrysochroa birmanensis* var. *doigii* Brendell 1912. I was twenty-three years of age.

Lying full of notions in bed, I got it stuck in my mind that millions of brown people and yellow and white and black people were parading my name through their cities on placards, talking only about me and my jewel beetle and its kingly shoulders, its green mantle and Cleopatra eyes. Their small talk at mealtime was full of it. Doigii! For all posterity! And I so young!

'Who's the great big peacock, then,' said my mother, to dampen the conceit that was making the walls of her house bulge.

Two weeks after Norman's cable I received a letter from his publicist, a Mrs Amy Carson.

The ribbon spool must have been loose in her typewriter, for many of her characters were tipped with red, like cinnabar moths. Or the excitement of writing to me had made everything bounce.

'We all find him so cute, and have nicknamed him Wiz. I asked if Wiz was a he. They told me Yes, but it wasn't quite as straightforward as that. I hope you weren't thinking of him as a girl! Now I must be serious or I shall be out of a job. The fact is that the museum is working up an exhibition of which Wiz is to be the centrepiece . . .'

She was doing a poster, in which I was to feature, photographed 'in a characteristic costume, if you please'. Lewis's in Oxford Street had a good jungle background; they snapped me in my shorts and helmet, butterfly net poised. Amy got this into a number of popular American magazines. The story of our sojourn in the rainforest, the sensation of Hpung's murder and my capture of Wiz in the baroque post office of Chaungwa caught the imagination. Over two thousand people showed up on the first day he was exhibited. Amy sent me press cuttings. I was the most famous naturalist in America, she said.

The most famous! Hartwig Goetz – well down the list, among the plankton. It was a good feeling. I plumed and preened myself all over gloomy London, especially in the Darwin. At home I was insufferable.

Here let me praise my noble, generous mother, so harassed by the fates, and give thanks unto her for the gift of life, which I regard as an honour. I was told of her death on the platform of Smolensk railway station. Pneumonia, that was what my cousin Nicholas said.

Eleven

I T WAS an acquaintance of Igor, my great-uncle, who tipped us off about the Russians' expedition to Turkestan. For many years there'd been rumours in the Darwin Club. The collection of bird skins in the Academy of Sciences in St Petersburg had been damaged. Had the rain got in? Was it the heating? Or was it really the case, as alleged, that Brandt, the curator, had sold the rarest skins to a dealer in Hamburg who happened to be his brother? There were always tales on the go. But now Mother heard via Uncle Igor that the Academy had actually received the money to do something about it. The word 'received' had been underlined in red ink.

This was always the point with the natural sciences in Russia, which were much spoken of and the subject of many collections including royal ones – but rarely the recipient of State funds. That scene from Gogol's later, destroyed, volume is ever applicable, where a candidate for the civil service is asked to solve a problem that is stated as follows: 'Given a scheme, a promoter must secure the finance for carrying it off. Compose a secure defence against all promoters.'

But now the Academy actually had the money for a three-year trip working out of Samarkand to assemble the definitive collection of the passerines of Central Asia. It was in their pocket. How to get it into mine, that was the trick.

Goetz had the ear of people who counted at the Academy. I was more or less Russian. We had international reputations. But it was Wiz who clinched it. I was the man in form and there to prove it was Wiz, gathering new admirers every day. So the job became ours, subject to an interview at the consulate in Bedford

Square with Zhdanov, the head in Britain of our Third Section. His eyes, obscured by the thick lenses of his spectacles, moved murkily over us as if they were slivers of jellyfish. He related in vicious tones how much his family had suffered in the uprising of 1905. All the terrorists had come from Germany. Their propaganda sheet, *Iskra,* had been printed there. He looked threateningly at Goetz. 'This is what comes out of your country to bite us. Why should I grant you a visa, Mister Goetz? How do I know you may not have the inclination to be a terrorist, that you do not have this disease?'

I was sorry for Goetz. He was a naturalist, a student of beauty and Linnaeus. Soldiers at frontier posts he could deal with. Bureaucrats panicked him.

'But I've been here so long that at last I dare call myself English. Only a speck of German remains. A speck, sir, – *ein kleines bisschen . . .*'

'There, one hundred per cent German,' said Zhdanov in triumph. 'But I see you have employment capturing birds, so I suppose you are harmless. My wife likes birds, the sort that lives in cages. They're the easiest. However, I don't suppose your people concern themselves with canaries.'

With poor grace he filled in our passports, single sheets of paper measuring fifteen inches by twelve. The way he stamped them was so curious – a sideways, furtive, crimping motion. It seemed to say, 'See how far that gets you.' I imagined him selling papal indulgences in the square at Padua.

At lunch in the Club some wiseacre remarked that the tools of trade of the naturalist are identical to those of the terrorist: rifle and gun, knives, cyanide and arsenic. This made me think. We could be delayed interminably if we used the railway system of Europe. It was a standing joke that more Tsarist police agents were on it than travellers. So we went by tramp steamer, through the Mediterranean. When we got to Smyrna, Goetz suddenly decided that Troy was too close to miss. 'Antioch and Ephesus too. I wish to see these places while they still have a smell of the Bible and one can visualise things as they used to be. I'm getting old. My health may collapse, my luck likewise. Where do you want to rendezvous, skipper?'

We decided to meet at Kattikurgan, a small garrison town

on the edge of the Turkestan desert, roughly midway between Bokhara and Samarkand.

There was a difficulty between us concerning the Russian calendar, which operates several days behind the rest of the world. We agreed that it was thirteen. He wrote down the date of our meeting on the flyleaf of his journal: May 28th, 1914. He said he'd arrive from Samarkand on the second train.

When I made fun of him for specifying the train he'd be on without seeing a timetable and having a thousand miles and two mountain ranges to cross before he got there, he retorted, 'All railway stations must receive a minimum of two trains daily in each direction. There are travellers with morning urges and travellers with evening urges. If they all go the same way – but that's foolish even to consider talking about. What I say is logical. There will be a second train, Doig, and I shall be on it.'

It was the way we planned our expeditions. Except for Russia, whose frontiers were notorious, we could have gone anywhere in the world without a passport. What constricted our movements were not borders but natural obstacles: mountains, deserts and rivers, in that order. When collecting, our speed was negligible. But on the hoof, as a general rule, we would reckon to cover a thousand miles a week in railway country and the same distance in a month where we had to use mixed transport. The least reliable conveyance was a boat. Whatever the means of propulsion boats always have the potential to go slower – because of the wind or the absence of wind or the tide or the current or the shoals or the waterfalls. Never completely trust a boat, that was our rule. Goetz's calf muscles were a constant reminder of the truth of his adage: 'Walk steadily to travel quickly.'

A Turk of the same build as himself carried his baggage off. Goetz was using the commercial-sized airtight salt jars of Messrs Cerebos to store specimens such as snakes and the larger insects. I'd offered to take them all myself. But he was certain he'd alight on something worth collecting. He'd wrapped half a dozen in sacking and roughly boxed them. The Turk went down the gangboard with muffled chimes ringing on his shoulder.

On the quay Goetz turned and shouted up, 'Don't sneer at me, Doig, I'll be there. The second train, going from east to west.'

I travelled on to Odessa and thus to the Crimea and Uncle Igor's cool, colonnaded villa, the design for which had been lifted from one of Diocletian's palaces.

My cousin Elizaveta had just been staying with him. Uncle Igor could do nothing but talk about her. On several occasions I asked his opinion about the international situation and in particular about the Russian policy with regard to Serbia. The nearest I got to an answer was this, which came with a shake of his old rouged cheeks: 'I never heard such a foreboding consonant as that "b" in Serbia and that's as far as I want to think about it.'

He would say nothing about war or politics. Happiness came most easily to him when he was sitting in his arbour of vines with his Vichy water and medicines, staring at Elizaveta's photograph. It was the best one ever taken, a close-up of her dark, angular face as she stepped off the running board of his Astro-Daimler.

But he must have been one of the few people in Europe not brooding about the political situation. When the second west-bound train arrived at Kattikurgan on May 28th, the possibility of war was all Goetz could talk about.

From forty yards he hurried towards me, this thick, crumpled naturalist, this absolute connoisseur of beauty, breaking into a trot after a few paces so that I believed he must have vital news, like an outbreak of the plague. I too began to run. Other passengers had descended, portly gentlemen in robes, turbaned in many colours. Goetz and I converged erratically, swerving through them like a boy and girl hastening to declare a passion.

He put his hand to his breast as he got his breath back. 'Not as young as I used to be . . . listen, skipper . . . yesterday in the bank in Abramovski Boulevard I met a German, a merchant. He had a newspaper, some days old, which he lent me. In it I saw reprinted the speech of Germany's Chancellor at the time of the Army Bill last year. His words were so ruthless that I've memorised them. "We are not bringing in this bill because we want war but because we want peace and because, if war comes, *we desire to be the victors*." These are the words of a man begging for war. It cannot be otherwise. When I gave the paper back I asked the merchant his opinion. He looked at me as if I was some stupid pig farmer from Holland. "Of course, what else?"

'Then we went to the Civilians Club and had some beers together. But only Russian beer, light stuff not worth talking about. Anyway, I wanted to tell you this before we start our work. You're the leader. It may be that you would wish to take some special action, that's what I thought on the train.'

I had the same feeling then for Goetz as I'd had when he was being questioned by Zhdanov: that he should be kept well away from the unalterable baseness of mankind. Here was someone who'd sleep happily amidst the most venomous snakes in the universe yet pale to ashes at the prospect of human bloodshed. He was truly shocked by what he'd heard. His eye-whites were stark and so magnified that his face looked unnatural.

He said, 'I'm too old to fight. Thank God, for I could never kill a man.'

'What about me?'

'Ja, you'd kill alright.' His jowls shook with a little mirth.

'So what should each of us do if it comes to war?'

Goetz considered me. The natives were flowing round us in a noisy stream. He said, 'That depends on the balance of your patriotism – are you a subject of King George or of the Tsar? For me there is only King George.'

He remarked there was time enough for one of the Powers to step back. No one would start fighting before the harvest had been gathered: September, say, if the year was normal. He said how disgusting politicians were, that they'd ruin us before they'd finished. This required so little comment that we let the subject lapse. It drifted away into the soft desert dusk as we strolled up the platform to his baggage.

We spent the night in the front room of Kobulov, the station-master, beneath the glow of his household ikons. Goetz was sleeping poorly, moving around a lot and speaking words or even half sentences. I knew all the signals by heart. But I was the leader now and mine the more important sleep. I woke him. The subject that was exercising him was War and Patriotism. How much could the State demand of its citizens? Could men be legally compelled to fight, even if the cause was odious to them? The words came rushing out. He was greatly disturbed. He'd only been in a state of semi-sleep: 'Touching the clouds having a foot on the ground,' was how he put it. What was needed was a new and invincible Truth to which all men could subscribe with an easy conscience. In place of battle standards there should be banners of Christ; in place of marching songs, hymns. (I should mention that he was a devout Lutheran.) In this way the blind pursuit of soldiering that was the curse of England and Germany would wither to nothingness. The armies of the future would be spiritual gatherings seeking One Truth.

'Then go and join one,' I growled. 'That'll cure you quickly enough.'

Twelve

STATIONMASTER PAVEL Kobulov was vital to us. He'd been stuck at Kattikurgan for twenty-eight years, having arrived there as foreman of the gang laying the rails. One evening the surveyor and a commissioner had come rattling up the line on the platelayers' bogie, which was pumped by hand and could be heard a mile away. They got out their map and said, Here there will be a station: who's the foreman? Pavel was a tall, clean character who stood up straight. It was enough. He was appointed stationmaster on the spot, even though he had no maths.

It had taken him six years to sell his first drum of tickets. The railway auditor couldn't believe it and had accused him of fraud. The experience had scared him stiff – taken years off his life and turned his hair white. But now he'd got over it and had learned the tricks.

He dealt with only six trains a day (four civilian and two military). He was delighted to have the chance at a second occupation.

The greatest practical difficulty for any naturalist in the field, after locating his quarry, is to get his specimens home. Naturally it is also important to dry, eviscerate and prepare them; to do these things thoroughly and without short cuts, which is not always easy. To be birding during a migration, as we were in the following year, leaves few of the twenty-four hours for eating and sleeping. Cleaning a bird, skinning it, inserting the shaping materials as required, and sewing it up again takes thirty minutes. There can be no interruption once the job is started or the ants will take over. By day we would select, stalk and kill, usually with a blowpipe. In the evening I would prepare a meal while

Goetz fed our animals. If the light was good we'd write up our journals while everything was fresh in our minds. Then we'd settle to the exacting job of skinning the day's bag, sexing the birds and analysing the contents of their guts – by lantern, by the stickiness of night, smeared with sweat, a fur of mosquitoes swaying on our forearms. Then we'd check and recheck the information to go on the label and try to write it out without smudges. Sometimes, in important cases, one of us would paint on the label a match of the bird's plumage colours. These can take on a different hue when seen six months later on a February afternoon in St Petersburg. It is vital for a scientist to know what the bird looked like in situ.

Much of a collector's reputation rests on the quality of his skins. If it's impossible to imagine that the bird in question ever flew, sang or raised a brood of young, then his efforts have been wasted. The skinning style of one man is quite different from the style of another. Curators recognise them instantly. There's no hiding at the topmost level of museum work.

So, it's three o'clock at night in the Kizil Kum. The annual bird migration from India is in full swing. The air is full of them, from the mountain passes of the Hindu Kush to where we are. Their purpose is to breed. For this they seek prolonged daylight, space, and ready supplies of food and water. From Turkestan they'll spread as far north as Siberia.

For Goetz and I the day is already twenty-one hours old. We are camped in the snow-fed marshes where the river Zarafshan runs to waste. There is a wilderness of saxaul and tamarisk thickets here that give excellent cover to most of the species we're after. In them live also the small, melancholic tigers of Central Asia. We are coming to the end of our stint of skinning. It's not good for Goetz, who next year will drink an entire bottle of brandy by himself to celebrate his fiftieth birthday, to work these hours for six weeks without a break. Therefore I do much of the skinning alone, while he sleeps. But tonight he is busy searching again for the Truth about the war that he foresees. He is bothered about Patriotism and wishes to discuss it. We talk as we go along, with long pauses since scalpel work is delicate and we have to concentrate.

The night is never quiet. There is a constant murmuration of voles and other small mammals among the saxauls. There are the owls that hunt these sounds, and the cock nightingales and the sleeping noises from our donkeys that are related to snores. We hear the frantic squeals as a wild pig, which was happily rootling through the mud for fleshy young tubers, is jumped by one of the tigers. Whenever this happens, a short and poignant silence falls upon the desert. We are all imagining death, even the voles.

We hear the stars whisper to each other tidings of dawn. We stretch, yawn, clean and store our skinning tools, hook the skins to a pole standing in a bucket of water, check that everything is listed correctly in our journals and collapse onto our sturdy Army & Navy beds in the same clothes that we have worn for two weeks. Every other morning we'll pack the skins in a cotton shift and leave them with the headman in the nearest village, whom we'll also inform of our future movements.

The rest is up to Kobulov.

His son-in-law works at the Kommercheskaya Hotel in Samarkand and has access to a daily supply of wooden wine cases. It was he who found that a claret case fits inside a champagne case with a tolerance of an inch all round – a double skin and so perfect. Kobulov employs someone to follow us collecting the skins. He then despatches them by train to St Petersburg. (We have Priority labels printed with the Imperial eagle.)

All the stationmasters on the Samarkand loop keep in touch with each other via the electric telegraph to warn of approaching auditors or gangs of ne'er-do-wells, or to assist in the common cause of enrichment. Even five hundred miles away I found that Kobulov's name did the trick.

In the village he got us a couple of baggage donkeys for our guns, ammunition, traps, the lime green Skyproof tent, our skinning equipment and personal stuff. The purchase of our two riding donkeys he left to us. All riding animals are a personal choice.

Mine was a biscuit-coloured animal with teeth like yellow doors that I named Bathsheba. White donkeys were unpopular in these parts. The colour was thought to indicate a lack of stamina, like chestnut in a horse. Kobulov said that anyone seen riding one would instantly be labelled a Baghdadi, meaning metropolitan and effete. Bathsheba's hide was as stiff as buckram. Clouds of dust rose from her flanks whenever I thrashed her. She carried me for almost two years, my feet never far from the ground.

Her heats – she was quite regular – were torrid affairs of thankfully short duration. The moans with which she attempted to pierce the desert's stony heart had a tragic quality, a sort of I-might-die-you-know tone. In vain did she cock her ears for the trumpet call of male ardour, flap her stumpy tail, and scent the wind for a suitor to whom she could present her pink, primed, pear-drop keyhole. Because she was so regular I was always able to get her away from company when it mattered.

Her ears arched inwards. The length of a young carrot would have covered the distance between them at their tips. The hairs on the outside were mouse. On the left ear they disguised an immense dry wart. Within they were pale and downy, very near to white.

When the sun was searing the back of my neck (110 degrees was common in August) and rock-shimmer was creating extraordinary mirages in the desert, like undulating sheets of glass or mica, I would sometimes take an easy leaning on her withers. The heat, the glare, the dust, the monotonous joggle of her action would make my mind reel. Looking out through the archway of her ears I often glimpsed Elizaveta. It was her eyes, always her strong black eyes that the genie granted me first. Then would come the dark hair en brosse, the tendrils of left-over hair on the nape of her neck, her trim bold figure – but one can only dream of so much when astride a moke.

Thirteen

A N HOUR'S riding and we were beyond the melon patches and
tiny vegetable fields of Kattikurgan. A little farther on we
left the bund of its main irrigation ditch and entered the desert.

The sky was dull. Once out of shelter the wind's yellow
tongue assailed us, making the saxaul bushes whistle and the
bundles of dead blow-weed scamper like rabbits. My cheeks
stung with the grit it was carrying. Goetz put on a pair of dust
spectacles.

The big Russian forty-verst map is a secretive document. It
did not even hint at the many settlements and villages that we
later happened across. It allowed that Europe was on our left
and China on our right, but that I knew anyway since I was
following true north on the compass.

I don't know how intelligent birds really are: how apt their
judgement is, even in their speciality. Oftentimes I have thought
my imitation of their song to be terrible and have been embar-
rassed to hear myself. But so long as I remained in concealment
I found they'd come in the end. The fools! As I said to Goetz,
would you stand for it if a Martian came croaking up to you
and said he was I?

And the birds of the Zarafshan swamps, perhaps tired after
flying a thousand miles from India, are as gullible as the rest.
Phut! A three-foot blowpipe is a cheap way to kill a bird. Skinning
it also becomes easier than when it's been shot.

The ball, which is the size of a marble and is best made of
a dense soil such as clay, must fit snugly in the pipe or windage
will occur causing it to deviate from true. If you've been
waiting motionless for a couple of hours among sand flies

and mosquitoes for the particular specimen of Sykes's warbler that you need to complete your age sequence, you do not want windage. The air must be stored in both mouth and lungs and produced from those places simultaneously. It is not enough to be pop-cheeked like a cherub; the air will simply be insufficient. The correct noise when the ball leaves the pipe is round and dull, nothing like the cork from a bottle. Anything suggestive of a guitar being strummed is the sound of windage.

Another tip is this: keep the pipe on a level plane when you take aim. The vertical distance between its line of fire and the line from your eye will then always be constant and you'll be able to correct your aim easily. Move your head rather than the pipe.

Phut! – the target drops, upon a muddy slope, in front of its friends. The limp bundle of feathers is plainly in their view. For a moment the considering heads eye the corpse. Then they quickly resume the search for seeds, or insects, or the pallid spindly worms that inhabit the ooze of the Zarafshan. Of grieving there is none, or inquisitiveness or investigation. What counts is food, not death.

Also: the striking hoopoe (I can never see its crest without also seeing Achilles in his helmet) is the stinkiest nester in the universe, far worse than any of the fish-eating birds. Why? Are they alone in having no sense of smell? Or are they alone in not caring? What advantage accrues to them thereby?

There are birds that migrate through the Himalayas at fifteen thousand feet. Why not fly round them or through lower passes and avoid overworking their tiny lungs?

Perhaps it is a mistake to suppose that they should be intelligent in the same way that we are. Perhaps it is we who are the dunces. Their brains are capable of putting into effect unassisted exercises in navigation, harmony and athletics that in a human being would make that person a god. Yes, a god and no less than a god. But we suppose ourselves superior because we have souls and consciences. Neither has ever been seen. But we are sure we have them and that they distinguish us from the lower orders.

I wet my lips for another treacherous love song:

Tsweep, tsweep
Cherry do, cherry do, cherry do . . .

Phut! I can hear the sound yet. It is a reminder of the halo of glory with which I crowned myself, of the itch of purpose that kept me at it, of the time I swanned round Turkestan in the certainty that the Orlov Medal was mine for the taking, that the two-handled golden urn that went with it in perpetuity was already on my mantelshelf.

Fourteen

THEN WAR was declared. For us it happened in the following manner.

With winter came the intense, scorching cold of a continental climate. A thin sun by day, deep frosts by night. Our Skyproof tent would stand up by itself even after we'd knocked the pegs out of the ground. Instinctively Goetz and I crept in from the desert to get snugger with humanity.

We made camp about a mile outside Bokhara. The city still closed its gates every night. We did our collecting right up to the base of its mud brick walls, from which the sentries would watch us.

On this tinsel-bright morning of December I'd gone to shoot a couple of mallard for our dinner. The air was like glass and perfectly still. I could make out the fissures zigzagging up the dun wall. Below the turrets that jutted out at regular intervals were black streaks of ordure. On the ramparts were the Emir's soldiers in tunics that were an unmilitary shade of green – pistachio is what I recall. I could see their belt buckles glitter, I could see the cigarette the sergeant was smoking, I could hear him scolding one of his men, even though he was quarter of a mile away.

There were many swampy holes, old clay pits, round the city that the wildfowl loved. The second duck I shot fell out in the water. I waded in to retrieve it, up to my waist, feeling with my feet for snags and thinking about Guinea-worm disease, which is a killer in Bokhara.

Cold! It was cold enough for Judas that morning. My scrotum was on guard, was as tight as a walnut.

But I was going to get that mallard. It was my dinner.

Suddenly there was an inkling of jewellery bobbing in the corner of my eye. The men of Bokhara wear raiment of every strong colour. But this man I looked up to see riding above me on the bund was like a garden. He could only be the Emir. On his head was a turban of crustacean green, a little pointed, a little oniony, and below his deep collar, which was a red shade, his robes fell away in cascades, each fold or pleat having different angles of pink and green stripes. His horse, an Arab stallion, was tripping along vainly, hot-hoofed and half dancing as he held it on a longish rein. Its bridle was leafed with silver and the saddlecloth embroidered in gold. It curved its neck, fiddled noisily with its bit and trumpeted white steam from its glaring nostrils. The Emir's robes came down to his ankles. His stirrups were like leather coal scuttles. He rode very upright in his saddle. As the animal capered along the top of the bund, the clean winter light flew off the Emir's costume in all directions and dazzled me. I stood in the pool holding the wet mallard by the neck and shading my eyes, the better to perceive the extraordinariness of this man and his horse that so filled the barrel of the low winter sun.

Among and around the horse's legs were four or five rough-coated dogs with good bone at the shoulder. They were to flush the game. It was their day out. They knew it: shivered, trembled, looked piteous for all the time their master was halted. A few yards behind them a man on foot held a leash of three feathery salukis for the chase. Last rode the hawksman, in a plain white robe, carrying on his gauntleted right wrist the red-hooded killer, a goshawk.

They stopped, this gay cavalcade, and looked down at me. Their dust hovered and settled.

The Emir laughed – marvellously white teeth, like icing on top of his beard. I, dripping and freezing, laughed back. We exchanged greetings and then, leaning forward in his saddle, he spoke seriously, too fast for me to catch it all. Was it about cholera? Kobulov? What exactly was he saying? He pointed to his soldiers. He read a newspaper. He fashioned a universe with his pink and green striped arms. He traversed a machine gun. I understood – it was war.

'When?' I shouted.

'August in your calendar,' he replied. He listed the countries that were fighting. He spread wide his fabulous arms. 'But what can we do?'

'Leave them to it.'

He laughed again. Then he gave a command and they rode on their way. The man with the salukis hitched his robes round his waist, and set off at a loose lollop, his long golden thighs easily keeping pace with the horsemen. A chieftain and his retinue, man and his oldest friends, off for a day of sport in the desert, coursing the hare and hawking the marsh pheasants in the same way as generations had done before them, unchanged in any detail for five hundred years, since Genghiz Khan brought them the stirrup and made everything possible.

Away it went into the sand and scrub, that colour plate from the book of history. Away, away, with never a backward glance.

As it happened, that was the last occasion we touched Bokhara for ten weeks. I wanted to complete our survey of the western, and relatively barren, section of the desert before the spring migration arrived from India. When eventually we did return, the pulse merchant from whom we always bought our supplies plucked at my sleeve. There was a man in the city looking for me, sent by the railwayman – meaning Kobulov.

The message had passed through many hands since leaving the Crimea: Count Igor Rykov, my great-uncle and the possessor of the Rykov fortune, was dying.

Fifteen

Elizaveta came for me at the station in Eupatoria in Igor's Astro-Daimler. It was eleven years since we'd last seen each other, at the farewell party on the platform when Mother and I went to London, into exile. I looked her over critically as she swung her long legs out of the car, carefully placed an olive slipper into the dust, brushed aside the chauffeur's arm, and with a cousinly smile – half friend, half duty – kicked off into the decreasing space between us.

We embraced with a slight reserve. I hunched over her, being six inches taller.

I said, 'How is the old bastard?'

Smiling she replied, 'Alive and well. He only wanted attention. He takes care to get nothing but curable diseases. I'm afraid you've wasted your journey.'

We took our places in the car. Presuming he would find a fellow enthusiast in another man, the chauffeur slid back the window and rattled off for my benefit the owners of every car in the Crimea and the models they possessed. The governor of Simferopol had a forty-horsepower Braun, made in Vienna; the police chief in Kerch had a yellow Panhard Levassor . . . There were twenty-two altogether, of which he'd driven all but three. He chattered away, glancing at me in the mirror every time he told a joke to make certain that I'd understood it.

She stayed silent. Even if she'd wanted to make a speech it'd have been difficult against that competition. It can't possibly have been all she said during the journey to the villa but this is the line I remember: 'So, you've grown up, Charlie. Thank God.'

She was being Igor's hostess, also representing her absent

brother, Nicholas the progressive farmer. She'd made herself at home in Igor's Imperial villa, cast off her grey nurse's uniform and surrendered to the gentle spring sunshine of the Crimea.

The loquacious chauffeur drove us along the winding coast road, under the archway surmounted by the iron Rykov wolf, between the light pink clumps of oleander, to the severe door of the villa. He took my bag from the dicky, set it down and drove away.

She said in a superior way, as if she was matron of the spa, 'It's time for their siesta. You'll have to carry it yourself. On no account awaken our uncle. It's the only time he can sleep.'

Uncle Igor was my gaunt, stooping, mauve-cheeked great-uncle. Four times a year he would call on us when we were living in Moscow, travelling between his Crimean lands and his palace in St Petersburg. Nanny Agafya told me proudly that he was a 'plutoman'. But I never saw anyone so miserable. Central to his health were an ivory enema syringe and large round blue pills for his faltering heart. A relay team of messenger boys scuttled continuously between the pharmacy and our apartment bearing small packages labelled 'MEDICINES – URGENT'. The only people to relish his visits were the servants, to each of whom he gave on his departure a solid gold five-rouble piece for their troubles, which were considerable.

Sometimes Elizaveta's family would ask to stay when Igor was in residence. Mother was firm: the head of the family must have his privacy. So I would just observe her when she came from her hotel for a meal. Surreptitiously I would consider the nuances floating around her that my youthful comprehension couldn't penetrate.

'It can happen like that,' Mother said airily when I taxed her about Elizaveta's slimness and her dark features, both so different in character from the pink and stalwart Russianness of her brothers.

'A throwback probably,' said Father, who was reading the *Textiles Gazette* in his armchair. 'Egypt is the future, you know.' He lowered the paper, which had a picture of a new ginning machine on the front. I was bent forward studying it, trying to figure out what did what. 'Just think of her as a normal cousin, Charlie, that's the easiest.' He started reading again. 'Yes, Egypt by gosh, how they could grow the stuff with a bit of training.'

Whack, they closed the lid on her ancestry, and there I was content to leave it. What her father, my uncle Boris, had got up to as a widower had no relevance to my life. But was she content to return the favour and leave me with my secret? Oh no. She was always a pest – a great scratcher of other people's scabs, no sense of fair play at all.

She knew, because her brothers had told her, about the competition I was having with my parents' toilet – a Doulton: 'The Simplicitas – factories in Paisley and Lambeth.' She knew what I was after, to trace the entire course of those fat, black, Gothic letters in a oner. No short cuts, no cessation of flow to restore the pressure, and no skimping when my faltering arc came to tackle the 'y' of Paisley, which had as many loops as an anaconda. Every letter had to be faithfully described. I would drink tanks of water in advance, until I was red in the face.

Nicholas and his brother Viktor, who would sometimes squeeze in with me as invigilators, had informed her all about the Simplicitas and the defeats that my sharp, boyish stream had suffered.

So when Uncle Igor had departed and all the Smolensk lot came to stay, what was the first thing she did? Bang bang bang on the toilet door, rattling its polished brass knob, poking around in the keyhole with something from her hair.

'How far have you got? Why are you groaning like that, have you burst something? Shall I get a maid to go for the doctor?' – all in her screech that told everyone what I was up to.

She was a skinny, noxious girl, Elizaveta of Smolensk. She told on me when I kicked about the mounds of carefully raked leaves in the Alexandrovsky Gardens. She spat into my boiled egg when I reached over for the toast. She ripped the heroic frontispiece from my favourite book, *With Clive in India,* Henty's best, which Papa had just given me for my birthday. Her behaviour was abominable from the very first day I met her. Cousin, ha!

And while I'm trawling through the charge sheet, let me recount the incidents at Brest Station, at our farewell party.

It was winter. Apart from travelling on Train No. 1, the train for diplomats and couriers, Mother's principal conditions for agreeing to go to England were an entirely new wardrobe, five thousand roubles in the scarlet hundred series, each note to be ironed, and a party for *le tout Moscow* on the station concourse. Of course my father went along with this. He may have had, as my mother once alleged, *une main baladeuse*, but he also loved her profoundly.

Everyone my parents had ever known was there. The party grew noisier and noisier. Elizaveta was in the thick of it. She hopped and squealed, stamped on a cake with her fur-trimmed bootee to see how far the cream would fly, and miscounted our trunks to make us panic – so demurely, with such cat-eyed innocence: '*Tetushka*, auntie, weren't there meant to be seventeen of the big ones?' She told the porters we were English aristocrats – baron-lords, she said, and ripe for mulcting. She shrieked with laughter when their gangmaster pursued Papa for a larger tip. She told everyone about me and the Simplicitas. And all the while she was preparing those immense, make-believe tears, as if she really cared that I was leaving.

How I loathed her that evening! How I was yearning to strangle her, inch by lynching inch, with a tourniquet fashioned from the chic pink scarf to which her age did not entitle her. Alone and glowering in a corner, I was making plans for her death via a cauldron of simmering tar into which I was about to lower her slim girliness, by the ankles, upside down, drawers round her head, when suddenly, as she was on the point of screaming—

Out of the snowy night, past the left-luggage office, there marched the Macrimmon my father had hired, bagpipes blazing, kilt swinging, glengarry and blackcock feathers at a virile rake. Our guests clapped and shouted and hollered, I mean they went berserk. Bravissimo! Maestro Pushkin! Chukov, who was in love with Mother once a week and was by then completely pickled, whisked his opera cloak over his shoulder and cavorted goat-like after the piper, twiddling and pumping, tapping out the rhythm with a patent-leathered foot, imitating the man's every move and making a noise that we could guess was perfectly execrable. The habitual station drunks and vagrants started bolt upright from their benches, rubbing their eyes, utterly bewildered. Tchukov began to bait them, bending down and making his bagpipe noises right into their faces. A quarrel ensued which was solved only by the intervention of the stationmaster and, more effectively, by the arrival a few minutes later of our train.

Sixteen

B UT THAT was now a long way behind us, eleven – almost
twelve – years ago. We were no longer children, or spiteful
or precious or desperate to embarrass the other. We'd got Igor's
smart pinnace and its blue-capped crew to take us along the
coast to Sebastopol and then to Balaclava. A peasant had driven
us in his cart up to the ridge overlooking the battlefield. The
day was glorious. The short turf on which we sat was studded
with wild yellow crocuses.

'Do you remember how fervently the old soaks crossed themselves?' I said to her.

'Of course, they feared the worse,' Elizaveta said.

Her eyes, which I'd always remembered from my youth as
peremptory, had widened and softened to a dark brown colour
that matched her suede belt. They were examining the arrangements inside a crocus, resting quietly upon her high cheek bones,
their long lashes very prominent from where I was sitting, on
her right. Her black hair was cropped short (the hospital had
shaved her to the skull when she started). But her voice, that
was what got to me. It had changed completely and was now
low and evenly spaced, a rich gliding sort of voice.

'Wouldn't you?' she continued. 'You're snoring away over
your disgusting dream and all of a sudden it's interrupted by
this terrible screeching. What would be your first thought? You'd
think, This must be tremens, it can't be death with a noise like
that.'

She was stretched on her side, a white-shirted elbow denting
the turf, the back of her dark head just then cradled in her hand
so that her arm was part of two distinct triangles. She was

gazing down into the valley, which was speckled with sheep.

'Boltikov was so repulsive the way he attached himself to your party. Huge, like a mountain. All that sugar he must have eaten—'

'All that money he made—'

'Imagine inviting yourself and then doing nothing but boast . . . Anyway, he's dead. Blew up, pop, some sort of seizure.' She waved a hand to where a couple of vultures were starting to dismember a live lamb. We could plainly see its frantic jerking. 'Such sordid birds. You must know why we have to have them.'

'As scavengers,' I said.

We agreed how unpleasant they were; cumbersome and clanking, with jealous, speculative eyes, like Boltikov's. I said that the sound their wings made when they took off was like someone rapidly opening and closing his umbrella to work the rain off it.

At this she looked at me with her eyes a little wider. Perhaps she was wondering what else might be in a naturalist's mind. She said, 'Igor told me the other night on the terrace – you'd gone off after a moth – that when he was a lad, old Prince Gorchakov, who commanded the army, told him that after your cavalry came to grief, he saw a team of vultures turning a wounded man over with their beaks. To get at his rectum, he said. Apparently it's tasty to a vulture.'

'To all carrion,' I said. 'He told *me* that it took three years after the war for the songbirds to return to what had been the French sector. They shot everything that flew.'

She picked another crocus. 'This hateful war, our own – what's going to happen?'

'Soldiers will die, politicians will not. Other things too, which at the moment we cannot possibly discern. More things will happen than we expect, certainly not fewer.'

'You're not going to be one of those soldiers?'

'No. Why should I attempt to be killed? Goetz and I have discussed this often. We can never settle whom either of us is to be loyal to, since we are half-castes.'

'That's convenient for you,' she said.

'You mean selfish?'

'Yes, but not in a critical sense. We all have to look out for ourselves. The hospital is full of soldiers who've obeyed blindly. A month ago we had a man whose stomach was slit from side to side. We could see his intestines. We could even see the tapeworms moving around. As I ground up the phenacetin for him – it's for headaches: so cruel to give him hope – I thought, Why don't the other men run away when they see this sort of thing? So I'm not blaming you . . . What about afterwards, when there's no more blood to be spilled. What'll it be like then?'

'When we're as white as veal?'

'Well?' she said. She always hunted a bold line conversationally.

'The principal change is that I shall become as rich as Boltikov. It wouldn't embarrass me at all. I'm completely Russian in that respect. Having a thousand serfs to do what I want would be paradise.'

'How are you going to make this fortune?'

I explained about breeding the plague flea and milking it for serum. From thinking about how ruthless I'd have to be to succeed in such a business, I must have used the word, for she interrupted me: 'A ruthless man – I like that.' Her eyes challenged me. 'What ruthless men have we had in the family since the Founder? My father – grandfather – Igor – pfff! And now . . . Nicholas is the worst, wasting all his time trying to get the peasants to farm more efficiently. They take his money and do nothing. It's they who are the ruthless ones. It's not as if his money is all his, in any case. Some's mine, for my marriage portion. Father said so in his will. Why should he be able to throw it at those people? But I'm a woman. It's not for me to go against my brother.'

'Don't be silly. Tell him it's your money, that you need it.'

'You do it for me.'

'You're his sister.'

'It doesn't matter. You're the ruthless one. He'll pay attention to *you* . . . It's high time there was a ruthless Rykov. Someone must plunge the daggers.'

Seventeen

'WHY DO you think Igor told me about the vultures?' she asked, frowning, her thin filleted eyebrows curving like millipedes. 'It's not a nice image.'

'Because you're a nurse and might be interested? I don't know. I've always thought of him as a strange man.'

She rose, smoothing her long blue cotton skirt. She was wearing lawn tennis shoes. 'Is this all we've come to see, a battle-field? I don't call it anything very special. Let's go down and get the boat to take us home. I'm leaving the day after tomorrow. I promised the hospital I'd be back by the last day of March. And Igor's giving a dinner for me, or have you forgotten?'

'Why's he doing that?'

'For agreeing with him that he was desperately ill and behaving with remarkable courage . . . Eight courses, many wines and all of them French, a footman behind every chair—'

'Scratching himself.'

'Probably – and the Rykov silver on the table. Not often we've seen that, is it, Charlie! The original pieces . . . think of it, the sparkle and the wealth!'

'I'd rather not. It could have been yours – or mine. It's wasted on him.'

'I agree. So let's consider it ruthlessly. How heavy is the whole service? How would we get it to the station? The car's too small. How many men to bribe to transport it for us? How many to guard the carriers? What's its actual silver content? See, I can think like a man. Are you really ruthless, Charlie Doig?'

That voice, so pure and low – so why do I mention it again. Dark questing eyes, teeth as white as my Bokharan horseman's, her fine-boned fingers always busy at something, perhaps now a habit after hospital work, winding bandages and spongeing shit off the distressed. Looking to be a countess and likely to be very good at it if the money were correct. That's what I thought when she said 'ruthless' for the third time. We began to walk towards our cart on which the peasant was slumped sideways, dozing. She moved well, on firm slender ankles. Her scuffed canvas tennis shoes kept obtruding into my vision. I reduced her from countess to a lower rank.

A few yards from the cart she stopped me. Her face was illuminated by mischief and amusement. Her smile gave it an impression of circularity and made her ears stand out from her head. She didn't laugh – she really wasn't an overtly merry sort of person: she explained things through her expressions. She said, 'You're such a professor, so serious about your work, I had to make a little fun for myself . . . the vultures, do you want to know why Igor told me about them turning the wounded man over?'

'Why?'

'Because there's no one in his house prepared to listen to his stories any more. They've heard them so often. They walk away, even his steward, and there's nothing he can do as he's not agile enough to corner them. Even his doctor won't listen to him – it was he who told me all this. And Igor's frantic to talk about the old days.'

'And?'

'But I listen because I'm in his debt.'

'How, what's he been doing for his god-daughter?'

'The pearls, Charlie, the pearls . . . Igor's in love with me. He's going to hand them over at dinner. The Tsar's own pearls, which the Founder probably slipped into his pocket without a glance because it was all he could do to keep up with the flow of gifts. They're vast, cousin, *vast*. Each one is as big as La Pelligrina. The largest must be almost three ounces.'

She put on a swanky walk, waggling her hips, twirling her sun-umbrella; pouting, coquetting me. She extended her hand, dibbled her ring finger at me and threw out her lips. 'It's the diamonds next, darlinka.'

'You whore, you little whore,' I yelled.

She laughed, thumbed her nose at me with both hands and ran towards the cart, turning halfway to see if I was coming after her. Her small tufted breasts pressed at her shirt pleats. I could make out just enough of them to imagine their pull and slap. I caught her by the wrists. The roof of my life slid back and she entered. Her lean dark face was framed against the bluest of skies and a ziggurat of soft white clouds, a face so powerful in its musculature, so capable. It was the most wonderful experience I'd ever had.

So that was where it all started, in the spring of 1915, and there was no remedy.

Eighteen

CHANGE YOUR woman and you change everything. The rules of behaviour and attitude are instantly altered. Unencumbered men deal freely with each other. A woman shows up and soon there's a falling-out.

Of course Elizaveta was a thousand miles from Samarkand, and she wasn't yet mine. But Goetz knew. There was something different in my manner. He could smell a rival.

Other things were changing around us as well. The war had caused self-doubt. Young able-bodied Russians, the sons and grandsons of the original settlers in Turkestan, had been conscripted, railed out to Europe and not heard from since. The price of goods imported from metropolitan Russia had more than doubled. The everyday soft, dirty brown sugar had virtually disappeared. A lump of refined sugar had become a luxury. Officials had been through the villages handing out blue rationing cards. People were saying, 'What, can't we eat as much as we can afford? What sort of century is this?'

There were tensions, mutterings, and a new restlessness in the bazaar tea-houses. Ideas were now widespread that at the beginning of the war only students had dared promote. The fact of Muslims being exempted from conscription meant there were more of them around to grumble. I'm not saying that Samarkand was seething, only that people no longer joked to strangers about the Third Section.

It was to the Civilians Club, in the Russian section of the city, that Goetz and I always went when we got too stinky and needed the company of others. Because of the anti-German sentiments around I introduced him as Fellowes, a Londoner. It was quite safe as he spoke so rarely to people who weren't scientists or naturalists. An Englishman might have spotted him for a fake but there were none around.

The Club had tall European windows with sun-bleached maroon curtains trimmed with some sort of industrial lace; carpets and armchairs of the same colour; many flies, and a troop of elderly Russian waiters, perhaps convicts who'd served their time in Siberia, whose strength was so clearly waning that any decent person wanted to jump up and do the job for them.

Outside, on one side of the entrance, a verandah enclosed in fine copper gauze had been tacked onto the building. On the other was a hitching rail.

It was here, at a table on the verandah, on a warm, shimmering morning full of birdsong, that Goetz and I sat down to breakfast. He'd brought his old canvas grip, which he placed beside his chair.

One of the antique waiters hobbled after us. He unfolded our napkins. The linen, which was none too clean, trembled as it was fumbled across the table by his long yellow fingers. Goetz moved his grip to the other side of his chair. I stared at him. His heavy face seemed to be unnaturally buoyant. The dullness in his eyes had gone. They were sea-water green and sparkling.

What was it? I said, 'You found something new during the night. Let me guess. Not a moth, that'd be too easy—'

'Your powers of observation have improved, Doig. Well done. What's happening is that in an hour I'm getting on the troop train to Krasnovodsk. Then Baku, the Black Sea and Constantinople. Berlin within a fortnight, if I'm lucky with the steamers. A month at the outside. I'm leaving you.'

He paused to see my reaction. I had nothing to say. There were no words handy.

'I had counted myself ninety-nine parts English. But last night I had a dream in which someone whisked back a curtain and there, painted in miniature, I saw on display the whole of central Berlin. Each of the street names had been painted on a scroll that unfurled at the place you were thinking of the moment that you looked at it. The city was perfect, the most complete application of science, method and public welfare that a fairminded person could wish for. My home, Doig, my home! I sat

71

up. I'd gone to sleep with the lamp on. The flame was as steady as a rock. That showed me my decision was correct . . . And here I am. I can't stand reading about the war and doing nothing any longer. I must help my nation, not specifically against you English or our friends here but in a general way, to protect her against her enemies. I can drive an ambulance or be a bicycle messenger. I'm in good condition, despite my age. The medical board will be sceptical. It's their duty. There's no point having old men like walruses in the line. But they're bound to see the sense in what I say . . . I don't mind what I do so long as I can help my country.'

'Why do you want to be killed for no reason? If it was climbing a rock face to get a bird wholly new to science, that's one thing. But signing up to fight . . . that's pointless, that's like volunteering to go insane. And where does it leave me?'

He looked at me with his new joyfulness. 'Call it my sense of patriotism being too active. I refuse to quarrel . . . We're done, you and I, Doig. Maybe our entire profession is done. When the war's over people may say, What do we want bird skins for? Let's spend our money on guns . . . So there it is. Berlin's where I'm going.'

At this moment we were joined by a dealer in animal hides who also used the Club for a wash and brush-up. He was a powerful, virile man, always dressed in a sheepskin, with a leather belt from which hung all the accoutrements of manhood: horse-pick, sheath knife, a small branding iron and a fleam for bleeding his pack animals at high altitudes.

He was halfway to sitting down, his hands on the arms of his chair, when he took in what Goetz was talking about. He stared aghast at him. 'What? Fight? Doig, cut his tendons. He'll be grateful to you in five years . . . Listen, my friend, I love the Tsar and his German woman and the grand dukes, the whole stupid pack of them. Who else is there? But God preserve me from wanting to die for them. I mean, die . . . What's a man of my vigour to do when he's dead? It's a waste, that's what death is. And Berlin – Berl . . . NO!'

He kicked back his chair and rose angrily. 'So you're not Fellowes, the nice English naturalist, you're someone else. You're a bloody German. Then go and die. Tomorrow isn't soon enough. I can't bear a man without a sense of independence.'

Goetz rose neatly. Overnight he seemed to have become leaner. He bowed to us both, still with that look of contentment in his eyes. The Club had done his laundry. There was a crease in his white shirt and his shorts had been pressed.

He told the outside porter he was going to the station. The porter signalled a phaeton from the rank. Turning to me, Goetz said gaily, 'I bequeath you all my *togs*. The right word at last, *ja*? Everything I've left behind is yours, Doig. Get that woman. Godspeed, my friend!'

His backside and black-stockinged calves ascended the step. The phaeton sank. He took his seat, lay back and crossed his legs at the ankle. He raised an arm to us – I can't say that he waved. Then he was gone.

'I'm not alone, no one likes Germans any more,' the skin-dealer said. 'Especially the Tsarina. The people call her *nemka*, the German woman . . . So you haven't been in Moscow recently? No, I didn't think so from your outfit. Things are looking bad there. Prices just go up and up. You could get to the moon on them. Good second-hand boots complete with laces are impossible to find. People will kill for a bite at an apple. Same for butter and eggs. The farmers won't sell. They say, What do I want money for if I can't buy vodka? I've said I love the Tsar and I do but why does he want to prohibit drinking – in Russia! When I first heard of it I said, Vodka forbidden in Russia? Here, pinch me, kick me . . . It's the end, Doig. The people won't stand for it. There are riots everywhere. You stay in Samarkand with your birds and beetles.'

He ate, snapping his jaws voraciously. 'You're lucky, you've another country to go to. Sew your luck into your pants and keep sitting down. Someone may try to steal it.'

Nineteen

B UT WHEN speaking of my luck, he failed to touch wood or invoke the usual deities. Luck was affronted. My life, which since I'd started out with Goetz had been buttered with it, began to fall to pieces – onto the ground, buttered side down.

It turned out that Bathsheba had got herself nailed by a jackass. Her huge rimed eyes simpered at me. She laid her head against my ribs and when I declined to scratch her poll or tug her bandy ears, snortled deeply in her throat and butted me. She'd have carried me alright. Donkeys didn't come gamer than Bathsheba. But I couldn't hold myself responsible. She was like a balloon, and the Orient is full of narrow doorways. What if I lost my temper and kicked her because she couldn't get through one, or because she'd been overtaken by some whim of motherhood that I hadn't comprehended?

So I said goodbye to her. First Goetz, then Bathsheba.

The skin-dealer went off into the Pamirs for the early crop of skins. Thus I became without friends, and that in a city where women were tricky.

Moreover, I found that my work was no longer so compelling without Goetz. The shambling old pedant! What a fuss he'd made about the simplest thing! But I missed him and the exactness of his methods and the gruff airing of his knowledge of an evening. Had I ever called him Hartwig? I didn't think so. We'd been Doig and Goetz to each other from the moment we'd met, in the library at the Darwin Club. I began to dwell on this. An opportunity had been lost – but for what? I grew listless and easily found reasons to stay in Samarkand, where I at least had some sort of company.

Neither last nor the least painful: I was kicked by a horse while walking through the *registan* or marketplace and suffered a fracture to my right tibia. I thought wrongly, This caps everything. I was so sorry for myself. Even when the Russian doctor came to see me at the Civilians Club and said, 'If you think you're in a bad way, you should see how our soldiers are compelled to fight,' I was convinced I'd had it for all practical purposes.

I longed for Elizaveta, to hold and consult. Letters were futile. She'd sent me only one, from the Pink House. My good and trusted friend, Kobulov the stationmaster, who was acting as my postman, had steamed it open and read it, probably aloud to his family. In it she told me how Nicholas, her half-brother, was thinning out the attic lodgers so as to reduce costs. Times were bad. He knew he wasn't acting honourably. Only two of them remained. One had made a pass at her. How should she respond?

'Why do women write such stuff?' I'd asked Goetz. 'She's twenty-six and never been short of an answer. Why ask me? What's she after?'

He wriggled coyly, delighted that I'd taken him into my confidence. 'She's lonely, just her brother with her and some servants . . . Oh yes, the hospital work, that has to be taken into account . . . I don't know. She may want you to think she's lonely.'

So I wrote back and told her to stab him to death. Rip, shoot, drain off his lust somehow, that was my advice.

At the time I'd thought, I should get over to Smolensk and bind her unto me. But my contract with the Academy of Sciences had a year and more to run. I believed it could wait.

Twenty

You know how people like to say frightening things solely in order to test how frightened they are themselves. One day the Club's outside porter said as he handed me my crutch, 'Men who've been on the railway of late call themselves not travellers but survivors. Everything's collapsing. Even the pigs'll want to get out by the time this war is over. There'll be nothing left to show we were ever here. Mark my words, sir, not even an old sow wiping the mud with her tits.'

Well, I thought, You're just a windy old man blowing off, and hopped round the corner to the Imperial Bank in Chernaevski Prospekt. This is what an invalid does in a cosmopolitan place like Samarkand when he's out of sorts. He goes to check on his money and have an agreeable conversation. The day has to be lived.

The bank was a pleasant villa with high, airy ceilings. The manager, a plump flowery gentleman from Odessa whose name was Simeonidis, did his business on the ground floor and lived with his family on the next.

He rose as I was shown in. We had some talk. But it was less casual than before. There was a lot of white round his eyes, which were as tight as buttons. I smelt bad news – but for whom? He started up again about the war. I cut him short. 'Stop beating about the bush and tell me the worst.' Sighing he pulled out of his desk a letter from the Academy.

'See, they actually bothered to write. They are honourable people. The money will be sent – but later. If they'd wanted to abscond, would they have written?'

That was how I heard that the Academy had stopped paying its collectors.

I was shocked. If I could be treated in this way by the Academy of Sciences no less, where would the rot halt? What other institutions might cease payment? The Empire itself – what would happen if Russia ran out of money? I searched for information in the banker's eyes. They were as black as boot polish and showed only my own reflection. I looked round his clever face for a clue. There was more going on there than I'd heard about so far. I thought, That letter's a smokescreen. Then suddenly, You're about to jump ship. You've heard something on the bankers' grapevine. Kobulov gets one sort of news first, from the railway telegraph. But you, my friend, are first with the most vital news of all: what people are doing with their money. Perhaps, I thought, the Academy was not the only one to have stopped payment . . .

I considered his wife, whom I could hear playing the piano in the room above. Did she know what he's planning? *Or is he going alone?*

Out of the whole idea, that was what stuck: that he'd fixed something up with an Afghan trader and in a month would have become Mr Michelis passing through Peshawar – looking for business opportunities, sir.

I closed on him. I picked a thread off his lapel and I said, 'You're going to make a run for it. You know something I don't.'

He looked at me blandly. The pudgy, manicured hand that held the letter was steady. His dark hair gleamed with an oily lotion. I took the letter from him. He bowed slightly.

Twenty-one

M OTHER SAID to me on the train carrying us into our
English exile, 'Come, I want to eat chocolates, and I need
to be among my people.'

She slipped her vanity case into the pocket of her stole, picked
up the bag with her magazines and Einem chocolates, and set
off down the palpitating corridor to the restaurant car. The
carpet was green, a worn patch outside each door. Boltikov was
airing himself in his doorway, taking effete puffs from his
Northern Lights cigarette. He shrank his millionaire's stomach
to let us pass; offered Mother a bow, inclining his head and no
more. His lips crinkled to open a conversation – with regard to
our *charming* party, I've no doubt – but Mother walked on,
flapping away the perfumed odour of his tobacco.

Putting her hands behind her back, she waggled her jewelled
fingers at me. I slipped my hand into hers, manoeuvring my
palm until it was snug.

The candle shades were scalloped in rose. Our chairs were
the same green as the corridor and had black piping. Mother
straightened one of the shades and considered the menu in its
silver frame.

Thinking of Boltikov, I said, 'How do fat men bow correctly,
to the Tsar, for instance?'

Absent-mindedly, poking through the chocolates on their
yellow paper boatlets, she replied, 'The very fat, the very old
and the arthritic have special dispensations. Also those who've
been wounded. When they extend the left leg, they're permitted
to lean on it with their left arm. Sometimes they grip the left
wrist with the right hand, as a support. I enjoy watching men

78

bow. You can tell which are the arrogant and which the humble. Do they also abase their eyes? That's another point.'

'What about left-handed men? Do they bow differently?'

She took out her tweezers and deftly pinched off the almonds and the caps of purple sugar and laid them out on the table-cloth in two ranks. She didn't stop doing this as she said, 'But why should they? *Ils ne sont pas frappés d'incapacité.*'

And then, 'Boltikov is such a completely odious man, so irre-deemably *snobi* . . . If you ever have to bow, bow low. Always remember that. Make it good. Bow as if you yearned to kiss the soil upon which the man's standing, and do it slowly.'

Seeing Simeonidis's paltry bow, which Mother would have deemed an insult, I recalled that railway scene in its entirety. He could say anything he wanted but I knew he was for off. He'd reached the point of no longer caring what I thought of him.

I said, 'I'll take Goetz's money as well as my own. Don't forget the interest at the new rate.' Giving him no time to inter-rupt, I went on to specify the currencies I wanted it in and the denominations.

He smiled, which I took as acknowledgement that I'd been right. 'Don't take the twenty-dinar note, the purple one. There are too many around. Traders are getting nervous. How would you like your monies, sir? Some people going on a journey sprinkle the larger notes through a sack of rag cotton. The shape of the sack is not associated with wealth. Or I can put them in a wrapping of canvas from the market, which is easier to carry – but is recognisable.'

Then his lips went all smooth like marzipan and he said, 'I'm told there's a white swallow nesting on the mosque of Ulug Beg. My instinct tells me that would be a great rarity, Mister Doig, sir. A man who was busy catching it would have less time to observe the follies of their fellow humans . . . Well worth the, er, effort . . . of a keen naturalist . . .' His voice fell away as a maid came in with two demitasses of sweet coffee.

When she'd gone he didn't return to the white swallow but began to tell me about the party that he and Mrs Simeonidis were going to have to celebrate her name day. Everyone in Samarkand above the rank of lower captain was going to be invited. The governor and his staff, the important policemen, the jeweller . . . Vodka would be served in a separate room. For those who couldn't get their nerve up to break the law, the place would be swimming with *champanski* and the sweet, fiery white wine that was made by his friend Mr Filatov.

'Shall I remind them that the vines responsible for their enjoyment came originally from the Rhine, from *Germany*? I think not. I want this party to be talked about favourably.'

Above our heads Mrs Simeonidis ceased playing. She let the piano lid fall with a thud. The floor creaked as she walked to the window.

Simeonidis coughed into his fist. 'Actually I think our party will be talked of in Samarkand forever.'

I thanked him for the information about the bird. He tried to pass me my crutch but I refused it, saying I'd sit where I was and watch him parcel my money.

Twenty-two

A TRAIN OF Bactrian camels swayed down the long expanse of the marketplace, pushing to one side the traffic in donkeys, horses and small hooded carts. On one horse sat three men, the father having the saddle and thus guarding the four dead chickens that hung by their yellow feet from the pommel. Beneath the mosque walls were the barbers' stalls. A little apart were the fortune-tellers – then some musicians – then a man selling shawls, and cloth for turbans – then the birdcages containing the fighting quail, the canaries, and by itself a goshawk belled with silver that glared insanely at me as I passed. Amid the dusty heat and vendors of almond and pistachio cakes and the hadjis in green turbans and the multicoloured throng I advanced awkwardly to my favourite tea-house.

On the table was an earthenware pot holding a lilac tulip from which a hoverfly had just turned away. Before me rose the vast green and turquoise mosque of Ulug Beg. Mosses and flowery tuffets and stunted oleanders sprouted on its dilapidated wings. The flap of the tea-house awning cut off the top of its dome from my view.

My bad leg was resting on a chair. The flies were darting at me to drink from my sweat. From behind came the hum of chess games, the clack of dominoes, quarrels, theories and histories. Women went past in their long grey parandjas, faces obscured by veils of black horsehair. Their trencher-fed hips swayed lusciously and maddeningly.

I poured my tea from a pot stamped 'Made in Benares'. Sipping it, I wondered if the departure of Simeonidis would depend on the moon. Probably, if he was going to ride out. He didn't have the figure for a horseman. But how else was he to get to Peshawar? What a squawking there'd be that morning when Mrs S. awoke alone . . .

Then I saw it. Not a swallow but a swift, *Apus melba*.

It was flying low and straight down the gay marketplace, as white as a snowflake, as fast as a bullet, its muscular angled wings drilling a tunnel through the air. It veered a point or two. It was flying directly at me. My heart awoke with a bang. The power! The beauty! O unspeakable God – on it flew, this albino, this priceless fluke, speeding at my eye, a blur of white against the turquoise of the tiles. It banked to avoid the awning and went screaming over my head, literally so, for this chee-chee-chee, a saw-edged scream, is the only language of the swift. A whiffle of windswept feathers, a flash of its purplish shanks tucked up against its belly – and it was gone, its wings curved like scimitars as it disappeared down the black throat of the covered bazaar.

That lightning should strike twice . . . my beetle and then this . . . but how was I to capture it? I beat the crutch against the table leg in my frustration.

A shadow took my light and stayed there. I looked up.

He was about twenty-five, one would have said a Mongolian. Square-faced, stocky, unsmiling. Brown, granular skin with a clump of long dark hairs on his chin. He was dressed in Russian working clothes: leather sandals, blue trousers and blouse, a loose cotton jacket. He had thick dark rolling hair, and eyes that fell away at the side. They were the knackiest eyes I'd seen in a man.

He appraised my leg. 'You want that bird.' No question mark.

I nodded. I was crazed for the albino. There couldn't be more than one in the world.

'Alive is not possible.'

'What would I do with it alive? Put it in a cage – in prison?'

His face was unreadable. He said, 'If you want it you must pay me one hundred roubles in cash.'

I said it was too much. How would we stand if he spoiled the plumage? But he'd been spying on me and had seen my expression as the swift went scorching over my head. He knew all about Goetz and myself, that we killed birds for museums.

82

He'd been to the library and discovered the correct Latin name for this swift. To rub it in, he told me the name in Hindi as well – *badi ababeel*. He said it was one hundred roubles regardless. There was only one price. He'd bring it to me in such a condition that I'd believe it to be still sleeping.

'You pay me now,' he said. 'By hand, not on the table.'

I asked him his name. 'Kobi.' He'd been brought up by missionaries and so spoke excellent Russian.

'Without a past?' I said, feeling a kinship.

'My parents – dead. My past also. Only the future is left to me.'

He refused my offer of tea and took the money. Then he left as noiselessly as he'd arrived, a matter of the disposition of shadows. I watched him thread a path down the marketplace, oozing through the crowd and the animals as water does between particles of soil. He spoke to no one; a solitary man, a killer making his way was the thought that reached me.

Twenty-three

O F COURSE he got it. Shinned up onto the mosque roof and nabbed it on its nest. We cleaned and packed it together. Kobi had slender, agile fingers. He knocked up a little box for it – calling it a coffin with sly humour slipping from the corners of his liquorice eyes.

'What do you want now?' he said in his forthright way.

And I did have another requirement.

The Academy had abandoned me. My father's death had ceased to be a scourge. I had reached the end of my inherited momentum. Goetz had gone one way, Simeonidis was going another. I had a broken leg. During my bad hours I'd looked inside myself for additional stores of knowledge and found that in the matters of tranquillity and contentment, and love and friendship, I was destitute. All around me there was warfare, repression, and edginess. I was insufficient alone. It was time to get out of Samarkand and join my Russian family.

'I want to be your assistant,' Kobi said. 'I like that work.'

I couldn't explain my feelings to him. We were too new to each other. I said that I was going to Smolensk, that I had kin there. 'It's my home,' I said, trying the word out. I thought of my childhood; of Elizaveta, of my cousins Nicholas and Viktor and of the Pink House. 'Yes,' I said with greater confidence, 'I'm going home.'

He didn't ask if he could come with me. What he said was that he'd need an hour to gather his belongings.

'Wait,' I said, 'I can only pay you when I have money.'

'How else could it be?'

'So why would you come with me?'

'I'm young, call that my reason.'

He returned with a bedroll containing clothing and a few more essentials. At his belt was a sheath knife. He showed it to me straight off – Sheffield steel, the best. His missionaries had given it to him when he left them. What for? He didn't yet know, but in saying it his eyes again gave me a squirt of humour and cruelty combined. Then we went to the station to see what was doing.

Trains were scarce. Passenger trains in particular had almost ceased to exist. We had my two ponies, my gun, some bits of baggage, and the last case of specimens for the Academy. My Imperial travelling papers proved useful, also the contact with Pavel Kobulov. On the basis of these we got passage on a military train, leaving Turkestan by Orenburg rather than the southern route. We found ourselves space in the horse wagons with the grooms.

The locomotive crept over the interminable steppe, panting not chugging, for which it was left with inadequate strength by the oppressive sun. We rolled back the sliding wooden doors on both sides of the wagon. It was an improvement, but we still fried. Soldiers would get off and walk beside the metals to give themselves something to do. We stopped frequently, God knows why, perhaps because the engine was boiling over. Then the men would catch up and climb aboard and recount what they'd seen and whom they'd spoken to, as if they'd been off on a month-long patrol. Whenever we crossed a river we'd halt to let the grooms form a line and fill their heavy wooden buckets with water for the horses. The heat distressed them terribly. They had to stand for the whole of those two weeks. Their ribs heaved metrically, while from their drooping miserable heads strings of dribble swung to the motion of the train, lengthened and eventually fell. We shovelled their dung over the side but as there was no bedding, their urine was absorbed by the planks. No amount of swabbing could remove the acrid stink. They drank prodigious quantities of water whenever we offered it to them, and developed sores.

There were other civilians on the train, commercial men of the stamp of Simeonidis moving round the Empire in an attempt to gain an advantage from the situation. One of them, who described himself as a jobbing plunderer, had travelled in China selling suction pumps. In that country, he said, the train-drivers refused to work at night. Passengers had to sleep on the ground or in hostels.

The vast landscape dawdled past under a sandy sky, the colour of an old lion's pelt. A favourite game was to have someone sit towards the back of the wagon and then to bet on how many seconds would pass before that person called out that some agreed landmark had completed the passage from the left hand to the right hand of the open door. Many *makhorka* stubs were produced from many boots, puffed at and then gambled away in this fashion. (It was remarkable what the soldiers kept in their boots.) We swung our legs over the edge of the wagon, smoked, watched our saliva blister on the metals, cracked lice with our thumbnails, told lies and chaffed the men who were walking. By night it was much the same. Men could sit and gaze for hours at the red bloated moon that seemed to be anchored above the steppe by a hook and cable.

For whatever reason, the grooms had the skill of contemplation. They'd repeat hundreds of homely adages and stories in respectful voices. One I remember concerned an ill-treated wife who was walking home to her parents at night and saw reflected in the village pond a moon with the countenance of the husband who'd been faithless to her. She waded in to strangle him and drowned.

Said Kobi immediately, 'Did she cry out, That's my husband and I'm going to kill him, otherwise how did anyone know it was her intention? She might have been wanting to bathe herself.'

No one could answer this. 'Don't spoil the story,' someone said.

Kobi wasn't going to give up. 'Well, there must have been someone who heard her. And why didn't that person try to save her?'

'Because it was her husband himself who heard,' came a mellow laugh from the shadows.

One young man spent the time composing verse with only one rule of scansion, that every fiftieth line had to rhyme with moon (*luna*). He charged a friend with remembering the poem as he went along – which that friend was able to do, for the peasant's power of memory comes with his mother's milk. Someone else had a balalaika. Bit by bit this vast, sad epic was set to music. Every night the day's work would trickle away into the velvet darkness of the steppe and there be lost. That was the predominant feeling on the train – lostness. None of those men expected to see their families again.

There was no fixed time for sleeping. Since there was nothing else to do, we slept when we felt like it. On our bedrolls, on the stinking planks, with saddles for pillows.

So I thought nothing of it when I began to feel constantly drowsy and tired. Headaches appeared and then a rash on my chest, and on my palms and soles. My thirst knew no boundaries. I would go round the horse buckets, sticking my head right inside them, lapping at the water or spooning it into my mouth without much regard for all the scum and soggy bits of flotsam. I was the one who was an animal.

I became delirious. I was at the mercy of my mind. I can recall nothing whatsoever from the last five days of the journey. Death would have been completely uneventful.

Twenty-four

THE FIRST anyone knew of my coming home was when two of the wretched Smolensk station horse-cabs were sighted shuffling up the drive that winds prettily beside our river. The horses slowed to a walk as they met the gradient where the drive climbs and curves to the gravel sweep outside the Pink House.

Halfway up this slope, which is not severe, is a splendid pair of lime trees, very Russian in habit, that are known as Gog and Magog. Here a track branches off to the stables and carriage houses and grooms' quarters.

My cousin Nicholas, who'd ridden in from the fields only a few moments earlier, was wisping the sweat off his horse with a handful of straw. Timofei, his old groom, had his arms full of the saddle and girths that he was about to put on a fresh horse.

(Elizaveta took a long breath. She was about to start the action.)

Nicholas heard the rattle of the vehicles. Running out into the middle of the stable yard he was just in time to see the cavalcade disappear round the corner of the Pink House. In the first cab were two passengers. In the second was their baggage; and tied by a rope to this cab were two thin and dusty ponies. He jumped onto his mare and cantered bareback in pursuit, cutting the corner at Gog and Magog so that he arrived on the gravel at the same time as the cab-drivers halted.

A Mongolian stepped out, totally disregarding him. This man reached inside the cab and took out a leather gun-case. He marched over and deposited it to one side of the front door. He returned, hauled me out of the cab and supported me to a bench. By this stage Louis, Nicholas's butler, had arrived and was standing speechless in his green apron, hands on hips. The small Mongolian pointed a forefinger at Louis and then at me, indicating he should look after me.

Here Elizaveta allowed herself a modest digression.

It was 1916, at the peak of our brief, ripe, Russian summer. Death and the demands of economy had reduced the attic lodgers to a single person, Bobinski, the old tutor. It was he, on the lookout as ever for a novelty, who'd spotted the two cabs coming up the drive beside the river. His head went back and forth as leaning from the window of his attic room he followed Kobi's movements to the door and then Nicholas's movements towards Kobi. I was recognised. The questions among the female house servants at that moment were, so Bobinski reported to Elizaveta: who was the Asiatic and when was he going to have a bath and get his hair cut as then he'd be really quite handsome.

She smiled down on me. 'I don't expect you ever thought of Kobi as handsome.' Then she continued.

Nicholas said to Kobi: 'Who the devil are you?'

In his slightly accented Russian, Kobi replied, 'We've come from Samarkand, both us and the ponies. Doig is ill to his boots. I work for him. Help me get him into a bed.'

That, as Elizaveta explained to me a week after the event, was how the play opened, the prologue. Later she discovered more. Kobi had nursed me to Moscow, worrying that I was going to die at any moment and be pitched off the train. He'd been in as much of a fever as I had. (But of a different nature, she added, reverting momentarily to her nursing profession.) At Moscow he lugged me and the horses and the baggage across to Brest Station. Whenever there was any sign of trouble with soldiers or officials he waved my papers at them saying, 'On the service of the Tsar, make way there.' With the last of my funds he got the whole caboodle to Smolensk. But where to go then and how to get there? He had no address, only the name Rykov and the feeling he should be looking for a large house. He marched over to the cab rank, took the first driver who seemed to know what he was talking about and promised him that Nicholas would pay.

'He has a genius for something,' Elizaveta said.

'Adventure,' I replied. 'He'd be happiest trying to ride a comet.'

I was in the quarantine room, where last I'd been as a child with mumps. The window was open at the bottom by a foot and the tan blinds lowered to halfway. The July sun was entering straight from the garden, bearing all the remembered sounds and odours from my youth. Outside I knew it to have burning northern vigour. But here, inside the room, it had become lazy. Everything around me was soft and drowsy, as summer should be, like a love poem, or a meadow before the haymakers get to it. By my bed was a glass goblet and in it nodded harebells from the field, as blue as the heavens.

She left my side and sat down at the small desk beside the window to write a letter. Her hair was as short as I remembered it and her voice as grave. The sunlight bouncing off the Fantin-Latour that had taken over the wall outside was dyed with the faint, most delicate pink of its petals, which it brushed across her left cheek. The right one was in shadow, blocked off from the sun by her strong nose, which was that of a Saracen as well as her father Boris.

No calligrapher was Liza. Her pen ripped across the page like a fretsaw, dealing out troughs and pinnacles ruthlessly. After about ten lines she had to change the nib. She wrote with her head at a slight angle. She was wearing a white blouse with leg-of-mutton sleeves; long grey skirt; black belt and stockings and shoes. She'd been at a hospital meeting in the morning in Smolensk, driving herself the eight miles there and back in her neat little gig. Sitting bolt upright, I was sure. Not a slumping girl, this.

The scent from the rose was exquisite. It had colonised the room. Every particle of the air was charged with it, and the sheets, and Liza's skin when she bent over me with the medicine spoon.

I wanted this woman. I wanted her wholly for my own.

A small china bowl of pot-pourri was on her desk. She stirred it with the end of her pen, dribbled some through her fingers. 'A woman friend told Nicholas about this rose and then bought one for him, having it sent from Paris. His wife is the stupidest woman I know. Helene said that accepting the rose from this woman was tantamount to adultery and went back to her parents in Moscow, taking their two boys.'

'And Nicholas, what did he do?'

'He hasn't changed. Moaned about his boys, the last of the male Rykovs etcetera etcetera. Otherwise not very much. His suspicion now is that she's working up to request that he divorce her. That's much more of a worry to him. He'd have to raise another loan on the estate.'

'Not worth the Fantin-Latour then.'

She shrugged. 'Helene's not the woman he thought she was . . . But it makes wonderful pot-pourri.' Again she trickled the petals through her fingers. 'It's the rose from which confetti is made.'

This was how she introduced to me the subject of her fiancé, Count Andrej Potocki.

Twenty-five

THINKING I felt a flea, I said to her, 'I thought you got them all?'

'Yes, Sonja and I between us. You were in a coma. We washed you and hunted out all your little friends, both crawling and hopping. Nicholas said we were wasting our time, that you were certain to die. It was louse typhus that you had. I see a lot of it – in the morgue, dead men. Count yourself lucky, Charlie Doig.'

'Who's Sonja?'

'My maid.'

She went back to her writing. 'I must finish this letter. It's to our patron, the Grand Duchess. I'm complaining of the shortage of beds and medicines. Things are so bad that we have to lay the men out in the garden. In the winter, imagine it . . . That's what we were talking about this morning.' She took care with her signature and printed her name in capitals beneath it. She blotted it, briskly made the blue silk ties of her letter folder into a bow, and put it under her arm.

I said, 'Why did you come here to write it?'

'I thought you'd be asleep. Sometimes I need the calm of this room.'

'No other reason?'

'No. You wanted me to say, so that I could be with you?'

'I believed myself to be favoured.'

'I won't talk about it. Whatever I say you'll think badly of me – that I'm doing it just for the money. You've got to remember the circumstances – my age, and the fits I used to get. I need the solidity of marriage.'

She had her hand on the doorknob. I said, 'I remember Andrej. He used to look up your knickers when you were on the swing – when you were just a girl. He's a pervert. Your life will be a misery. Ask Nicholas if you don't believe me.'

But the moment I said this I knew I was wrong. Nicholas would have bitten his tongue off sooner than do anything to obstruct an alliance with the wealthy family of Potocki.

She said sharply, 'At least he's a fighting man,' and left before I could defend myself.

All those Potockis came from the Polish borderlands. Andrej's father had been a famous friend of my uncle Boris. Whenever he went to Moscow to transact his business he'd leave his son and daughter at the Pink House. Andrej was slight, sinewy, reserved, brainy. He'd sit on the bank watching Viktor, Nicholas and myself attempt the construction of a tree house and then with a few key words state the correct procedures. He had a mass of black tousled hair that he never combed. He pretended it was electric. We never made fun of this absurd claim for a very good reason: if you watched his head when he was arguing at full stretch, you could swear its individual hairs were vibrating. It was obvious that each fibre was growing directly out of his brain and that he was telling the truth.

His particular ally among us was Viktor.

They joined the same line regiment of cavalry when the war broke out. We can imagine the two friends jangling down the summer road in 1914 to thrash the Hun; pennants fluttering, lances buttoned, squadron by squadron of colour-matched chargers, for that was how the chief of staff, an amateur water-colourist, liked it. Viktor was killed at Tannenberg on the first day. As if to avenge him, Andrej did more than survive. He came out of the battle unscarred, his ears ringing with the roar of glory.

Time and again in those days of chaos he risked his life to extricate his dwindling command from one tight corner after another. Despite his efforts to break out he was driven back into the forest and there surrounded by the Germans. He had barely a hundred able-bodied troopers left. He called them together – beneath a gigantic oak tree according to Louis, who had all the biographical details of the hateful romancer – and asked if they were of a mind to surrender in the morning, 'as if we were common foot rabble'. His men, who liked nothing better than to have a column of infantry choke on their dust as they trotted past them, growled their dissent.

That night it rained and thundered, which in August means rain on the Burmese scale bucketing out of an inkbag sky. When it was at its blackest, Andrej led his men in single file out of the forest and straight through the German lines; dismounted, the horses' hoofs muffled and their muzzles bound with strips torn from the soldiers' shirt tails.

By sun-up they were safe. It was too wet to get a fire going: they lounged naked in a clearing while their clothes dried. Then they rode north-east – waveringly, for the terrain was complicated by the forest and a succession of large lakes. They met other stragglers. Within a week Andrej had gathered five hundred men. All went well until they reached a lake far wider and longer than any they'd met so far. The scouts rode for a day in each direction without being able to see its end. Mosquitoes came off its swampy margins in clouds; Lithuanian mosquitoes with thoraxes the size of thimbles. Every species of noxious insect was present beside that lake. Horses and men went wild from their biting. But how should they pass it, on the east or the west? Andrej's only map showed the concept of the lake but no solution. He tossed a coin. Tails – the eagle. He gave the order to march west.

Nicholas, who was telling me the story as he couldn't trust Louis to get it right, continued: 'Appalling. As bad as having to cross the Pripyat marshes. Not an acre of decent country the whole way. Brackish, quaking mudflats. Then thick willow scrub, then a vast bay to be traipsed round with a dead sort of river going into it that the men had to wade across with the water up to their armpits and bubbles of poisonous air coming to the surface with every footstep. Horrible black water. Insects like piranhas, night and day.

'At length they reached the end, which was marked by a small bald hill. They'd had their eye on it for miles because a hill was extraordinary in that region. Andrej was determined to climb to its summit, to impose himself on it, to take his revenge for what they'd suffered from the mud, the insects and the dense reed-like grasses that grew to eight or nine feet and had leaves with edges that could draw blood.

'His Zeiss binoculars magnified ten times with a lens size of forty millimetres. Through them he saw below – for the land fell away quite sharply – a splendid mediaeval manor house, timbered authentically with numerous shingled roofs that were interrupted by rows of triangular dormers in the attics. He could make out the marks where a moat had been filled in. On all sides of the house were lawns and allées. He had to crawl forward to see the stables and offices, which were directly below him.

'There were figures moving round – soldiers. On studying them more closely he saw they were German officers. He'd stumbled across a rest area for the cream of the German officer class, a free brothel for the victors of Tannenberg. It was to the east that he should have turned.

'He counted two croquet lawns and six lawn tennis courts. A class for athletics was taking place. Young women in gloves and carrying parasols were watching from benches. He saw a croquet player invite one of them to take his shot. He took up a stance immediately behind her. As she struck the ball he gave her a terrific buffet with his loins, at which all his friends laughed. In a thick flowerbed, some tall white flowers were being smashed to pieces by two, maybe more, bucking bodies. He contrasted all this with the condition of his own troops. His plan was complete by the time he squirmed backwards towards his men, who were without exception hungry and angry.

'There was never the smallest difficulty with the engagement. The guards were killed at their posts and the telegraph operator shot neatly, head over heels, as he ran to his wooden operations hut. You can imagine the rest. Where Andrej was most artful, one could say merciless, was in getting his men away sober. They took with them the six most senior Germans. After a couple more weeks and a few skirmishes – the Huns going insane when they discovered what he'd done, you understand – he arrived at our own lines. He rode up to the chief who was soaping his balls standing in a canvas field-bath, saluted and said, "I've brought you General A, Colonels B, C, and D and a couple of also-rans. Potocki reporting back for duty, *sir*!", fairly roaring the word 'sir' at this suddy, stupefied, hairy-bellied old pink man.

'Don't you see it, Charlie? A ready-made hero exactly when we needed him. Perfect! Our little playmate was whisked back to St Peter – damned if I'll call it Petrograd – to be paraded round the capital. Got an immediate transfer to the general staff – to the Garde à Cheval. Absolutely top of the pile. And now – for God's sake don't go and tell him about her fits. He hasn't an idea. I tell you, it's as big a coup as old Rykov's. Five thousand acres of sugar beet plus pin money plus jewellery. All she has to do in return is wear nice clothes, feed his friends and bear his children. That hospital stuff she does, it'll have to go and no bad thing either. I wouldn't let my cattle near it.'

Nicholas bent his sunburned face over mine and kissed me on the cheeks and on my lips. His were chapped and salty. 'I can't believe my luck. All my problems with Helene are at an end. Andrej'll see me right – or make her see reason.' He gave a menacing little grunt. Then, 'I'll be able to buy a new bull, perhaps more land. Get that leg of yours a bit better and you'll be strong enough to walk around with me. There are a couple of meadows I've always had my eye on . . .'

He ran his hand through his thick wheaten hair. Laughing boyishly, 'Don't go telling Liza what I said. But you have to admit, it's come at a good time . . . A fairy tale!'

'When's the wedding, then?'

'Whenever he wants her,' he said in a hoarse whisper.

Twenty-six

EVENTS MUST have space to develop. No good ever came of pressing them too closely. When they're ready they'll let you know. At that point the art of dealing with them lies in having a sense of promptness.

So I let the affair between Andrej and Elizaveta take its course, which was entirely by an exchange of letters. Timofei, the coachman, would fetch the mail from Smolensk two or three times a week. Sometimes Louis brought Andrej's letters to the drawing room when I was there with her. She never rejoiced to have them: would inspect the envelope carefully, as if the handwriting was that of a stranger. I pretended to be indifferent, though naturally I was delighted. Time was on my side. Mightn't he try another adventure and get a bullet in the throat?

My leg mended fast. I spent the tail of the summer naturalising around the Pink House and showing Kobi the lie of the land. He was bunking in Popovka, the village of about forty families that serves the Pink House.

Let me give you an idea of the geography.

Popovka is eight miles from Smolensk. To get there from the railway station you go past the market and over the Dniepr on the ancient, five-span bridge. Care must be exercised since there's barely room for two carriages to pass and it's a long way down to where the pleasure steamers are berthed. Through the gateway in Boris Godunov's walls, up Suborny Hill with the cathedral on the left and so on past monuments and history until one hits off the Popovka road beside the Roman Catholic church in Molokhovskaya Place. Then the eight miles: either dusty or muddy but always rutted, curling through undulating, heavily wooded countryside, the road being wide enough for a farm cart and no more. This area is the forest of Popovka.

It belongs mostly to Nicholas, a straggling swathe of oak, ash, chestnut, birch and willow, all self-seeded. In winter it appears hollow and sinister: dark gallows frames edged with snow. Ravens circle. Crows dip their heads and issue their echoing cemetery calls from the tops of dead trees. There are wolves, foxes and deer.

The only timber of value, a section of planted fir that abounds with red squirrels, is owned by Nicholas's neighbour, Mikhail Baklushin.

At mile four there is a wayside shrine to St Nicholas, patron saint of travellers. The flowers are tended by every passer-by.

At regular intervals woodmen's tracks disappear into the forest.

About a mile before the village of Popovka, upon turning a corner, the forest ceases for a space and there one finds Zhukovo, an oasis of verdant pasture with the only decent soil in the area, a nice dark loam to a depth of three or four feet. (Elsewhere there's a shallow mixture of clay and sand with a sour yellow colour that doesn't drain readily and is hard on both the ploughmen and their oxen.) At Zhukovo there's a nice old timbered manor house, cottages and a herd of gleaming black Scotch cattle.

These spend the winter in a long barn. The side giving onto the road has been artfully constructed of different coloured bricks to suggest a Greek colonnade.

Mikhail Baklushin, the owner of Zhukovo, is my godfather. He's a rotund, jolly, surprising man known to every person around as Misha. One of his ancestors had the good fortune to own a brickworks at the time of Napoleon's invasion. A boast of Misha's is that the Baklushins and the kings of Sweden are the only families in Europe to have lived for a hundred years off the fat of Napoleon. He's referring to the profits his great-grandfather made when Moscow was rebuilt.

He's unmarried, wears foreign suits with off-white shoes and has made it his business to rescue from the peasants all the chickens mutilated when they're scything their hay. He can't bear to see the fowl hopping around the street growing thinner and thinner. An old carriage is placed outside his house for their convenience.

He reads Sherlock Holmes in bed and rises late. Then he puts on a bright silk dressing gown and goes out to feed his chickens and speak to them. This procedure is easily visible from the road. He's been doing it for so long that when he's ill and can't go out, it's noticed and commented on instantly.

His housekeeper is a younger sample of the Bobinski tutor type: educated, impoverished, and without ambition. They have a good relationship, Misha and this man.

A famous incident once occurred concerning Misha. He had a brainwave, which he explained as follows: from then on every word spoken on his farm during the working day was to have one meaning only. This would promote simplicity, accuracy of speech and purpose, and thus an increase in profits, which he would share with Vasili, his long-serving stockman.

'"One word, one meaning", that's the name of the decree,' he said to Vasili as they stood in the kitchen. 'Keep notes of it, now. I'll be asked to describe it in a book one day.' He had quite a bit more to say about the system and all the time, according to Vasili, he kept dabbing behind his ears and round his neck with an apple-scented handkerchief.

Uncle Boris was speechless with laughter. 'Millions are now within Misha's reach. Loaf is no longer going to mean to idle round in Misha's pay, cow is only to mean a creature with four legs and four udders, bull—'

'We know about that, my dear,' said Mother.

'And mortgage is only to mean debt,' said my father George, who was the most professional borrower of all, though we didn't realise it at the time. 'Why don't we try Misha's game for the day and see if we become happier – eliminate what's superfluous, straighten it all out. "One word, one meaning". Is that to be our slogan until the dinner gong . . . ? Yes, my darling? I see you wrinkling your nose.' This he said to my mother, grinning. Then, 'Boris, what are we to do about our ladies? What on earth's to happen to the female race in Misha's crisp new world?'

'That's enough, George,' said my mother. 'We can concentrate if you make it worthwhile for us. But what will it solve? Haven't you enough happiness as it is? And the arguments you men will get up to – I can't bear to think about them. It's a silly idea.'

Mother's remarks put my father in his place. Instead a boy was sent round to Misha inviting him to English tea (by which uncle Boris meant staying for a couple of days) so that he could give us a talk about his heroic plan. This was for the sake of politeness.

However, the boy was detained in Popovka and reached Zhukovo too late. Misha had departed to catch a train to Moscow.

Twenty-seven

T HE REASON the message failed to get to Misha can be stated simply – the tavern. The highway stops in Popovka. Tracks do continue through the forest to the next village but the road itself ceases. The tavern operates as a sort of turnstile for anyone entering or leaving the village. It butts onto the road so intimately that a horseman can be handed his drink from the window.

The boy was spotted as he ambled past sitting sideways on a carthorse. A man shouted out of the window, 'Where to?'

'Zhukovo. To Misha's.'

'What for?'

'"One word, one meaning" – the *barin* is going to explain it.' Of course he was hauled in for questioning.

Everyone with business at Popovka or at the Pink House is observed as he passes the tavern. His apparel, wealth, temper, class, company, probable length of visit, all are noted and recorded in Popovka's collective memory. And when he leaves the enclave, this also is noted.

Whenever my parents and I were driven to the train at Smolensk, I would shrink back from the window and try not to be seen from the tavern. I hated the silent scrutiny from behind the small square panes of oil paper; the dulled and bearded faces staring at the coach dashing past. In fact I never entered the place until now, when Kobi and I would feel thirsty on our strolls. The pine walls and ceiling were blackened by tobacco smoke and the years of conspiring that had taken place since it last burned down. The darkness was striking even on a sunny day. The light admitted by the oil paper was grey and gritty. You'd never have been able to tell the colour of a man's gloves as he rode past. But the topers would have had a good enough notion of what he signified from the way he sat his horse.

Opposite the tavern are the church, the priest's house and an unwalled cemetery. The church descends in three levels from its golden cupola to the porch, which has a large wooden gate onto the road.

I cannot remember a time when the priest wasn't loathed by the villagers. This was a long-standing emotion directed mostly at his office. But of course it caught him as well.

Popovka has one street. The houses are two-roomed and built of wood. In cold weather the owners hang a second set of windows on hooks on the inside and stuff the gap between them with oddments of wool, paper and fur. The year that Uncle Boris had a clear-out every one of these windows was crammed with the brittle yellow pages of obsolete French novels.

Behind the houses are the vegetable patches, kennels and sheds for geese and chickens. The wealthier peasants, those who are farming in league with Nicholas, have wooden stockades in which they secure their livestock from wolves in winter. The timbers are never sawn to a uniform height. Seen against a frosty sunset, their top line goes up and down like a piano score.

Everything is too sunk in tradition to achieve any progress, that's Nicholas's habitual complaint. 'They won't kill pigeons in case they kill the Holy Spirit, and Fyodor Fyodorovich told me last year he would never consent to use a mechanical reaper as it would be dishonourable to his horses. Many believe that the yield from the rye has nothing to do with good husbandry but everything to do with the dark spots that appear on the sun. They say these have a regular cycle, and reel off the years of the bumper crops to me. Of course the upshot of all this is that the harvest is preordained and there's no point in working at all. I say to them, Why then should I try to teach you? Is it to be scythes and pitchforks until we die?'

Liza, reporting this to me, commented: 'The fact is that they're far better capitalists than he is. Nicholas cannot bring himself to be professionally greedy. He's not poor enough, there's too much of the aristocrat still in him. He's weighed down by his conscience and the eighteen thousand serfs that the Founder owned. The peasants know this and exploit it. When he does his accounts he rushes into me exclaiming, "But where's it all gone, sister? I'm *bleeding* money."

'But he continues to let them have land at stupidly low rents, even though every spring they run whining to him, trundling their paunches before them, saying they've got no seed corn to plant as they had to eat it in the winter to stay alive. "Oh, *barin*, your honour, a loan for a twelvemonth . . . . I swear by the Mother of Christ . . .""

Such is Popovka.

The road continues from the village for half a mile, when it arrives at a turning circle of cobbles. These aren't rounded sea cobbles but sliced ones, as that's how the stone hereabouts shatters when addressed with a sledgehammer. Between them grow clumps of a lovely pinky-purple scabious. I've seen as many as two hundred arguses at a time drinking from the puddles and feeding on the plant – a wonderful twitching brown carpet. Even the surrounding air was spangling, as if it had been polished by all those butterfly wings.

The only exit from the cobbled circle is through the great archway that the Founder built to commemorate his patriotism and acumen, which is a rare combination and well deserves a monument. It is crowned by the Rykov wolf. 'Think Well' is the family motto.

Beside the archway is the gatekeeper's lodge.

The road to the Pink House is well bottomed, good for any weight. It curves round the shoulder of the high ground on which Popovka stands and then dips between the oaks until it comes out into a pleasant river valley that's four fields long and two fields wide, the fields having been laid out methodically to measure ten English acres apiece. In spring the road's rich in primroses and dog violets. The male brimstones, in their high yellow livery, guard their territories with darting vigour.

I'm asking you to visualise yellows and greens above all other colours, and the corrugated boles of oak trees as you're rattled down the drive. You're sitting behind Timofei who's wearing his best hat, his station one, which is like the black funnel of a steamer. The colours of April appear all the brighter because Lent is done with and laughter has been reborn.

The river – let us be generous and call it a river and not some-thing lesser – is slow and oily and as wide as a strong catapult shot. Frogs, herons, and by summer the grey migrating cranes, make it their home. It's exactly as Mother remembered it, where the stable horses come to be washed on the name day of their patron saints.

A humpbacked stone bridge takes the drive across it. Then it loops back along the side of the river before heading up into the bowl at the top of the valley where the Founder planted his settlement. On both sides it's shaded by poplars. The eight English fields, which are reserved for the exclusive use of the horses on the estate, are on the left of the drive. Count a mile from the lodge to the Pink House, two miles from Popovka.

I omitted to say that a large reason the river deserves to be called that is because it's the residence of swans. We've inspected each other on numerous occasions when I've been exercising my wasted leg muscles: I with frank admiration for their stately way of going, they flirtatiously, glancing sideways at me with their languorous, red-lidded eyes.

'Now, a swan that also had eyelashes would have the world at its feet,' I remarked to Liza one evening. 'Imagine if it decided to eat in a restaurant. Even a waiter would run to its table – would sprint.'

We'd been looking for chanterelles – idly, because the woods were well picked and it was getting late in the season. Now we were walking beside the river. Andrej was visiting the Riga front. Out of sight is out of mind.

She was strolling with her arms folded across her breast. 'There's only one restaurant left in Smolensk now. I went there with our new director yesterday. Nobody came to our table for half an hour. He said after a while, "I believe these waiters would be quite happy to kill us." What do you say – do you agree with that, Charlie?'

'Isn't that the dream of all waiters in our country? Our advantage is that we're intelligent enough to realise that when it's a question of us or them, it's we who must shoot first. Their sense of class will make them hesitate – fatal. We don't have any inhibitions of that sort. Survival is the only proper measure of cleverness.'

'Survival . . .' She stored the word away.

'Perhaps that's how waiters feel everywhere in the world. For all we know they may be yearning to pluck the lid off the chafing dish, pick up the revolver concealed below the potatoes and go, Bang, that'll teach you.'

At that moment we reached the bridge. Our escort of swans gave us come-hither winks as dark as melted chocolate and paddled on, taking the central span of the bridge where the current was strongest. I touched the balustrade with my finger (it marked my goal). We turned together. And there it was, one of those damned queer things of that year.

For in looking towards the house, up the broad, slightly rising valley, we saw that the whole land before us, the fields, the grazing carriage horses, the wings of forest on either side and the forest behind the house, had been set ablaze by an immense bank of flaming clouds. As far as the eye could see, the sky was on fire. From Popovka to Warsaw, from east to opulent west, molten metal was pouring from the mouth of the sun, yawning as it prepared for night.

We stood in stupefaction. The swans came back through the bridge to find out what had happened to us and were instantly feathered in flamingo pink.

Liza cried, 'Look at Xylophone, Charlie – quick! Pink as a trout! . . . Oh my – pink one side and grey the other! Do you suppose the other horses are wondering what's wrong with her? Are they asking, "Has she a disease? Do we want to be in the same harness?"'

She looked at me, her face made radiant by the evening glow. Love roared gurgling into the chamber of my heart and flooded it. All that had been brewing since we sat above the battlefield of Balaclava among the wild crocuses rose to the surface, forcing the stopper out.

I grabbed her by the ears and pulled on them. 'Marry me instead. He's disgusting. You'd be backing a loser. Be honest with yourself.'

She considered me. Our strong noses were inches apart.

'You might as well say yes now. I'm going to get you sooner or later. I'm determined.'

She took back her ears with a flick of her head. In her face there were three parts of curiosity to every two of amusement, in which I also include an air of confidence such as is natural for a beautiful woman being wooed. 'You can tell our grand-children, He almost pulled my ears off when he proposed. It hurt so much that I gave in. To become Mrs Doig was less painful.'

'Love, what of that?'

'You're saying that I don't love you? Don't be ridiculous. Why else do you think I want to marry you? Do I have to spell out the word "stars" before you can see them?'

'So I have to imagine love, is that it? Well, I don't have to with Andrej. He bombards me with it: jewels, money, furs, smaller gifts—'

'What do you mean by that?'

'Trinkets for the castle — horses, coaches and so on. Bric-a-brac you might call them.'

Now she was laughing at me. I wound myself up — but just then we heard a horse trotting down the drive. I dropped my hands and turned.

It was Nicholas who rode out of the oak trees, my honest, dutiful cousin who would have been ideal for Tolstoy in any story that revolved around the agonisings of a liberal landowner. He'd been to renew his loans and was in his town clothes. He swung his right leg over the pommel and slid to the ground. His horse sighed and shook itself.

'My dears, you've no idea what a day I've had. The terms my bankers are demanding this year — I might as well go to the Jews,' — he switched his look from me to Liza — 'you know, Kugel in Pochtamtskaya. At least they know how to leave a man with his dignity. Whereas a Russian banker will take everything he can get his hands on as security, down to the gravel on one's drive . . . So as of today I've got a new motto: Never be gloomy. It's either that or slitting one's wrists . . . I met Misha on the way back and invited him over. Tomorrow, I said. We've been living like mice for too long. Let's open some wine and have a laugh for a change . . . That's the sort of day it's been.'

He smiled frankly on us. He had such a decent face that to witness him depressed was to feel depressed oneself. The gap at the top of his two front teeth was wide enough to take an apple pip. It was always a good sign when it was in full view. He made a good-natured shooing gesture to Liza. 'We'll catch you up in a moment.'

He took me by the arm. 'I didn't want to speak out in front of her . . . My worries, Charlie, they breed like rats. At the mortgage office – that was bad enough, but then – it was the latest news in town: Brusilov has started to fall back. As long as he was victorious, the idea of Russia supreme was in the ascendant. People would say joyfully, "He's just like his name, bristling and bustling." That's not what you hear now. You know what it means when they say "fall back". It means he's in full retreat. Morale has never been so low. Mutiny in every regiment. The Tsar – hopeless. Feeble when he needs strength, arrogant when he should be tactful. Lets the monk get away with anything, just because the brute tells him his son will live. Such terrible lies! Doesn't it hurt him to tell them? My friends say he never washes and that he's had every single woman at court. He just reaches out. They don't even struggle. It's disgusting, I tell you.

'The whole thing's boiling up for disaster. You wait and see this winter. St Peter's got too large to feed except by rail. And who's using all the railway wagons, eh? Exactly. Soldiers, horses, ammunition. Food be damned, unless it's for the horses. The Tsar gets sozzled on wine every night having forbidden his subjects ever to get sozzled on vodka. His German wife lets herself be screwed by that stinking shitpricker of a monk – in the orchid house! Yes! He pushed her up against the glass so he could show off to the gardeners while he had her. Do they think our people are without sensitivities?'

I told him he was working too hard. He should give more responsibility to the village elder.

He continued: 'So I was riding down the drive and consoling myself with my new motto when I saw you with Elizaveta. She wouldn't have told you so I must. She's had another attack of *le grand mal* – a fit.'

'That's what the doctors said? When did it happen?'

'When you were in the desert. I think it comes from the stress of working in the hospital. It's what she says herself. So I've ordered her to go there less often. That was right, wasn't it? I do my duty by everybody. But especially in the case of Elizaveta – our future, Charlie, yours and mine – you see what I'm getting at . . .'

'Even a blind man could.'

'She can have a thousand fits a day once they're married. Go gently with her, Charlie, that's what I mean. Don't provoke her. Dear Christ, the catastrophe that would be if he backed out . . . Now, we'll pretend we were talking over the farm accounts and which peasants should have loans for the winter.'

She said nothing as Nicholas, plucking shiftily at his short beard, took longer than was necessary to explain our need for privacy. Her eyes were dull from the certain knowledge she was hearing a lie. She rubbed the gooseflesh on her forearms, put on my pullover, and as her dark head burst through and Nicholas at last shut up, said in her rich low voice, 'So, Charlie, you said you were determined. True or false?'

Nicholas looked from me to her and back, but neither of us was giving anything away.

Twenty-eight

TOGETHER WE walked up the slope to the Pink House and the remains of the gory sunset. Nicholas's horse trailed behind us with its head among its hoofs and its eyes closed.

'Like a plate of raw mince,' Liza said, nodding at the sky.

'Not with the black stripes. Order of St George, that's what it is,' said Nicholas crisply. 'How many of them does Andrej have by now – half a dozen?'

Timofei had been watching out for him and came stumping down the track from the stables, walking on the sides of his boots, ankles and knees bending outwards. Nicholas tossed him the reins of his horse. 'There you are, old fellow. Give it an extra bowl of mash tonight. I'll take the chestnut tomorrow.' He hesitated. 'No, I'll come with you and see if Fyodor Fyodorovich has started to thrash out the straw yet.'

The groom was bent over feeling the horse's legs.

'Devil take it, Timofei, why do you always nanny me so? Their legs should be made of wood so I could ride them as I wanted. Don't glare at me like that, old fellow. Never be gloomy, that's my new motto. You should copy me. What would you do if I purchased a motor car? I wouldn't need you, would I? Think about that.'

Timofei said scornfully, 'You won't get a motor car as you no more like modern than I do.'

They walked off chatting, the horse also more cheerful now that the stables were in sight.

'So, what else did you get out of Igor?' I asked Liza lightly. 'The diamonds? Some nice rubies?'

'So that's why you want me?'

109

'Of course.'

'What a way you have with the ladies, Mister Doig . . . You're still determined? I could hear bits of what Nicholas was saying. Outdoor men speak loudly.'

'Do you mind?'

'His telling you – no. Having *le grand mal* – most certainly. The hospital doctors said, Sorry, we just don't know . . . What happens? Describe it, you ask? The first thing is the screaming around me in the hospital. It disturbs me intensely. I think of pain and somehow this spreads from a single human (which is me) to a village, to an army, to the nation and I see them all running away from it, trying to shake it out of their heads. The worst for screaming is when there's just been a major battle. We're always low in anaesthetics. Sometimes we have none. The surgeon has to make a choice. To one man he says in effect, You will scream. To another, You need not. The men don't know what the surgeon's decision means to them. But I do, and I start to feel the pain for them. Also there is the fact that I'm involved in causing them that pain. That's when I had the last fit. I know all the moves my mind will make as I walk up and down the rows of the wounded.'

'Did you roll around – foam?'

'Don't, Charlie.'

'Just curious. Isn't it better to have it out?'

'So it doesn't frighten me any more? Thanks.'

The black belly of the night was pushing the evening sky down into the trees – tatters of pink and pearl, salmon and its skin. Venus watched beadily from somewhere just above Popovka as Russia, so unimaginably huge, so wooded and rivered, so heavy, so clumsy, so cruel, rolled onto its side and snuggled down.

Wood smoke was drifting through the air. From the pleasure grounds the haunting song of a flycatcher bobbled to and fro, gorgeously defiant among the vulgar chimes of the blackbirds going to roost.

In the desert at this hour rocks crack like bullwhips as they start to cool, and the soil, relaxing, shudders and sighs.

We were standing shoulder to shoulder.

'Listen – the flycatcher.'

'The little trickling noise?' She sighted down my forefinger as I pointed in the direction of the bird. She closed her fingers round my wrist, trying to keep my hand steady. (The way she did that, one finger after another, like a piano exercise, not seizing or snatching.) I inclined my head so I could brush my cheek against her hair, angled it to kiss the warm, furry nape of her neck. Her fingers tightened on my wrist.

What happened next was that I heard the unsurpassable sound of *Monochamus galloprovincialis* whirring – steaming – bellowing – up the hill behind me. I whipped round. I didn't push Liza away, or knock her, or shove her. I never saw her stumble. Believe me, history. It's true I heard her cry out, but by then I'd committed myself to the timber beetle. Its wings were going like mad, its long gangly legs splayed out like a crane fly's. Huge, wand-like antennae, longer than the creature itself, were scenting the dusk, looking for love, for the greatest story there's ever been.

'Like us, Lizochka, like us!' – I stretched out my hand for her as the beetle bustled away into the darkness.

But she was ten yards away. Anger had her, she was beating at the air with her fists and shouting – 'I piss myself, that's what I do. I slobber down my chin, I collapse and the hot piss runs down my legs and out onto the floor for everyone to see and I writhe around and have to be restrained. Put in a jacket – yes! like a lunatic. I'm repulsive, that's what I'm like when I have a fit. You wanted to know. You asked. I'm telling you.'

I ran over to her but she palmed me away. 'That's what you did to me just then – because a silly beetle was flying past. You know why I agreed to Andrej? Because I want intelligent company for my life, and protection when I'm ill. With Andrej I'll have children. I'll be the mother I've never known. I'll bring up my family decently and in comfort. What better ambition could a woman have? Not just now but ever since time started for us.'

'How was I to know it wasn't another Wiz? I make steady money from him. Already I have more fame than most men when they die.'

'Most civilians.'

'Oh, so it's back to bold brave Andrej and no one else counts, is it?'

'You're a remarkable fellow, too. Is that enough?'

'Mine's the only star to follow. Throw him over, Lizochka. He's a dirty little man.'

'Too late, Charlie Doig. I saw what I'd become a moment ago. A life on the move is a life of danger. Something would happen to you. Then I'd be desperate. I can't abide the thought of being an old woman and lonely and poor.'

'It's the money. You were always after it,' I said harshly.

'I was born within earshot of it. It makes a handsome sound. Why would any woman consent to live where she can't hear it? You can't embarrass me that way.'

We'd wandered off course, into the pleasure grounds, though I didn't recall bending to unlatch the hooped, rusty, waist-high gate for her. The night was opening up its shop. Stars were rising out of her hair, springing up like sparklers to form a tiara for her dark head. A baby moon clothed her, its silvery light fluttering between the trees and making a pool round our shadows which it had sketched, all squashed up, upon the old lawn tennis court.

I said, 'We'd make a good team, Lizochka. Better as man and wife than as friends.'

I was trying the affectionate tone, as between cousins – which of course we were.

'He is to be my husband,' she said simply. 'I have a good bargain to offer the man who can afford me. There's no point not being honest with oneself. I shall bear him as many children as he wants, make a worthy home for him and be faithful. My temper is medium—'

'How often?'

'Badly, once a year. I could do better if I had to. But I think there's a minimum that's natural. Not to lose it at all would be inhuman. Andrej – I haven't discovered about him yet. There'll be faults, we may be sure, just as our Lord Christ made us.'

Our quarrel had withdrawn out of sight. I forbore from reminding her how he'd pushed her on the swing – from in front, to admire her silken groove, to estimate angles, depth, fertility, consequences. Count Andrej Potocki with his riches, his bravery, his electrified hair and his Order of St George, first class. Damn him to hell! Damn him and his luck and his sugar beet!

My head went back and my nose went up and I said, 'I'll win you somehow. This is rubbish about family comforts and dying adored. You're a far bolder woman than that. We were made for each other.'

It was all so obvious to me. I felt like a lion-tamer or a dare-devil pilot when introduced to a beautiful woman who's in love with the same risks as he is. What else can they do but strip off their clothes and fall on each other? No alternative has yet been found. Caxton, railways, the Gatling gun, by none of these has the human race been so advanced as it has by men and women falling on each other.

I started to speak along these lines but Louis came out and called for us. I placed my heart in a jar and with a light, confident finger tapped down the lid, which was perforated so that my love could breathe.

In the hall the gigantic blue-glazed stove was knocking out the heat. Liza took off my pullover and smoothed down the tufts of her dark hair. With a wan smile she handed it to me. Standing there, I had this extra thought: add stuntman to the list and she and I will couple furiously in the air, like a pair of white swifts, and produce a prodigy who'll be named Daniel Doig. Oh my heart, my young heart! How I heard it going – sizzling! I put my arms round her waist and swept her up. 'Ouf!' she gasped as I swung her round. She didn't know what to do with her hands at first. Then she made them into fists and beat at me – seriously, lips compressed and her eyes hard.

I brought her back to the floor. I said, 'That was for Daniel, our first child,' keeping my arms around her.

She had to smile, though she tried not to. 'You should come and work in the hospital. Optimism is always needed there.' Then that maid of hers, Sonja, appeared and they went off to the kitchens together to see what could be found when Misha came.

Twenty-nine

BOBINSKI MUST have had a patronymic but the use of it had withered away during the course of his fifty-five years at the Pink House, together with his hair but not his appetite, which astounded everyone because he was a thin, pale man of fragile appearance, something like a papyrus. He'd taught French and English to three generations of Rykovs, plus a little botanical Latin for farming purposes.

Louis was the newcomer in the house. Uncle Boris had rescued him from a footman's job in Moscow. Once a year he returned to France to see his mother. He was comfortably built with a head of strong brown hair, an eagle's-wing moustache and a soupy complexion.

Between him and Bobinski there was constant skirmishing. It was Louis who'd started to call the tutor Bobka and then Bobby.

In the event Misha Baklushin couldn't come to the feast as he was bedridden with a strained rib. The only guest, therefore, was Bobinski. He came down the stairs into the hall punctually at five thirty. Louis headed him off as he advanced upon the drawing room. The discussion, which echoed off the marble tiles in the hall, concerned whether Bobinski should be announced by Louis as he went in.

'You, my fat friend, should remember always the butler's adage: Be seen and not heard,' – and with these words Bobinski entered the drawing room, wheeling round and shutting the door on Louis in one rapid movement, the tails of his frock coat swirling up to show the shiny backside to his trousers.

He was in exceptional form. He reminisced freely and wittily about Nicholas's father and grandfather, drank all the wine he was offered without seeming greedy, ate splendidly, and made fun of Louis.

Louis's dark eyes watched him forking through the warty, parsley-speckled dumplings.

'Now, Count, as for the marriage of your half-sister to Potocki . . .' Bobinski said, taking his time as he chose a couple of dumplings and steered them into a harbour of red cabbage that he'd prepared with a view to spooning the whole lot out together.

'*Dépêche-toi*, Bobby,' said Louis. He flexed his fingers and sprang the dish – made it hop. A little jet of gravy spurted over the tutor's cuff, which he affected not to notice.

'. . . would it not be advisable to have something arranged unconditionally?' he said. 'To – ah – encourage haste in the proceedings?' Louis laid his free hand on the back of Bobinski's chair and stifled a yawn.

'Monsieur, you just watch your step when Count Andrej arrives. Manners like that and he'll have you sent to a military school where the peasants are whipped until they learn how to be proper waiters. Now take your hand off my chair immediately . . . Count, once you have a date you can arrange for the choir. Of course you'll use the cathedral . . . really, my advice would be to press the gentleman . . . the longer it's left the greater the chance of him being killed too soon.'

'Please, Bobby,' Liza said. 'And you're the one who's always speaking of the importance of manners.'

Even Nicholas frowned.

But Bobinski plunged on. 'We must snap him up. These awful days will end and when they do families like yours will need money more than ever before. The losses! Think of the horses we've already had taken. It'd be a crime to let him escape merely through acting too casually.' Turning to Liza, 'You must be like Desdemona, my child, and talk him out of patience. Make yourself ever more alluring. Yes – ah – *knock* it out of him.'

Louis came out from behind his butlering screen. 'If Count to be killed tomorrow, he should have the lady today. No mistake he should. Get baby started.'

I looked across the table at Liza. She was sitting quietly with her eyes turned down. I thought her face unnaturally white.

Bobinski said to Nicholas, 'A war is being fought. He could be killed while we're sitting here.'

'No need to tell *me*,' Nicholas flared. 'I've lost my brother. I've told Andrej he can have her whenever it suits him. What more can I do? We don't want to press him so much that he takes us for some petit bourgeois.'

'But the choir,' persisted Bobinski. 'Your sister deserves the best in the province. You don't want to be landed with the old growlers.'

It was the corner of her mouth that I first noticed – jagging, twitching. She stiffened. Her eyeballs, prominent anyway, were staring at a point on the wall behind me. I jumped out of my chair and ran to her side. I placed my hand on the point of her shoulder. I could feel her quivering, vibrating like a telegraph wire. Urgently I broke into another speech from Bobinksi and told Louis to fetch Sonja. I'd been hearing her washing glasses in Louis's pantry.

One of us on either side, we raised her from her chair and guided her along the corridor to one of the downstairs bedrooms. Sonja rushed away and returned in a few moments with a fire pan. The hot coals were lolling against each other, sending up acrid fumes. She tipped them into the grate, sprinkled some handfuls of curly birch peelings on top and laid the kindling. Again she rushed out, with a whisk of her drab grey gown. Her strong black shoes sounded prissy on the planked flooring. The side door grated. She was going to pick from the wood stack at the end of the verandah.

Liza's black eyes were staring up at me, glazed with shock. Her face had a bluish tinge. She was holding her head rigidly. Everything else was trembling violently. Her dress was moving as if she had mice in her underlinen. I pulled up a chair and began to stroke her arms.

Sonja entered. I continued what I was doing. I said, 'Look, she's relaxing. I think it makes her warm. That must help. You must know what this is – her illness?'

Turning, I looked at her thoroughly, wanting to flatter her since she was an important link to Liza. I saw a woman of about twenty-five with brown, pulled-back hair, a pale jowly face and sloping shoulders. Her breasts hung like bags of wet sand. She had shadows beneath her eyes as big as pennies, indicating troublesome menstruation. There can't have been a plainer woman in Popovka.

I glanced at her red hands, thought of them hunting out my lice – prising my buttocks apart.

Her voice was a surprise, being smooth and educated. 'It's another fit. It'll go on for several hours like this. That's what she said when she warned me about them.'

'I wonder what brought it on like that,' I said.

Sonja said, 'I must see if she needs changing. You have to leave.'

As I was closing the door on my heel, she ran over and pulled it from my grasp. Poking her face into mine, her eyes goggling angrily, she burst out, 'How can you ask such a stupid question? You all did it, you're all guilty, you men with your licentious jokes and then your talk about the chances of that' – she paused – 'that *aristocrat* getting killed. Do you think I couldn't hear everything that goes on? You were talking about her as if she were a pig at market. Not once did any of you ask what *she* thought. What concerned you was the money she was bringing in. I couldn't believe it. I wanted to rush in and stop you. Is she a prostitute? I wanted to put this question to each of you in turn. But I'm only a servant. I've learned to keep myself to myself – and to my mistress. So leave us. You've done enough harm.'

I was astonished that she should speak to me like that. I said as much. But I said it to a closing door.

Nicholas ran up to get the news. I asked him about Sonja. He didn't know much: the choice had been entirely his sister's. I told him what had passed between us. He wasn't interested. He'd taken Bobinski's words to heart and was considering how best to hurry along Andrej.

'Oh good, as long as she's being properly looked after.' He flicked his fingers and went to the drawing room to write Andrej a touching letter.

Without Liza and her parlour games (which he adored), Bobinski soon fell asleep. His head was to one side and from the back of his throat came dry, creaking snores. A sheath of white hairs rose from under the collar of his shirt and circled his scrawny neck like the frilled paper round the end of a lamb cutlet. Soft, bent and childlike, he occupied his wing chair. His mouth was soft too, from repeating all the stories he'd heard in his time, stories that probably went back two hundred years to the time of Peter the Great.

The fire settled in the hearth, the pen scratched, the snores mounted.

I, however, was considering the assassination of Count Andrej Potocki. Not practically but in general, as a beautiful aspiration. One can have too much of the Goetz mentality, of three courses of virtue at every meal. Goodness is artificial and acquired only with much effort and purpose. A man who is honest with himself is entitled to his full share of sin. Was it a crime to want Potocki dead?

It was too powerful a question for that somnolent room. I went out and sat in the hall, opposite the big blue and white stove, beneath a thicket of roebuck antlers.

Thirty

M Y LEG only needed constant work to become firm again.
Kobi and I had been in the habit of walking daily to and
from Popovka and through the forest. But with winter came
short days and difficult conditions underfoot. I didn't want to
slip and crack the bone a second time. I took over an empty
room near the kitchen in which to get fit.

It had snowed on this particular morning. I was on my way
to exercise as I sauntered down the passage past Liza's rooms.
I'd never been inside, even as a child. They'd always been her
private lair. Whenever she ran there sobbing, we knew the game
had been too rough. None of us had dared follow, least of all
Andrej Potocki to whom, as a guest and not of our blood, there
was a social barrier at the entrance to the family's sleeping quarters. I really don't recall anyone getting into her rooms, even
her girlfriends.

The door was ajar. I thought to get an inkling of what it
could be like between us in fifty years' time. There was curiosity
– temptation – love – all that was human. I mended my pace,
checked behind me for Sonja and stepped smartly in. I released
the doorknob silently, fraction by fraction.

Then I stopped dead. I half-whistled (air without noise). For
here was Aladdin's cave.

Chinese scarlet were the walls, the scarlet of a warlord's
banner, a parrot's poll, a northern sunset. A spectacular ripping
scarlet from the black planks to the uncomplicated cornice,
which was likewise black. These were not ladylike colours, not
of the lady I believed I knew. I stared up at the ceiling. In the
centre – at the core of the earth – was a sun lapped by curling

tongues of flame that had just spat out a galaxy of small white puffballs. Was it smoke? Were they clouds? I was too stunned to choose. What was going on? Scarlet, for the woman who thought her fits were caused by blood and screaming! Perhaps it was her idea of an anti-therapy: that the shock of awakening in her scarlet tank would scare the attacks away. You could see the brushstrokes rippling through the paint, which made me think of waves, and turbulence, and thus my woman's energy.

So scarlet was it! Go to, Liza! I shouted as if cheering home a racehorse. Go to! Who would have expected it of someone so calm and smooth, with skin like alabaster . . . A drum roll of love sounded and beat upon me, filling all the long dry solitary cracks that lay sprawling in my character. Lizochka, *dusha moya*, my soul, my love!

Elizaveta! I spoke her name, lingering greedily over those rare, late, gentle consonants.

I picked the ragged doll off her pillow and strolled into her boudoir, stroking its threadbare locks, which were made from real hair.

The bookshelves were black as well. Now that I was getting into the swing of her mind, this seemed an entirely proper way to connect the floor to the cornice. Her books were in Russian and French, novels with paper spines the same colour as Nicholas's summer jackets. There were other objects on the shelves: a photograph of my uncle Boris posed before a studio background of a palm tree and an ivy-tendrilled balustrade; a death-edged photograph of Viktor in his cavalryman's uniform; dried fronds in a vase; a lime green porcelain pot, an ivory Buddha, and a group of wooden platters on stands – rough, peasant work, the scenes painted in violent orange tones of villagers performing their daily duties: the fetcher of water, the hewer of wood, the besom lady flicking dust from the tavern door.

Was I right to discern the Popovka tavern? Might Sonja have done them? Was Liza her patron?

But now the most serious consideration of all presented itself. It had to be asked. Was I myself too drab for this strong, bright woman?

It made me giddy just to stand there. Inside my head was a

spinning disc of scarlet and black. All was awhirl. The noise of the colours was like Burmese labourers beating out tinplate. Was this what I was going to have to live with? I felt swamped by my surroundings. I flumped into a chair. For I have yet to describe the rest of the furnishings, I mean the curtains, the counterpane on her brass-railed bed, the chair coverings, the carpets on the floor and a couple hanging on the walls. None were in soothing colours. They were all in the bold rectangled designs of the Caucasus, spangling with reds and blues, blasting broadsides from every corner of the room.

Who was this woman? Did I know her? Could I ever know her?

'So what is the answer, then?' I asked myself aloud.

The door flew open, well enough to have taken the hinges with it. Scuttling at me, fist upraised to strike, was Sonja.

I saw it in an instant, the slattern's crush on a bold and beautiful woman. I laughed at her, ha ha ha into her buck-toothed rabbity face, which was popping with jealousy. 'Are you so pally with her that you've forgotten how to knock?'

'Brute,' she hissed. 'You'll never get her.' She clenched her hands, her big red knuckles of ham.

'One of us will – but it won't be you.'

She looked wildly around to see what I'd been up to. 'If you've so much as touched any of her belongings . . .'

I saw that she had a rip in her brown woollen stockings. It started at her ankle and disappeared up her skirt. 'In the woods, were you? Cold, I'd say. A girl'd need a good reason.'

'You're just trying to avoid answering,' she said, ' . . . sir.'

I pointed above her ankle. The wool had burst and I could plainly see the clumps of her dark hair.

She pressed her skirt against her bottom, arched her back and looked down. In doing this she showed me a long streak of a dusty, greenish colour as if she'd been leaning against a tree. What would she be doing in the forest at this time of the morning, at this season, with snow on the ground? I watched her face intently.

She said nothing but folded her lips resolutely over her long teeth, as if by concealing them she was able to conceal the deceit that was all over her face.

I jumped up and before she could stop me pressed the back of my hand against her cheek to get the temperature. 'So what were you doing out there, you lying bitch?'

She tried to hold out on me, trading blinks. But in my life as a naturalist I have often had to wait for more timid creatures than her to come to my call. I bided my time, swinging my foot to annoy her. Presently I noticed perspiration gathering at her hairline.

'Soon you'll be sweating like a June bride.'

She started. What sort of nerve was that I'd hit? 'You have no authority to enter her room. She would have told me.'

'You should stick to being a lady's maid.'

Then she played her ace. 'I know when they're getting married.' She uncovered those teeth, cocking her lips into a foxy little smile of triumph.

'When?'

Of course she didn't reply, but continued her horrible smile, her eyes boring into me. 'If I'm excused from questioning, I'll come back to do my duties when you've gone, *sir*.' She made me an exaggerated curtsy, using both hands to spread her skirt.

'How did you find out? Did she tell you herself?'

'She isn't alone in it. There is also her lover, the aristocrat.'

What was it about her? That half-educated accent, the false servility, the shrewdness, the hint that she had information concerning Potocki that none of us had access to – what was going on?

I said, 'You haven't told me what you were doing in the woods.'

'That's my business. And don't think you can get the Count to dismiss me. Only she can do that – my mistress.' With a brisk nod of her head she was gone, leaving me halfway out of my chair, boiling with anger, my eyes bulging like a bulldog's testicles.

Thirty-one

A WAR WAS destroying men of all nationalities, stoking its furnaces with their corpses, ramming them in, each man's head up the arse of the one in front and their grey toes sticking through the grating for the rats to chew. Being especially consumed were my countrymen, who'd been driven back on all fronts – by the Austrians, by the Germans, and by other nations whom they'd traditionally despised.

Somewhere close to the above there was living in a smart and appropriate billet my boyhood chum, my rival. I wanted him in that furnace with all the others. Alternatively I desired that someone would come forward with proof that he had heredi- tary dementia. Or was in the final stages of syphilis – the nose and a doctor's ticket on the same salver. It was with absolute sincerity that I longed for his death. I scanned the newspaper like a hound.

It was our only source of information. Nicholas also read it avidly, in the evening, sometimes aloud to Liza. The censor's office in Smolensk was a benign one: victories were not inflated and reverses not shovelled under the carpet. The paper would there- fore speak of temporary retreats for tactical purposes, temporary bread queues in Petrograd, and temporary agitators whom they termed *bolsheviki*. This suited Nicholas, who had put himself in an impossible situation, that of being suspicious of good news and crushed by bad. He would himself act as a second censor when reading to Liza and would thus usually tell her nothing but pap.

One evening she taxed him about his right to do this. She was old enough to be married off: was she not old enough to make political judgements for herself?

His reply was typically obtuse. 'If you believe that only terrible things can happen then they will. That's why we have censors, to smooth everything out and remove the rubbish. A steady progression of events is what people want, especially women. Nothing too sudden.' He lowered his voice and leaned towards her on the sofa so as to make everything confidential and realistic. 'There's any number of psychologists who support censorship. The most reputable men in their field, actually.'

'Name them.'

He opened and closed his mouth like a fish. His little blond beard quivered. Of course he couldn't. I doubt if he could have named a single psychologist in Russia.

She looked at him icily. 'You should stick to what you know about.'

This was a slap across the chops. He flushed, but said nothing.

She went on to say that he'd changed the Rykov motto from 'Think Well' to 'Think Stupidly'. Didn't it feel like a second visitation of the jacquerie of '05? Did he want to have the house burned round their ears? Shouldn't they do something? Couldn't they at least *think* of doing something?

'What sort of thing?'

'Going to the Crimea – to Uncle Igor?' She was looking at him without flinching.

It was too much. She was questioning his position as head of the house. He crimsoned, he bridled and foamed, and standing straddled above her roared about duty and deserting the colours at the hour of greatest danger. There was more, to do with Potocki and getting rid of a deadweight from his house – at last. He was crude beyond belief, being angry because she'd said what he ought to have been saying.

She went upstairs. We heard her calling for Sonja. Then and there she had Timofei drive her into the city, in the middle of the night. In the morning she sent word to Nicholas that she'd work at the hospital until her wedding and then leave the Pink House forever.

'I never knew she had such a temper,' he said to me after reading her note.

Now there were just the two of us. At breakfast he'd put on a good show of cheerfulness. But after he'd ridden out he'd retire to his office and give himself over completely to gloom. His motto was sent to the graveyard. By evening he'd be completely addled. He'd go to the far end of the drawing room to immerse himself in the paper. He'd go along the print with his finger, pulling nervously at pieces of his beard. He kept a wind-up Konig phonograph down there. At his worst moments he'd listen to the *Stabat Mater* of Palestrina, groaning, with his head between his hands.

I understood now how it had been for Liza before I came back from Turkestan. How had she endured his moods and his history lectures, his inane remarks, even his clopping farmer's tread along the corridor? It was time to shake myself up. Popovka did not have good prospects for me at present. What was I to aim for? It seemed to me I should start with the Academy, and the sooner I did this the quicker the improvement would be.

Straightway I walked through the snow to get Kobi. He'd found a widow in Popovka and was living with her. 'Tigerman' was what they called him for he was lithe, leathery and had a dangerous look from the manner in which his diamond-shaped eyes appraised you, as if he were a hangman estimating your weight.

I went to the widow's house and told Kobi to get ready. We were going to go to Petrograd and pay a call on the Academy. 'Try our hand at some business again,' I said.

'Don't take him away for too long,' said the widow, sensually. She watched Kobi as he strapped on his belt with its Sheffield steel knife, then fluttered around him, helping with his coat, finding his boots.

'You'll take care of any money they give him, won't you,' she said to me. 'If something happened, I don't know how I'd live . . . Those poor soldiers of ours, having to put themselves up to be killed for fifty kopecks a month. Fifty! For a loaf of bread! *Barin*, you're a clever man, can we be sure the Lord Christ will make them all heroes up there?'

'Shut your mouth, Mother,' Kobi said. He put on his great-coat and fur hat. 'Even the mention of fifty kopecks a month makes me ill. I wouldn't sell my spit for that . . . What fools there are to be found.' He hoisted his knapsack and nodded to me that he was ready.

Thirty-two

B UT WE never got past Zhukovo that day. We were only a hundred yards down the road from Misha's house when we met the man himself coming back from Moscow. His red face shone from his carriage like Christmas.

'News! Hot from the press! Come and share it with me.'

I demurred. He insisted – he implored – even his coach-horse joined in by bowing its neck and scraping at the road gravel.

'Look, there you are!' he said.

'It's hungry. It wants to get out of the traces and have a good roll. The horse has got nothing to do with it, Misha.'

But this is provincial Russia we're speaking of. What was the Academy compared to neighbourliness? Timofei backed our carriage the whole way down that hundred yards to show off his skill with horses and we piled out amid a squabble of Misha's mutilated chickens who came instantly to his whistle, the halt and the one-eyed alike.

Both sides of his porch were stacked with firewood, splashed with white fusillades of chicken shit where they'd roosted. He led me into the pleasant, chintzy drawing room while his house-keeper got the samovar ready.

'Of course we'll win, Charlie, and then all the hardships our men are suffering will be blotted out for eternity by the days and nights of drinking and the rape of the German wench. Glory is for officers. For their men – firm white flesh like crab meat, preferably still kicking. Or black, or any other colour.'

We got ourselves comfortable. Then he launched into his news. He'd been staying with an old flame in Moscow. She had a school-hood friend whose brother was important in government . . . What he'd told her was absolutely *scandalous*. It concerned the artistic nature of War Office regulations:

Every cavalry regiment must have not fewer than sixteen trumpeters.

Odd-numbered hussar regiments must have only black horses; even-numbered only greys. Dragoons were to ride chestnuts, and uhlans, bays. Horses with white socks were to be segregated from those with blazes. For important parades irregular white markings were to be painted over.

'Because, said my lady, they're indicative of character flaws – i.e., not to be trusted in a charge, which is ridiculous for Russians to pronounce upon, we who have more flaws than rotten ice. In their defence this brother person had pointed out that the Shi'ite Arabs also dislike white markings, especially white on diagonal legs, which they have a name for – *shipraz*. Hussein who was the son of the Caliph Ali who was the son-in-law of the Prophet was killed riding a horse with these colours . . . I think I did well to remember all that, eh Charlie . . . hey, damn the tea, let's have some wine. This sort of talk is depressing. A few more Brusilovs, that's what we want.'

He got a bottle of Crimean wine out of a painted wooden drum and squinted at its label. 'I never believe them when they say things like "First Prize at Paris, 1887". You don't get sausages saying "First Prize". Or cheeses. It's just another example of modern lying . . . Well, here's to my godson – long life! Beautiful women! An easy death!'

He was a laughing, corpulent, cork-faced man, short of wind and not agile. Luck, in the form of an inheritance, had favoured him from birth. He'd been repaying it from the moment he discovered he had the knack of amusing people with his stories. He frothed himself up in the manner typical of a Russian landowner with unexpected guests. He was determined to get the news from the War Office off his chest.

'And the battle wardrobe of our Deoprazny Hussars, which we would rate as the elite cavalry of the universe were the blood-lines of its officers and of its horses to be combined, must make one despair. Can we hope to beat the Hun if every officer has to wear white gloves and dress uniform when charging? Can we hope to beat *anyone* if these officers wear corsets so they'll be slain with a pretty waist and a pouter-pigeon's bosom?' He looked at me slyly. 'In some officers the bosom is, ah, pronounced. In fact many have bosoms you could milk, the idle dogs. That's what you get from lying around all day. It's obvious most of them are pederasts. Lev hints at the regimental duties that young Rostov was being lined up for when he was killed. You read the text more carefully next time. *War and Sodomy,* eh, Charlie! . . . Look, here's a story that'll amuse you – but first: what do you say to a flask of my raisin vodka? You wouldn't consider it too vulgar? . . . These prize-winning wines, I must teach myself not to even go near them. The purest swill in Russia . . .

'So, it was like this. Last month I went to a meeting of our Smolensk *zemstvo* – full council, everyone very serious. We did our business and were standing around afterwards in this tiny room, almost a cupboard, where we get our reward of a glass of swill. No vodka of course. Strictly forbidden.'

Mikhail Baklushin, my godfather, winked at me with a fat pink eye. 'Six bottles between forty of us – an outrage, boy! – and naturally we all wanted to get to it first since we were hoarse from speaking nonsense. The man in front of me had his arms going like the devil in the scrimmage and I heard him mutter to the chap on his left, "Got to get there before Misha. Nothing left otherwise."

'"Our friend the Popovka Falstaff," said his companion.

'"How do you mean? He's so fat he's like a toad."

'"Precisely. Falstaff."

'"Oh, I heard flagstaff the first time."'

Misha stood himself against the door jamb and thrust out his belly, which was encased in a waistcoat of dark green brocade with four fob pockets. It rode up as he placed his hand flat on the top of his head, and showed through his bursting shirt a slope of grey woollen pantaloons and the fork and buttons of his braces. 'Let me see how much I've shrunk in the last year. What I lose in height is rearranged round my waist, that's how it seems to me.'

Moving away he eyed his mark. 'But Charlie, what a gorgeous tale! Me, old Misha, the tubbiest man in the province, being described as a flagstaff! I said to them, Thank you very much, very witty, but keep the toad at home next time. Good, eh! But pity poor Jack Falstaff, I cry whenever his name enters my mind. They shouldn't have brought him into it. If I have a dream about Jack I cry in my sleep. At the end, where the king cuts his old companion – it's too much for me. To ribbons! Mortally! As if he was carrying a week's shit in his breeches – horrible beyond words – the action of an out-and-out sadist – my pillow's sopping wet when I wake up.' He reached over and placed a soft hand on my sleeve. 'I am Sir Falstaff, that's the irony of it.'

'It was within the power of the king so he did it,' I said.

'Exactly! Let's have another little glass together to drink to the feebleness of kings and governments. May they totter and lurch and reel and sway – but not quite fall over. A small staggering government is best for its citizens.'

'Short-sighted but not blind.'

'Oh rather!' He beamed magnificently at me, a sun rising to its peak. 'I'm reading Sherlock Holmes – in English, Charlie, so be proud of me. Very slowly, with the dictionary, in bed every morning. There's some silly woman and it's her line: "Oh rather!" A bit common is it, like my raisin vodka? Let's get some *zakuski* or we'll be incapable. Don't be concerned about your men. They'll be hard at it with Vasili.'

The reason I decided to return to the Pink House instead of staying with Misha: there was a scrunching frost and the sky glittered like a funfair. It was a night to be out.

Kobi and Timofei were in as bad a way as we were. We stood around pissing into the brittle leaves under Misha's majestic sycamore trees, all of us, swaying, hands in our pockets, hoping for the best.

From the dilapidated carriage that was used as a hen-house a cockerel with a distinctive voice shrieked into the milky night, perhaps supposing dawn had arrived.

'Old Stumpy, a good friend but given to fighting . . .' Then Misha said, 'Look, we all know that the finest jokes in Russia come from Odessa. So let's go down there and hear something amusing for a change instead of all this talk about bloodshed. Enjoy some warm weather whilst we're about it. Tomorrow – what's wrong with tomorrow, Charlie?' He tucked away his cock and groaned, 'But the wine's so awful down there. I mean swill is too polite for the Crimean wines. And the journey . . . the trains are full yet they can spend days doing nothing, just standing at the platform. I heard of a man who took a week to get from Kiev to Odessa. What's gone wrong with our country? What's to be done about it all, boys?'

Kobi said, 'Before I came to Smolensk, I never drank.'

Timofei was counting the stars in a low voice. 'Forty-seven, forty-eight and a tiny speck of a thing which may be something on my eyeball but let's count it anyway – and next to it is number fifty.' He turned to Misha. 'You know, *barin*, it's a long time since I had any reason to count to fifty . . . As for your question, I don't know what's to be done by us ordinary folk. The people who're making such a nuisance of themselves, they're not our sort.' He too shook out his cock and stowed it away in a nest of grey undergarment and cotton wool. 'It's God's will, that's what it is.'

'Nonsense!' cried Misha, 'that's just being defeatist . . . So what shall we do now?'

Someone will know why we fell in with his urging that we pay a midnight call on his black Scotch cattle. He was proud of them, their sheds were just round the corner of his house, it was as bright as day, we were drunk – well, those were the reasons, I knew them all along. But it was stinking cold just the same.

We walked briskly, each of us trailing a stream of vapour. Tallow candles as fat as a man's thigh were on top of the pillars in the shed. Bathed in their dingy yellow glow the cattle looked up at us from their bed of straw, jaws rotating, an expression of total indifference on their faces. We lined our forearms along the top bar of the wooden gate and with the thick turdy smell of the cattle yard in our nostrils, silently construed the differences between man and beast.

Misha said to Timofei, his neighbour on the gate, 'You can count to a hundred here if you feel like it.'

'They look happy, not like my master's cattle,' he said.

'The Count doesn't know how to love them, that's why,' Misha replied. 'There's no point in having animals unless you love them. They know when they're loved. Then they prosper. The cows come in season regularly and smell attractive to the bulls. Bulls are like us, they need to feel wanted before they give of their best. Then they inseminate the cows deeply and accurately so that when the calves are born they're feeling around for the teat within minutes. But first you have to love them.'

'Not for me,' said Kobi.

'And you have to love them also for their effect on the land-scape. Nicholas's are so many colours that they say nothing to the eye. But mine, shining solid black against the green of summer . . . They're my harem of Nubian princesses.'

At that moment there jumped up from the pen on the far side of the shed Vasili's eldest son, whose turn it was to be the nightwatchman. He'd been sleeping in the straw alongside the cattle. He came nervously towards us, brushing himself down. Misha shouted at him not to bother. He halted, scratching. He said it was time to put the tar on the old cow's hurt. He was speaking to himself really, still full of sleep.

We turned round, reversing our positions by leaning back against the gate and putting our elbows on the top rail.

The moon was blazing down on us. The shadows were sharper than the sharpest silhouette. I could make out the loose thread hanging from a cuff button of my greatcoat. I was taught that black and white were the only colours possible by moonlight. But the blues I could see! There were half a dozen shades of it, the adjacent blues of plums, of damsons, of blackberries – an orchard of blues, without even counting the murky blue of Timofei's coaching coat. And in the middle reaches of the sky, on the edge of the moon's main force, there hung another blue – a haze, like a veil, that was the colour of paraffin. Ah! The breath of wonderment came from our mouths like smoke. The ancient wooden manor house of Zhukovo, the cattle sheds with their eccentric brickwork, the stars like hay seeds – 'Russia, oh my beloved,' I heard again my exiled mother's lament. Such beauty! Our voices were stilled by it. Misha took his hat off and held it over his heart

In front of us, in the yard, were six great elmwood troughs. Kobi was the first to notice. Pointing at them he said, 'I can see six moons.' We hoisted ourselves off the gate and walked over.

The water had frozen after the moon came up and trapped its reflection beneath the ice. Six moons, one for each trough, glittered at us. Straw and stalks of hay that had been floating on the surface were caught in the ice. The moon appeared to be chewing them. Each moon had a slightly different expression according to the way its ice had formed: bland, scarred, or wrinkled like the skin of a pudding.

'Drowned,' said Misha, 'full fathom five.'

Timofei bent right down, putting his hands on his knees. 'I'm not going to be tricked. I'm not a simple. It's the moon shining off the ice. Drowned, *barin*! You're making fun of me.' He put his hat back on, stretched and yawned. 'Drowned! You rich people know the funniest things to say.'

We'd warmed up a bit. The drink was starting to rise again, like scum. We swayed back to the house and our carriage. The old horse's whiskers were individually frosted and stood out like a sparse white bush or like the painting in Popovka church of Christ's crown of thorns. He was a wonderfully patient animal that day.

I said to Timofei it was a crime to have left him out in the cold when we were all enjoying ourselves. He said it didn't matter, the mud on his coat would have kept him as warm as he wanted to be. He climbed onto the box.

Kobi and I got inside. But Misha had something private to say to me. I stepped down, nearly missing the step. We went into the porch where the housekeeper had left a night candle.

'I didn't want to speak where there was any chance the men might hear. The apropos is – your fellow – the oriental, Antonio – well, I didn't have it directly from him – of course not – but in a round-the-sugar-bush way I learned that you were – ah – my dear godson, friend, neighbour – that you were *interested* in Elizaveta. Which is good – excellent – except that she is already affianced. Therefore, something has to be done to clear the way for you. Now, this is the point: what you have to understand is that this Potocki is as slippery as a pig's foreskin. He beats his women, he beats his soldiers, he beats his servants. Gambles. Owes his creditors a fortune. Land will soon start walking away from him if he can't keep the Jews happy. I hear these things, Charlie. I can't resist listening . . . So, take a sword to him and hack him down into the gutter. We, the citizens of Popovka, will applaud. That's what I wanted to say!'

'But if that's how it is for him, why doesn't he go after an heiress?'

Misha placed his hands on my shoulders. 'My dear child, what other heirs does your uncle Igor have? Do you take Potocki for a cretin?' He shook me gently, swaying me to and fro. 'Get her for yourself, Charlie. You're our sort, not that Polish scoundrel. The Lord Christ preserve us from all Poles . . . Oh, it would make me so happy. Liza's such a – a – lollipop. "Bending down to the lad's height, Holmes said: 'I'll give you sixpence if you go into that shop and tell the man in the skullcap you've come for the purple lollipop.'" Adorable! I adore the sound of your English words. Of course Holmes never said anything so silly. I made it up. I just wanted an excuse to say "lollipop" and have someone hear me who could understand.'

He gave a terrific snort. 'For God's sake get her, Charlie. Russia will never have seen a party like the one we'll have . . . I must go and lie down. Happiness, it upsets me so very much.' He flung his arms around my neck and we embraced and kissed each other on the lips.

Thirty-three

B UT THE next event, most horrible: Goetz was dead.
We reached Petrograd two days later. I walked into the
porter's lodge at the Academy and handed the man my card.
He knew immediately who I was. And the very first thing he
said in response was this: 'Your old friend Goetz has gone to
the stars.'

His death had been natural. He'd signed up as an ambulance
driver, had got out to shovel snow and had dropped in his footprints from a heart attack. The head of the Academy, Tarasov,
had come down from his office to tell the porter. It had been
among the obituaries in the quarterly *Proceedings of the Natural
History Society,* a copy of which had reached them from London.
My name had been mentioned extensively, which was how the
porter knew about me.

He saw I was troubled. The wet snow was sliding off Uncle
Igor's mackintosh cape. He took it from me and hung it up.
Then he ushered me into his sanctum and invited me to sit
beside his tiny coal fire until I was composed.

So it had come to this, the sorry world. My mentor, the repos-
itory of so much wisdom wrung from so many unrepeatable
experiences, Hartwig Goetz, the survivor of malaria, snake bites,
earthquakes, floods, hernias, overturned rafts and a charging
elephant, had absconded with his genius to the kingdom of the
greatest naturalist of them all. Memories knocked into me, stum-
bling over each other as they jostled for focus. Dead, my heavy
humourless friend with his sun helmet and black elasticated
stockings, with his weakness for brandy, with his piercing
comprehension of beauty and thus of magic. Dead!

'Old stories coming back,' Kobi said with sympathy. He was in the doorway watching me. I'd often talked to him about Goetz. He knew everything that had happened between us, from our first meeting at the Darwin Club to the breakfast in Samarkand when he resigned. He had Hpung's murder by heart.

'He was fearless. He'd risk anything, suffer any illness if it added to human knowledge. The museums should club together to put up a statue of him. He saved them millions. Faked-up firsts, faked-up variants, fake bones, fake feathers, fake faeces – Kobi, he could even tell fake shit from real. When I was starting with him, we got two tins of the stuff from a museum in California – don't look like that, it is so. Someone was pretending there was an unknown bird in Alaska and wanted money to track it down. Whenever there was an argument, the message went out: send for Goetz! A true and honourable man.'

'Your best friend?'

'Friendship – it wasn't like that. I loved him.' I said the words spontaneously, as they arose.

'All the world lives squashed up in a tent like happy friends. One night a gale blows it away. Then war.' He gave me a funny squinting look, maybe apologising for the elegance of his philosophy.

I spread my hands before the fire. The old question returned with a vengeance: had I ever, even once, called him Hartwig? Had we ever had one intimate conversation – uncovered ourselves – been as close as *that*? Yet I loved him. Now dead, a rickle of grumpy bones in a hole in Silesia. Was there some odour about me that meant I could never bind with those I loved? Grim Jesus, what a morning.

There were intrusive voices. It was Tarasov, come to take us upstairs to his office.

The wide staircase echoed to our footfall. Corpses of curled-up woodlice, the yellow mouthpieces of Kapral cigarettes and portions of leaves strewed the marble on either side of the carpet. At least half the lustres in the chandelier weren't working. The pipes were cold and the windowpanes spiky with bursts of frost. Tarasov was wearing gloves.

I said, 'Where are all your people?'

'I have two porters left, both old men. The rest have been

taken for the war. So far as the office staff are concerned, we have reached an agreement: they need come in only on the days I permit heating, of which there are two each week. By this method the work of the Academy goes slowly forward and my people are free to labour at staying alive. Coal, firewood, food, decent clothes for their children – such things are not found these days without a search. Often without prior information. I myself – but we must all make sacrifices. I shan't bore you.'

He was a short, patient man: an administrator, he made no bones about it. He knew nothing whatsoever about natural history. The only aspect of my work that he understood was my energy. It was a point he admired in all his collectors. To march across a desert, to go unclean for months, to work twenty hours a day during the high season, to do all the things Goetz and I had taken for granted – even to consider them from his armchair gave him a migraine, he said with a wrinkle of a smile.

As for the money, even when it was paid to them by Government it was too little. And when it wasn't paid . . . he proffered his hands, turned them palm up and delicately parted his fingers to allow some imaginary essence to go to waste. 'I can only apologise, Doig. For as long as I could I paid the staff here with my own money, the private money of my wife and myself. But there came a time – one must draw the line somewhere. Collectors were far away and my family needs pressed . . .'

I could have pushed him for my money on the spot, but I liked his cut and I wanted employment.

'Of course,' he continued, 'what interests you most are the specimens you sent back. Alas! I must tell you that they are still in our storeroom, still unpacked. The tragedy of my position is that I'd be wasting my time going through them. I wouldn't know where to begin. People do that for me – when I heat the building.' Again we had his modest smile. 'So we are behind with our programmes.'

Music was his first love. He'd only trained for museum work to get the salary. Seeing my chance I moved the conversation to birdsong, giving him examples. He quickly offered us the job of unpacking and cataloguing our cases.

May I make myself a compliment here? It is that while we were at the Academy we improved its economy by a factor many times greater than our pay. Where a problem is concrete there is little that two men of determination and versatility cannot effect. All desire for purification of the slashed humours of my heart was fulfilled by these weeks of cold, hard work, which commenced with killing 104 rats in the basement.

I found one sauntering down the stairs as I came out of the storeroom, so fat that he was hopping down them like an old man, step by step. They have thin skulls, rats. One tap was enough. Then I called Kobi and we made Tarasov and the *kazachok* or odd-job man and the porters help us, for the rats were eating everything in the basement. I thought of my poor father and laid about me with a vengeance. We tied our trousers above our boots. Rats'll run up your leg, even your bare leg, when they're hard-pressed.

It was a good start. Tarasov came out of his shell. Thinking about my white swift, I asked him if the Academy was still buying. It was what the three- and ten-rouble notes in his desk were for, he said.

'Small notes, that's all I need. I can pick and choose from the collections I'm offered. You'd be surprised – they're decent, well-connected families that are selling.'

'What if they've got a rarity and insist on gold roubles?'

'Then it's, Good morning, sir. No one else will buy these goods. You can be sure they've already been round the dealers. They always accept my offer in the end. You see, Doig, they're leaving the city for good. Getting out, they say to me. *Getting out in time.*'

He cocked his head on one side to gauge my reaction to his emphasis, *in time*. He wanted my opinion without actually having to ask me outright for it, which might have appeared treasonable coming from a man in his position. He wanted to hear me say 'What, you mean in time to save their lives?' and then to answer my own question.

I felt a burst of sympathy for this would-be musician who'd paid the staff from his own savings. I was honest. 'You're asking the impossible. How can I know what would be right for your family, for your wife and children, for instance?'

'Isn't that the truth! There's more to it than Yevgeny Tarasov! There's a daughter as well as a wife. We're the happiest household in my street. Everyone is envious of us. I leave at the same hour in the morning and return at the same hour in the evening. If I don't they worry their heads off. I open the door – they're waiting! They rush to embrace me! A meal's on the table, my slippers by my chair! And now . . . Doig, you must tell us what to do, you've been in tight spots. People are terrifying them with stories about strikes and gangsters and these anarchists who say openly that they'll take everything from the likes of us. And the stories about the monk . . . We're both men, I don't need to say any more . . . they also say she's a spy, that she's being paid by the Germans – all sort of stupidities that have to be false when you analyse them carefully. But the effect is pernicious. No smoke without fire, my womenfolk say meaningfully.

'Is something *big* happening, that's what I must know. We could sit it out at our dacha, grow our own vegetables and pretend it's Yasnaya Polyana. But I don't want to lose my life. I'm not a brave man. I'm not ready. So what we should be doing? Tell me, Doig. I beg of you, be candid.'

'But I don't know any better than you what'll have happened in a year's time. Perhaps I too should be getting out. But for the moment I want to make some money. Are you any different?'

Then I turned the subject back to Goetz. There was still a lump in my throat. I had to speak about him until I'd exhausted my sense of loss. 'His sort of honesty and scientific scrupulousness may turn out to have disappeared entirely when the dust settles,' I said.

'Dust! Ha!' exclaimed Tarasov with his little smile. 'I fear you'll be proved right. At bottom all war is a form of theft. The lawlessness moves out of the trenches and becomes generalised. Everyone turns their hand to crookery of one sort or another. The Goetzes become rarer and rarer. How will it end for the Academy? I don't know. Science cannot exist without honesty. Ah, Goetz, are you blushing up there? I hope I'm talked about like this when I'm dead. What was his forename?'

'Hartwig.'

'Hartwig – not a name one meets in Russia at all.'

A porter brought us a tray of tea glasses. He and his mate

had sold the rats, instantly, for five roubles – as they came, in the hessian sack with its trail of dripping blood.

'More like twenty-five,' Tarasov said when he'd gone. 'His sort are always afraid of being caught by some unknown impost. They were plump, too. A family of four would last a week on them. There are other basements in these old buildings, Doig. We should draw up a schedule for our hunting dates.'

Then he wanted me to tell him more about Goetz. I gave him the whole story, starting with Agg and the British Museum. His eyes were fixed on my face throughout. At the end I said, 'But, Yevgeny Alexandrovich, this is what is extraordinary: we actually spoke very little – as you and I are speaking now. We were always Goetz and Doig to each other. Therefore the depth of my feelings for him are a surprise to me.'

'Something else is going on inside you,' Tarasov said. 'There are certain pieces of music that can be guaranteed to make an audience tearful, even army veterans. Tchaikovsky was adept at producing this sort of effect. With you it's the reverse. Your emotions were alive this morning. Fluttering around looking for somewhere to alight – and what should come along but the death of Hartwig Goetz.'

Thirty-four

W E KILLED more rats, Kobi and Tarasov himself being the leaders of the team. Our little administrator was vicious at it, the terrier we didn't have. Word spread. We could have set up as a butcher. One morning there were six housewives waiting when I arrived for work: large, scarved women with waterproof bags so that no telltale trail of blood should follow them home.

Of course Tarasov said nothing of this activity to his ladies. When he locked the double doors at night his hands were clean and often contained a small gift, which he would have wrapped himself.

Our trade in rats was Petrograd writ small in those last months of 1916. The tension was so thick you couldn't have sliced it with an axe. The wildest stories raced from street to street. Single shots were common at night. Policemen were seen less frequently. Burghers hurried fearfully to their homes and their most telling conversations concerned which regiments could be accounted 'safe'.

At the same time the chic and frivolous became more so and packed the nightclubs until dawn.

Somewhere the Tsar was reigning. At a long table in a portrait-lined chamber he was sitting alone, in a brown leather chair, signing above his title single-sheet orders that still retained the curl of the typewriter barrel. In a nearby anteroom a dozen of his ministers were quarrelling furiously. In a third sat the Empress of All the Russias writing birthday greetings to her husband's foe, her own first cousin. In a fourth were courtiers plotting the death of Rasputin, the Empress's favourite.

This, or something similar, was what we all imagined about the unknowable process of government. We knew how difficult the situation had become. We longed for a firm, sensible hand. So we fabricated a story that contained all the necessary elements. The question of the greatest interest was whether Nicholas was signing the orders fast enough or whether speed had become irrelevant.

Count Igor, with whom we were staying, had just turned eighty. He had a butler, Joseph, who was in his fifties; a steward – a swarthy bullying fellow; a coachman, four gardeners and a motley of house servants. He may have been infirm but he was neither gaga nor had he surrendered the wish to enjoy his life. Though he seldom went out of his palace, he'd become restless if one of his servants didn't give him an up-to-date report on the stroke of every ormolu hour.

'What news? What news now? What are they saying today, is it to be guns or butter, quickly now, boy.'

There was a day on which a pranking footman took it into his head to tell Igor a tale of the tanks he'd seen rolling down Nevsky Prospekt with factory workers marching behind them wielding scythes and flails. I returned from the Academy to find Igor balanced on the edge of a curule chair in his hall, robed and wigged, his cheeks plastered with an especially bright strain of rouge. Between his knees was his walking stick – hands clasped on top of it – chin resting on his hands. With two powdered footmen in the shadows behind him – an extraordinary sight.

He handed me the speech he intended to deliver to the mob. 'There *has* to be a change. It's been too good for us. All my life I've been saying, I cannot continue forever to be so lucky. But how will it happen? The difficulty for an old man is to distinguish the trivial from the important. I don't want to be thought windy. I don't want my neighbours to be still laughing at me in a year's time. On the other hand it may be that today I shall perish. If this is so I desire to die with dignity. Here, tell me if you think I've judged my speech right.'

I wasn't going to poke fun at my uncle or tell him what the mob would do if it had a mind to. I had Joseph mix him his martini, got out the cards and we settled down to an evening of piquet, at which he excelled.

How does one know for certain that history is lurching off in a different direction, that it's making a right angle as opposed to a slow bend? Are there infallible signals it always emits? In what quarter does one look for them? In short, how can a citizen actually *know*? This is what I was debating that night as I lay in bed in my uncle's palace.

And late the next morning, which was December 17th, I discovered the answer.

It was a heating day at the Academy. At about noon there was a commotion – doors slamming, quickened footsteps, shouting. Down the main staircase, two at a time, sprang Tarasov, across the hallway and down the iron stairs to our office below.

'The monk, the monk! Have you heard, Doig – at last! The Lord has listened to us – we're saved!' His voice rang down the passage. He burst in, our little administrator, and flung his arms upwards. The waistband of his trousers rose. I could see his white hairless shanks and his maroon sock suspenders. 'May he rot! May he pay for his crimes for all eternity!'

Thus did I learn of the previous night when Prince Yusopov had dined Rasputin on poisoned Madeira and cyanide-filled gateaux; shot at him when he showed no sign of succumbing, missing him twice as he crawled away from the wrecked meal with the tablecloth draped round his shoulders; shot at him again, this time winging him in the buttocks, and having thus disabled him had had him trussed with the iron ringlets of an anchor chain and stuffed through the ice into the famished Neva.

Tarasov read out the news three times to reassure himself. He scampered around like a clown, leaping to and fro over the suit of wagtail skins that we'd laid out on the floor.

We had a stenographer with us that morning so that I could dictate entries for the Academy's catalogue – a woman of formidable size and mien. But Tarasov was not to be denied. He had her put away her pencil and notepad and grasping her by both hands hugged and danced her round the storeroom floor, throwing off toots and ripples of the national anthem as he went.

He dumped her heavily on her chair. 'The shipwreck's over.

We're saved, the monk's had it' – he yanked open the door and ran back up the stairs.

Igor in his palace was the same. 'It's the only change that was needed. It'll be back to business as usual after Epiphany. We Russians have seen these things before, a hundred times. Think of Pugachev and the panic everyone was in.'

Straightway he began to make plans for moving his household down to the Crimea. It was where he preferred to spend the winter. It was only because of the present crisis that he was in Petrograd at all. And now the monk was dead . . . He wouldn't come to Smolensk for Epiphany but he'd come for Liza's wedding – his god-daughter. He'd always enjoyed the drive through the woods when the snowdrops were in petal. What was the date? Had it been fixed for certain? We must be certain to tell him when we got back after the Christmas festivals.

Thirty-five

S HE'D RETURNED. I smelled her Soir de Paris the instant I
stepped into the Pink House. It lingered on the stairs and
in the doorways, maddening me. The quarrel with Nicholas was
still festering. She'd returned only to get married, as she'd said.
She took her meals in her rooms, outside which Sonja sat like
a babushka, knitting and guarding. Even when Liza went for a
walk, Sonja was at her side, blotchy and scowling. I grew to
detest the sight of her.

I made it my business to bump into Liza. 'My future is with
another man. So adieu.' I saw it in her every expression.

Nicholas had invited Helene to come from Moscow for the
holiday, bringing their two sons. He was having difficulty
borrowing the money she was after and wanted to talk some
common sense into her. But when she arrived it was without
Leo and young Nicholas because of the risk of the train being
blown up. For her own poor body, she didn't give a straw.
She'd borne the children, done her duty, was scrap. Her boys
were the future . . . But this selflessness was shown to be
utterly bogus by the fact that she'd brought her own soap and
could speak of nothing except her health. I'd forgotten how
miserable she was. She went around with glittering eyes,
hunched, searching for dirt in every corner and under every
valence. When she did offer an opinion, it was always on how
badly the war was going. She had praise for none of our
generals, not even Brusilov. Armageddon was only a question
of when. After three days she announced she was leaving.
Nicholas had not dared even to broach the money question
with her.

It was in the morning that Timofei took Helene to the station. In the afternoon, when Nicholas and I were slumped with relief in the drawing room, we suddenly heard a terrific hullabaloo circling the gravel.

Louis went out to do the honours. He didn't close the front door properly behind him. The wind came whistling through the house, on it the noise of a cockerel baying with all its might, as if seeing the moon for the first time in its life. It clattered its wings. It was the bird called Stumpy – and Misha – and . . .

'. . . his mother, Madame Lydia,' said Louis in the doorway. 'They have come to stay.'

Misha entered first, dressed in a shaggy brown raccoon over-coat. Underneath he was wearing cream flannel trousers and tan and white brogues. 'It's so mild that I couldn't decide if it was summer or winter. So I came prepared for both . . . Doesn't Mamasha make herself look beautiful? She got bored of me, you know. She says my piano is out of tune. So she can't prac-tise and . . . well, thus we are here.' He sighed good-naturedly, his stomach heaving. 'It's true. Thus are we here, out of her boredom.'

Misha's mother was the same shape and about half the size of Misha; a sloping amphora with a well-powdered face and a little black tit of a hat tied beneath her chin. I had to bend at the knees to kiss her cheek.

'Who wouldn't get bored with my son?' Then Lydia Baklushin embraced us both with full, confident kisses and plumped herself down, looking to be entertained.

Nicholas called to Louis to bring us a tray of afternoon tea, English style.

'Where's the bride, then?' asked Lydia.

None of us knew. I thought she'd be in her room.

Misha threw himself into a deep chair and crossed his cream-coloured legs. 'Thank God that repulsive monk was dealt with. Someone should have done it a year ago. I say that to everyone I meet, whether I know him or not, to show how strongly I feel. He could have brought the house down round our ears. Now we can have some sensible policies.'

'No politics, Puffsy! You agreed.'

'But that was hours ago. What are men to talk about? Be

reasonable, Mama, or I'll take you back to Zhukovo and leave you there alone.'

I supposed he was thinking about the travelling arrangements in the pause that followed. His rolling eye went up and down his mother. But what he said, very mildly, was, 'Of course we must talk about politics. These wretches in Petrograd are the difference to us between life and death. If they fail us in the great affair of the war—'

'If they fail us, yes . . . ?' It was Nicholas, wanting to be worried.

'Terrorism also is a part of politics, whether one likes it or not. Men are influenced by bombs. The question is simply this: who has the power? If the war goes poorly – well, use your loaf, Nikolai Borisovich.'

'That may be the case for men but it has nothing to do with me,' said Lydia. 'I'm born, I get married, I produce for my husband a bone-idle son, my husband dies and then I die. Mine will be a typical story of our times. Politicians – I blow my nose on them. What can they possibly have to do with a woman's life? You must talk about your chickens instead, Puffsy.'

Misha sighed. He nodded us towards the billiard room, to which there was an entrance from the corner of the drawing room.

But as we were getting up we heard the tap-tap of Bobinski's stick on the hall tiles. Yesterday he'd stumbled on the stairs and taken a hurt. He limped in, having been attracted by the sound of guests.

'Were those your *chickens* I saw looking out of the carriage?' he asked without any preliminaries of greeting, planting himself in front of Misha and thus with his back to Lydia, who was tucked away at the back of her armchair.

She gave a slight cough. Bobinski whirled round. Full of confusion, he clicked his heels and bowed to the waist, which only had the effect of making us all look at his shoes, which needed a good polish.

'*Mille pardons, Madame.*' He stuck his bad leg out to one side and struggled down into a kneeling position. '*Mille pardons . . . mille pardons, Madame la Comtesse,*' offering his old dry lips to her hand. Clambering up, he backed out of the room –

glancing over his shoulder for the furniture and bowing at every other step, his cheeks pink with embarrassment and his hand pressed to his heart.

In the doorway he encountered Louis wheeling in the tea trolley.

'This is like a good farce,' laughed Misha. 'Don't go on behaving like that, Bobby, for God's sake. She's not the Tsarina, not even a countess, though she'd like to be. She won't have you walk to Siberia. Will you, Mamasha, you'd never do that to Bobby. If it were me, on the other hand . . . Come on, Bobby, come on, stop looking as though you'd never seen a woman before.'

Bobinksi apologised to everyone in turn and was made much of.

Louis made room for the tea things on the circular morocco-topped magazine table.

'What, Louis, tea maid now?' Bobinski said, getting his nerve back.

'The other staff are engaged in the kitchens. Sonja is with Miss Elizaveta. They are discussing the wedding. I thought it better that I myself brought in the tea.' Louis addressed himself to Nicholas to save face. Bending down he rotated the plate of madeleines until Lydia Baklushin could reach the one with scarlet and green icing that she'd pointed at.

Nicholas said to me, 'It's so strange, when I don't see Sonja, I don't even think about her. She's the most forgettable person I know.'

The next morning we understood what the closeting of Liza and Sonja had been about. A black motor car arrived flying from its bonnet the insignia of the general staff. Its wheels spun on the loose stones as it ascended the slope by Gog and Magog. The horses were just then being walked out by Pashka and Styopka, the stable boys. Both animals and humans lifted their heads and looked on in silent amazement.

The car drew up sleekly and wealthily, its fat black tyres making the gravel murmur. The driver opened his passenger's door and stood to attention. I watched as Potocki dismounted, looked around, and stretched.

It was obvious. He was there to claim my Liza for the

Christmas festival. To make her drunk, to devour her, defile her, debauch her at every point of ingress.

He was in the full uniform of his regiment, the Garde à Cheval: white tunic, white trousers with a wide red stripe down the seam, gleaming calf-length boots. His shoulders were looped with gold and his chest striped with a warrior's ribbons. He was shorter than I remembered, about the same height as Liza, with a baby belly from sitting in an office. An anxious face, clean-shaven. His hair was still electrified but now there was less of it. It was like a horseshoe round his bald crown.

I don't know where Nicholas was. Skulking somewhere in case Liza threw a fit on the doorstep and bust his bowl of expectations. I myself went out to greet Andrej.

His eyes were grey, soft yet thorough. We embraced; we sized each other up. I searched his face for the decadence of a gambler. But he was not as Misha had said. He was every bit as decent-looking as one would imagine of a hero and a patriot. I could think of nothing to hold against him, except that he was going to bed my woman for which I hated him so much that I was quivering.

He said, 'I've heard about your work from Elizaveta. We've both come a long way. One can never tell what's waiting to hatch within one's schoolmates, isn't that so, Charlie? When all this is over you'll come and spend a season with us. Our families – it'll be a good union, me and Liza. I hope I can prove myself worthy of the honour.'

Louis came out of the house with a case in each hand and one tucked beneath his arm. As the driver was stowing them away, Liza walked out in her travelling furs. Behind her was Sonja, pale and with spots round her mouth.

Sonja asked the driver in a bossy way if he'd got all the suitcases in the car. He opened the luggage compartment and showed her. Liza, her arm through Andrej's, waited until Sonja reported to her. The three of them quickly said goodbye to me, and then to Lydia, who'd just appeared.

Louis ran out of the house with a furled umbrella, which he handed to Sonja. Liza asked Andrej if she should send Louis to look for her brother. Andrej said they shouldn't waste time. He and Liza got into the back of the car, Sonja into the front. The driver went round checking the doors were properly closed. The car glided down the hill, past Gog and Magog. The last I saw was through the rear window: Andrej unpeeling the fur stole from her neck, which he kissed. Snooping should be abolished, it's so hurtful.

Thirty-six

A FTER THE festival I went back to Petrograd with Kobi. His widow was only too glad to have him as a wage-earner.

For my part I was waiting for a miracle. 'Where the hell have you been?' That's what I was going to yell at it.

Returning from the Academy one afternoon in February I was met by my uncle Igor. He'd been waiting to see me turn in at the gates. I walked across the courtyard and past the statue of Diocletian, conscious that he was standing on the steps above me. He led me into the house by the elbow, saying nothing. He pointed to the console table on which the incoming and outgoing post was placed.

I saw the buff woolly paper of a telegram – a lengthy one.

It was from Nicholas. Elizaveta was to be married to Count Andrej Potocki in Smolensk Cathedral in five days' time. The bridegroom was going to be staying at the Pink House beforehand. Celebrations would be low-key. The exigencies of war were to blame.

Kobi scrutinised me as I read it out.

'Already his sugar-beet money is at work,' Igor said, referring to the fact that so long a telegram had been accepted for transmission. 'But does it mean no wine, no music, no dancing? Obviously it does.'

For Igor as for Bobinski. The years were rattling on. Every party was their last one, every half chance for amusement had to be snatched. Igor had been peeved to begin with. Now that he had me in front of him he became shrilly voluble. Liza was his god-daughter: she'd had the Rykov pearls off him: she was his heir. She *owed* him a party. He wanted to polka, he wanted to see all the old measures being stepped before it was too late. 'About the war, that's just an excuse and a pretty thin one too. She's ungrateful, that's what it is. She hasn't any time for her elders now that she's hitched up with Potocki.'

He fell to sulking. He shuffled round the palace in his slippers, barking at Joseph and saying repeatedly that he'd have nothing whatsoever to do with it.

'You're young too, you go off and have your fun. I'll hold out here as best I can.'

I was not huffy. The crisis was at hand. I wanted to be there. I *had* to be there, to suffer such mortification as was to be my lot. Before my eyes was a tablet and on it was chalked 'The price of ambition is suffering'. Then I'd get out and start again in another country.

The next day we said our farewells to Tarasov and drew the last of our pay. I tried him with my white swift. He smiled as if knowing all along that I had something up my sleeve. 'How pretty it is,' he said, trailing his finger down its spine. 'You wouldn't credit how many ornithological prodigies I've been offered this month. The last was a white rook. Every Russian knows a rook's as black as sin, yet here was a white one on my desk. What did I do? To the lady I said, No thank you, madam, not even if you gave it to me. I would regard it as an insult to nature to accept the idea that I could ever see a white rook perched in a tree. So I shall thank you and say that I know swifts are black. Let us part as friends, Charlie.'

'Yevgeny Alexandrovich Tarasov,' I said, 'I accept your decision: one, because you are an honest man and deserve well; two, because it is in keeping with this bad phase in my life. But I must tell you that a white rook is possible and my white swift is genuine. Admit it, you know nothing about ornithology or albinism . . .'

Etcetera until darkness came and it was time to get ourselves to Nicholas Station and onto a train for Smolensk.

But when we got to Znamenskaya we found nothing had moved since midday. The usual array of stories was on the go. A wagon carrying munitions for the front had slipped a coupling and overturned. No, it had been carrying cattle – or horses. They were careering, terrified, all over the tracks. Troops had been called in to shoot them, in the dark . . . No, it was just normal incompetence: the station's coal bunkers were empty.

Silently Kobi and I sat at the station bar, drinking, watching and listening.

We were not alone in our predicament. Entire families were trying to travel. Not just parents and their children but aunts, uncles, servants – all the outliers. Perhaps, I thought to myself, when these conglomerates succeed in leaving the city there'll be no one left in Petrograd with their surnames. Whole units of tribal existence dispersed around the globe . . .

I asked one man how long he'd been there. He sighed: 'Since two, when we had hot soup in the restaurant. But with the Lord's help we shall leave soon. To Odessa. And then? The United States of—. I can't bring myself to say it. It's too presumptuous. God knows how we'll get there.'

For the young children the excitement of the occasion had vanished. They'd long since given up going to look at the board. Morosely they sat sucking their thumbs. They said nothing. Their dulled eyes regarded those who passed with curiosity but no fear. They were plump bourgeois children, ignorant about a land of wolves except in fairy tales.

Not so the unmarried aunts and uncles who were living on the fringe of the family. They had no illusions. It was flight, nothing less. They never strayed far from the parents and covertly watched them like hawks in case the train should suddenly arrive and they were forgotten in the stampede: in case there wasn't room for everyone and the question arose of sacrifice.

These were not poor people. What I was seeing were the middle sections of the mercantilist class, educated people who had some communal instinct for when the incompetence of government had become, like a disease, untreatable. As the owners of capital they'd learnt to be on the lookout for jealousy, to keep constantly under review the most vital commandment of all: *get out in time*. Some would say it shows confidence to move one's family from one land to another. But that was not what I saw or felt at Nicholas Station that night.

The overhead station clock moved inexorably forward. Disillusioned, the groups made their arrangements for the night: shoved the aunts and uncles and servants to the perimeter and assigned the bench, their thickest rugs and mama's patient lap to the first-born son. But even as they dozed they were straining their ears. What was going on in the marshalling yard? Would they ever get to hear the longed-for chuff and toot from Train No. 7? Fantasies perverted the rationalism of their well-ordered minds – and kept the cold at bay: the winter sun in Odessa, the famous jokes of its citizens, the theatres, boulevards, seaside promenades, hairdressers, cafes and especially the shining brass plate at 1, Kazarmenny Pereulok where resided Mr J. H. Grout, the Consul of the United States of America, a country so fabled that even to admit aloud that it was one's destination was considered unlucky.

There were quite a few of us at the bar: army officers, commercial travellers, humbug men working the carriages with their five-kopeck tricks. We drank bad-temperedly, swapped lies, and coarsely chaffed the tarts plying their trade from the shadows. None of us expected trains to arrive at that time of night, be turned round and sent out again. We were men of the world. We were used to dealing with practicalities. A railway timetable was a theory, nothing more. What really concerned us was this: had the bolsheviks so completely infiltrated the railways that they could grab a munitions wagon whenever they wished?

Kobi was on my left. A Lieutenant Borisholov was on my right. The question arose yet again. (The station was eerie without the roar of locomotives. Our human voices filled only a portion of it.) A middleman in toiletries said, 'I don't believe it. If they could control the railways so effectively they'd close them down with strikes. I would. Then our armies couldn't be supplied. Finish! Which of us could say what the result might be – the Tsar might be forced out . . .'

'Keep to the railways, my friend,' growled Borisholov, 'or we might start thinking you're a radical too.'

Turning to me he said, 'So many civilians have no idea of reality. All they want to do is lock the door and pull the blankets over their heads. The truth is that the bolsheviks are playing with us. I've seen what they did to an officer who became unpopular for making his men carry out his orders. They stripped him and tied him to the branch of a tree by one ankle – better sport like that. Got hold of his free leg and stretched him open. Then they cut his testicles off. I was the one who found him.'

Leaning over me, Kobi asked, 'How did you get enough revenge?'

Borisholov eyed him. 'Is he with you?'

'Yes.'

'We shot the first twenty of his regiment that we got hold of. No trial. In public. Singly. I expect it did no good but we felt better for it. The soldiers who castrated the man had probably slipped away into the forest. It's what they do. The colonel reports them as missing in action or not returned from leave, anything that can't be blamed on him. The word "leave" is in itself a joke. The men laugh in your face when you mention it. What happens when they go home? They find another man screwing their wife and they can't even get drunk properly. Drink is the only other pleasure they know. Drink as in anni-hilation.'

'Yet you're going back to the front,' I said.

Borisholov thumped his glass down on the zinc for more. 'It's safer. I can sense through my skin what's happening around me. Here you can never tell. Your enemy may be the man from whose kiosk you've bought a newspaper all your life. There could be a sniper hiding behind this chimney stack – or that one. If you're a soldier you can't help thinking how simple that'd be . . . This wine was pissed by a fox. I've got something better in my pocket. Tell your fellow to watch our stuff and you and I'll go for a walk.'

The night passed, not cosily at all. Towards dawn a number of things happened.

Thirty-seven

T HE FIRST concerned the station clock, which had stopped
during the night. At six o' clock the morning shift of porters
started. People began to be about – I mean a clear distinction
could now be made between those hurrying off to do a day's
work and the class of night folk who haunt every station in
Europe, who position themselves close to the toilets and cannot
even think about sleep until dawn.

Three men from the new shift, each of them carrying a fifteen-
foot section of wooden ladder balanced against his shoulder
blade, walked with careful steps down the central platform. They
hooked the sections together and extended it to rest against the
girder to one side of the clock. One leaned back against it, his
arms folded. They were waiting for a fourth party.

A number of passengers gathered about them to observe
proceedings. Never had anyone known a clock in Russia receive
such prompt attention. I heard a woman say it was a sure sign
of confidence that the trains would soon be running normally.

The clock had two faces. Some men in the group began to
discuss the mechanics of the piece. Did the whole thing split in
two or did each face open independently?

Borisholov said wearily, 'One man will hold the ladder while
his mate climbs it to examine the parts that are usually faulty.
He'll call down to the foreman who'll walk slowly back to the
supervisor's office. The latter will send for an engineer and
someone who understands the electrical components. A total
of twelve people will have been involved by the time the clock
is again working . . . Hey, look over there, look what's come to
exalt our lowly company.'

I turned to where he was pointing. To my astonishment there was the tall figure of my uncle Igor floating onto the concourse followed by his steward and two footmen, each escorting a porter with a heaped barrow of luggage. He was wearing a silk top hat; a dark, close-fitting, ankle-length overcoat; full make-up, tight black leather gloves and galoshes. Round his neck was a silver fox, in his hand a cane.

'By the four brothers of Christ,' breathed Borisholov, his jaw hanging, 'and his good-for-nothing sisters . . .'

Igor halted and looked about, tapping his cane petulantly. His steward was holding the tickets, the ends of the pink paste-board showing between his gloved fingers like the tongue of a sleeping hound. Nonplussed by the silence, the party stood there.

Borisholov nudged me. 'Are they begging for disaster? There's rioting in the street and they expect to get away with looking like Louis the something?' He straightened himself and shouted out, 'Hey old man, made your will?'

I said to him, 'That's my uncle.' I walked over to Igor, who hadn't heard Borisholov. He showed no surprise that I was still there. He'd had a change of mind. Not about Liza – he was still convinced of her ingratitude – but about the need to see all his relations before it was too late. He'd cabled Nicholas to keep his favourite room for him.

The rouge was brilliant on his cheeks. Beneath the yellow-green light of the gas lamps it was the colour of a special geranium. The bristle round the curve of his jaw was layering into a soft white pelt, the whiskery stuff of an old man. From beneath his dyed eyebrows he glared around at the waiting passengers and the man up the ladder at the clock.

He said to his steward, 'Go and find someone in charge and discover what's happening. Act humbly. Remove your gloves and don't elevate your jaw. But mind you speak with authority or these traitors will think you're of no account. Use my name.'

His steward rammed his gloves untidily into his pockets. He undid the buttons of his topcoat and shambled off like a prize-fighter.

Igor turned on me: '*Humbly*, run after him and repeat the word. Before he gets us into trouble.'

The steward hadn't been gone more than five minutes when

a rumour took shape that an express for Moscow would depart from platform four – the central one, with the clock on it. I witnessed its birth: a young woman rushing away from the porters' cabin gripping her hat, blonde pigtails flying, her fat thighs struggling to go as fast as her brain was urging them. I could judge its progress by the wave of noise and activity that rolled though the station as sleepers awoke and leapt from their benches, their hair like tussocks of wind-blown grass, and straightway, as if they were just continuing a dream they'd all been sharing, started shouting at each other, 'The clock! Make for the clock!'

The babushkas got their charges onto their sleepy feet and hurriedly began to pack up the encampment. Sewing was stuffed into deep bags of ribbed maroon velvet. Fistfuls of knitting needles spiked their balls of coloured wool and disappeared in seconds. Husbands whacked down their hats and crouched at the ready over the suitcases, hands curled round the leather grips.

'Where to?'

'To the clock, idiot, as fast as you can.'

This was a scene repeated twenty times on each platform. Igor said calmly to me, 'Look how it's always the women giving orders in a crisis. I'd have more confidence in this country of ours if it was ruled by a woman.'

Within minutes everyone who'd gone to Nicholas Station to travel to Moscow had gathered on platform four where, astonishingly, the clock had been restarted and was showing quarter to seven. Even some who weren't travelling anywhere near Moscow were among them. There was a feeling of desperation, that *any* train would do so long as it took its passengers out of Petrograd.

The steward bustled towards us, his black-stubbled face showing how pleased he was with himself. He'd discovered what we already knew, and had a policeman in tow to escort Count Igor to his first-class compartment.

To get to the right place for first class we had to process – parade – down the length of the platform.

We were as follows: Kobi and myself, Borisholov and a couple of other officers, the steward, the footmen in breeches who were

157

guarding the porters with the luggage barrows, and in the midst of the group my great-uncle Igor, skimming along with his strange walk, his top hat towering above everybody like a periscope.

There were no curtains over these people's minds. The policeman put an additional edge on their curiosity. Their crimped unslept eyes passed over most of us without comment: we were small fry. But when they alighted upon the Count and his powdered footmen and the policeman, they grew malicious. I could see the change: the film of weariness being yanked off like sticking plaster as the narrowing eyes dissected the top hat, the silver fox, the flesh-pink breeches of the footmen, and the quantity of fine leather baggage, every piece stamped with a black 'R' and the Rykov wolf in gold.

Who is he? Why should he be guarded and we not? Is he a politician, one of those arrogant, incompetent, squabbling cowards? Did he vote for the war? Is he responsible for the death of my son – or my brother, or uncle? Thus the connections were made. There were no murmurings, just these harsh and hating looks. Calculations concerning wealth. Jealousy. Alarm lest Igor's presence on the train might attract a bomber. And thus to fear.

A small printed notice on a gaslight informed us we were at the right section for first-class passengers. The train arrived. Igor's baggage was dealt with. He tipped the policeman and his footmen, dismissing them with a flap of his dangling glove as if dispersing gnats. Then he went into his compartment to lie down. The steward and I exchanged looks of relief as we heard him fumbling with the lock. We went to join the others in an open carriage, one down from Uncle Igor.

Borisholov produced a pack of cards, which he gave to the steward to shuffle. He unfastened his holster belt, took out his revolver and laid it on the table. His fellow officers did the same. The three of them were sitting with their backs to the first-class carriage and thus had a clear view of anyone approaching.

His revolver was a Luger Kriegsmarine, nine inches long from tip to toe. I picked it up, chuckled it in my hand, aimed it through the window at a porter. The barrel was graceful and deadly. One knew immediately that a bullet that went down it went straight.

'Magazine takes eight,' said Borisholov. 'Parabellums. Ejects the empty and reloads itself. Pretty . . . I had it off a German officer whom I took prisoner – in the days when we took Germans prisoner.'

'Ammunition?'

'Universal.' He exchanged seats with one of the other officers, so as to be on the outside, next to the aisle. 'There are some thugs on this train that I wouldn't want in my regiment,' was what he said, and he checked that his Luger was loaded.

We started to play cards.

Kobi went to sleep. He had no instinct for card games. And I thought he was still asleep when I completed the trade with Borisholov of my white swift for his Luger Kriegsmarine plus all the ammunition. With one hand I slid through the wreckage of the cards the light wooden box that Kobi had made for the bird. Borisholov took the swift out, showed it to his brother officers and kissed the top of its head.

'For my father's cabinet. His knees will go soggy when he sees it. We are both of us optimists – here, where it matters.' He slipped his hand inside his blouse and patted his heart. His face grew light and his soft brown moustaches began to twitch. They seemed to radiate a special bloom, like a woman's newly washed hair, as he contemplated the pleasure his father would receive.

'First viewed coming head-high down the marketplace in Samarkand? Oh, I have the scene so clearly.' He curved and darted his hand in imitation. 'I'll give it him tonight. We'll get drunk. This bird is too noble for someone like you to own. Think, it can fly three times as fast as this train goes . . . My father will have a beautiful object to admire and you, who are at odds with the world, will have a weapon to defend yourself with.'

'And you, my friend, will have to find another German who wants to surrender, which may not be so easy,' said one of Borisholov's fellow officers to him.

I protested but Borisholov would have none of it. 'You're in a hopeless situation with a woman. You're on the way to her wedding to another man. What are you going to do? Gallop away from the church with her kicking in your arms? Of course you've lost hope.'

I drew Luger and ammunition towards me; three square buff boxes holding twenty rounds each. I stacked them on top of each other. Despite the waxed paper between each layer, the bullets chimed lightly. Something made me glance over at Kobi – it had been he who'd captured the swift. His diamond eyes were fixed on me; hard, unblinking, stripping me down to the gristle.

Thirty-eight

WHEN WE reached Moscow Igor went to the Club de la Noblesse for the night. Kobi and I billeted at a hotel beside Brest Station, so as to be handy. A little after dawn a train was flagged for ten o'clock. I telegraphed to Nicholas to have two coaches and the luggage wagon wait for us at Smolensk station from three o'clock onwards.

I need to be precise about this day.

When I pulled back the curtains I saw in the room opposite, across a narrow brick courtyard, a man whose stomach was ribbed with dark hair pulling up the shoulder straps of his long woollens.

I went out into the street and angling my head took the measure of the unattractive Moscow sky, which seemed to contain an extra dose of smoke particles that morning. I said to it, 'No thank you, day, go and dump your stuff on another man. Pick on someone who can take it.'

For breakfast I had two herrings, pickles and thin tea. After this I used the hotel's blue-tiled squats. They were built on a platform about nine inches off the floor. The dividing stalls reached only as high as a man's waist. My neighbour, also buttoning his trousers, said to me across the partition, 'The shit-holes here are more poisonous than anywhere I know. The whole of Moscow must run down a slope into them.'

I tried to buy a newspaper at the station. The ink was smudged. Every copy in the pile was the same. I thought: someone is concealing information from me, and that information will be – Potocki is dead. I ran out into the street shouting 'Dead! Dead!' like Tarasov when he heard the news about

Rasputin. A hundred yards away I found clean newspapers. Of course there was nothing about Potocki being dead. His filthy Polish tool would be up her after all.

Then our train arrived and on the dot of ten it departed, its punctuality striking every passenger as extraordinary and even ominous.

By now my sentiments for Igor, Nicholas, the Baklushins, Kobi, for everyone except Liza, had deteriorated to the point that I didn't mind if I never saw one of them again. As the train trundled to Smolensk at its pathetic moribund speed, things became steadily worse. I didn't sulk or get bad-tempered. I spoke civilly to everyone. But all along it felt as if my heart was being slowly hauled out and snipped to pieces in front of me. By the time I stepped down onto the platform at Smolensk I had determined to forget the rest of the day before it happened.

That day was January 29th, 1917.

The wind was small and bitter from the north-east. Towards the horizon the sky was layered in different tones, some ash white, others approaching the black of thunder. But above my head and around me, which was where it counted, it was as grey as a corpse.

The ground was hard and the ruts frozen solid.

A steam piledriver was at work in the goods yard. Its regular thumping was blocked by the armour plating of the sky and compelled to return to earth, at which point it released a faint sigh, or echo. The noise disturbed me, being difficult to define. I was so burdened by my dejection that I was ready to be unsettled by anything. Leaning over I shook my head violently, as if this echo were an insect that could be shaken out of my ear.

I knew I'd acted odiously by bartering away the white swift. Geographically it had been the last link with my father. I doubted I would ever return to Turkestan. The bird was part of that era so intimately connected to the Darwin Club, to Goetz, to Wiz, to museum work – to all that I'd accomplished in my life.

Betrayal, loss, desperation – I needed a miracle to rescue me. But it wasn't at Smolensk where Nicholas, pale and constrained, was waiting. After greeting Uncle Igor he took me aside.

My mother had died a month ago, at her home in Fulham, from influenza.

I felt nothing. Fate had already got me by the scruff of the neck, like a newborn kitten. I was so certain of being drowned anyway that another piece of bad news was without significance. The piledriver was battering away at my ears. It was not in my power to think for myself. I couldn't even swear that I'd heard him correctly. I asked him to repeat what he'd said.

He began to weep. On my behalf, because of my failure to do so through these other circumstances. I watched him do this with curiosity. 'Your dear, dear mother . . .'

This made me angry. Just because *his* mother had been a nonentity who'd been forgotten half an hour after being buried didn't mean he could claim mine. He hadn't seen her for twenty years. All he was interested in was getting Liza declared Potocki's countess. My poor destitute mother was just a blob in his mind.

I said to him, 'Keep your dishonest tears for yourself.' I slipped his fumbling embrace and went blindly through the station rooms towards the cab rank – speaking to Nicholas like that had set me off, had opened the floodgate of my self-pity. I walked quickly so that he couldn't catch me up. There was another man between the double doors – a shadow in my blurring vision. Mechanically I stepped to one side – as did he. We tried again – a dance. Tears pouring down my face, I looked up. It was Andrej Potocki.

And now I want you to know what this man said to me, this cavalry officer and God alone knows what sort of bigwig who'd stolen my woman, who'd been lit up by the heavens in a golden sheen of glory and riches, whom I hated.

In his precise and militarily pompous voice he said: 'Last month I was taken by an English destroyer from Arkhangelsk to Wick, in Scotland, where I caught a train to London. There were four of us. I was the junior. The purpose was to discuss the development of the war with certain British officials. I also went to see your mother, who always used to have sweets for me in her pocket, as if I were a pony. She was weak. It was turning to pneumonia. I think she knew she hadn't long. She'd been clearing up and had found a box of your father's most personal relics – their marriage certificate, a fob watch inscribed to *his* father, that sort of thing. I've brought the box with me. I'll give it to you when we get to Popovka.'

He grabbed my arm urgently and his soft blue-grey eyes grew wide and intense in a manner that made me understand why his men had followed him after the defeat at Tannenberg.

'Your mother – when I saw her in London I said to myself, This woman is the essence of Russia. All that Russia signifies to our class is present in this one person. Sometimes one must leave something and return to it in order to see it plainly and without varnish. Your kindly, generous mother, who'd brewed a samovar for me and made a cake and bought some Russian wine and cried Russian tears when I left, she was everything to me. Everything! When I tell soldiers what we're fighting for, I think of your mother. Bless her. May the Lord Christ take her unto Him.'

We spoke, my rival and I. Through my tears I thanked him. I hated him less.

But it changed nothing.

I went out into the stinging wind and submitted to the death-coloured sky that was pressing down on my spirit and forcing it into the soil. I passed the ranks of horse cabs and the women in under-chin scarves selling cigarettes. I walked with head bent against the wind over the Dniepr bridge and followed the new tramlines up Suborny Hill. The golden globes of the cathedral where they were to be married were on my left. I was looking for drink, and found it.

I was at this for an hour. Then Kobi sidled up alongside and informed me from the corner of his mouth that Potocki and Count Igor had gone off in the best carriage. Nicholas and the steward had supervised the loading of the luggage wagon and then followed in the other carriage. We were to make our way to Popovka as we wished.

'I suppose that means back to the station for a cab,' I said, as we stood on that icy street.

'No, he's immediately behind us,' Kobi said. 'The same man who brought you home when you were ill was at the station. He recognised me . . . Doig, the Count told me about your mother. Was she very lovely? Did you have good feelings to her or did you insult her like some sons do? I would like to have had a mother.'

My foot was on the cab step when he said this. My weight

had gone most of the way through my body and was moving down my leg. The cab was tilting towards me. I was about to put all my weight on the step.

I looked back at Kobi, the orphan I'd picked up in Samarkand, who'd got me to the Pink House and saved my life, who'd never known his ancestors, who they were, how they swore and spoke and smelled. I looked into his face. I took my foot off the step and put my hand on his shoulder—

The explosion was terrific. The very sky tottered.

The cabby reacted instantly, while we were still gaping. 'The dynamite store in the yard, sure to be. Quickly there, jump in before the police put up roadblocks.'

He kept to the backstreets, normally teeming but now suddenly devoid of activity. In an instant windows had been shuttered and barred. Mastiffs slid their snouts sideways beneath padlocked yard gates and snarled at us with teeth of pitiless white. A boy in flannel shorts, rumpled stockings and a workman's cap pelted helter-skelter out of a lane, across the street in front of us without looking and straight into the house opposite.

The cabby turned to Kobi and said, 'That lad'll have been taking his auntie a message about the explosion. I know her. She's mainly deaf, though one can never be sure.'

He was looking over his shoulder to see how Kobi would respond when a file of Cossack cavalry trotted smartly out of a side street. They halted, facing us.

Savagely the cabby hauled the horse's head round.

It was bad timing. A stack of dynamite had just exploded and there we were about to run away from a dozen Cossacks in long grey-brown coats, rifles slung across their backs, each with a coiled knout in his fist – tough, dark, whippety men aching to lash someone's bones to the marrow.

'Stop!' I shouted at the cabby. I grabbed him by his ear and pulled on it as if I was pulling at a stuck doorknob. He gibbered at me. But he got the horse to stop, broadside to the Cossacks. They were about twenty yards away. The soldier in charge – three stripes of braid on his cape – summoned me imperiously, with a wave of his knout.

Kobi stayed with the cab so the fellow didn't get any ideas about bolting. I walked up to the soldier. Cossacks have their own system of ranks. I called him sergeant. He didn't object. I said we were travelling to Popovka, where we were guests of Count Rykov. I showed him my papers.

His horse was as eager for trouble as the sergeant. It set up a terrific grinding with its teeth and shook its head, rattling its bit and spattering me with flecks of whitey-green foam.

He leaned down from the saddle. His yellow eyes devoured me as if I were a mouse. He twirled his knout and caught the thong expertly.

'I don't know your count or countess or any such bitch round here,' he whistled through his ragged teeth, 'and if I did know your count I'd call him a coward for not fighting our enemies. Same as yourself, a coward. Same as your Chinky friend over there, a coward. Know what we're doing? Blocking off this bit of the city while the police do a drag. Like bolting rabbits out of corn. Bang bang.'

His smoking eyes were shrivelled by hardship. Holes had been drilled in his head for them. The flesh all round was puckered where they'd been forced in. His face was as small and wrinkled as a monkey's, topped with a ridiculously large regimental cap that stuck out over his ears like the eaves of a roof.

His men edged closer to him, bunching for the fun. The horses jangled their bits, tested the iron of their hoofs on the cobbles.

'That's what's going on in this part of Smolensk. But we could change our minds, Mister Friend-of-the-nobility. We could catch cowards instead. So you run off to your dainty-arsed count. If the street's not empty by the time I've picked my nose I'll have my men whip the scabs off your back as was done to our Lord Christ.'

I ran. I ran like anything down the deserted street and leapt into the cab. It was already on the move.

Kobi said, 'They'd have minced you.'

The cabby said, '13th Army Corps. Every one a Satan. That's why you don't see many women in the street these days.'

I said to him, 'Why did you say it was the dynamite store? Terrorists would have stolen it, not blown it up.'

'What does it matter where it was? The bolsheviks are under everyone's bed, that's my meaning.'

166

I told him not to speak like an idiot. So he repeated himself, slightly differently. 'But, *barin,* what does anything matter? Look at my horse's ear. Most of it's gone. Has anything about the horse changed because of it? Is it less of a horse? Of course not. You or I, intelligent men like us, would say an ear is important to a horse. We'd be wrong. So if an ear doesn't matter, what does?'

He'd bought the animal from the cavalry, at their annual cleanout. It had been used to give recruits sword practice at clay figures placed on top of a line of posts. The riders had to gallop weaving through the line and take the heads off the figures first on one side, then the other – forehand and backhand. 'What they say, those Cossack barbarians, is that if you swing the blade properly it goes right through the clay so cleanly that you'd never know it had touched it. The blade *sings,* that's what they told me. But the man who had this horse was a clodhopper and he swiped one of its ears off. So it had to be sold. Has it made a difference? Not a pennyworth. See what I mean? Nothing matters really.'

I said my friend Mikhail Baklushin at Zhukovo had chickens missing their legs. But the cabby wasn't interested in that, only in what he was talking about himself.

Thirty-nine

WE EXCHANGED a winter's afternoon for the darkening forest. The road wandered in five or six tracks to the ford over a deep-cut stream. We went awkwardly down the bank, through water that came to the axle hubs, and up the other side. The tunnel of trees stretched in front of us.

These were Misha's firs; straight, trim and correct. Snow clung to the branches. They sloped gracefully away from the trunks like skirts and their tips swept the margins of the road. Since Misha drew an annual income from them the road was kept in reasonable shape for the timber wagons – a new skim of road metal, properly built culverts, a top-side ditch. We bounced and jolted on the frozen ruts behind our one-eared horse. The two coaches and the luggage wagon had left faint marks in front of us in the snow.

After two miles we came to the end of Misha's plantation. Now the ancient style of forest took over: birch and oaks – white on dark, slim on stout – and the chestnuts that knocked Timofei's hat off in the summer.

We hadn't gone more than a short distance when Kobi said to me, 'Count Nicholas is coming. Galloping.'

'Where? You're seeing things. He'd never leave the baggage alone with the carters.'

I was slumped in the back of the mildewed cab with my arms crossed and my chin tucked into the top of my greatcoat.

The day was closing in on us. The light sprawling through the oaks had a green tinge drawn from their bark. Nothing was growing under the trees except brambles, stunted berries and those quaking mosses that are fond of bog water. There was a suggestion of sprites, of an awfulness to match my mood. That's why I told Kobi he was seeing things.

'You wait, Doig,' he said.

The cab-horse flickered his surviving ear.

'There,' said Kobi, leaning across me and pointing.

The cabby hauled in, pushing to one side of the road to give Nicholas room. 'Someone's in a hurry,' he said.

Through the dank underlight Nicholas galloped. We heard his shout. He disappeared from view as the road went round the contour and cut into the back of the ridge in front of us.

'Broken axle,' said the cabby. 'Coach gone off the road, bound to be.'

The pale flash of Nicholas's shirt: why should he be riding in shirt sleeves in January? And it was never the axle. Timofei was a stickler for inspecting them.

Then his face was at the window, his sweating, frightened, haunted face. His neckcloth had gone, his collar was wide open. Blood was on his neck, printed in fingermarks, and on his forehead. It was on his hands, which looked like meat, and on his forearms and God knows how, on the white blaze of his crazy-eyed horse.

He leaned panting against the side of the cab. His mouth filled – he turned his head and vomited down the door panel. He spat out the bits: wiped his mouth on his arm.

'Have you got a pistol?'

I showed him my Luger.

'Then for mercy's sake hurry up and shoot the animal. The bastards! It must have been down a culvert and triggered by someone hiding in the wood. I'm going to town for the soldiers. We can catch them yet. The bastards! The cowardly stinking *suki*!'

He rammed his spurs in and disappeared into the firs.

'Dynamite store be damned – as fast as you can go,' I shouted at the cabby.

His beard went lop-sided as he produced an ingratiating smile for us. Now was the moment the fool chose to argue, believing he'd got us in a pinch. Bolsheviks – police – soldiers – papers – his permit – the endless trouble for him and his family . . . thus his wheedling as he sat in front of us on the box, not offering to budge. So I got out one side and Kobi the other and we slung him down the verge and into the brambles where he set up a great yelping. Kobi took the reins. One-ear went well for him, head up and looking all around it. I expect it remembered having been in the cavalry from the smell of the blood. A bugle call would have done just as well.

I'd say the time was about half-past three on this January afternoon when we reached the scene. A little sunset pinkness had crept into the sky, an underlay of fleshy tints behind the drifts of grey. In the glade where we halted, the air was perfectly still and green, and bitter with the stink of cordite.

In front of us was the luggage wagon, deserted. Then the carriage Nicholas and the steward had been in. Then the wreckage.

No living person was visible. First thing I said to Kobi was, 'Where are the baggage men?'

'Legged it,' he said without hesitation, surveying everything.

The bomb had been placed in a culvert that took the stream under the road where it made a steep bend. That way the coach that Andrej and Uncle Igor were in would have been going at its slowest. To judge by what was left of the wreck, it had been detonated beneath Timofei.

'Two men,' said Kobi. 'One to give the signal, the other to fire it.' He depressed a plunger.

I didn't see how else it could have been done so accurately.

The explosion had ripped a huge crater in the road. The grass had been blackened and branches ripped off the oaks leaving scars so stark and white that I thought at first glance they could be pieces of flesh. Other branches were broken and hanging down limply, attached by a twist of bark. Looking upwards I observed that a hole of perfect circularity had been created in the tree canopy. Through it I could see the first star of the night.

Typed papers were plastered round the trunks of the oaks like posters for a new set of civic laws. Blown from Andrej's business case – had he and Igor been discussing the war? – and still gripping the bark. Torn, disfigured, charred at the edges. The scarlet Imperial crest was there, upside down, a paper with Andrej's signature, something headed 'Memorandum' – 'Report'

– 'Final Draft'. A document I couldn't make out had been speared by the jagged prong of a branch.

A piteous noise came from the foal of the trace-horse whose back parts had been broken. The two had been among those hidden by Timofei from the Remount Commission. This was an outing for them. I expect the foal had been gambolling beside its mother, sticking its nose into the snow and examining everything with its wide glistening eye. Now it wanted to get at its mother's milk but whenever it got close it smelled the gore and danced back out of range, revolted. It was hysterical – bleating, crying, pawing the ground, its nostrils distended.

There was no sign of life in the mare's eye, though its diaphragm was still pumping. I put my pistol in its ear and shot it through the brain. The sound rang out in the empty forest like a pick striking metal. The heap of carcass tensed. Its legs stiffened, and it died.

Kobi cut a length out of the traces and fashioned a halter. I caught the foal round the neck and we tied it to a tree. The creature stood there shivering, looking from us to its mother's milk-bag with uncomprehending eyes.

This is how it is with the unexpected. There are the initial moments in which one forms the photographic plates for memory storage. Then one attends to whatever practicality sends out the most powerful demand.

The foal dealt with, I turned my attention to the coach.

My first thought was that the detonation had been a yard premature. For the shafts and box were shattered and of that good man Timofei no identifiable lump was visible. Even his impregnable dark blue greatcoat had been blown to smithereens. Had a bomb of that size gone off under the passenger part, the coach would have been in matchsticks and the fate of its occupants beyond doubt.

It was lying on its side, mangled, torn and splintered. Nicholas had had it tarted up specially for the bridegroom. Now its fresh green paint was scorched and the wheel rims gone: the spokes hung loosely, like a derelict umbrella. The window on the top side had been blown out. The Rykov wolf, so carefully picked out by the paint shop in the golden lozenge of the door panel, was totally disfigured: its haunches had been smashed and its snout and piggy eyes besmirched by nitroglycerine. The only undamaged part of it was its ribcage, which by itself looked like a cat's.

How did I feel? Was I horrified? Bewildered? Squeamish? Keenly interested, that's what I recall best. Keen and growing keener by the moment. The possibility of a glorious death slapped me across the face like a douche of spring water. My skin stung with excitement. My heart raced, shaking my ribs with its vast leaps.

Andrej – gone?

Kobi was on top of the carriage, gingerly dismantling the wreckage to get at sound timbers. He didn't want the thing to collapse beneath him. He called down, 'There's someone inside. I can make out his hand.' I climbed up and joined him, standing on the edge of a leaf of the springs. But there was only room for one of us at a time.

'Dead?' I asked.

'Looks it.'

'Who?'

'Count Igor, I think. Once I can get my arm properly inside, I can clear away the mess and see better. Skin's all flabby, though.'

'There should be two men in there.'

'I know that,' Kobi said, looking at me in a certain way. (He was fishing round with his hand, his face flat against the panel.)

The problem was that the rear cross-member securing the chassis to the coach work had become unseated. The bolts at one end had sheared and the free end of the tie had got wedged into the road. If it collapsed the vehicle would fall to pieces. We didn't have to be engineers to realise that. Kobi was right to go slowly. But I was hot with impatience, I was like a sinner desperate to find the key to heaven before it gets too dark. 'Hurry up – here, it's quicker with two,' and I began to wrench the planking away so forcefully that the whole edifice rocked.

Kobi, who by now had got his head and shoulders inside the coach, called up, 'Be careful, Doig.' A little later: 'Only one man, Count Igor.'

I didn't believe him. I pulled him out and got in there myself.

As for the horse, so for this harmless old pederast. The blast had caught him at the knees and shattered him from the fundament outwards. I mean shattered, not just bruised. I could make out his rouged cheeks at the bottom of the death trap. His face was unmarked. But the rest of him was a bloody mash.

I got Kobi to pass me a stick. I prodded Igor around to see if there was anything of Potocki somehow squeezed in beneath him. It wasn't edifying, poking around in that loose flesh. I was glad my mother was dead and not seeing me.

The exercise was unprofitable: it was all Uncle Igor.

I was disappointed by this turn-out. I'd puffed up my hopes – crossed the 't' of his death – already taken Liza into my arms. I'd felt the lithe length of her body against mine. Andrej had been pushed at her, I'd been her real love since that day at Balaclava. We'd embraced in a state of delirium. Total victory had been mine. I'd married and occupied her. All this had I done in my mind. But now there was no corpse – and no victory.

He couldn't have vanished. Come on now, Charlie, do some thinking. Had he got out unharmed and walked to Popovka with the steward? I didn't think so. Had he been thrown yards away by the blast? The steward would have dragged him somewhere handy . . .

The steward, that was it. I had to consider his actions. He was the key.

He'd gone. Therefore he'd known Potocki to be dead. If he hadn't been, he'd have stayed with the injured man until Kobi and I arrived. That Andrej was dead was the sole tenable conclusion. But where was he then?

I thought, suppose he'd been up there on the box with Timofei, chatting, joking, sharing the reins, showing what a good chap he was? Well, if that were the case, I ought to be looking for very small pieces.

I peered more carefully into the upper branches. And before many moments had elapsed I came to understand that the bomb had not been detonated even an inch too soon.

One: snagged in the crotch of two branches and virtually the same colour as the bark, the brownish-green panel from the back of an army officer's greatcoat with the two buttons still attached. Kobi fetched the hatchet that our cabby kept under his seat and cut down a sapling. I hoisted him onto the lowest branch from where he could climb within range. Stretching, he fiddled down the scrap of coat. It fell flopping from branch to branch and as it did the dark yellow moiré of its silken lining winked at me and filled me with encouragement. That wasn't the style of Timofei's coat, my God it wasn't.

I needed more. His pocketbook, epaulettes, the box containing Liza's wedding ring, even the balding head with its atoll of electrified hair – I needed absolute proof of his death.

'Someone's hand,' Kobi said, pointing down into the brambles. 'Timofei's?'

I said we'd make a pile of the oddments, parcel them up and hang them in a tree until morning. Night was coming in fast. At some stage a doctor and officialdom would appear, directed here by Nicholas. But what if it wasn't until the morning? What if the wolves ate the evidence overnight? Andrej was no use to me as a missing person. I wanted him in the ledger of the dead. If he got into the history books as a victim of the terrorists, well and good. He'd have his footnote and I his woman, which was the better trade by ten million roubles times ten.

Forty

THERE ENTERED my mind a conversation with Goetz in Turkestan. He was washing slime off his forearms after dealing with some skins; standing in his shorts, stockings and boots at a pistachio-green enamel basin resting on a wooden stand. I was cooking our meal, upwind so the smoke would keep the insects off him.

'You know that the best collectors in the world are doctors of medicine? No question of it. They're nerveless, you see, Doig. They observe everything related to life and death with both dispassion and curiosity. How did it happen? What went wrong? They always want to know. Macabre doesn't come into it — can't. Science is supreme.'

I remembered that remark of his as Kobi and I tried to match our haul of limbs. We were in a hurry. I had to prove beyond the shadow of a doubt that we had the remains here of two men and that one of them was Potocki. And I had to have the evidence assembled before some minor official arrived with ideas of his own.

The most encouraging clue was the first one we found: the hand with Timofei's thumb. For he'd been the Popovka fiddler and had the flattened thumb pad of the business, from a lifetime stopping his strings with it. Kobi lit the lantern on the front of the cab and we noted the characteristics of that thumb: a wide brown stump with the nail well down the quick and ingrained with dirt. I said to Kobi, 'Nothing like Potocki's.'

Nor was it. We soon found Andrej's right index finger, the tip stained with ink, and his left hand complete with his little pinkie and signet ring.

We arrayed them side by side beside the lantern. I could scarcely restrain my glee. Kobi said in the most matter-of-fact way, 'You can tell from the fingers who had the happier life.' I glanced at him. He was quite serious.

There was the sound of creaking leather and the bustle of horses. Out of the darkness of the fir trees our Cossack patrol of earlier trotted briskly. The trooper riding beside the sergeant was carrying a storm lantern swinging from the hook at the end of a pole.

We stood back from the remains. The sergeant stared suspiciously around him with his yellow eyes. His gaze came to rest on me. 'You again. Trust my luck. Why not some peasant that I can arrest and sell back to his family?'

I walked over and laid my hand on his horse's bridle. I explained what had happened and what we'd done so far. I said I was afraid the wolves might carry off the body parts in the night. 'Good,' he said several times as he counted up all the things that he and his men wouldn't have to do.

He nodded when I asked if he'd witness my identification of Potocki's ring finger. He dismounted and picked up the hand. He inspected the ring under the lantern. I thought he was going to draw it off and pocket it, but he just tossed the hand onto the ground, so casually that I was compelled to stare at it: rather podgy, the veins still blue, a flap of bloody skin hanging from the wrist tendons. Kobi turned it over with his foot to prove he was the sergeant's equal in callousness. I leaned against a tree, got out my pocket journal and in the back wrote down the circumstances of Potocki's death. I read it out to the sergeant. He nodded. We both signed it, he with his name in full – Pyotr Sergeyevich Vastok. He picked the hand up and held it out to me. 'Say goodbye to him, then.' I said it'd bring me bad luck. But Kobi thought it a fine joke and shook Andrej's hand vigorously. The Cossacks standing around were also amused and a couple of them shook it in order to be able to tell their sons they'd shaken hands with the war hero Potocki.

Vastok climbed onto the spring leaf and stuck his head into the wrecked carriage. He withdrew it and peered down to me with his snakelike eyes. 'Dead.'

'Count Igor Rykov, my relative.'

'Tell me the names of the other dead men again.'

'Timofei the coachman and Count Andrej Potocki from the general staff.'

'Two aristocrats, one bomb. Another victory for the bolsheviks. Who gave them their information?' He jumped down, flicked his head at Kobi. 'What about him?'

I said he'd been with me every moment for the last three days. Everyone knew the marriage was to take place in a few days. They must have had someone watching the station.

'And ridden out in advance of these men and chosen the place? Hidden themselves and the bomb? Never. They had prior information.' The sergeant dismissed my idea with a wave of his hand. 'Thank the Lord I don't have to worry about that. Killing the bastards is my job . . . Form a line, men, and pick up every piece of the bodies that you can find. Hurry, it's getting cold.'

At that moment one of his troopers walked in his bandy-legged way into the circle of light. He'd scooped up some clothing and now had it spread over both forearms, which he extended to us like a tailor proffering a sample. He even made us a little bow.

I could have kissed every pockmark on his brutish face. For what he had draped over his arms was a ragged portion of one leg of the trousers Andrej had been wearing that morning: the unmistakeable regimental trousers of the Tsar's Garde à Cheval – saintly white with a fat seam of scarlet braid. No one could possibly dispute the fact of Andrej's death now.

With delight I told Vastok whose they were. He said he'd already agreed the dead man was Potocki. Why was I so anxious? 'You think you'll get his woman,' he said flatly. 'Either his woman or his money. Or his horses. You stand to get something, that's obvious. Maybe it was you who arranged it.'

He raised his large flat cap. His head was shaven except for a black forelock, his Cossack chub. He smoothed his hand over his nodular skull and settled his cap. One of his men spoke to him. Vastok jerked his thumb at me and said, 'He did it. He wants the woman.'

Forty-one

THE STEWARD arrived with the Popovka men from the other direction. They had a wagon laden with bedding, lanterns, ropes, shovels, crowbars and food. A little later Nicholas turned up on a fresh horse, leading the way for a young doctor from Smolensk who was driving himself in a covered trap, a little box of a thing.

I made a joke to the doctor concerning the mix of limbs and the place for a pedant in the proceedings. He regarded me strangely, much as Kobi had done earlier. Nicholas overheard me, for I was in good humour. He became very stuffy. He was clearly upset, and not really speaking to anyone – certainly not taking command of the situation. The Popovka men were eyeing him slyly as they waited for orders. I could see trickling through their minds all the money, coin by coin, that the Rykovs had lost by this spectacular failure of the union with the Potockis. I had an urge to go among them whispering, But don't forget Count Igor's dead too . . . his pockets rang like church bells when he went for a walk . . . *Bozhe moy,* the riches of the man . . .

The parleying continued: Nicholas, the doctor, myself, the sergeant of Cossacks. The rankers were standing around smoking. Nicholas carped and criticised – glared at the torn soil – sat down on a log and fell silent. After a while I told him it'd be midnight before we got anywhere at this rate. When he started to whine about his bad luck, I took over. I got the soldiers and the Popovka contingent to form a new line and thus we swept the entire area, banks and bracken, stream and marsh, until the doctor declared the corpses complete – or complete enough.

He agreed with me about Potocki's remains. I got him to sign my statement also. Then he made parcels of the bodies, which he tied to the roof of his trap. Having done this he set off back to Smolensk, the Cossacks following him.

Of course the road had been rendered impassable. We unloaded the baggage and carried it round the crater to the Popovka wagon. The frosty moon shone as sharp as a cutlass, confusing the lanterns and throwing out long, swaying shadows. We could have looked like prisoners on the road to Siberia.

Nicholas and I walked together behind the wagon.

The extent of his problems now became evident. He'd been an idiot. He'd put all his ready money plus some borrowing into various joint farming enterprises with the Popovka peasants. They'd rattled the prospect of a good profit beneath his nose and gulled him ruthlessly. To finance the wedding and Liza's dowry he'd gone not to his usual lenders, the Agricultural Mortgage Corporation, but to Kugel & Co. in the Pochtamtskaya. There was a point here he didn't fully explain. I think it centred upon the anxieties of the Mortgage Corporation. Anyway, they'd only lend a proportion of the sum required whereas old man Kugel had been most obliging.

'At a cost but at least I didn't have to worry about not getting the money at all. It wasn't a good deal. My friends do nothing but boast about how they got a quarter per cent knocked off here or an extra sixty days credit there, but I . . . However, reflecting upon it as I rode home, I thought, It serves me right for having spent Liza's dowry on my own projects. So I thought better of myself for having recognised this fact.'

Potocki had later agreed to share the cost of the wedding. But nothing had been written down – and now he was dead. It was weighing heavily on Nicholas. The Pink House was full of food, of every luxury that could still be purchased in Moscow. He'd had to pay cash. He faced a loss of a good fifty per cent even if he could get Belov's to take their stuff back. What could he do? There were still eight months before harvest. He'd also borrowed against the crop itself. So if the weather was like it had been two years ago . . .

It would have been a dismal tale on anyone's tongue. But Nicholas would have me believe that bad luck had singled him out for special treatment. He walked with his head bowed. He could think of nothing favourable to say about anyone – including Liza.

'She could have had him weeks ago if she'd put her mind to it. Now he's gone and got himself killed. It's even possible she may be too compromised to get another man – you know, Charlie, too *soiled*. She might be carrying his child. Think of that.'

This reminded him of Helene and Leo and young Nicholas, and of the Rykovs in general. The illustriousness of his family history pressed down on him. If things went on as they were, he might have nothing but debts to leave his children. He'd be best to sell the Pink House – retire to a district where he was unknown – even to take his own life, if he had the courage to do it. His anxieties came out in the jerky speech of a man sinking ever lower in his own estimation.

Morosely he enumerated the possibilities. It was horrible listening to him. He was so feeble at the point of decision.

For the third time he said, 'But what shall I do if it turns out that she's pregnant?'

I stabbed my finger at his chest. 'I'll marry her. I'll take all these worries off your plate.'

We came to an abrupt halt in the brilliant moonlight. He stroked his lower lip. He looked at me intently.

'Is this an offer made for family convenience or were you all along secretly . . . you know . . . her suitor?' He was looking at me with his face on one side. The weakness had vanished. Already he was making new calculations.

'Take it as you find it.'

'What a tragedy that could have been . . . But Charlie, how your pulse must have raced just now, when you realised what had happened! Eh, Charlie boy, eh!'

Then sharply: 'She'll have you?'

'Why'd I say that otherwise?'

'Of course she'll get Igor's fortune now . . . Tell you what, I'll agree to the wedding as long as you promise to support me. You'll have enough money.'

I laughed at him. 'I don't need your agreement. You couldn't stop us if you tried.'

He put his arm round my shoulder. 'I don't know how that slipped out. It's all the tension that's been building up within me. Let's just be three good friends together – three cousins, even better. Have her whenever you want, Charlie, just as I said to poor Andrej.'

Forty-two

THE WAGON-DRIVER was chanting a song concerning the unexpected death of a lover. Standing up, stamping his right boot at the moments of emphasis, he was making the most of the long, melancholy notes.

Nicholas strode up. 'Enough of that boys, enough of the past. It was God's wish, wasn't it? Let's give thanks we're still here. Someone sing a cheery tune to get us home.'

I said to him in an undertone, 'Have some respect for your sister. They'll think she's a whore if you just wipe out Andrej's death and pretend it won't matter to her. Have respect also for Timofei, who was a well-liked man.'

'We're going to be three jolly cousins together, old chap Charlie,' Nicholas said. In that light I thought he had glass eyes they were so shining with triumph.

I wanted to say to him, You're the greediest man in Popovka, and the most unprincipled and despicable. This is the second time that you've sold your sister – once every six weeks that amounts to.

That was what I said to him with my expression. To myself I said, I shall wed Elizaveta Rykov in place of Potocki and straightway take ship to the United States, to Norman Joiner and the museum in Chicago.

Yes, we would marry immediately. I would walk up the aisle wearing Potocki's boots and after a short honeymoon Liza and I would become another of those families camping on the platform on the chance that a Train No. 7 would at some stage arrive and whisk us to Odessa. Then to Marseilles – New York – and so in our gliding cream and brown Pullman through the roaring stockyards of Chicago to Union Station. We would emphasise our Russianness, paint ourselves as the naturalist and his aristocratic love match fleeing from the barbarians. Lizochka would play auction bridge, impetuously, at afternoon parties of jealous, lynx-eyed ladies. Husbands would return early from their discount brokerages to feast upon her beauty, her nurse's sympathetic eye and her rolling-river 'r's. I'd have to associate with men of learning who wore brown suits and celluloid collars, but for half the year I'd rough it and grow old on the trail, as Goetz had done. Uncle Igor's fortune would see us through the hard times.

I began to make a reckoning of the hard times we'd have. Allow seven days a year for her fits and their consequences, five for my recurrent bouts of typhus, five for arguments, five for tantrums, ten for when the babies come, five for the visits of sheer bad luck plus a general allowance of ten per cent. Thus six weeks of every year could be ruined – annulled from the records. It was too much.

Paring it down: Dear Lord, preserve Lizochka and your servant from hard times. She is the only woman I can love. She deserves the best you have. Make me listen to her. Give her easy births and loving children. Hear this prayer, Lord Christ.

I was ready to explain all this to her, that it wasn't going to be easy on account of our afflictions. However, I'd pleaded with God. I was full of strong and original lines why she should marry me.

She listened for a bit. Then she interrupted: 'I'll only do it if I can hear your heart beating as you enter the room. You've got to want me impossibly.'

'But I do!' What else could I say?

'Not convincing. I'm having nothing to do with you if this is another of Nicholas's schemes. I understand them now. I don't want you to even touch me unless it gives you an electric shock. That's how it should be. That's proper love, not the sort that lawyers arrange.'

'As it was with Andrej?'

'Nicholas's work from start to finish. He knows nothing about women.'

We were in her room, surrounded by the Chinese scarlet,

amid the sweet perfumes of birchwood burning in the hearth and of the daily hashish pipe that she had taken to smoking to dampen *le grand mal*. It was evening. I'd spent the day rehearsing my lines. The wedding arrangements were still in place. Nicholas had been spreading the news about Liza and me to force our hands. Everyone was astounded by the twists in the tale and sniggering behind our backs. Kobi reported that the villagers were going round saying as Vastok had that it was I who'd been behind the bomb. 'Look at him, pinching the dead man's woman without any sense of shame. Who else could it have been?'

Sonja had been so disgusted that she'd taken her papers and left, the little prude.

Somehow her name now entered our speech. I told Liza she was better off without her, saw the look in her face and sped off at an angle, hoping she hadn't been listening properly. She had. She bridled immediately: drew herself up: poked out her Saracen's nose. God she could be so beautiful.

But it had been a mistake speaking against Sonja and it was useless trying to retrieve it. Women are so difficult. It's far easier to rectify a mistake made when luring a bird with its song. One wrong move with a woman and you've got to spend hours coaxing and cajoling and even bribing them to look at you again.

'Gradualness is the great point with women,' my mother used to tell me. 'Don't snatch, Charlie.'

But to marry this woman was top of my list. I'd said it once and I said it again as Liza started to tell me about Sonja's intelligence and how wrong I was and how presumptuous. I told her what Mother had said about gradualness. I said I'd been as gradual as I was going to be. I told her flat that I wasn't going to be refused, that yes or no was too full a choice. She smiled slightly, a movement of her lips.

The scarlet walls and black bookshelves, the hot colours of the Caucasus, they swirled around me with the tang from her hashish. I was intoxicated by them, by the tumult of my love and by my own energy. I wanted to eat her – to gain possession and have at my disposal her body – her entity, everything she was made of, bones and skin and spirit, guts and juices. I was on the point of bursting. My arms trembled to grab her. Only the lack of consent restrained me.

'We'll leave in a balloon for our honeymoon and conceive our first child at a height of five thousand feet.' It was the continuation of a previous whim.

'Don't be facetious. That's the sort of thing Nicholas would have said if he'd had enough wit. Listen, Charlie. A woman exposes herself and gives everything that's most vulnerable about her when she accepts a man. She must take her time, judge him thoroughly, judge the quality of his blood and the prospects for children and happiness.'

'That's being pompous,' I said. 'You've known me forever. Remember the Simplicitas?'

'I knew Andrej too.'

'Good brave man, Andrej. But he still looked up your skirts when you were on the swing.'

'I never didn't wear knickers. Your Nanny Agafya would have had me struck by lightning.'

'But he's gone now. Whereas I am here, asking that you marry me and come to America. Why shilly-shally?' I took a step towards her. 'Let's do it. That's where the future is. We're good together. God in heaven, Lizochka, you've only got to think about what's happened – Andrej, Uncle Igor, the state of the country, revolution being openly talked about, even abdication. Why wait? Are you crazy? . . . Oh *dusha moya,* my beautiful love, I didn't mean it like that, forgive me that I'm crass,' and I raised her from the chair to her stockinged feet and fixed her solemn eyes.

'Why didn't you say anything when I was betrothed to Andrej? Was it just chance that you left it until Igor was dead – until I inherited? Are you sure this isn't Nicholas again? Sonja was right, you can never trust men.'

'I tried,' I started, but she'd spread her sails and was scudding along.

'What about it then? What were you doing all the time I was being estimated for pedigree duties? Do you think I wanted to marry him? That his sugar beet was such a draw? Duty, that's how Nicholas wore me down. Duty, the noble line of Rykov, what society expects, comfort in my old age – night after night until I was exhausted and gave in. Where were you when I was in need, Charlie Doig?'

Raising my voice, 'Stop gabbing and listen. Remember that evening the timber beetle flew past? What do you suppose I was saying?'

It was too much. She exploded, pushed me away, thumped the boards with her foot and yelled into my face, 'Beetle! An insect flies past and you chuck me away! Your so-called lovemaking stopped dead in its tracks, like a raindrop hitting a windowpane. Oh no, Charlie, you can't get away with that . . . All I was after was enough encouragement to put Andrej aside. Then a beetle goes past under your nose – and – and – '

She had her fingers crooked in talons to claw me. Her nipples were taut beneath her blouse, an ounce of gunpowder in each. Tears the size of gooseberries were rolling down her cheeks, her lips were buckling. 'A damned common beetle was better than me' – that was what I heard, and then I snapped her into my arms and clung to her as a stormbound mariner clings to the mainmast and puts his trust in God. We were shivering, both. I vowed never to mention beetles within her earshot. I called her my angel, my jewel, my columbine, my meadow pipit, my lady of Krakow, my treasure trove, the mother of my children.

'I always knew we were meant for each other. Always! Daily!' – 'Grow your hair to your waist and make a cradle of it for me to rest in, like Moses' – 'Out, *grand mal*! Out, out, I abolish you!'

Such were the endearments I murmured and shouted. She smiled and smiled on me, stroked my cheeks and swore it would have come to this, even if she had gone off with Potocki. It was how love matches were made. It was how the world operated its levers, even though it was sometimes slow to interview all the applicants and get them paired off. So many lost souls searching for love! Queues of them! Ladies in this line, if you please . . . gentlemen must remove their hats . . . if you don't mind, sir. We kissed, made our jokes, wallowed like hippos in our conjoined emotions and kissed again and again. We built a house (wooden, very Russian) and furnished it exotically. We lined our children up on the brown turf of our summer-parched lawn in order of height and age and discovered a difference of three feet two inches between the glossy poll of Daniel, our firstborn, and Sibylla, the baby, who wasn't really a baby at the time we imagined this but a plump little lady of six who would be pushed on the swing only by her mother.

She had a tongue like a gypsy's that went halfway down my throat. With open palms I frotted her gunpowder nipples until her eyes grew as large as plates and her adam's apple began to quiver. I was primed, eager as a dog, as full of go as any man just rescued from the brink.

But I was too forward. She was a woman of grace and at heart demure. She held me off. It was to be husband or nothing.

And there was another reason beside her own moral inclination. Her mother, the lady from Krakow, had given herself to her father out of wedlock and 'no good ever came of it. Look what happened. When she died giving birth to me, everyone said that was why she died. She departed this earth in ignominy, which I would not wish for myself. You take me – you fall down the stairs and break your neck – how am I to account for young Daniel when he arrives? Your mother was right – gradualness, my darling Charlinka.'

The dinner gong boomed, three times sternly, as was Louis's custom.

'Marriage, then hourly, then America.' I kissed her mouth hard.

And Louis, as if he'd been listening at the door for the last two hours, took it into his head to deliver a pattering crescendo with the gong mallet that culminated in a single magnificent reverberation, like the final and most spectacular rocket at a firework party.

Viva! The betrothed couple!

Forty-three

I SHUT NICHOLAS as completely from my mind as I could. Liza and I were the possessors of great happiness. We wished only for hosannas, and spoke them to each other with our lips and our eyes and the swollen gestures of lovers.

However, in supposing that I'd just slip into Andrej's place going up the aisle I'd planned too wildly.

It was two days after the assassinations, in the late morning, that we were visited by a harassed detective inspector who'd been sent down from Moscow. With him were a local inspector and a stenographer. (I had thought the latter to be only the coachman – which he was, but he'd learned shorthand at the Smolensk Institute in his evenings.) They'd inspected the scene and come straight on.

We were questioned one after another in the drawing room, Liza going first. She came out quite pale, shaking her head, and hurried away to the kitchens to arrange for the samovar and *zakuski*.

Bobinski too was summoned for questioning, which delighted him. He dressed up in suitably sombre garments that had belonged to a previous lodger, now deceased – a fallen lawyer. He had Louis announce him, throw open the door with a flourish, and in he tottered on his cane, his scant hair watered and his eyebrows soldered to his forehead.

Misha was last. He was no time at all. The stenographer emerged looking for a quiet corner to go through his transcript. Then Misha stuck his head out and said they'd finished, we could all go in now.

We started with the forest itself. The inspector from Smolensk

188

said it was seething with deserters from the army, with anarchists, and with the general criminal riff-raff that the prisons were now inadequate to hold on to. That every miscreant in the province took refuge in Popovka forest had been a universal assumption for as long as I could remember. Uncle Boris had spoken of them, how useful the tame ones were at haymaking time. So what was new? We looked from one inspector to the other.

'Tell us something we don't know, whether you've apprehended anyone,' Nicholas demanded, tossing his head of fair hair. We were impatient. For a policeman to hold back on secrets is a terrible disappointment.

Thus it came out, fortunately when Liza was still away from the room, that Sonja, her maid, had been arrested as an accomplice. She was in custody in Smolensk. Her interrogation had already commenced.

'Third Section, though we don't call it that now. But an identical body with identical methods. Results will be quick.'

'Gratitude!' squeaked Bobinski. 'The family takes her in, treats her like one of their own and then – just look at the strumpet. She deserves everything she gets. You ask Louis about her, my goodness. He has an opinion.'

Indeed he did. Shaping his lips, he wafted it towards the inspectors like an old connoisseur of debauchery. 'It's my belief that she has a sexual disorder. A number of times she made advances that I repelled. Then one day she grabbed my hand and applying unimaginable pressure led it down to her pudenda—' He broke off as Liza returned with a plate of angel cakes.

'I'll bring in the *zakuski*,' he said and left the room as fast as he could.

'I omitted to tell you that we have in fact arrested your maid Sonja,' the Moscow inspector said to Liza. 'I wanted first to hear what these other gentlemen had to say. There is no doubt about her involvement.'

'Why do you say that?'

'She was the only person who knew exactly what Count Potocki's movements were to be. Because of her position in your service.'

'Apart from myself.'

'Indeed.'

'Apart from a dozen members of the general staff.'

'Indeed.'

'So you agree that she wasn't the only one.'

'Of course, I have said so. But there is far stronger evidence that I cannot disclose. Anyway, the Third Section have her. Rest assured that we shall soon know everything. The Count will not go unavenged though we have to move both heaven and earth.'

She rose and ran from the room. I would have followed but Misha stayed me. 'Give her some time by herself. These are great blows she's having to take. I know, Charlie, there's always you to help her, and thank Christ for that. But women . . . take my advice, I've known a few.'

Bobinski's eyes were stark with excitement, about a foot out of his skull. 'The villain, the minx that she was – but how did she get the information out of this house? Have we thought enough about that?'

I said that I believed she met someone in the forest. I'd seen marks on her dress, and a rip she couldn't, or wouldn't, account for.

'That's it! Do you hear that, Inspector? It's all the proof you need. Hang her immediately, that's what I say.'

'What Bobby means is at least hang someone,' Misha put in laconically.

'Andrej deserves it,' Nicholas said. 'He was a hero to the whole country. His march after Tannenberg – can you remember the excitement in the capital, and the crowds, and how proud and grateful everyone was? If no one's executed for his murder the whole of Russia will want to know why.'

The samovar arrived. Soon after, Nicholas asked Louis to lay two extra places for lunch. Liza never came down. The history of Sonja filled all the spaces in the short winter's day.

Together with her name there was much talk about the armed soldiers wandering around the cities seemingly unattached to any regiment. Most would have known how to plant and detonate the bomb. Some might have taken pleasure from killing Andrej just because he had a safe post on the general staff and a yellow silk lining to his greatcoat. I knew it for a fact. One only had to glance at the factory strikers in Petrograd or at the soldiers on the trains, in short at starving, exhausted, jealous citizens, to understand that many unthinkable actions become possible when hope is drained from existence.

I found myself repeatedly whispering the magic incantation of 'America' and as soon as the policemen had gone I ran upstairs with the drawing-room atlas and smothered Lizochka with my schemes.

We rubbed noses, bubbled our lips together. 'After the funerals, after we're married,' she murmured. 'One thing at a time, as you're so fond of saying. What difference will two weeks make?'

That was how long it took. It was wartime, and people accepted that different customs should apply. But Andrej and uncle Igor were men of distinction. No lime-slaked pit for them, though I would have gladly settled for something less grandiose than the three-hour service in Smolensk Cathedral we had to endure.

What am I to say about those two lost weeks? The combination of fatalism and lethargy that seems to breed in Russia like cholera bacilli in an open sewer drove me frantic. Even my darling was not immune: would flick through magazines or plump up the cushions on her bed and puff a little hashish. She said she was developing a passion for roses. Why didn't we go and live in England in some cottage *ornée* with an immense Maréchal Niel trailing all over the walls? Everyone knew about England and its roses . . . It was as if the future having been settled, she could put her feet up.

Nicholas was hopeless. Only two subjects interested him: the value of Lizochka's inheritance and how to avoid speaking to Helene, who'd come down from Moscow for the dual events. He cared about no one but himself. I understood that quite clearly now.

Misha, my urbane and loveable godfather, moved between the Pink House and Zhukovo, speaking amusingly to everyone and lifting not a finger to help.

So it was I who had to shoulder the greatest burden of the arrangements. I found myself collecting surprise remarks to inject like stimulants whenever Liza, or Nicholas, or Misha, or even Louis said something like: 'Next week, Charlie, let's leave it until then. Today would be unlucky.' Or if a particular saint's day was coming along, the patron saint of love or luck, they'd be likely to say, 'Why don't we do everything then? We'd be setting out on the right foot.'

Going to America was completely submerged by the effort of steering these very different engagements upon which I balanced precariously, like a logger keeping his raft of timber in one pack. Only when the two sets of obsequies had been completed and the family crypts sealed could I clearly see the prospect of my marriage to Liza: the two of us at the altar, the ring, and the beautiful words of accomplishment.

By this time I was on my knees with fatigue. Also tense, shivering, with an emptiness behind my eyeballs as if a network of caves had developed there.

So when Kobi came down from Popovka on the morning of my wedding to warn me that a troop of armed deserters was encamped nearby in the forest, I told him roundly to get out. I swore at him. I told him he was scaremongering in order to steal my thunder. In a crouching, bad-tempered way I bore down on him. 'This is my day, the day to beat all my other days,' I snarled at him.

Forty-four

F EW OF our guests came back from the cathedral. The road
through the forest had become notorious. They didn't want
to be reminded of the murders. The idea of going back at night
was loathsome. They feared that they too might end up speck-
ling the upper branches of the oaks like an unseasonal flush of
leaves.

Nevertheless guests there were and with a purpose, and what
was cardinal was that Lizochka and I were that purpose. Come
the late afternoon you would have found the blue-tiled stove
roaring away in the hall as with Liza at my side I kissed and
embraced all who came within reach. I was the blissful bridegroom and shortly I'd be lording it over the banquet that had
been planned for another. Excelsior! I raised my eyes and
signalled to Pushkin in his heaven. Now I know the source of
happiness, old father!

I didn't give Andrej a second thought. I never dreamed of
calling up to him, Hard luck, or some such tripe. It's a mistake
to let one's feelings get over-soft or in any respect pretty. That
way lies diffidence and indecision.

Nicholas had invited a few of his peasant farmers from the
village. They stood in a solid group, combing their beards with
bent fingers, shifting their feet and covertly examining photographs of the last generation of Rykovs, the knick-knacks and
the furniture – mentally compiling inventories and valuations.

Their wives stood close to them, trying by frowns and rasping
whispers to deflect the shots of peppered vodka that Louis was
urging on them.

Bobinski had a number of jokes that would have been deemed

scurrilous in Uncle Boris's time. But the changes in morals had eroded their pungency and now he dished them out, one per male person, as he circled the room tittering.

Bobby: white-tufted chin, emaciated nostrils, skin like papyrus, stooping, the pensioned tutor in worsted stockings and knee breeches helping out his adopted family.

Nicholas: out of character in a frock coat, gappy-toothed, with lumpy red hands like his farmers, prowling among the throng with skin-deep laughter, thinking of the money going down the drain and who was going to drive his sorry-looking wife to the railway station the next day. Not a scrap about us.

Kobi: by no means turning away Louis and his vodka. His widow – a proud woman and by her build a lusty one.

Oh, friends crowding round us and people I'd never met and the heat from the stove and the vodka and the red faces and from our own happiness, oh, this was an apt and lovely world! I caught Kobi's eye and saluted him, meaning by it that I apologised for my rudeness to him in the morning.

We went in to dine – caviare on warm *kalach*, milk-cap mushrooms flavoured with saffron, sauerkraut and whortle-berries, graceful fillets of sturgeon, woodcocks' livers on steeped toast, roast boar plugged with cloves, real French wines, Einem's chocolates, and to crown it all, a gift from Misha, half a dozen bottles of Tokay, the 1874, the archangel of wines.

Mishenka Baklushin! Dearest Misha!

His face was the colour of a bursting tulip. The contours of his stomach made one understand more about the function of legs. He was wearing two waistcoats, in case he got bored with one of them or spilled his food on it. The topmost was cream with roses picked out in gold silk and a hem of light blue – to suggest the summer, he confided to Liza. And the under one? she enquired nosily. His laughter made the buds of candle-flame quiver. He wouldn't say – well, he might – for such a delicious bride – for his godson – for the two finest people in the world – but the truth was that it clashed with his countenance and so she'd understand it if he said nothing more – at which with another huge laugh he displayed the article in question, a garment so pale and puffy except for its bright green buttons that it might have been intended for a warm shirt. The Popovka men looked on with amusement, it being well known among them that Misha had had the fancy for it only last night and had given the village tailor an hour to get it done.

'It's for when I cry,' he said, his eyes already starting to brim. 'I can weep and snuffle on it – and then give it away. It was only two roubles. And you all thought it was going to be as purple as my nose! Lizinka, my darling, how I shall miss you! My darling! My darling!'

They embraced and hugged, both crying.

Presently all the foods that Nicholas had squirrelled away for Andrej were swayed into the room in tureens and on platters held aloft. Beer and wine were served by Styopka, the younger stable boy, jug in one hand, bottle in the other. He poured them so merrily – slopping out the good French claret as if it was beetroot juice – that by the sheer vigour of the flow he over-turned the glass of the man opposite me. Great shouts of joy, sufficient to bend the rafters.

Voices began to be raised: 'I tell you, Arkady Semyonovich, that the field you call Poor Furlong and I the Widow's Acre should never have been planted to rye. The soil is not unsuitable. Its character, Arkady . . .'

'The best bull we ever had round here was old Thunder, remember? Hurdling that fence of pea-sticks to get at the black-and-white heifer? Remember how he took it, boys, remember? Like a racehorse, all his hoofs in the air at once . . . the size of the hip on him . . . what stock he left . . .'

And the man whose glass had been knocked over leaned across and said happily to me, 'That girl of yours, Sonja, was hanged this morning. Tried at eight, hanged at nine. Rope must be cheaper than bullets. And if you think also of the time saved by not calling out the firing squad . . .'

It's rare when a conversation that shouldn't be heard isn't heard. This was one of those occasions. I leaned over and kissed Liza's ear.

Some hours later Misha got up to say he was going to share with the finest audience in Russia 'a very good safe joke. The safest joke in the province,' – he kerfuffled his whiskers – 'told me the other day by my old auntie.' Everyone knew he'd just spoken three lies for their personal delectation and laughed dryly.

'I'm keeping it back as a pledge for your orderly departure. Our friends Charlie and Elizaveta have before them fifty years of life together. They need an early night. It's a long way, fifty years, isn't that so, ladies?'

'What's this about the ladies?' It was the man opposite me again. 'If I were to be starting right over again, I'd take my wife's sister. She does a man better. Let's hear no more about how the ladies feel. It never goes well when the hen crows. You all know the proverb.'

'When'll we know to go home?' asked another.

'First day of Lent.'

'At an exact hour, on the stroke, that'd be the most sensible thing.'

'That's what I like to hear,' boomed Misha. 'Simplicity. One word, one meaning. When you hear the bells of my falcon you'll know it's bedtime.'

'What does he mean?'

'It doesn't matter. Drink while you can. Take advantage of good fortune.'

Misha let himself fall backward; plummeted onto his chair, on which he bounced upon landing; a man made large by the magnificence of the evening and his own gusto.

Liza said to me with full red lips, 'If there were only one word allowed, what would we choose?'

'I'll tell you later,' I whispered and I cut up her sterlet and placed the first snowy flakes on her fork, which I guided to her lips. Everyone cheered. We were unashamedly in love amid the guttering candles and paraffin lamps and the scent of birch-wood in the hearth and the roaring gossip of the revellers.

We drank toasts in the province's purest illicit vodka. I myself drank a million. Misha said it wasn't his joke, that was still to come, but here was a question on a different plane: why didn't someone invent a perfume for women that copied the aroma of lamb cutlets fried to brown in a pan of onions?

'Why not? What man wouldn't want to rummage her instantly?'

How Misha laughed! How we laughed with him, from the sheer pleasure of seeing his belly heave and the sweat disappearing into his rolls of chins and jowls to emerge seeping over the edge of his collar.

'You should be the inventor!' someone shouted.

'Invent a new world for us, Misha!'

'That's it, one world, one meaning—'

'*Word*, Arkady you fool, *word*.'

Once more the room shook with laughter. This was a vast philosophy they'd hit upon. Eternity was too short to settle such a matter. No matter, the ecstasy of argument was in their eyes, and it would have been dawn before they left if Misha hadn't now given his signal. Louis was standing by the door. Misha motioned to him with his forefinger. Nodding, he slipped out of the room.

Moments later there was a sharp, pungent, whistling explosion from the terrace, a noise that was all the more shocking for being completely unexpected. A number of people ducked, or anyway cowered.

Misha called out, 'My cannon – my little brass *falconetto*, last fired for the coronation of His Majesty. Powder by itself, no ball. No risk of injury.'

'I suppose that's what he meant by his falcon,' someone said gloomily.

'The jig's up,' declared Fyodor Fyodorovich, the village elder. 'On your feet, brethren.'

'What's that good safe joke of yours, Misha?'

'My cannon, of course.'

Chaffing Louis, patting his head and chucking him under the chin, the couples went out to their wagon. Styopka reeled off to fetch their horse.

They were carrying their own mounting block, by which the wives had to climb up onto the wagon. They'd done it for the journey down and now it was time to reverse the process. But it was discovered that getting onto the wagon after a banquet of roast boar was by no means the same as getting off it when hungry. There was talk of pulleys and ropes and fat stupid women. The horse was led up and backed between the shafts. The wagon jolted; a lady got a nasty knock on her knee; ancient ill-humours began to surface beneath the flittering moon.

Suddenly Nicholas, whom everyone believed had retired from the evening, rushed out of the house and shouted, 'Off with you, you've had enough out of me.' He flapped his hands. 'Go away. Go back to your homes. Every single one of you.'

The benches they'd got from the inn were facing backwards. Stoutly the wives sat there in their bundled coats and shawls, watching Nicholas. The injured woman rubbed her knee with a circular movement.

The driver spoke to Fyodor Fyodorovich, who was sitting on the bench behind him. Fyodor said to Nicholas, 'The wedges are still under the wheels. If your honour would throw them up to me it would be the quickest way.'

Nicholas spun on his heel, his mouth working. 'You do it,' he said to me brusquely. The wagon rumbled off down the drive, a gallery of white unmoving faces staring at me.

Forty-five

NICHOLAS WENT inside without speaking. Liza and I were alone. The noise of the wagon hung in the night, the stones rattling beneath its iron-shod wheels.

Ghostly clouds were moving slowly over our heads from behind the house, brushing past the moon. Above the forest there were darker ones waiting, banked up. Not many stars had bothered for our wedding night. But I could see that those looking our way were green with envy.

She shivered. We turned to go in. On the top floor, we saw a candle approach the window. Behind it was Bobinski's white face, distorted by the imperfections in the glass, like a moon in a rippling pond. Wavering, it looked down on us. Then he drew the single thin curtain.

She caught me by the lapels. Dark hair, eyes, eyebrows, a wing of shadow falling across her cheek from the porch lantern. 'Let's make a start on our children. We've only one lot of fifty years.' She tugged at willing me, and folded her body against mine, the whole length, even as far down as her knees, so that she was stitched to me. She said, 'You've knees like a gorilla's. Here are the miles they've carried you' – she leaned back and rested against my arms. Her two fingers began walking up the front of my coat – 'mile after mile, mile after mile, one mile, two miles, 149,000 miles scowling at the backbone of Mister Goetz in the fierce Charlie Doig way. Grunting. Behind you two ogres shimmers poor Hpung. Then: ho! what beetle can this be looking so dapper?'

I caught her below the knees and swung her up, tossed her a couple of times to show that I had arms as well, and bore her into the house.

Misha and Louis were discussing the evening in Louis's pantry. I could see their two profiles and on the table a wine bottle.

I carried her up the broad staircase to the first-floor landing. 'Every girl should experience this once in her lifetime,' she said, smiling up at me. 'But will it hurt your leg?'

I denied it.

She said, 'In my father's time this was where all the pensioners would gather to watch what was going on in the family. Strangers and the doctor fascinated them. They were sometimes a great nuisance, like barnyard fowl.'

'Shhh.'

Our bedroom, which was over the hall, was the room traditionally reserved for important guests. Lamps were burning in the alcoves on either side of the door. I pushed the door with my toe and closed it with my heel. Cream beeswax candles filled the room with their warm light. A blue hyacinth from Misha's hothouse was on her dressing table. The fire had declined to an even glow. Louis had had the warming pans removed from the huge feathery bed just before we came up. Dried lavender stalks had been stripped into the coals. Their perfume was everywhere.

'Better than the smell of lamb cutlets,' I said.

'Hurry,' she said. 'With us it's every moment that counts.'

I let her down. We knelt and prayed before the ikons. Then I snuffed the candles and started to unclothe Mrs Doig in front of the fire.

Had he bored a peephole in the floor, this is what the person in the room above would have seen, starting at the double windows and working towards the bed.

The wooden shutters had ducks and geese carved in them that admitted pokings of the sky's milky grey light. They didn't extend far into our room. The man upstairs would have cursed as they petered out at the marble washstands.

Next he would have hit a strip of darkness. But he couldn't have failed to notice the gleam of what lay beyond and would have passed through it eagerly, thus arriving at the pool of licking firelight in which we lay. There he'd have witnessed the clumsy haste with which I mounted for the first time the woman who was now my wife.

So what had there been a hundred such peepholes, each with its avid eyeball? We wouldn't have cared.

In any case the man upstairs was Bobinski, and as I was putting out the candles I'd heard the snap of a drawer as he folded his clothes away, and the lilt of a wine-filled couplet in his squeaky voice. Then the tap-tap of his bedstead against the wall as he settled down. Later there was the slippered shuffle of Misha coming upstairs – the clack of Louis turning the key in the front door. But I may be making some of that up, for I was deranged by my love for Lizochka and could think only of her body naked beneath mine.

Forty-six

O N MOMENTS when time stands still: in the souls of all women when their children are born. At the news of unseasonal deaths or of deaths encompassed by strangers. At visions and conversions – Saul on the dusty highway to Damascus; Pierre Bezukhov seeing Moscow afresh, through the eyes of a man who had visited the bottom of the pit and survived; Bernadette at Lourdes. Blindingly, evoking in one marvellous instant some previous journey of the being – upon the first sight of a painting, at a singular phrase of music, at the drift of long-forgotten perfume, at all unexpected revelations of beauty and thus of truth. At the onslaught of genius, at the unlocking of a conundrum.

At the capture of Wiz, in that steamy post office in western Burma, let me not omit that.

On the crocus-strewn hill above the battlefield of Balaclava, when Elizaveta, in her long blue skirt and tennis shoes, conquered me.

Time halts in its tracks and our selfishness with it at all such moments. The minutes, the hours, even the days are suspended by whatever god deals with these practical aspects of magic. To say that they are then dangled over our heads ready to be dropped when things have turned for the worse is to be cynical. Magic exists. It is before us every hour of the day. Nature itself is a crawling, fluttering, hopping, humming encyclopaedia of magic. And nothing that I have mentioned can surpass the magic of the moment at which a man first enters the body of the woman he loves.

'And when he had opened the seventh seal, there was silence in heaven about the space of half an hour.'

If infinity were possible to grasp, that was my opportunity, on the brown bearcubs' skin before the embers of the fire on my wedding night. I was afloat in space, at large amid the constellations, circling effortlessly on a rocket fuelled by happiness. Hulking over her, pressing into her body with my thick haunches, I splashed her with tears of joy that I was unable to control. I called her twenty-five names that were new and beautiful. I kissed her loving eyes incessantly, and her strong-boned nose and her warm mouth and her chin and her ears until my lips were bruised. The other noises we made were the practical ones of loving – pleasure, disbelief, a slapping stream, plunkety-plunk. At my discharge I let out a shuddering cry of triumph for I knew, in exactly the same way as a convert is assured of his faith, that my steaming bolus of sperm had spied her egg and was, even before I finished shouting her name, zooming towards it like a torpedo. I strained against her thighs, so firm, so white. I kept my eyes closed and counted out loud to fifty, when I was sure they'd fused. Her fingers were spread across my buttocks, pulling me into her, making doubly certain.

Thus was Dan Doig conceived. Proudly we smiled on each other in the firelit darkness.

'One word, one meaning.' We spoke the words simultaneously, kissed and clambered into our enormous lavender-scented bed.

Forty-seven

S HE MOVED, stealthily, so as not to awaken me. I was a thousand miles away, dreaming of Goetz being carried in his
sedan chair along the hill track in Burma. But he'd grown much
larger, and his hairy nostrils were trained on me like gun barrels.
I woke with a start. 'Is it time? Dawn?'

'I have to do something, my darling. Go back to sleep.'

'Where are you going?' I grabbed her arm.

'To piss.'

'Why didn't you say so?' By now I was quite awake.

The fire had died out. By contrast the light coming through
the shutter holes was stronger. She got out the chamber pot and
took it over to the window. She stood, naked, looking through
one of the holes. 'I don't like what I see of tomorrow. Snow or
rain, perhaps both. Let's not move from here, Charlinka.'

The luminous glow of night was coming through the shutters. I could just pick out the wolf of the Rykovs loping round
the contour of the pot, one heraldically raised paw stretched
towards the handle.

She squatted. My buttock (by which I mean her buttock on my
side of the pot) bulged over the rim thus obscuring the ears of
the wolf. I don't know how this happens with women. Standing
she had such neat, contained buttocks. I'm just reporting what I
observed. This was our first night together and some things were
strange to us both, especially to my virgin queen.

'It's so cold over here,' she said. 'Snow not rain.' She frowned
in concentration as the urine hissed out of her.

'Not so hard, Lizochka, for God's sake! You might dislodge
it.'

She scampered back. I raised her side of the blankets. She dived into my tent and my arms. 'Men, you're so stupid,' she grumbled happily.

We talked of our love and going to America – whether we'd try to get Misha to come with us. 'He'll never leave when his hyacinths are blooming. He might say yes, but he'd back out at the last minute. Later in the year and it's the fruit season and then his pet hydrangeas.' She folded herself more cosily into my side. 'He'd be heartbroken without snow. He adores watching it fall. He's too old, too settled, too Russian. There's only one way he's going to leave Zhukovo.'

We lay there, my bride and I, all toasty in the warmth of our love. Outside it was snowing. We could tell by the silence.

We discussed Kobi. I said he'd never get on over there: the language, and him being such a rough diamond. I said a bit more about him – her breathing grew rough. She was asleep.

But I – my brain had switched to Alert. The room seemed like a furnace. And when I did fall asleep it was to another sequence of unpleasant dreaming. Before it had been Goetz. Now that we'd talked of going to America I had to rehearse that journey as well. For some reason I ordained that it should not be via Train No. 7 to Odessa but through Germany we must travel, to an emigrant steamer departing for America from Bremen. I saw the three of us being crammed into a train packed with Jews, fugitives like ourselves, and the German delousing cubicles where we were robbed of our money and papers. I observed closely the prison-camp conditions in steerage. I wept in fury to see my Lizochka brought so low.

At the last I saw our dead child being pitched overboard, flicked off a mat into a choppy sea of cucumber green. Doig, the chaplain called him, the surname alone, for he was only one of a number of children who'd died in the night.

It should have been a relief when I awoke, sweating, but the taste of my dream remained. The dawn of a Russian winter was in the room. It had washed my bride's gentle face with a repulsive mealy colour. I crept to the window and peered out through one of the ducks carved in the shutter. A ledge of snow was on the sill. On the ground there must have been six inches. It was still snowing, wet, lazy flakes the size of a tablespoon head. Mist was halfway down the trees, drifting across them. Everything about the house was quiet. I had the feeling of abandonment, that Liza and I were the only people remaining.

I gazed down at her, the mother of my child. Then I stole out and went along the corridors to my bachelor room, where my ordinary clothes still were.

The terrace plants, the herbs and thyme, which had perked up since the last spell of weather, had once again been clumped by the snow. The barrel of Misha's *falconetto* was moulded in white, except in the shelter of its mouth where there was only a dusting. A wren had been in not long before. The triangles of its spidery toes were clean and clear. It had alighted on the tip of the barrel, leaned over to have a peek inside – and hopped down. Peering out at winter with knowing eyes, it had defecated and left.

Snow is so destructive of the well-balanced mind. On the one hand it builds up resentment because of the personal restrictions it imposes – and on the other astonishment at its power and beauty. The Russian mind has been formed around the properties of snow.

There was no birdsong. They were mostly staying up at roost, puffing out their breast feathers to make extra layers of insulation. Why should they waste their energy on getting about? Wait until it warms up a bit, until the earth rolls an hour or two nearer the sun when a little judicious activity might yield a meal. Be sensible, not like man. If one had to be a bird on a day like this, best to be one of Misha's cripples, shuffling round a warm hay shed never knowing what titbit might next fall to one's beak.

Though rats would be a danger to them. They too like warmth. But there never has been a day in history when rats were other than a danger. They are too similar to men: besotted by fighting, either for food or for the moist raptures of Miss Laycock – the monosyllable. Was it twelve times an hour, was that how often Zincke had estimated their virility?

In this mood of mine, which was fundamentally joyful and made irritable only by a restless sleep and a horrible dream, I passed among the trees in the pleasure grounds – white pillars decapitated by the mist – and suddenly the thought swirled into my mind that by impregnating Lizochka and therefore renewing the line of Doig, I had at last, conclusively, avenged my father.

It was fourteen years ago, to the month, that he'd died by the agency of a rat.

Well!

I immediately felt more cheerful. I blew my nose into the snow and reviewed the necessity of shaving. I'd take the girl her breakfast in bed – withhold it if she argued – have a go for twins – and then know a lower peak of sensuality, eating warm new bread with cunty fingers. It was how twins were conceived, in separate sessions? She was tall enough to carry them without difficulty. Thinking about Dan and his brother curled up inside her, I looked round to see if the kitchen fires had been lit.

They had not, so I continued. I was walking down what we'd always known as the archery lawn. It was wedge-shaped with summer borders of hollyhocks, delphiniums and lupins on either side. At the end of the taper a white wooden gate led into what Uncle Boris used to call his 'mature' garden, meaning an area of shrubs and ornamental trees that the gardeners didn't have to bother about. It was on the archery lawn that Andrej had again been the hound, shouting to his sister, who was collecting for us, that there were no more arrows to come and then shooting one, zippety-zip, into the turf at her heel.

No, Andrej, that was not a nice thing to have done. Thank you for scooting off to heaven. We both know that Liza is better off with me.

I pushed the gate open, creating a pleat of snow on the far side on which it stuck. In front was the wellingtonia, the first in Russia, that had been planted by Uncle Boris's father, Konstantin, to commemorate the great man's dying. Patches of shaggy rufous bark stuck out from the plastered snow. I walked through the archway hewn in it with downcast eyes, awarding marks to Andrej for each aspect of his behaviour and then marking myself for it. Of course it was a false exercise, for I had no intention that he would turn out superior.

I noticed that my friend the wren had preceded me here also. Again the spinsterish toe marks – but oh, when one thought about it, what lustrous eyes the birdie had! And it so tiny, no heavier than a green muscatel grape! Eyes sharp enough to be enlisted for the Inquisition! Much sharper than my girl's – I thought: will she squeal when I lay my frozen hands on her, and so I came into that part of the garden that led downhill to the great swathe of rhododendrons and the rusted manorial gates that marked the boundary of the pleasure grounds.

Again I looked back at the chimneys. There was still no sign of life. I decided I'd walk as far as the ford.

It was the hinge that I heard first, as taut as a scream.

I stood stock-still. Snowflakes settled on my eyelashes. But not a single part of me moved.

A horse snickered. Thump – that was its punishment.

I reckoned he was about thirty yards away, on the other side of the rhododendrons. I could see nothing of him. All I had to go by were the sounds. There are people like that, never silent, noise growing parasitically on them like a fungus. I waited.

Then – the swirling of a string of phlegm round his back teeth – gathering it into a ball – and the rasping thwap of spit.

I hated this man immediately. I sensed it for mockery, that mustering of a whitey-grey, tobacco-streaked plug, for contempt of all who lived within the pale marked by those gates. Riding into the garden of another man at dawn wasn't something done on a whim – for an excursion.

Straightaway I was like an animal protecting its young. Liza was waking and stretching, feeling the warmth on my side of the bed to judge how long I'd been up. Soon she'd be emptying the pot, folding back the shutters, lighting a lamp or two, esti-mating the day, thinking about that breakfast . . . and I was at the bottom of the garden listening to the sounds of an unknown man on horseback who if he desired could be in her bedroom while I was still floundering through the snow. I had no hesita-tion. I hated him for trespassing on my honeymoon, for defiling the home of my love, for being invisible – a threat. I hated him absolutely. He was a danger to me. I could smell the stink coming off his animal groin. I didn't need to know why he was here or anything about his appearance, his nature, his religion or his political views. That he was, was enough. I rammed the hatred into my heart and pressed it down with my thumbs until it had filled every wrinkle of the sac.

I was in the middle of the glade, exposed on all sides. But I stood my ground. This was the path he'd have to take. Hands on hips I waited for my enemy amidst the falling snow.

Forty-eight

I T WAS not one man but two. They were fifty yards away, not thirty. White storm capes, the pelts of their ponies dark beneath the mottling snow, their sly, cautious movements – it was hard to pick them out. It was only by a plummet of snow knocked from a branch that they gave themselves away. Once it had fallen and no bird had flown out of the tree, I was able to piece together the mosaic.

Two of them, small men judging by the height of their ponies. Rough fur hats or *shapkas*, one of them black and one white, dark scarves, the capes spread over their ponies' quarters. Rifles slung over their shoulders – clumsy Nagants, the wood going to within a few inches of the end of the barrel, just enough room to screw a bayonet on. Black stubble, days of it, running with the grain of their jaws, heavy round their mouths. Troglodytes, driven out of the forest by the weather to gather food.

Or for some different purpose.

My Luger was in our bedroom.

It was Shubrin who came first out of the trees. The second man, Glebov, was riding in his tracks. It was Glebov who'd spat. He did it again as I watched. Raised his head, looked directly at me, and spat.

I didn't budge. I held my hands behind my back. They should come to me.

They were bundled against the cold. Hunched, dirty, unslept, defeated. Riding anxiously, not at ease with their ponies. I thought, they're new to these animals – or infantrymen. There were only two ways for the ponies – to turn right around or to continue the way they were going, towards me: the rhododendrons were like a high green wall on either side. These men shouldn't be having to push at them and snag their mouths. Horses aren't fools. No creature with a man sitting on his spine can afford to be a fool.

So who were they? Raiders from the forest would have come in a gang.

But there were just two of them, two small dark men.

Glebov pulled out and drew abreast of Shubrin as they reached me. Leaning forward, one shoulder huddled against the snow, he rested his forearms on the pommel of his saddle and studied me. Insolently, blue eyes narrowed beneath their slanting lids. He was wearing black skin gloves. His was the white *shapka,* on its left side the scarlet cockade of his regiment.

The ponies kept blinking the snowflakes out of their eyes. After a bit they dropped their heads, sadly, an action that included some expectation of a blow. They were unclipped. Their winter wool was curly, like astrakhan. Beneath their bellies it hung in hairballs clotted with ice and mud.

Glebov went on staring at me. The other, Shubrin, was acting as the leader. A younger man, possibly soft: pudgy cheeks, teeth too white, his bearing too agreeable.

It was Shubrin who told me their names and their regiment – a cavalry one with a middling reputation. Their colonel had been Prince Balachovsky. That was how he said it, in the decidedly past tense.

'What happened?' I asked.

'They got him,' Glebov said. 'What else do you think could have happened?'

He needn't have said it like that. 'How?'

'Some of the men were having a meeting in camp. Balachovsky marched over and told them to get on with their work – which was to do with watering the horses. The ringleader, a man called Stolz, said they wouldn't listen to him until he'd reduced himself to the ranks – become their equal. He said, Never: what would you do without officers? They caught him and sliced the epaulettes off his uniform. "Well, how do you answer now?" said Stolz. Balachovsky said they could cut his throat before he'd do what they wanted. And they did. They looted the chaplain's quarters and drained the Prince's blood into a silver chalice. Then they gave it back to the chaplain saying, "There you are, the blood of the lord."'

I said, 'That's the sort of story one reads about savages in anthropology books. Were you there? How did Balachovsky's throat look?' I was remembering Hpung.

Glebov replied, 'I was out on patrol, trying to find a way to outflank the Germans. The regiment had buried him when I got in. I never saw his corpse . . . It was chaos. The Germans were pressing us hard.'

I said to Shoubrin: 'Did you see any of this? Is it true about the Prince?'

But he belonged to a different company from Glebov and Stolz. He'd heard about such an incident – and then – it was true, the Germans had attacked and he made a run for it just as the regiment broke. His voice was tired.

Impatiently Glebov said, 'Let's get to the point. It was half dark when the Germans attacked. Stolz was yelling at his group of conspirators to desert with him. One of our men had got hold of a machine gun. He was threading a new belt of ammunition. I said to him, "Do you believe in our Little Father and the holiness of Russia?" He said, Yes, who else is there? I said, Then turn your gun on Stolz. He said, Why? It was too much to explain in a short time so I kicked him out and did it myself. Shot him and Stolz. They came after me, my own men, but it was easy to escape because the Germans were in among us and everything was in confusion. That's the point, our escape. That's how we come to be here, damned hungry.'

Shoubrin took over. 'The bolsheviks are like the worst slanderers with their lies. What they call the truth is the complete opposite to what any reasonable man knows it to be. But they put it so cunningly that people who are illiterate are immediately persuaded – as if they've had a vision. The "sweet lepers" was what our adjutant called them . . . Anyway, I got out at the same time as Prokhor Fyodorovich,' – he jerked his thumb at Glebov – 'we met in the forest. I almost shot him, thinking he was coming after me. We joined forces . . . Headquarters said, "You two are invaluable because you really know what people like Stolz are capable of."'

'They've sent us out to recruit,' Glebov said. 'We can tell the peasants the truth of how it actually is, and the danger we're in from these revolutionaries.'

'Why Popovka?' I asked.

'We picked it on a map. You're to recruit in the sector east of Smolensk, they told us.' Glebov threw back the corner of his cape to get at a *makhorka* cigarette. 'They're going to pay us a bounty. Ten roubles for every man we bring in.'

His blue eyes looked me over. 'You're worth ten roubles.'

'That's not the way to beg a meal,' protested Shoubrin. To me he said with an engaging look, 'I don't really know anything about this fellow. We just found ourselves in the same mess. Two heads are better than one – you know. Pay him no attention. That was a silly thing to say, about recruiting you. Besides the innkeeper told us that you travel on Imperial papers. You're an important explorer, he said.'

'And that your wife is your cousin, which according to geneticists – ' Glebov drew heavily on his cigarette, which he had cupped within his palm to keep it from the snow. He appeared to be sucking his knuckles when he inhaled. He expelled the smoke lazily – like a monarch, another snub in my direction, '– is improper, not to say harmful to future generations. That's the way you get lunatics.'

I said to him evenly, 'Do you want a meal or don't you, cunt?'

'Rocking lunatics in the cradle, that's what you'll be doing,' he said, rolling his eyes and looping his tongue into a grotesque imitation of a cretin. 'But that's your lookout . . . I could have shot you as you stood here. From the wood.'

I thanked him for letting me know.

'Perhaps you don't hear about the war that's going on. Perhaps you don't much care for fighting.'

'Why would you have wanted to shoot me?'

'Because your gloves are better than mine. Because I'm hungry. Because I want your woman. Because I want to sleep in a soft bed. Could be anything.'

'You call those good enough reasons for shooting me?'

'Who said anything about good?'

'What we call civilisation.'

'Listen. You asked why and I said why. I might have said, Because I don't like the look of you. It's a reason.'

'What else did the man say to you in the tavern?'

'Only one word that was interesting – food. We'd been riding through the forest all night. Stopped for a couple of hours in a woodman's shelter. As cold as being on a planet. Had to pick the ice out of my horse's nostrils or it'd have suffocated. Not even a morning turd on the go when we reached Popovka. I pulled the innkeeper from his bed and said I'd shoot him if he didn't have a meal ready in fifteen minutes. That was when he said it – food.'

'He was just an innkeeper, your usual coward,' put in Shubrin.

'I said to him, I can't eat words. He said, Of course not your worship but if you rode on down our street you'd end up at the Pink House where you'd find the bits of a wedding feast still on the table. So here I am, *Doig*, dirty, tired and hungry.' He produced my name with an ironical flourish.

Shubrin said, 'We beg a day of rest, nothing longer. In the name of the Little Father, our Tsar Nicholas, for the future and greatness of Russia, we supplicate thee.'

It was the traditional entreaty.

Glebov ignored him. He said to me, 'You never answered about why you're not fighting.'

He looked me in the eye: in a straight line, as straight as it comes. He was still leaning on his pommel, a gloved hand swinging from the wrist. Staring into my skull, as I was into his. We were like criminals competing for the same patch; agreeing on nothing except, in this one long concentrated glare, upon our hatred of each other. At the same time probing for hints as to technique and indications of character defects. I thought, He must have hated me as instantaneously as I hated him.

Why? I had a reason: to protect my woman. But what reason could he possibly have?

Shubrin said, ' Finished with each other?'

Glebov said, 'He hasn't answered me. Ten roubles would buy me a whore.'

I went up to his pony standing so dumbly and jerked at its bridle. 'You know why. I carry Imperial papers. Also typhus. Now go to the kitchen and get them to heat the bathhouse.

Hand over your clothes to the women to be powdered. One louse is enough,' and I shot him between the eyes with my look. 'Walk your horses.'

They dismounted, both of them. Glebov was about five four, five five: up to my chin without his *shapka* on.

Glebov said, 'You still haven't answered. I'm odd, I like answers.'

'I'll slice your lips off if you want.'

Shubrin made pacifying gestures with his hands. Glebov, nodding and sneering at me, kept his mouth shut. They started to lead their horses up the glade to the Pink House.

It was snowing much harder now. The fires were going in the house. I couldn't see the smoke in the snow but I could smell it. The wind was rising. As we came into the stable yard, tongues of snow were already reaching out from the pillars. It was where it always drifted first. Styopka was at work on them with a heavy wooden shovel.

Glebov brushed past him, not speaking, not even looking at him. He went straight to the wall by the mounting block. He threaded his reins through the first in a row of rings, tied a hitch and put his saddlebags over his shoulder. He said to Pashka, the older of the two stable boys, 'Check the oats for rats' shite.' Then he marched off stumpily towards the house, looking foolish in his storm cape. It had a long swallowtail shaped to lie easily on a horse's back. It trailed along the ground like a ballgown and left a ripple upon the fresh snow.

'You'll have to carry your train when we waltz,' I shouted after him.

Shubrin said, 'I don't understand why he behaved like that. He's really a very clever man.'

Pashka spat. He was untying Glebov's clumsily knotted reins with numb fingers. 'Couldn't even tie a pig up.'

Forty-nine

NICHOLAS WAS in his office when I got in, being buttered by Fyodor Fyodorovich and another peasant for his generosity last night. The latter had his beard bent into his mouth and was chewing on the end of it, his eyes fixed on Nicholas.

'You always exaggerate,' Nicholas said to Fyodor. I thought there was a bilious greenish tinge to his cheeks. Or perhaps it was the combination of the paraffin lamp on his desk and the dim morning light. 'Just saying thank you is sufficient among friends.'

I said, 'When people have had a good time they like to exaggerate. It puts a polish on what they enjoyed most.'

'I suppose so,' Nicholas said.

'If only we had the likes of Thunder again,' Fyodor said, 'you know how cows love to have a good-looking bull rubbing against their flanks – they become quite placid and would give such milk that your honour's calves would be worth a hundred roubles at six months. We could hire him out, as we did Thunder—'

'You never told me about that,' Nicholas said sharply.

'*Barin . . .*'

'No, you never did. Do you think I'd forget it? What happened to the money?'

'Here, in this very place, I myself counted the golden roubles onto your desk. Two piles of five, ten golden coins. How pleased we both were! Surely, your honour—'

Nicholas waved them away and put his blond head in his hands. From the wall behind his shoulder a photograph of the Tsar regarded his discomfort with bearded sympathy.

Passing me by the door, the Popovka peasants bowed and

made deft, humorous enquiries about my health and that of Liza. Had we slept well? Had we quarrelled already? Was that why I was astir?

I asked if they'd seen two men ride through Popovka early. They'd stopped at the tavern and then taken the track through the wood and over the ford.

They looked at each other. 'We heard them go past,' said Fyodor. 'That was all. It was too soon for me. I did more living last night than I should have.'

I sat down opposite Nicholas and said jokingly, 'You shouldn't have hung onto Andrej's grub for so long. Not as fresh as it was a fortnight ago. You should see yourself.'

He had a way of rifling you with his strong blue eyes until you looked away. Not saying anything, the stare doing the job by itself: the artifice of an idle or weak-minded man. I let him get on with it. If you gave way on the small things, you could do whatever you liked with him on the big ones.

He suddenly said, 'I think I have to vomit.'

'Stick your finger down your throat.'

He returned looking brighter. 'You may have been right about the food – I shouldn't have skimped like that – do you know, Charlie, what just occurred to me? Whenever you ask two peasants a question and they look at each other before replying, it's because they're cooking up the answer. In just one glance they agree on every lie that has to be spoken. Remarkable . . . Now, these two soldiers who want to stay . . .'

I explained about Shoubrin and Glebov: what I'd said to them. For twenty-four hours and no more.

'Oh – oh, let's think about it. Good families, would you say . . . ?'

I was saved from having to answer by Louis's knock. Pashka was outside with the carriage to take Helene to the station. Nicholas leapt to his feet. 'Thank God someone remembered – if she had to stay any longer – Charlie, you'll give support if she goes for me, won't you? Say I've been vomiting? Won't you, old chap Charlie?'

Pashka had harnessed the high-wheeled winter coach, which didn't have rubber tyres. It was spartan inside as well, having a hard bench and no armrests. Helene started to protest, making all sorts of squawking noises, like one of Misha's chickens. But the more she yammered the more courageous Nicholas became. We bundled her in and told Pashka to get on with it.

Louis said there hadn't been a sign of Liza yet. I looked up at our window. The shutters were still closed. I tossed up a bit of gravel, then another. She came to the window, my darling, white-robed and expectant, waving her lovely hands at us and beaming.

We went in, Nicholas saying, 'I hope to God Pashka doesn't get blocked by the snow and have to bring Helene back.' In his office he started up about her again. 'She's bleeding me dry and teaching my sons how to do it as well. They only care about my money – my own blood, Charlie! She's made them into strangers! What is life doing to me?'

He rose from his chair and threw his arms round my neck, sobbing. 'How have I gone wrong? Whatever I do, other people do the same things much better. If I'm a failure at forty-two, what shall I be at seventy?'

I said he shouldn't brood so much, alone in his office. It was at the back of the house, by the laundry room and the door that led out to the stable – without creature comforts – a sunless solitary hole. I took his arm. We walked past the domestic quarters towards the drawing room.

The hall stove had been fired but its warmth had yet to spread. In one corner was a table and a couple of deep chairs for people putting on their slippers or waiting for the weather to clear. We sat down. Louis passing, I asked him to bring us some chocolate.

'So, what's to be done about these men?' I asked.

'Go upstairs to Liza. Make the most of her before you start collecting troubles like mine. We'll speak of the soldiers later – this evening.'

'Now. They're already in the kitchen.'

'Oh, Charlie, how should I know what's to be done? It's all too much – too much, too long, too endless. At least if you're poor the decisions are fewer . . . What's your opinion?'

'Kick them out.'

'To Popovka?'

'Farther.'

'I don't know . . . Anyone on Imperial service deserves a

night's rest and some decent food. Just because one was cheeky to you . . . You should have slapped him down, right away, that's your fault. And we don't know that they're *not* of good family, do we? . . . We'll give them a couple of nights and then send them away. There! We'll have fresh company at dinner. It'll stop us getting melancholy shut up by ourselves.'

I said to him, 'Nicholas, there's two of us here who don't need more company.'

But having solved the immediate problem, his mind was wandering away to look for thicker gloom. 'The generals should get a proper grip on their men – shoot as many of them as they need to. And Stolz and the chalice – I still can't believe it. Russians just aren't capable of such an act, not our sort. I suppose Stolz was one of the urban scum. That's the difference. You take any city regiment and you'll find it riddled with Stolzes. But in the villages you'll get Russians of a very different colour. Look at Popovka. I know, a tiny example, but that's what our country is made up of, lots of tiny examples. Our friends should have no difficulty recruiting in the villages with a story like theirs. What was the head money again?'

I told him – ten roubles. Immediately he reverted to his usual preoccupation with money. He was like a shopkeeper worrying himself to death over a missing pair of bootlaces. He talked of getting the Cossacks from their base in Smolensk to beat through the forest. How much he'd have to pay them, what the bag might be . . .

I asked him how he thought he'd get the bounty money actually paid to him. His mouth turned down. 'It's that arsehole Trepov at the Treasury, not a rich godfather,' I said.

'I'd forgotten about him . . . It was only an idea. These are hard times and I must consider everything . . . well, that brings us up to date. Tell Louis the attic'll do, where those parasites spent their lives devouring my inheritance. That's where it's all gone, Charlie, I'm telling you. This is how my father reasoned: what shall I do today? Answer, have a good time. Tomorrow? Have a better time. Next week? Have the best time ever. At least I don't have that cross to bear. It's become impossible to amuse myself however hard I try. Nothing's funny any more . . . Oh, just see to it all for me.'

Fifty

Glebov and Shubrin were in the kitchen. Misha was having breakfast at a little table in the drawing room, in front of a weak fire: ham, two sorts of yellow cheese, both from Popovka, a bowl of apples from the loft, tea with cherry jam. His napkin was tucked in at his neck. He wiped his mouth, reached up and kissed me.

Louis was slapping up the cushions. They'd obviously been carrying on the chat they were having last night. I told them what had happened in the garden.

'Pah! You Russians!' said Louis angrily. 'Don't you have any other speed beside fast and slow? I want to get things straight again. I have the plan laid out in my head better than any general. This room first, having moved the furniture, then move the furniture back . . . Now here are two more men stamping round the house calling for God knows what. Russians! Is there nothing in the middle rank of speeds that'll do? I'll leave and then you'll wish you knew how to behave better.'

Misha said calmly, 'Sit down with me, my fine friend. It's the snow that's putting you out of sorts . . .'

'Never! It's the mess.' Louis shaped his waxen hands expressively. 'The snow's like a virgin! A bride!' He touched my sleeve. His dark fat face was suddenly alive with pleasure, from ear to ear, as if he was going halves with me in my romance. He said, 'I saw her! I was passing her door. The chevalier in me cried out – I couldn't resist! She said, "Are you trying to starve me?" I had a tray sent up immediately. Oh, Mister Charlie, what are you doing down here when the most delicious winter peach is waiting for you?'

I took the stairs two at a time. Nine strides across the landing where the pensioners were wont to gossip. Whoof! I flung myself across the bed with a thump, at which she rose involuntarily, pillows, magazine and all – levitated.

She'd finished eating. There was a fleck of egg yolk at the corner of her mouth, which I scraped away with my fingernail. A zest of chocolate was on her breath.

The tray was on the floor. She was lying propped against half a dozen pillows and cushions, reading a copy of Country Life with an advertisement for Fry's cocoa on the back cover. She had a shawl round her shoulders. She looked at me over her scarlet-framed spectacles. They came from Paris, the same train of thought as the scarlet walls of her room, and the black book-shelves and the painted ceiling.

The shutters had been folded back. The snow was falling thickly, making the air completely white except when an eddy of wind burst a gap in it through which one could glimpse the speckly darkness of trees. The fire had been lit and was in good shape. There were two full buckets of coal – enough until the evening. Between the fire smell and the breakfast smell was her perfume: Soir de Paris, light, sharp, delicate, like a tangerine.

And when I undressed I found another smell, that of her body, which was imprinted upon the sheets and the pillows and rose to my nostrils like the aroma of warm pancakes. Was it of her skin or was it of the organs that her skin enclosed? Had sleep stoked them with energy? Was this what I could feel, radiating through her pores? I stuffed my nose into the crook of her neck, casting off her shawl.

Reading, or pretending to read, anyway affecting disinterest, she stared hard at the page.

'It's for my English, for when we get to Chicago. This is a report on a motoring tour from the tip of Scotland to the bottom of England – the left-hand corner. 874 miles, or Moscow to Petrograd and back again. That's all it is! Puny! Like living in a cupboard!'

'My mother said exactly the same when Pushkin told her we were going to live there.'

'I read it and I said to myself, Is that really all there is? They must have missed out some provinces. I've changed my mind. I don't want an English rose garden. I want a ranch,' which she said with curling lips. I raised her spectacles and put my hand over the eye that was peeking at me. She fluttered the lashes against my palm.

'So, only a ranch,' I said.

'It's putting a very reasonable price on my virtue. I'm a ruined woman now.'

'Not even Pushkin went that far. Mother got a first-class rail ticket to London, a new wardrobe and fistfuls of red notes but no ranch. I saw the notes, helped her count them. Then she wodged the lot into her purse and went shopping alone.' I was slobbering into her neck and her ear, taking nips of skin here and there. 'Ruined! On the contrary, my soul, brought to perfection.'

'Sensible her. Where did she go shopping? Paris or round the corner to Muirka's?'

'Oh, Muirka's. We always aimed for the blue flag when we needed anything. We could never have afforded Paris.'

'Afford didn't come into it with my family until our generation – Nicholas, Viktor and myself . . . I always liked your mother. When she told us a fairy story you knew she believed it as well. She would start to cry before we did . . . ooh, you do that so tenderly . . . I must concentrate on the magazine or I'll never be able to speak English properly. I'll be a disgrace to you. Here are some photographs, look, Charlie. The man wearing a driving apron – it wouldn't be difficult to create something more stylish. I could do that. Make the design and find some poor people who want sewing work . . . Or do you suppose it's really an old coaching apron he's got on? In which case he needs another. Cars aren't the same as coaches. How do I get hold of Igor's Astro-Daimler?'

'Hard to ship it from the Crimea to Chicago. There's a war going on at sea.'

'You have to use your hands in a quite different way in a car,' she said. 'Have you ever driven one?'

I was growing impatient. I spoke in a droning mutter through lips glued to her ear: 'One day I'll drive you through Chicago naked except for a fur coat.'

'Who's naked, you or me?'

'You. I'm wearing a yachting cap.'

'Open tourer? Like this one here, the Dion . . . ?' She speared a trembling finger at the magazine, stirring up her perfume and driving me to the edge.

'Yes. I want to boast about you, show you off to the crowds.'

'So I'm half naked in the car and you've got that cap on with the badges. Bound to have flags and anchors somewhere. You can't do *nothing* to me now, not looking like an admiral.' The red frames tilted, slipped an inch down her long nose. The lovely truffle-dark eyes were liquid with mirth and love. 'I'm getting cold. The wind's rushing up under the fur coat – into the sacred grove. No one's watching us. There's no big scandal. People just want to get home. It's winter. What happens next?'

'I'm unbuttoning your sable from the top. Like a lecher. People are certainly looking now . . . Remember, it's only a three-quarter coat. We're all thinking about the grove and hoping, No goose pimples. For your sake.'

'Is that the third button you've just undone? Is the crowd panting now that they can see my little bosoms? They're all rosy in the cold.' This came out of her in a low murmur. The magazine was drooping.

'Tell them to stand back from the car, to give us some air if they want to see the performance. I'm too occupied. Be strict. Issue a commandment. They'll like that.'

The magazine flopped to the floor. I heard the double click of her French spectacles being folded away.

I threw back the covers to expose her belly – the vital dimple and the ivory skin beneath which Dan Doig's soul was flexing. I kissed it, I kissed everywhere, and then her tufted breasts and back to her throat. 'Are they standing back yet?'

'That's it, folks, you've seen enough for the time being – stand back from the car – please – *please* stand back. High explosive is being carried.'

I cupped my hand between her legs. She was as wet as a pail of oysters.

'Come inside me, my sweet Charlinka. Fill me, blot out the daylight.'

Fifty-one

I HELD HER fingers at shoulder height as we descended the polished elm wood staircase, matching each other's steps.

'As if you were leading me out for a quadrille,' she said, smiling across.

Steam was coming off me like a horse. I could feel it blowing through my pores: pride, vanity, conceit, hope, ambition all driven to the surface by the ardency of our love. I was dripping with happiness. We would conquer the world! We would live to a combined age of 180 years and die simultaneously, a multitude of bold deeds behind us, in the presence of an untold number of spawn and underspawn.

Pace by pace we came down those gleaming bare planks, wide and shallow, that had been hewn to the Founder's specification almost exactly a hundred years before. Four generations of Rykovs had come down them, three of them in their coffins. But I refused to think of Nicholas. My bride was sparkling with the dew of love. Her lips were shining with its droplets, were puffed out so that they had the appearance of some tropical fruit that grows so extravagantly in the lull following a downpour that a foot-traveller yearns to plunge his teeth into the succulence of its creamy flesh and gorge himself, sticking his nose right into it and coating his whiskery chin with its juices.

I have lived in the Kizil Kum desert in temperatures of 110. I have ridden my donkey Bathsheba out of it and so arrived in the shaded gardens of Samarkand among peaches and apricots and vinous products. I know what ripe-breasted fruit can do to a man already turned by mirages. I know about visions, both for myself and how they take others. On that evening the opulent lips of Elizaveta were telling a story that was an epic, and I was the only man there who could read it.

Thus did she come down the stairs from our marriage bed: slim, dark, glowing, generous – perfect.

In a skirt of dark brown houndstooth from London (a gift from Andrej Potocki – ha!), a blouse of peony pink to set off her short raven's hair, and with the Rykov pearls in a double loop round her long bare neck. 'Too ostentatious?' she'd asked, playfully working the pearls round her palm like a salesman. Not today, we'd agreed, not on this of all afternoons.

Not this afternoon, not any other! Elizaveta my pearl, my angel, my very world. I loved her above all the Creation. Had I had only one empire, it would have been hers in an instant. There, take it! Take my map chest! Take my ingots, my navy, my regiments of grenadiers! She was more beautiful to me than the sum of all the most beautiful women to have existed. Tap tap went our feet in unison on the polished boards. We halted for the tenth time, both conscious of the moment, desperate to prolong it. Her knuckles came easily to my lips. As I kissed them, one by one, I looked along the sleeve of her pink blouse into her eyes. Can I say that for the first time in my life I understood womanhood? Unbleached, in its only true form? Can I be trusted on this, I with my coarseness and big bones and lumpy knees, to recognise what is not made plain to all men?

I'm not saying that every secret door was opened for me. I wouldn't know what the whole amounts to. A woman will proffer different things to a man than to another woman. But that was the notion that came to me from her staunch black eyes as we descended the staircase: that she was the top woman. I was as proud as a pig of her.

Louis, the romantic, had removed the five-stemmed candelabra from the dining room and placed them in the alcoves on the stairwell. Their flame-tipped fingers flickered in the draughts and put a shine on the dense grain of the panelling. They imparted an aura of holiness, too, reminding us that it was only yesterday we were married.

In recognition of this I stiffened my back, imagining that I'd swallowed an umbrella, which was what Nanny Agafya had ordered me to do whenever I slouched. Smiling, replete, upright – I cocked my chin.

Then I did a stupid thing and afterwards said a stupider.

The face I made at Liza can only be described as a smirk. I knew it for that the moment my words came out: 'Potocki wouldn't have been up to it. It's one thing to look up the skirts of a girl on a swing—'

'He's dead, don't say that.' She crossed herself, humbling me with her dignity. Then she whispered, 'Thanks be to God.'

I took this for a public communication between her and me, as confirmation of the thought behind my ungracious words. I blew out my chest. I was the man who'd won the hand of Elizaveta Rykov. The rest of them – nowhere! I'd smashed up the pack of her suitors, I, Charlie Doig, the son of a cotton-broker – the winner, number one. I snatched up her hand and whisked her down the four remaining steps as lightsome as a bird. Footsteps sounded in the corridor from the kitchen – entered the hall. With a sweep of my free arm, I said to Glebov, 'Meet Mrs Doig, the lady all other men must dream of in vain. Count yourself lucky to have seen such beauty.' (She started to put pressure on my arm, uneasily.) 'In the entire library of wives, there is only one frontispiece – my Lizochka. We were married yesterday.'

He'd put on a fresh uniform, crumpled but clean. He'd gone to the baths, slept, shaved, eaten and was standing there plumply, depopulated of lice and with his dampened eyebrows arching upwards at the tail like horns.

To Liza I said, 'This is Junior Captain Prokhor Fyodorovich Glebov, our guest for the next two nights. When last I saw him he was less presentable.'

Glebov bowed to me. He bent his head over Liza's hand. I studied him closely.

What I saw was not different from the morning. I knew that as soon as he straightened and I looked into his eyes, which were a hard, mineral blue-green. Perhaps he was small for a cavalry officer, I don't know enough about that. Certainly Liza was taller than him by two or three inches. Well muscled for now but would probably go to fat. Feet not much bigger than a woman's. Face – short, round and made heavy by a constant air of disapproval. His hair was black and thick, starting to go off in the centre, like Andrej's. I supposed him to be about thirty. There was a caged vigour about him; not in any particular detail but in a general emanation of purpose, of energy being held in storage. Even here, when he should have been rested and relaxed, he put forth an aura of tension.

He looked Liza up and down as he released her hand. I thought, I was right to hate this man.

I said, 'Better than Madame Glebov, I'll be bound.'

That's what I mean by saying something stupider. I should have kept my trap shut and my head down; hidden away my bride; let Glebov pass through my life, opening the window for him to leave as one would for an insect.

He looked right into me. He opened me up, not prying but scrutinising, like an inspector of souls. He was trying to get something away from me. Had he selected me personally? Had he and Shubrin turned up at the Pink House by design? I was swept by the conviction of danger pending. It wasn't going to be money, my revolver, my travel permits, anything simple. He was out for something altogether less easy to protect.

There were complicated issues in those eyes, which now that the light was coming onto his face from a different angle I saw to be bluer and paler than I've stated. I thought to myself, But perhaps he has such an air on him all the time. Maybe his parents were cruel to him and he regards the entire world with suspicion. Perhaps it's not me, or Liza, or the Pink House that he's after.

Lizochka took my hand. She pressed against me, shivering. I said, 'I'll get your house jacket in a tick, my sweetheart.'

Glebov said, 'About your enquiry concerning Madame Glebov, she was killed two days ago in the defence of Russia. A few hours before you were married, I believe. As for her beauty, no one can be beautiful in a grave.'

'I could never have known.'

'No? I shall go for a walk before the light disappears completely. I wish to see more of my host's property.'

'What nerves he must have,' said Liza as he walked away. 'Two days ago. I wonder how she was killed.'

'If it's true.'

We watched as he went out of the hall into the vestibule. He had on a mallard-green tunic (from which he pulled his *shapka*), baggy grey-blue breeches with red piping, bast slippers. He began to rummage through the assortment of boots and coats that had piled up over the years. He attired himself in a cloak; chose a blackthorn from the stick rack and stepped into the snow without a backward glance.

'It's not often that you see a cavalryman actually walking,' Liza remarked. 'They prefer to do everything from the back of a horse. Andrej had short fussy steps, as if he was afraid of falling over. And that was even after two years of desk work.'

I closed her mouth with mine, hurriedly, smudging her lips, for Misha was coming out from the drawing room. He was sketching a catchy little melody, something by Mozart.

'Well, dearest Liza, what do you make of our new friends?' said Misha. 'I looked out of my bedroom window this morning and I saw this young man hurrying to the house when he should have been dealing with his horse. I thought, The scamp! – and went back to bed. It was far too early for me.'

Fifty-two

GLEBOV WAS rarely in the house. Shubrin, on the other hand, was never out of it. After a couple of days we established that he was, by trade, a billiards professional. Tubby and charming, he exercised his skills at the expense of Misha. As I passed I'd hear the click of balls and zing! as the scoring peg was whipped back down the brass rail to zero. Another fifty points to the recruiting officer.

And he drank.

'It's so irresponsible of him,' Nicholas said. 'I know we'd be a nation of alcoholics if we could. It's only the cost and this wretched decree that holds us back. But to behave like that when things are so bad . . .'

'He may belong to a sect that expects the world to end very soon.'

'Next you'll say he knows the date. You're always making fun of me. You deal with him. I'm making myself ill with worry. The war, lawyers, my wife, the peasants, money. It goes on and on. You do something to help for a change . . . Viktor and Elizaveta were always my father's favourites – especially Liza. I was the dunce in the litter. Whatever I did I did wrong. "Look what a mess you've made of it, Nicholas. Why can't you be like the others." I'm fated to be the black-and-white terrier that's always trying to copulate with a woman's leg and getting kicked to mince by the husband. It's not nice to know one's that sort of a person. I never asked to be a Rykov. There's only one way to go if you're born at the top.'

'Give it away, cousin, and declare yourself a pauper. Many of our countrymen do. Then they take to the road and become mendicants.'

'That's because they've drunk the money away, not given it. Giving's quite different. What I'm saying is, I was never asked. All parents make this mistake. What we should consider rigorously before conceiving a child is this: would I, the parent, be grateful for the chance to have a life spanning the next seventy years – do they look like being good ones? Are our politicians getting more honest? But of course such questions never get asked except by those who shouldn't be reproducing their type in the first place. Members of our liberal wing are such a grouping. Otherwise what happens is that the man's horny or the woman's on heat and reason goes out of the window. There should be a better way . . . Man should be cleverer than that . . . what, don't you think so . . . yes?'

His speech sputtered out. I took pity on him. We shared the same blood . . . I said, 'Come with us to the United States. Liza and I have decided. We're leaving in the spring. Come, Nikolai Borisovich, we'll all go together, a family of good Russians, driven out by desperation. We'd welcome you with us.'

'Who'd buy my land?' It was what he said, quick as snap.

'A speculator . . . Don't dismiss the idea outright.'

'And I'd be the Rykov who quit. All those serious Americans would talk behind my back and say of me, His great-grandfather saved Russia from Napoleon and he abandoned the entire estate because of some trifling unrest. Look how few years it takes for a family to become degenerate . . . Me leave Russia? That's not much short of impertinence.'

'Steady . . .'

'You do it. Your father – you're close to being an American . . . Now go and find out what Glebov's doing. He's always disappearing. I've got jobs for him. And for that wastrel Shubrin as well.'

It was Glebov himself who solved the mystery about what he did during the day. At noon, when walking over to the stables, I heard two rifle shots. By dusk he'd sledded home a roebuck and had it on the bench in the game larder.

'The mighty hunter! Nimrod himself!' exclaimed Louis, nervously watching through the doorway as Glebov knuckled the skin off the animal's dimpling rump, a small figure with bloodied hands and a narrow flensing knife gripped between his teeth.

The meat was welcome. There were many mouths to be fed. But Glebov never tried to put on a pleasant face when accepting our congratulations. Even when we were eating the venison, he shrugged them off. 'It's for the common good. How are we to live otherwise? I learned something about hunting from my father.'

When he made remarks like this it seemed to Liza that he was trailing the coat of his past before us, that beneath everything he was longing to talk about himself. But when she gave him an opening he reverted to the deer and said in a surly tone, 'I shot it in the belly, its guts were hanging out.'

I said to him one night, 'Why do you take such pains to behave offensively to her?'

His eyes conceded nothing. 'Is it wrong to speak the truth? I say not. We have a special duty towards it. We are the only species on earth that can distinguish between the true and the false. We should remind ourselves of this daily, that we are superior to all other beings.'

'And a duty to women also? Manners?'

He leered at me, as if bragging about some bestial act he'd just forced Liza to perform. 'She's old enough, isn't she? Men and women, what's the difference?'

He was daring me to strike him; trying me; tapping my character with his hammer to see where it was weakest. He had this way of arguing that was impossible to counter. Taken piece by piece, his propositions were simple and logical. Morality couldn't deny them – in fact melted into their arms. It was the impression in total that was so disagreeable, of a man who scorned every aspect of civilisation, by which I mean the accepted way of doing things.

To Nicholas and Misha he was curt and polite at the same time. 'But Charlie, he couldn't leave even if I ordered him to,' Nicholas said, referring to the snow. 'Anyway, why should I? He's our butcher. He's keeping us alive. Just because you've got a brand new bride you're on the lookout for insults. Don't be so spiky!'

But it was intolerable the way Glebov was behaving. To me

– his knowingness, the veiled insults, the challenges, his stealth-iness around the house so that I could never be certain he wasn't behind my shoulder. To Lizochka – the way he looked at her body was enough. He seemed to have a hundred eyes in his head, all of them making her feel uncomfortable.

His presence grew on me. I began to disobey my own rule and to be rude to him, at which he sparkled. So I took Kobi away from his widow in Popovka and had him come and live in the Pink House, up in the attic with Glebov and Shubrin. I told him to follow Glebov everywhere. 'Spy on him. Threaten him with your shadow,' I said.

Fifty-three

THE BAD weather continuing, Popovka was severed from the rest of the world for several days while snowflakes floated down from heaven like paper saucers. By the stable boys at our end and the villagers from the other, the woodland track between the village and the Pink House was sufficiently cleared. But that was all that could be done. It began to get on our nerves.

This particular morning, the drawing-room fire was reduced to a mere wisp. Snow must have been building up on the chimney head and preventing it drawing. Puffs of defeated smoke began to return and spread round the room, making us cough. Irritably I rang for Louis and told him to send someone up with a ladder.

Presently the two stable boys appeared outside, Louis pointing upwards and showing them what was needed. First they had a good look at us through the window. Then they set about extending the ladder and getting it balanced. Pashka shouted to Louis to come back and anchor the ladder while they went up. But Louis said it wasn't his place and came in. Pashka sent Styopka up. The ladder flexed as he climbed. Pashka leant against the bottom rungs and gazed into the drawing room, angling his head to see into all the corners, to see what each of us was doing.

There came a shout from Styopka – a question – an answer – and Pashka followed him up.

Soon pats of snow and semicircular sections of ice fell hissing into the hearth, making the ashes billow out. Misha and Liza moved to chairs at the back of the room. Louis came in carrying dust sheets.

'Too late,' said Misha. But Louis spread them anyway.

'Shall we try a few snowballs down it?' It was the younger, Styopka, who was speaking. 'A bit of fun?' We could hear him with astonishing clarity. It was what snow does to noise.

'Slates'd be better. Maybe kill one of them, the lazy robbers.'

'Why do you call them that? The Count pays me. Who else would?'

'Pennies, what they can't be bothered to pick up. If it's any good it's theirs, if it's not it's ours. That's the law. Speak against it and you're put away.'

'Shh! You shouldn't be talking like that.'

'You go to prison and disappear. Rot away slowly, like shit on a cold day. Remember the monk? He was a peasant like us. Then he got too grand, and under the ice he went. That's Russia. That's the sort of country they want us to die for.'

He spat down the chimney. He must have nearly put his head down it for the noise was like a cap detonating. Some soot trickled into the hearth.

'Our family's been here since the beginning. We remember everything. Are we meant to forget the injuries done to us? Never! says Mamasha, not till the seas run dry and not even then. You'd think that too if your father was exchanged for a greyhound.'

'You're right there, Pashka. You don't have to be clever to know that.'

'It could have been five minutes ago, even though it was seventy-four years. The Count said to his friend, "That's a fine dog you've got in your carriage. Let's see it take that hare." When it did, he looked around his fields and said, "You have that man over there and I'll keep the dog." In the evening the Count rode up to the shed where my grandfather was with his milk cow and said he was to leave next morning, at six o'clock. Eight days' walk to get there. The whole family went. The cow died in a ditch – it was before the grass came. They were away for three years and a month. The greyhound was still living when they got back. My grandfather was permitted to take it for walks . . . I'd have fucking strangled it! To be bartered for a dog!'

'But what a time ago it was, Pashka. All those years that you said. Nothing like it has happened in Popovka since, or in any of the villages around.'

'That's being simple. What matters is that my mama's father was exchanged for a greyhound. I'll remember it for a thousand years and so will my kids. If the Tsar himself offered me money to forget it, I'd refuse.'

'Are you sure he hadn't done something wrong?'

'His only crime was to be standing there when the Count looked round.'

'There must have been *something*, Pashka.'

'I swear, not a kopeck. He was a fine, strong worker. Steady in the field, never missed a day. Everyone liked to work at his side, you ask your father.'

'Oh I know what he'll say. That they were all good workers in his time, that we're nothing but lazy scoundrels . . . Should we put a slate on top to stop the snow getting in?'

'How would the smoke get out, idiot?'

The ladder began to shake again as Pashka and Styopka descended.

Liza caught my eye. 'America,' said her lips, noiselesly.

Fifty-four

'IGNORANT CLODHOPPERS,' Nicholas said. 'If they weren't, they'd have gone to the city to advance themselves, wouldn't they? What they're doing is what they have the intelligence to do. Eh, Misha? Tell me if that's not true.'

But that wasn't what we'd heard. For us it had been the speaking voice of history booming down the chimney. Misha and I drew off into the billiard room, Liza following.

(Shubrin, as a joke, had balanced a block of chalk on the tip of each cue in the stand.)

We played without attention, careless about angles and not scoring. The story about the greyhound had disturbed us. The conversation soon came round to the topic uppermost in Misha's mind: the events of 1905, which had occurred when I was an apprentice to Goetz, a world away.

'In general, the moment that weapons become cheap enough the peasants will obtain them and use them against our class of person. By peasants I mean also the deprived, the disaffected and the professionally unhappy, of which every nation has a group, customarily amongst the intelligentsia. But the peasants are the most numerous.

'At the time of that rebellion the army and the police had the situation under control. There was no surplus of rifles and therefore nothing being sold cheaply. So it got nowhere. But in the provinces where the harvest had failed there was serious unrest. People were starving. The night skies were red from the flames of burning manor houses.'

He continued: 'Arkady Drutskoy was the cousin of my dead

wife. He had an Arab stallion that he'd bought from Zimmermann, who goes to Constantinople every year to pick through what's been sent in by the tribes. It was a Koheilan, as pure as the finest gold. It was called Baghdad. Under fifteen hands, of exquisite beauty and temperament. All the peasants for miles around brought their primitive eel-striped mares to be covered by this stallion so that they might have more vigorous and valuable foals. They paid nothing. They even got free stabling for their mares during the period of their covering.

'One morning these peasants decided to join the revolution. They marched against Arkady. Not to his manor house – not at first, that is – but to his stables.

'They went straight to see if Baghdad was in its box. It was. They took it out. They ate it.

'It's true, Charlie. They slit its throat, skinned it and cooked it immediately over a fire in the stable yard. It was the first action of their revolt.

'Why eat the horse at that point? Isn't it more rational to make it cover all the mares you want and then eat it? I'm not saying it was wrong to have eaten it: they were undoubtedly desperate people. But it was stupid. Anyone with sense would have taken Baghdad for his own profit and eaten one of Arkady's ploughing horses, which are enormous and would have fed a host. I always thought it was the reactionaries who behave stupidly – but no.'

He twirled the butt of his cue and potted a ball with such power that it jumped out of the pocket. 'Arkady had his front door stove in with a battering ram which was one of his own oaks. He'd had to watch it being cut down, knowing full well what its purpose would be . . . You might prefer not to listen,' he said, turning to Liza.

'I'm a nurse. I've seen more horrible things than you have or ever will, if God remains our friend.'

'It won't – affect you?' I asked.

'Bring on a fit?' She kissed me, put her arm through mine. 'You've cured me, cured me forever.' She extended a hand for dancing and we did a little Scottish sort of fling and leap, she singing, '"Oh, Charlie is my darling, my darling, my darling, Charlie is my darling, the bold chevalier . . ." Your father used to sing that to you. Remember? I do. He loved you very much. Dear Pushkin, what a figure he cut!'

Misha said, 'At times like these we must be able to remember our Pushkins and Borises. Without family affections life is a waste of time. My greatest regret is that my wife was unable to have children.'

Liza smiled across at me.

'I promise to be quiet,' she said, sitting down on a wooden chair that was painted dark green and had red swallow-tailed butterflies curling up its slender, curved legs. She pressed her knees together, placed her hands on them – arms and back quite straight. 'You get another shot, Misha. It's a new rule for today.'

He took longer than usual chalking his cue.

'Go on, friend. I'll be twenty-seven on my next birthday,' she said.

'Here is another case, that of a lady in the province of Saratov with whom I was once intimate. I'll go straight to the point: the revolutionaries gave my old lover Nyusha thirty minutes to pack one suitcase for each of her children. One suitcase – thirty minutes! Exquisitely cruel! You have to admire their knowledge of psychology. Thirty seconds – easy. You cram a book into your pocket, woollens and money into your case and run. If they give you a day – another easy one. But thirty minutes! A fraction of time in which to select from the possessions of eight or ten generations. How could a woman do it – could you, Lizochka? – with a peasant standing over you in his sour sheepskin coat, thumbs in his belt, making comments about your choice, slowing you down, picking things out of your case saying "That's not worth taking anywhere," making you so nervous you scarcely dare breathe – could you? An impossible task, I say.'

I said: 'An exceptional man would have seen it coming and dug a hole somewhere and buried the best of his objects. Done it at night. Told no one. Run his sheep over the place afterwards to conceal the marks.'

'Who can say what's coming?' Misha demanded hotly. 'Do you have this power? Have you dug a hole?'

'No.'

'Thirty seconds, that was the best one,' Liza said. 'Grab what's useful and start at the beginning again. Ancestral memories are

237

like millstones that sink all but the really strong-willed. Look at Nicholas.'

'Well, I say you're wrong,' Misha said. 'I think of my dear friends Arkady and Niusha and their children and I weep for them. Oh, I know I weep for everything. I see it in your faces – ha ha ha, the old fool, his tears don't count for a kopeck. But think of the *agony* – twenty-eight minutes . . . twenty-nine . . . thirty! The suitcase is slammed shut by the peasant – perhaps chalked, because he's heard that that's what officials do – and now you have the torture of going round the house and saying farewell to all your old friends – the rejects. They hang their heads. They whisper to you, "I'm not good enough, even after two and a half centuries, *mille fois pardon*." I'd rather be led out and shot in my own garden than suffer as Niusha did. What would sleep be without my grandfather's bed? Or a walk without my aunt Maria's promenade cane that has the painted head of a cockerel? Horrible, horrible, horrible. It'd be no life at all.'

He cut savagely at his ball and sent it whistling round the table. 'I'd say to them, "I'm bound to die anyway. So shoot me now. Put me against the old brick wall in front of the peach tree that always has leaf-curl and has never given a fruit to anyone. I'll stand for you. I'm too fat to jump around or run away." That's what I'd say to the brutes. To continue living would be worse than the alternative, of which none of us knows the truth. It may actually be very pleasant.'

I was in a cavernous armchair of cracked brown leather. Liza was on her green pinch-legged chair. The room belonged to Misha, the only one of us standing, and to his thoughtful, baritone voice that filled every inch of space with his emotions, up to the cornices.

'I thought the Drutskoys had the easier time of it – no choices, you see. First there was the stallion, I've told you about that. Then the peasants broke down the front door with the butt of the oak. They made my friends watch as they ransacked the house. They overwound all the clockwork toys and pissed into the helmets which generations of children had worn in history plays. They burned the wonderful old moustachioed daguerrotypes, danced round the courtyard in the coronation robes that Alexander Alexandrovich had worn a century ago and sawed up Arkady's best furniture to make it fit into their ghastly hovels. Pieces veneered with our beautiful pale Karelian birch – imagine the scene. Worse than Breughel. A shepherd took offence at a collection of French porcelain shepherds and pounded them into paste under his boot. They cut up the tapestries with sheep shears to make them into blankets. They drank everything they found, that goes without saying. Even a bottle of Arkady's hair lotion, so he said.

'Here's another instance of their stupidity. Arkady had a pair of silver stirrups that had been the Tsar's gift at some great ceremony. What did they do? Instead of taking them to the smithy to melt them properly they threw them into Arkady's furnace. The idiots are still picking through the ashes.

'The stones of the mansion they took to build pigsties with, and the panelling and floors and timbers to burn on their fires; roped it onto their wagons with the carvings and shrines from the chapel which they themselves had used for their marriages. They took their own saints as firewood. To do such a thing is so unlike a Russian peasant I can only think a professional agitator had been working the area.

'They bared the site. Then they ploughed it criss-cross and sowed it with nettle seed so that Arkady and his children would have nothing but stingers to return to – no birthplace, no memories, nothing. They gave them a cart and a donkey and told them to go away forever.

'The greatest treachery was that Arkady had built a school for them as well as a hospital; was paying the salaries of a teacher and doctor; had even lent them money, as Nicholas has done here.'

'If he hadn't, they might have murdered them,' I said.

'But why? You do someone a good turn and he turns round and says, Here's my thanks, and shoots you. How can it be? It's beyond reason. In Arkady's province at that time it was fatal to be caught wearing a clean shirt even. Rope, river, or pitchfork, that was the usual reaction, whichever was handiest.'

'I remember that year,' Liza said. 'Father had just died. Nicholas stayed very calm.'

'After these events I thought to myself, What a noddy you are, Mikhail Lvovich Baklushin, that the only clever opinions you possess are from your friends' letters. So I began to read ferociously. Kropotkin. Hegel. Herzen. I learned phrases from them by heart so that I could shine in company and pretend to be an intellectual. But after a time I thought, this is tripe – I could have written it myself and done so much more clearly. It got to the point that whenever I saw the word "history" in this type of book I quivered like a dog that thinks he's going to be taken hunting. Because I knew – knew – *knew* that what they were about to foist on me for the hundredth time was the idea of "history" being responsible for some foul, execrable, bloody, obscene, nightmare of a deed for which the only person culpable was the person who did it. The killer with the knife, or with the rounded stone for bludgeoning – the perpetrator. For his own reasons. Nothing to do with "history", all to do with the exercise of power and the cost of guns. History is pish.'

He sank into the chair next to me. The room fell silent. He wiped his brow. 'Was I shouting? Well, damn Kropotkin and the rest of the scallywags. I've learned my lesson. Nowadays I stick to Sir Doyle.'

'Where did all this start?' asked Liza.

'I was telling Charlie that once guns became affordable to the peasants we could expect trouble. The next thing I knew—'

'Kropotkin.'

'In a word. The source of all our woes, my dearest Elizaveta. People should be allowed to think what they please but not to publish it. That's a dangerous game.'

'And now,' I said, 'after three years of war guns are in everyone's hands. The Jews are already getting out. I've seen them. In fact Liza and I—'

She interrupted me with a look and said to Misha, 'If you knew that what happened to Arkady and Niusha was going to happen to you, would you consider leaving?'

He frowned magnificently. 'Leaving – you mean leaving our country? Running away?'

'Yes.'

'Leaving *Russia*?' His tone was one of incredulity.

'Yes.'

'Of course not. You must be insane. What would a man like me do in France? My friends, my cattle, my hens . . . How could

I die properly with all those Jesuits around? Women who walk as if they're gripping a rare piece of porcelain with their knees – no farting after a good meal – how would a Russian like me survive? Descartes this, Descartes that, none of our common silliness permitted . . .

'Listen to my morning. My housekeeper brings tea and my dogs to my bedroom. I have at least an hour before they insist I get up. If the sun's shining I hum Strauss waltzes. I read Sir Doyle and look at the view from my window. I've looked at it on over twenty thousand mornings. It never bores me. Something is always a little different – or about to be different. Every tree, every bird, every cloud is my personal friend. In the spring, when the rooks are nesting, I become drunk with joy that God has arranged that I can share His world with rooks, which are the most human of all birds. I don't care if they ignore me. That they're out there squabbling in my elm trees is quite enough. French rooks would be intolerable. I don't know how, but they would.

'Only in Russia can I lie there as I please. The Americans would shout at me. Work, you Russian dog! Improve the world! Fulfil your destiny! But why shouldn't I stay in bed if I want to? Am I disobliging someone? I'm happy. We should all be happy. It's the whole purpose of living. Our government should pass a law entitled For National Prosperity: Not Work But Happiness. Then it wouldn't have any more trouble, I guarantee it.'

He rumbled, groaned and sighed. He stitched one frown after another across his face, superimposing them so that his forehead and cheeks resembled a violent ocean. Then he'd wipe the lot away with a single smile or recollection. Liza and I rapidly became acquainted with a multitude of reasons, the large, the small, the practical and the childlike, why exile would erode Misha's belief in himself and thus condemn him to a premature death. His chickens and Scotch cattle were joined by his showing of hydrangeas and the garden party he always gave to celebrate the fruit season. He'd trust no other person than Vasili to turn the potatoes in his cellar or the apples in his loft. French fingers touching them would be the equivalent of feeding him poison.

Here he found there was a quarrel available with French laundresses. They'd be certain to infect his undergarments.

'Come, come, Misha, explain yourself,' I said. 'By dressing up in them?'

'Possibly.'

'With what disease, then?'

'Syphilis. Everyone in France has it. Their politicians spread it like jam.'

'Don't be absurd.'

'Even though I'm blameless, I'll catch it somehow. The street boys will run after me and make fun of my nose as it starts to fall off. Then the disease'll take over completely and I'll ruin myself buying expensive furniture. You ask any good doctor and he'll tell you that that's what happens to syphilitics at the end. They buy indiscriminately – insatiably – the best – enough to fill five houses unless their heirs lock them up in time. So no thank you to France.'

But in all this we were just catching sprats. His greatest reason for staying at Zhukovo swam beneath our conversation, usually out of sight but occasionally reminding us of its presence by a swishing fluke of its mighty tail. I mean Russia itself, the vast and moody leviathan that constitutes the heart, the spine and the soul of its peoples and lets none escape.

'Enough. You go. I give you my blessing . . . I'll be lonely.' He diddled his fingers on the arms of his chair. 'I thought I might see your children grow up – visit me – spend their holidays at Zhukovo. But Chicago . . . Tell you what – no, I'm lying, I'd never get to the frontier. It's better to be truthful. My legs would give way, I'd be incapable of any movement – paralysed.'

His voice sank to a whisper. 'Not ever to see Russia again – piteous Christ no, it would kill me. Even thinking about it is driving a stake through my heart. I can feel it beginning to split. Not exile, Lord Christ, please not exile, ever.'

He tossed his crumpled face from side to side and began to howl, the hot fat tears streaming over his cheeks and his lips shaking.

Fifty-five

SHUBRIN CAME in without knocking, hoping that a game was to be had. He glanced swiftly at us. 'What's the matter?' He began tapping a ball round the angles.

Misha and I glared at him from the depth of our armchairs. Liza went on staring out of the window. None of us moved.

I said, 'How many men have you recruited in Popovka? Or is drinking all you're good for?'

'It's hopeless. Only an idiot would want to enlist. No ammunition, no food, no medicines. What's the point of preaching to them? Besides – the money – what's ten roubles these days?'

'A bottle of Moët et Chandon Brut Imperial,' said Mishka.

I said to Shubrin, 'So is everything comfortable for you here? No other little thing you might need?'

'I hate sarcastic people, Doig. We don't allow that sort of talk in the hussars. But if that's your idea of a conversation, let me observe that you're not doing too badly here either. Plenty of men in the trenches have typhus. Many have broken legs, if not worse.'

'And many'll soon be dead from these causes,' interrupted Misha roughly. 'What are you getting at, Shubrin?'

'Glebov was right. That's a reward of ten roubles sitting beside you. He's married to a Russian, had a Russian mother, has Russian papers, eats our food, uses our trains – why isn't Doig fighting? Got an aversion to it, has he?'

I said that was a strong word and hoisted myself lazily out of my chair. Smiling guardedly, he moved to a safe distance. I picked up a billiard ball and tossed it from hand to hand until he relaxed. The reason he relaxed was because he was thinking only about my hand and how quickly it could smash his face up. I manoeuvred to get the others out of the firing line. Then I hurled the smooth white ivory ball into his gob from about six paces and carried straight on with the momentum of my hand, which became a fist.

He screamed and clapped his hands to his mouth. Blood welled out from between his fingers in a most satisfactory way. I pulled open the door, swivelled him by the shoulder and booted his cauliflower arse into the corridor. 'Pack and go,' I yelled after him.

'Just go,' shouted Misha.

Shubrin tottered away moaning. Louis, who was coming to tell us about luncheon, drew in to the wall to let him pass.

We had soup and then cold venison cutlets, boiled potatoes, cabbage and pickled mushrooms. Nicholas was nowhere to be seen. Bobinski smelt the food from the attic. We heard him coming down the stairs. He stopped outside the door to straighten up, then entered saying coyly, 'Goodness, what a lucky chance.'

'As if you didn't know,' growled Misha. 'How long are those worms of yours? Stretch down to your heels, do they? Could you use them for bootlaces?'

We were the first people Bobby had spoken to that day. His prattle filled our ears until Misha told him to slow down or I'd shut his mouth for him with a billiard ball, as I had Shubrin's.

'Children, why didn't you say so before? I could have eaten in the kitchen. I'm not proud. They listen to me avidly – as if I were Socrates. But Shubrin . . . No! . . . How dare he say such a thing! . . . and that Glebov . . . I've never cared for either of them from the first. I'm as likely to be the saviour of Russia as they are. A pair of apprentice butchers, that's what I thought when they walked in. I'm glad I have Kobi sleeping near me.'

This was too much for Misha. He was brooding about exile and would have preferred a meal eaten in total silence. 'Give me a hush, Bobby! I have to think. The future – a great question has just been asked of me. I may have replied too emotionally. Your chatter is ruining my brain.'

'But the past is infinitely more rewarding! Let's talk about that instead. Who wants to know about tomorrow – oh, Mikhail Lvovich, please don't send me out, I so enjoy talking to intelligent people. I promise to be quiet. I'll hold my tongue with my thumb and forefinger.'

No one spoke. The shuffle of feet as we got down to it – the chink of soup spoons on china – the tap of Misha's signet ring. Several times he looked sorrowfully at Liza and myself, sitting together.

Suddenly Bobinski said, 'Look!'

A dollop of snow fell from the stiff sprig of the holly tree outside – then another.

'But it was so cold this morning,' exclaimed Misha. He rose, opened the window and stuck his hand out. 'Nevertheless, it's thawing. God give us a slow thaw and no floods. Well done, Bobby. Well done, the herald!'

Bobinski beamed like a paper lantern. Louis, who'd just brought in a plate of warm jam and pastry confections, said to him, 'What's there to be so pleased about, Bobby?'

'Put that down and get on with your work,' Bobinski said. 'Look after the big stove, iron the napkins for this evening, watch out for leaks in the roof. That's what work is, Louis, should you have forgotten.'

Of course Louis had to answer him back, and during this ruffling disturbance I rose and, standing behind Liza's chair with my hands on her shoulders, said into her ear – lips touching the warm skin – 'Now the snow's going, Shubrin and Glebov'll be going too. If they look like staying I'll throw them out myself, whatever Nicholas thinks.'

That's what I was saying, kneading her back with my thumbs and thinking about later in the afternoon, her creamy nakedness beneath me, when we heard the sound of Nicholas marching up the corridor from his office – clumping self-righteously. He still had his boots on – the house was his.

He took his seat at the head. Louis dished him up his soup. Nicholas crammed a whang of bread into his mouth. 'Thawing,' he said, cheek bulging. 'Thank God.'

He took a spoonful of soup. Pulling at his bread again, his mouth full of mess, he said to me, 'Kobi wants to speak to you. He's just come in from the forest. Won't tell me what about. Said, "I'm not your man." To my face.'

'"But you eat my bread and live in my house," I retorted.

Rain off an oilskin.' Nicholas jerked his thumb towards the back of the house. 'In the kitchen by now, I expect.'

Kobi and I went out into the servants' courtyard. I felt the air with my nose. 'It'll be a fast thaw.'

He said, 'In Popovka they're saying it's too quick: back to snow in a day or two.' He pointed to the clouds, which now could be distinguished from each other and were ranged across the sky in chevron formation, each bar taut and nearer black than grey. 'First, they say, we'll get some wind.'

We left the courtyard and its staring windows.

'Glebov: tell me about him.'

Kobi was wearing the padded, quilty garments of the villagers under his sheepskins. His leather boots were tied below the knee. He had on a *shapka* as snug as a helmet, well down over his ears. Nicholas had lent him one of his hunting rifles, a Mannlicher .256 with a wonderfully smooth bolt action. They were best friends to each other. He had it with him now, over his shoulder. It had a leather cap over the muzzle to keep out the snow.

He said, 'The forest is full of soldiers. I see their marks everywhere. The snow is new. A small number could not possibly have left so many tracks.'

'Living off what?'

'There are certain families in Popovka giving them food. Trading takes place at night. When the dogs bark.'

'Water?'

'Some springs are still running. At the worst, melting snow.'

'Go on.'

'There's a troop that Glebov visits. They look to him as their leader. Before or after the visit he shoots a deer to bring back here. As a pretext.'

'How many men?'

'Ten. They have a good camp. In the shelter, well hidden. A spring comes out of the mosses. They've cleared a pool, right under the bank. I nearly slipped into it. They light a fire only at night and then in a brazier. They don't shave or wash in case a stranger smells the soap. They bury their shit, however hard the ground – they don't do anything that might draw attention to them.'

246

'You were that close?'

'Yards.'

'What else?'

'Two army tents. The men were in a group outside them, listening to Glebov. He was making some sort of address the first time.'

'Any horses?'

'No. I think they keep them in Popovka, hidden in the sheds of the people who feed them. I've seen tracks in the wood and near the village. So maybe yes.'

'Which?'

'Yes.'

'Any machine guns?'

'Rifles only.'

'Did Glebov see you?'

His black eyes burned me with scorn. 'Of course not.'

'Anything else?'

Tiny creases flickered at his temples. 'Pay me my money first.'

'I will when I can. What was it you saw?'

But he wouldn't tell me anything until I'd given him two hundred roubles. He was as hard as when I'd tried to bargain for the white swift, at the tea-house in Samarkand. That's what he intended to have: two hundred – one price only.

It was in the house, in my money belt. It was due to him. But I didn't want him getting ideas about Uncle Igor's inheritance. I said I'd have to borrow it from Nicholas. His look mocked me. He said he'd wait, his information also.

When I returned he was in exactly the same place, staring up into the sky. He tucked the money inside his quilted coat. 'Glebov was never in a cavalry regiment.'

'How?'

'He knows nothing about horses. A horseman walks with bent legs, waddling like a parrot. But Glebov is like anyone in a city. His legs are straight. He opens them in the stride like someone who means to use his own legs and not a horse's. I would even say—' He leaned his rifle against the wall and thrust his hand down his neck, inside the padded collar. He glanced at the louse before cracking it. He nodded a couple of times in some internal discussion. 'Getting warmer,' he said. 'I would even say he has never been a soldier in his entire life. You know how they stack their rifles, one against each other in a circle? That's how they've got them outside their tents. But when Glebov arrives he rests his rifle against a tree. I don't think a real soldier would ever do that.'

'What do you think he is?'

'I thought of Bobinski when I saw him gather the men around and make them his speech. I thought of a school.'

'A propagandist then – an agitator?'

'Or someone pretending to be an agitator. A police agent would be possible.'

'A brave one.'

'But Potocki was a man of importance. The stupidest man in Popovka knew his name. The police would rejoice to catch the gang.' Again Kobi nodded to himself.

I said, 'They executed the woman Sonja for it. They've been seen to do that much.'

'A woman – nothing. The whole gang – a sensation.'

We took a few turns round the terrace, where the barrel of Misha's cannon was starting to drip. The wind was rising. Flecks of snow were flying off the trees. Soon rafts of the stuff would be sliding to the ground.

I said to Kobi, 'He might be both. You know how it is with the Third Section. They create a riot themselves so that they can then carry out a general policy of repression. The only thing that's certain is that he's not what he says he is.'

'He's dangerous.'

'Yes.'

There was a terrible calm in Kobi's voice: 'Let me kill him. Today, as he returns. I left him with his troop of soldiers. One bullet. No one will hear in this wind.'

'Police agents are always on a roster somewhere.'

'You forget, Doig. There's a war going on. His blood would dry quickly.'

Fifty-six

S HUBRIN SADDLED his pony and left that afternoon. Glebov didn't return from the forest. Kobi was after him.

There was nothing to enliven our dinner. The increasing wind made the shutters pull at their bolts. Strange roars and whistles came from the gaps round the inner sets of windows. Draughts cut across the room like scythes, and the carpets rose by an inch. A small portrait of Nicholas's mother, which in the Russian manner he'd hung beside what he said was a Caravaggio (a huge dark and furious thing of a man being robbed by footpads) fell to the floor taking a chunk of plaster with it. Bang! It entered our morose silence and our jaws fell silent.

I'd never known the woman, even as a child. People had ceased to remember her within a month of her falling from her horse. Her portrait was without charm: a green and white woman wearing a mousy hat and gazing out of the window – past a vase of lilac-coloured tulips on the sill – at hills and trees vaguely indicated on the horizon. Italy, perhaps.

I'd have put it out of its misery, burned it. Better no mother than that one.

Nicholas exclaimed with dismay, 'Mamasha!' He rose quickly from his chair and picking it up inspected the picture tenderly for tears, and damage to the frame. He tucked it under his arm – glared round as if challenging one of us to shout 'Good riddance!' When no one spoke he left, showing me as he closed the door a face so wretched I believed he could be thinking of suicide.

I told Lizochka this and went after him. But all he did was turn on me and bark, 'Why are you following me? Do you want my mother as well as my sister?'

As I was standing there nonplussed in the corridor, Kobi came out of the kitchen. He was soaked through. He left a pond at every footstep as he waddled towards me. Quickly I asked him for the news. Glebov had vanished off the face of the earth. Shubrin had left the district completely – had ridden into Smolensk. Kobi had nothing further to report.

When I returned to the dining room, Bobinski had gone to his room. Misha was on his feet, stretching. 'Tomorrow I'll go back to Zhukovo. It'll have forgotten what I look like. Vasili and his sons will come for my cannon and the chickens. Tomorrow or the next day.'

The wind was causing puffs of smoke to backfire from the hall stove, like wisps of grey hair from beneath an old lady's bonnet. Every timber in the house seemed to be vibrating as Lizochka and I walked up the stairs to our room.

Our bedhead was an immense affair of carved wood clasping in its centre a blue padded lozenge dented and discoloured by a century of distinguished heads. In the wall behind it was a metal shaft connecting a weathervane on the roof to a disc and a brass needle in the vestibule, so that anyone could read the direction of the wind and thus assess the temperature of the day without having to set foot outside the house. It must have been for the benefit of visiting mariners.

The vane was a dolphin with an arched neck. In a breeze it would oscillate with an indolent motion as though sporting among the seas of a warmer climate. But now . . . with every gust it twisted, rattled and screamed like a cat with its tail on fire. It was only a foot from our heads. A sinner being toasted in hell would have been quieter.

Lizochka was sprawled across me, her head on my chest. Between the screams of the shaft, I said, '*Dusha moya*, I insist we make definite plans for leaving before that thing drives me insane. Which day, at what time on that day, with how many cases. I'll need to go to Moscow to see what vessels are intending to sail.'

'If the agents know.'

'This'll be a rough trip. Not like going to Baden-Baden. No hatboxes, couchettes, sliced salami for breakfast, tickets in a folder.'

'Shouldn't we wait until you get a reply from your Mister Joiner – Norman?'

'I'll cable him then.'

'Charlie – must we do anything as drastic as this? Smolensk is my friend. I know the people, the churches, the tram conductors, the colours of the river – everything there is to it. I get frightened thinking of what lies between here and Chicago.'

'You won't have time to be frightened. We'll be on the move the whole time.'

'I'm just telling you what's cosy for me now that we're married. I'm like any wife, I want to nest. Anyway, there's no point in *cabling* Norman. The telegraphists do nothing but play cards and plot. Misha told me. Why don't – why don't we wait until there's a new government before deciding?'

'If it's a decent one why would we want to leave? A rotten one and we ought to have left in advance. Stop procrastinating.'

'The novelty of America is the only good reason for going there. We could write to our friends and get them to join us. America as a toy, think of it—'

'A toy! Sweet Mother of God—'

'Charlie, I'm very comfortable here. It's my home. I'm beginning to agree with Misha. It'd be good for Daniel to be born in the land of his forefathers.'

She was exasperating in that sort of mood. The unexpected was the only thing of which she could never tire. If it didn't exist she would invent it, and by a perilous line of reasoning come to believe her invention. Perverse she was, and neurotic and tantalising. But never common. I loved her.

Going back to her remark about the telegraph, I said, 'Maybe there's a point and maybe not. But I'll try it, tomorrow. I'll ride into the city and hand my cable to the manager in person. Tell him I'll wait until it's been transmitted.'

'Fold it in two and insert a present,' my love said drowsily, as if she was indifferent to the whole affair.

It was getting too much for me. I said, maybe shouting, 'Are we going or not? What's got into you?'

'I'm just being realistic,' she said. 'We wouldn't be the only ones. There'd be a swarm. If you're the boss of a garments factory in Chicago, are you going to be in a hurry to hire a naturalist? Norman is important to us.'

'That's more like it,' I said. 'That's being positive.'

'What was wrong with it before? Everything I said was completely valid . . . That noise the shaft's making – what's the name of the composer everyone's so wild about? He conducted his own music in Smolensk last year. It sounds like him. What was he called? It doesn't matter. It'll wait until tomorrow.'

She braced her palm against my chest and pushed herself off, back into her own territory. 'So long as we do something by the end of the week . . . Nicholas won't press us . . . We could stay here as long as we wanted . . . Now, Dan Doig, it's the sandman for you and me . . .'

A rustling noise came from her throat, despite the wailing inside the wall space. When she put her mind to it, she could sleep through anything.

I thought, somewhere there'll be a panel in the wall to get at this machine and oil it. I dressed roughly by the light of my candle and went up to the attics. Bobinski's room was directly above ours. Perhaps there was an entry point there.

Narrow stairs, entering the attic corridor nearer one end than the other. Small bedrooms and box rooms on either side. Four rooms down, on my right, Kobi was sleeping – or would have been if I hadn't given him a night off to rod his widow. On my left was Glebov's room, wherever he might be. Next to it, candle-light showing beneath the door, was Bobinski.

I went in. He was asleep, the side of his face resting on his folded and prayerful hands, the flickering flame chasing shadows around his papery skull. Innocence, not a maggot left in that withered frame.

The knotty old varnished pine boards were unbroken across walls and ceiling. Above the bed was a print of the Repin picture of slaves hauling a barge up the Volga. I leaned over Bobinski's dreaming head and tilted it – just in case. There was no panel. If anything the shaft was louder here than in our room.

He stirred. A tremor deepened the wrinkles in his forehead. He twitched the coarse grey blankets up to his chin. I puffed out his candle. That was the way that fires happened.

The wind was racing down the corridor. Shielding the flame of my candle, I went along to Glebov's room.

His blood would dry quickly.

The bed was carefully made. His better uniform was on a

hanger on a wooden peg. Two shirts were folded on a chair. The top one was cotton, good quality – too good to belong to a soldier or to a police agent. I looked round the spartan room. Was it you who blew up Potocki and my infirm uncle? Then Kobi should have found you and shot you like a rabid fox, his boot on your neck as he squeezed the trigger.

But why would he want to come back? Was it to get Nicholas or Misha? Then why so complex a ruse as this, why not a bomb from a safe distance? It didn't tally. It would be bravura on an operatic scale to have wormed his way into the Pink House as his victim's guest.

So maybe there was no connection with Andrej's murder and it really was coincidence that he'd fallen in with Shubrin and they'd pitched up with us.

Then what was he up to in the forest, consorting with deserters?

Nothing was wholly clear to me. Thinking of my wife: *Kill him then. Kill him and clear out.*

On the coarse drugget by the bed stood his indoor slippers, neatly. (They were ours.) He was reading *Notes From the House of the Dead*, using as a bookmark the visiting card of M. Neumann, Furrier, with a Moscow address. A relative? Friend? Dupe? A small sum of money in kopecks stood in three tidy columns on the small table.

'I despise money,' he'd said to Misha one evening in the drawing room.

'So do I,' Misha answered. 'Especially the brass coinage.'

'What did he say to that?' I asked Misha later.

'Looked at me as a scientist might, as you might look at a beetle. Wondering where exactly the pin should go in my thorax. Not a drop of humour to the man.'

I remembered that exchange as I stood there. The room was without humour or odour.

Idly I opened the table drawer, its only one. Two pairs of rolled-up socks, woollen underlinen both short and long, and a silver Maria Theresa dollar, obviously a good-luck charm. Beneath the clothes was a plain envelope, unsealed. I flicked it open with my thumb and drew out ten blue sheets, folded once, of small black handwriting.

Fifty-seven

LET'S CALL it a letter, though it had none of the usual formalities. The thoughts commenced in mid-flight:

The hairs that grow on your upper arms are a continuation of those on your back and those that crawl down your shoulders. They cease at your elbows. Temporarily, for they start once more as we get closer to your wonderful hands. The hairs go along your fingers as far as the nails. There may be men in Russia with hairy elbows. I don't know. You're the only man I've known. When you first covered me it was like being under a black horsehair mattress. But then I found your buttocks, which were only downy. I like that thick black hair against my skin. I wish I could be a virgin again and have you master me, ordering me about as I lay there like a white slug not knowing what to do or what you might like. Your hair excites me. I expect you can hear the change in my breathing as you move against my smooth skin. One reason is obvious. The other is that as I squirm I'm imagining that I'm being done by a caveman who's killed in order to get me. I'm worth blood! I'm the reward! I know this man'll stop at nothing in our lovemaking. It's that, together with your hair, that excites me and makes me act as I do. You are him, Prokhor Fyodorovich. You are my caveman and I tremble every time you swaddle me with your black animal pelt.

I sat down on the pile of Glebov's folded shirts.
Some of the sexual details that followed were frank for a

woman. All were written in the same matter-of-fact style, in the same tight, secretive writing. I had the idea of an active volcano being explored by a pioneer who descends into the steam, peering and prodding with his alpenstock whereupon the volcano snaps tight its jaws. Poor prisoner Glebov! Yes, that was what I felt. So intense was this lady, whom I saw at a break in page four signed herself 'S', that for a moment I pitied him.

Should she shave her pudenda? Would he like her a stone fatter? (If so she hoped it would be laid down on her breasts and not hang off her arse.) Did he like her best unbathed? Would he like to enter her by the moon-hole? It had become very fashionable, she said, during the monk Rasputin's tenure at the court. He wasn't to feel that he was obliged to have her that way. She just wished to feed her man's every desire and share in his pleasure thereby.

Some of her musings had a political tinge. (She imagined for a paragraph that she and Glebov were building a hut in their exile settlement in Siberia. A bee got caught in her hair: shrieking, she let go of the apron in which she'd been holding the nails, whereupon he'd had to teach her a lesson, right there, on the sweet-smelling but clogging sawdust.)

Many were religious: palm fronds, pilgrimages, angels of love, poverty itself a reward. It was wild stuff, the ecstasy of the divine. One might have supposed it written under the influence of a drug.

I sat on, warming Glebov's shirts, the wind rattling the doors and the ten blue pages stirring in my hand. Were they written by his wife, whom he'd told us had just been killed? Were they fake – a decoy, or ciphered for some key words in that apocalyptic tangle? He'd gone to no pains to hide them. I folded them carefully along their crease and replaced them.

I thought of the book he was reading. I looked round his monkish cell.

Glebov! I was closing in on him.

'I'll shoot his balls off,' I said and picked up the candle-holder.

Then I heard the footsteps on the stairs – wavering, teetering. They halted. A lumpy dragging sound took their place. He couldn't make it. He was coming up on hands and knees. He was drunk.

I blew out the candle and positioned myself behind the door. The Luger was in my room. I had nothing. But he was a small man, a dwarf, and drunk.

It was eerie listening to him crawling up the steep, narrow staircase. He was like some creature from the swamp out for a kill: slithery, determined, breathing hard.

At the top of the staircase he paused, trying to remember which way his room was. The thin boards of the corridor wall trembled; he was hauling himself up off the floor. Blind hands fended him off the walls as he approached. He got to Bobinski's room. His fingers scrabbled along the woodwork like mice. His footsteps – six inches back for twelve forward.

He stopped. He was thinking, is this Bobby's room or mine?

The night was bat-black dark, the wind roaring and whistling down the corridor like a locomotive in a tunnel. The weather-vane continued to shriek in Bobinski's room. I could see nothing. I flexed my fingers and wondered at what height his neck would enter the room. Was he so far gone he wouldn't be alarmed if I fumbled him? I thought of his fat neck. I brought it to the front of my mind, a pale hairy stub containing the repulsive life of Prokhor Glebov. I posed it for my chopping hand. No! Too hit or miss. I picked the places for my thumbs. Cheesewire would be better, and a hook to take the strain—

'Help me. Charlie, *please*—'

I crashed open the door. Her nightdress was dark blue but black was the stronger colour at midnight. The sob wrenched my heart from its lining. I stuck out my hand and felt for her. 'Where? Say where, quickly – quickly.'

The noise came from my left, farther away than I'd expected. It was of snow sliding down a roof, hastening as it went. I threw myself forward to catch her. Too late, she was heaped on the brown linoleum floor, crying, and it was her foot I had hold of first, a slipper with a pompom. Her ankle was bare. I made my way up her body, which was shivering like a quicksand beneath her nightdress. I found her face, cold and running in tears. She clung to me, arms of steel round my neck, mouthing gibberish. Bed was where she had to be. I pushed her down. I burst into Bobby's room and took his candle and matches, knocking the chair over as I did.

How could it have happened? Why had the disease chosen to visit her at this point, at the pinnacle of our happiness?

I got her downstairs to our room. She clutched my hands as I tilted to her mouth the dark bottle of elixir that Pflob, the apothecary, had made up for her. She gulped at it greedily.

It contained morphine. I don't know to what strength he had mixed it, I forgot to ask him. It quickly dulled her senses and let everything that had been at war within her fall back into place. She told me once that having a bad fit was like having church bells pounding in the cortex of her brain – jarring, jangling, clashing, so close to her soul as to push her to the edge of annihilation.

But this had been a minor attack with none of the humiliations that were possible. In half an hour she was breathing smoothly again. She wanted to speak about it, to exorcise it. She was lying in the centre of our bed, bolstered behind the shoulders so that she could lean against the blue padded bedhead in comfort. Her face was haunted in the candlelight. Deep shadows were around her eyes and in the lee of her nose.

'Why did it happen? A warning? Is it possible to be too much in love?' she asked.

'Never.'

'But there may be a natural limit to one's happiness, as there is to the length of the day or how far the tide comes in. Could the heart get filled up and everything after that just spill over and be wasted? Maybe that's where I'd got to.'

'Spill onto the ground for the dogs?'

'For all the animals. They depend on us for everything else, so why not happiness? One sees happy dogs and horses and cows. They're capable of happiness. I could understand how such a system would fit into God's scheme.'

'*Dusha moya*, if God's just, suffering will inevitably have good fortune coming along behind it.'

'Inevitably as a mathematician would define it? Like zero at roulette?'

'Yes. There'll be someone in charge of compensation.'

'Compensation only? You mean, no surplus . . . ? Charlinka, tell me your opinion: does God have a rule that the total of

257

one's happiness in life must exceed the total of one's suffering? I would so like to be sure that He does.'

'Not for peasants. Their means of happiness are small and their possible hardships very great.'

'That's why Nicholas helps them in so many ways. Thinking of their example is another reason why I should accept my disease without complaint.'

She smiled at me, full of repose and dignity. I was sitting in an easy chair by the fire. I'd gone down and fetched a basket of logs. I was resting my jaw on my fingers, listening as she washed the subject through her system. We were at one with each other. These were good moments.

She said, 'If only one could be absolutely certain of being rewarded for suffering, if it was like childbirth, for instance . . . People who are especially religious must have their prayers answered on some occasions or they wouldn't go on praying. We have to believe that God is reasonable. Therefore, can He have any purpose in making someone ill if that person is not to get a benefit from it?'

'But may He intend some people to be ill from the very start – to shoulder the burden for a hundred others? Another possibility: perhaps God just isn't.'

'Charlinka darling, this is how it must be: either there is no God and my fits are going to get worse and worse and eventually kill me, or He's going to compensate me properly. Not just a hundred roubles and a grumpy handshake, but something that would give me lasting pleasure, like good health for you and our children.'

'Dan Doig is just a fraction of the compensation.' I went over and kissed the black pools of her eyes.

'Mister Doig also,' she whispered, stroking the hair back from my brow. ' Mister King Doig, the father.'

'You'll have to be patient for the rest,' I laughed. 'But we're young, and when we get to America—'

Immediately her face grew pinched again.

'It's not exile,' I said quickly. 'We can come back whenever we want.'

'*You* can. But for a woman who's built a home and a family out there – why stir up the pain all over again? You're asking a lot of me, Charlie. You're not a proper Russian. You don't *know*.'

She was starting to get agitated again, despite the morphine. I wanted to beat my head against the wall. It was so obvious to leave, so stupid to dither and bicker. She and Misha and Nicholas, it was as if they'd formed a conspiracy. Hydrangeas of all things. *Hydrangeas*. Fucking hydrangeas and the fruit season and duty, which in the case of Nicholas was itself a mountain of granite.

I poured her another spoonful of Pflob's elixir. It was the last in the bottle. I said, 'I'll ride into Smolensk for more as soon as the snow clears a bit.'

She looked at me dully and with reproach.

The wind had dropped to a hoarse breeze. The shaft was giving off only an occasional rattle. 'Tomorrow,' I said. 'I'll go there tomorrow. A night like this'll blow the roads clear.'

She was ready for sleep. Her travelling clock said it was three in the morning. I got a pile of coats from the vestibule, heaped up the cushions from the daybed and made myself comfortable on the bear skin in front of the embered fire.

Fifty-eight

ITS COLOURS flickered beneath my eyelids, something to do with the Vikings. Soon my dreams were livid with all things red and black turning into red and a smoke-streaked orange, these being the flares of the landing party from the longship whose beak I could see grimacing on the dark water of the bay. I saw the rush of men, the swinging arc of double-headed axes, blood spurting from the split skulls of the priests under the terrific pressure of their intelligence, and the white thighs of their serving women as they pulled up their skirts to show the red-haired raiders the way.

But I heard nothing, which was strange.

An ice floe, painted brilliantly by the leaping flames, came steering past the headland reefs and into the bay. Its leaning mainsail was a sheet of flame and the other little gussety sails that it wore on top like castellations were flickering gas-lamp blue and yellow. A watchman gave the alarm and with both hands raised a brazen ram's horn to his lips. He was broadside on to me. His cheek filled. The horn vibrated with his effort.

Still I heard nothing.

The raiders looked up from their pleasures, glanced over their shoulders at the ice floe which was now a warship gliding into the bay under bare masts, finished their women off with frenzied thrusts and ran, leaping like giants over the seaweed-slippery boulders.

And now the noise was turned on for me.

Shouts were throughout the air, and farewell laments from the pregnant women, and the mewling of seals and the suck of the black night's tide. A pencil-thin strip of scarlet dawn lay across the horizon like a sarong. I had the notion that a clipper was approaching the bay, toiling in the wake of the warship. I screwed up my eyes. They were gritty with salt – I bathed them in a pannikin of sweet spring water handed to me by Slype, my old headmaster, who was holding ready for my use his black steel binoculars. I trained them on the clipper. It was laden with Franciscan monks who were to beat back the Viking raiders. They were gathered in the rigging, their brown habits doubled and tucked in at the waist – bare legs, alpine calf muscles like those of Goetz. They were speaking, but a language of which I knew nothing.

And all of a sudden into these dreams of mine, among a hundred sounds of fighting that I was trying to sort into their historical epochs, there tumbled a noise that was completely dissonant from the scene spread out before me: a tumbling rant of church bells, without shape or form, so insistent that it drove out all the sounds of the Vikings and the wailing women. Everything was expelled save for the raging bells and the clipper, whose crew of monks was spread across its rigging like a roost of buzzards, while the ship itself drove silently through a flat sea of ink. They were completely separate, the noise and the vessel. The clangour of the church bells became solid, a heavy violet curtain. Behind it the monks began to fade. They were waving goodbye to me, their brown-sleeved paws growing smudgy.

I became desperate. I thought, Why are they undertaking this stupid voyage when the Vikings have already left? Do they intend to pursue the longship to the edge of the world and slay them with godliness? Have they enough water on board?

I thought, Why are they waving to me like that? Which one of us is doomed?

Next I knew was the wretched light of dawn and I was cold and stiff and Nicholas was kicking me.

Fifty-nine

I ROLLED AWAY from him, onto my knees. I was still in my
dream. It was extraordinary that Nicholas should be standing
there, a greatcoat over his nightgown, a candle-holder in his
hand, shaking and blubbering. I couldn't help looking at his
feet. They were six inches away. I hadn't seen them uncovered
since we were children. They were white and slabby in the
gloom, like a plate of sturgeon fillets, his toenails as long as a
mammoth's tusks.

I said, 'Why are you kicking me?'

'The news . . . it's so terrible . . . I couldn't bear to be alone.'
His cheeks were puffy, his mouth like a child's.

'You'll get splinters,' I said.

But he just gaped at me, snivelling.

Kicking me awake and tortoiseshell toenails and the man
unable to control himself – I said: 'I can't help you if you don't
speak.'

Behind me Liza stirred in the big bed.

I rose and shook him by the shoulders. Through his tears he
repeated, 'It's terrible . . . the end . . .' But I didn't want Liza to
hear anything that was terrible at this time of the day, and she
having had so little sleep. I was dressed except for stockings and
boots. I grabbed them and shovelled Nicholas out of the room.

He was in a bad way. Suicide – or his slippers (he had a new
pair, he kept on saying) – or to go back to bed – or church and
prayer: he didn't know what he wanted. I got him to settle for
his slippers. That quietened him, that and having me around.
We went downstairs to the dining room. There were still plates
and glasses left from last night.

I said to him, Where was Louis?, but he didn't respond.

It was the warmest room in the house, being in the centre and with only one window. We sat down, not moving any of the rubbish.

He put on his whiney beleaguered voice. 'Louis has left.'

When I didn't reply but just looked at him, wondering how he would manage if a real calamity occurred in his life, he said, 'Someone must have ridden over from Popovka during the night to warn him. Servants always look after their own skins first.'

'Why not?'

'A good servant would inform his master first if there was trouble in the offing. It would be his duty. Then he got himself taken into Smolensk – at least he didn't steal one of my horses. That would have been prior to them ringing the bells.'

'I heard them in my sleep. But cousin, is it just about Louis you were kicking me?'

'The bells woke me up. I thought, there must be a fire at the inn or something. But they have their own water carts for that, and my bed was so warm that I stayed there. Though I was too ashamed of myself to go back to sleep. I should have gone to the village. I know I should. But I just lay there and considered what other reasons there could be to ring the bells.'

He started to blubber again.

I got angry. 'You're behaving like an infant. Tell me the worst and get it over with.'

'On and on went the bells. Then I heard a horse outside the window and one of the peasant farmers calling my name. He even threw a pebble up, while I was putting on my coat. I could only just make him out in the darkness. He shouted it to me, twice. I didn't believe him either time. I ran downstairs and barefoot into the yard, more or less as I was when I came to wake you. He told it to me again. I *had* to believe it, there was no alternative. Why would this simple man want to lie? I brought him into the kitchen and poured out a *lampachka* in the proper way. I felt there should be some formality to our drinking. Though why I should have cared about such a thing in the circumstances, I don't know. We drank together. We cried together, that's why I'm like this. Then this peasant and I, we went outside and got down in the slush and prayed for Russia and for every single one of her people. Then he rode off and I ran upstairs to your room . . . Oh, Charlie, Charlie, what's to become of us all?'

'Have we surrendered?'

'Worse! A hundred times worse! A million times, worse than our greatest writer could imagine. They must hate our class in a way we could never begin to understand. To have rejoiced like that can only mean hatred and fear. He thought they loved him everywhere. I expect he consoled himself with that knowledge when he went off to shoot pheasants in his doleful manner or when he leafed through his collection of postcards. He'll have said, "But they love me, it'll be alright in the end."'

'The Tsar?'

Nicholas went straight on, weeping and sniffing. He turned up the collar of his greatcoat. 'Yet even in Popovka, which is by no means progressive if you compare it to Smolensk, they rang the bells for an hour. Under our noses! How they heard of it in the middle of the night – that's another story . . . The fact is that he's gone. Our Little Father has stolen away. That's what all this concerns.'

'Don't be so histrionic. They were saying it's the only way out months ago in Samarkand.'

He said solemnly, 'Yesterday or the day before, Tsar Nicholas II of the Romanov dynasty signed a deed of abdication, sitting in a railway carriage at Pskov. Only the other day we were celebrating their three-hundredth anniversary. Now – gone. Took out his pen and signed where some general said to sign. Put it back in his pocket and lit a cigarette.'

'Who gets it?'

'His brother, the Grand Duke Michael, if he accepts.'

'After him?'

'God knows. Wherever you look there's chaos and ruin. What I prayed for kneeling in the snow was this: I said, Lord Christ, who suffered and was crucified for us, preserve us from a republic. I didn't say it pathetically. I know I can feel sorry for myself but not this time. I knelt upright, with my fingertips touching the bottom of my beard.'

'Some republics have worked. The United States of America is one.'

'Because they're all refugees, no other reason. Think what a republic usually means: bloodshed, instability and the loss of privilege by the ruling class.'

'Yes, the guillotine took care of many a privilege in its day.' The door had opened behind us. It was Misha in his dressing gown – black collar, cuffs and sash, black frogging across his chest on a pink field. He had on his yellow Turk's slippers. He'd watered his hair but his eyes were veined and heavy and his cheeks had a poor colour.

'So who will be our Robespierre?' He swayed on the balls of his feet, hands rooted in his pockets. 'I'll wager we haven't heard his name yet. He'll be hiding behind others, watching and listening, the eyes within a mask. Maybe he's not yet here, but in an attic in – I don't know where, some liberal capital like London . . . So the Romanovs have gone. Well, I'm fifty-eight and I'm not going. The rabble can come and find me. First they'll kill my animals and my chickens. Then they'll scratch their heads and say, We'd better polish off old Mikhail Lvovich in case he makes trouble for us. Aim! Fire! It'd take a blind man to miss me. Much less painful than a lump in one's throat or stomach. I've done well. I shan't complain.'

Nicholas looked at him hotly. 'That's a typical Baklushin remark. Everyone complains when they die. It's always too soon. What's a million times more important is how we're to live. Will I have to give my land to the peasants? My cattle? Ploughs, horses, everything that I have? How equal will I have to be? What will I live on?'

'But your debts will disappear,' I said.

'If they take your cattle, Misha, they'll take mine too. What'll I do with the three cases of drench in my office?'

'Drink them. You'll feel like it.'

'The whole thing . . . it just doesn't bear thinking about . . . What sort of constitution is the country to have? Who's to make the decisions?'

'Not our sort, we may be sure of that,' Misha said. 'We're to be the new Jews.'

'Exactly, prejudice at every street corner. Ah – but wait a minute – from now on every citizen is to have rights that can't be taken away. Yes, rights! So they won't be able to say, Hey, you're the Jews now and we're going to give you a taste of a pogrom, because if they do we can turn round and say, But we have rights, we demand protection by the courts. That's it, isn't it, that I'm to have the same rights as you or Pashka? . . . No, my worry is this, that *every* Russian is to have a vote in the new system. That means women too. Dear Christ, Helene with a vote . . . She'll use it spitefully, nothing's more certain. A pessimist would say it's the end. Adieu. Done for. Finished.' He drew his index finger across his throat.

'Glebov,' I said. 'He never came back last night. There's a coincidence for you.' But neither of them heard me.

'There's no need to panic, Nikolai Borisovich. Nothing's going to happen in a rush except for millions and millions of words. You know how it is with us. And then . . . things may change for the better. A glorious victory. Or something no one has thought about. Understand this, the cake's not baked yet. And revolutions never happen in cold weather. History teaches us that. You've got time to do what you want. My own answer to the abdication is this: I'm going to send for Vasili and go home.'

But his stance, his garb, the manner of his speaking, none of these suggested that he was going to do anything hurriedly. He slapped his cheeks. 'That's better, that'll get the blood moving. I'm not used to being awake at this hour of the day. Now, what's left that I can eat . . . ?'

Nothing was going to stop Nicholas. 'No no, we must do something *now*. Louis has gone. Why? Obviously there's a plan to attack us and he's been tipped off. Where's Kobi and my Mannlicher? Charlie, you're a professional shooter, how should we arrange our forces? Oh God, who ever thought it would come to this . . .' An idea came to him. He raised his hand – 'The Cossacks! The Smolensk Army Corps! Someone should ride and fetch a detachment – without delay – oh, but the snow . . .'

Slumped muttering in his chair, he dashed his hand across his brow.

On the table, among the scummed plates and dried bread rinds, was an unfinished bottle of Crimean rosé wine. Misha seized it by the neck and poured himself a tumbler. He walked over to the window, had a taste, pulled a face. He surveyed the terrace – half-melted snow, the dinginess of his cannon. He said something – a murmur.

'What's that? Speak up, Misha. It's important I know what everyone's thinking.' Nicholas tapped the table with a spoon for emphasis. When Misha continued to look out of the window, he went over and stood close to him – right at his elbow.

Misha turned slowly. He looked Nicholas up and down with his heavy eyes. 'Why is it important? You're too stupid to know even what you're thinking yourself.'

'I have duties in a crisis like this. I have to act for the good of all the Rykovs of the future. Consider every possibility, chart a path through the hazards, be leader and guide. Our family's been prominent for a century. Mine's the judgement to carry it for another century.'

'Piss and shit.' Misha upended his tumbler and slowly wiped his lips down the length of his sleeve. He pushed Nicholas out of his way with the back of his hand and made for the bottle. This time he didn't bother about the glass.

I sat watching them. Liza and I would stage our own abdication, even though I had to use force on her.

Nicholas exclaimed, 'A motor vehicle! If things get too hot for us up here we'll grab a lorry and motor south, to the Crimea. We'll take over Igor's villa. All of us. Liza's his heir, it'll be perfect.'

He had more to say, but Misha wouldn't let him, dismissing his scheme with a contemptuous flick of his fingers. 'You asked what I said. I'll tell you. You'll be a much wiser leader for knowing it. I said, "If only one could be sure of a bullet. A bayonet coming at my belly – or a pike – I'd be sick." If that wasn't exactly what I said, it was what I was thinking.'

Sixty

L IZA DIDN'T awake until midday. I went up to tell her about the Tsar and the letters I'd found in Glebov's room. She asked where Glebov was. I said Kobi was keeping an eye on him.

'He makes me shiver,' she said.

'Another reason not to delay.'

'But you haven't heard from Chicago.'

'Let's get there first and then worry. Sweet Christ, we have to get to Odessa, find a boat to take us to France – that's a life's adventure in itself and even then we're only halfway. To make a start, that's all I'm asking for.'

'It's not like biting an apple to have a taste. It's all or nothing you're after.'

'That *we're* after, Lizochka. You and I and wee Danny Doig.'

'Don't think you can blackmail me.'

'Get on with your argument, then. Reasons why we shouldn't leave tomorrow, numbers one to ten.'

'What I want to say is that I can't give you all of me. Every hair, fingernail, mole, limb, you can take these to America. But my heart stays. Today, tomorrow, forever.'

'You can grow a new one, an American heart.'

'This will always be its home. This is where it eats and sleeps and loves – here – in Russia – in this fabulous beast of a country.'

Dear God how I groaned. It made my water boil to hear her speak like that. Obstinate! She made a pig look like one of those rotting liberals in Turgenev who believe in tolerance and clemency.

I said, 'What's your price, Mrs Doig?'

She looked at me shrewdly. 'But you don't have any money. And you've said yourself that you'll have nothing to do with borrowing in case you fall into the pit like your father. So how will you pay my price?'

'You'll take a slip. You can't refuse me that. Payable at 180 days – no, make it a twelvemonth.'

'So quickly?'

'I'm confident in myself. So what's your fancy? Not many Russian husbands would be so gentlemanly.'

'We don't even have the word. Except in eating. *Dzhentelmenski nabor*. Gentleman's Relish, an English milord paste.'

'Well?'

'The price of "yes"?'

'Yes.'

This was a conversation I'd conducted leniently. But now we could fiddle-faddle no more. We were at the gulf.

She took my big hand, pretended to read the lifeline, and kissed the palm. She said, 'Exile, that's the only realistic word.' She stopped my lips with a finger. 'I know you said I could come home when I want. Did you hear that – "home"? You don't really have one, never have. Moscow, London, South America, Burma, Turkestan – the world. So you can never understand what exile would mean.'

'Home is what we'd make in America.'

'A lesser home. I know that in America they've got all sorts of things that we don't have here – more useful objects, more comfort, better doctors and medicines. It'd be safer for me to have Daniel in America. I agree with everything you can say. But it would be exile for my soul. That's it, Charlie.'

'But it's peopled with exiles,' I cried. 'As Nicholas said, the whole nation is made up of refugees like us.'

'It was the idea of America that gave me my fit. My heart heard what my brain was planning and retaliated. It'll happen again and again, bound to . . . I'm just an ordinary weak woman. Exile would kill me, Charlie.'

I took her hands. 'I'll get the best doctors there are in America . . . My heart, Russia is becoming dangerous for our sort. The grandsons of men who were exchanged for greyhounds want their revenge. The Tsar has gone. The sewage of the past will burst out and sweep across the plains and choke us to death. Maybe not today. Misha said it properly: not until they find their Robespierre. But soon.'

She lowered her eyes. I felt I'd weakened her resistance. I said, 'Alright, the day after tomorrow, then.'

'A respite, that's all I want. I never believed he'd leave us. None of those other Romanov men would have. They were all so huge. Tall men never give way. But Nicholas is so much smaller. Petity and trying not to be.'

We dickered on about her Russian heart. My saying that in any case half of it was Polish was ill received. (Bobinski went up to his room. We heard him moving around, the floorboards squeaking.)

She started to expose a monstrous argument, that the respite should last until Dan Doig was born. I told her not to talk balls. My temper rose – turned yellow, bilious, like a chemical experiment. I gave her a week to settle up with her heart. After that she'd go over my shoulder and I'd carry her to Chicago as a rug.

Sixty-one

'WHAT TIMES we live in!' – I spoke the words reflectively. It was evening, around six o'clock. We were sitting down to eat. Misha had persuaded a contrite Louis to dine with us: he hadn't had a thing all day. He was standing over him, pressing down on Louis's shoulders and forcing him into the chair. From the corner of his mouth he said to Bobinski, 'Well, Bobby, you're the scholar among us, aren't these strange times? Is this our Thermidor or isn't it? Will any of us be alive next month?'

Bobinski had been unable to grasp the momentous nature of Nicholas's abdication. He conceived of it solely as an historical fact, to be bracketed with its companion date, that on which Mikhail Fyodorovich Romanov had been elected to the throne of the tsars three hundred years before.

However, it had by no means escaped him that Louis had attempted to flee beneath the cloak of the night and been frightened back to the Pink House by the uncouthness of the crowds surging through Smolensk railway station. All day he'd been alternately cursing him for a traitor and wandering around the house plaintively calling his name. He put a bowl of soup in front of Louis with exaggerated deference.

'Were you in your slippers, Frenchman? Did you still have the curling tongs in your hand? Don't look to Mikhail Lvovich for protection . . . I'm speaking about your great funk. But when you got there – the crowd so boorish, eh! Language too strong, was it? Nasty pushing and shoving, was there, monsieur?'

Misha tried to nudge Bobinski away but the old man wasn't going to be crabbed like that.

'You have to be modern to get along these days, monsieur.

Modern means wearing a European suit and polished black shoes. Never brown in town – I expect that's what went wrong this morning. You've learned your lesson. Now you must drain the cup of repentance. To the last sip – of hemlock, tee he he . . . Back with your old friend Bobby, what a disappointment for you, monsieur! And at your age, when you're just beginning to think, What's left for me, what challenges and discoveries . . . Enough. Here we both are again. Welcome home, friend!'

Louis, struggling to rise, reoccupied Misha's attention. 'Sit there and enjoy your food or I'll get angry. It may be our last meal. What do you say, Bobby, Nicholas, Charlie? Will we be like the Drutskoys in '05? Will the peasants rise up now that Nicholas has abdicated?'

The words were balancing on the edge of his lips before springing off. Others were clustered in the air before him, like bees. We were sorting them out, each of us picking words that were interesting—

Clump – clump – clump. Cavalry boots came marching self-importantly up the corridor from the kitchen, stamping and scuffing.

Nicholas went to the door. It opened before he got there. It was the dwarf Glebov.

I looked at the boots that had warned us – drabbled with mud but at least he'd taken his spurs off. I looked at his short, hairy face, which told me nothing.

'I welcome you to our meal, Prokhor Fyodorovich,' said my Lizochka, rising from her seat with such exquisite control and courtliness that he could never have guessed.

She was wearing her long-toed scarlet shoes, a pair of baggy cream cotton pantaloons with a wide scarlet belt *au chef de brigands,* a cream blouse and a loose silver fox. At her throat was a purple choker on the point of indigo and lying like pigeons' eggs in its folds the full glory of the Rykov pearls. Mrs Gaudy I'd called her as we came down the stairs. She'd smiled, happy to be within her best colours. Not the entirety of her bottom but sufficient of it could be read from the unconstricted quiverings within those Turkish pantaloons. I yearned to be the chair beneath her and so, I could tell from their glances, did the other men.

She was as tall and slim as a statue. Holding herself perfectly and looking at Glebov like a friend, she said, 'Our food is your food. May God's blessings be upon all in this house.'

'Amen,' we intoned. I found myself bowing to Glebov, for the ikon was directly behind him. 'If you ever have to bow, bow low' – I remembered Mother's advice. But I was bowing to God, who only requires a dip of the head. I crossed myself.

We sat down: Glebov spoke. He'd had to go into Smolensk yesterday on some 'light' affair of business – a bill that had fallen due for payment was the suggestion – met a friend and become absorbed in the heady matter of the abdication. This he announced to the company in an unimportant voice. Casually, so to say. He looked round, saw that a place hadn't been laid for him, went through to the pantry and returned with cutlery, glass and a plate. He stuck his finger into the borsch and stirred it around to see what meat rose to the surface. He sucked his finger clean, helped himself and sat down.

We goggled at him in silence.

'Excuse me, Count.' He stood up and stretched right over the table to get at the lump salt, which he proceeded to grate over his soup between thumb and forefinger. He crumbled his bread, ate a spoonful of soup and said, 'It's a step in the right direction.'

'Have you seen Kobi today?' was what I said, also casually.

'He's in the kitchen, drying his clothes.'

Nicholas was white round the mouth with anger. 'What do you mean, a step in the right direction? Don't you realise what's going to happen now? It's kaput we are, Glebov. All of us and that includes you.'

'Apologies, I was referring to the soup,' he said smoothly. 'There was nothing to be had in Smolensk except bread and turnips. Only the rich can afford meat these days. Anyone with cattle to sell could become a millionaire.' He looked at Nicholas and then Misha: pale blue eyes veiled with mockery. 'Horses too. Hoarding has turned into a most profitable trade.'

'So what *is* your opinion of the abdication?' Misha said sternly.

'One thing's for sure, he'll have to pay for his train ticket like anyone else.'

Nicholas said to the company at large, 'But who's going to

rule? In 1905 no one could have been in doubt. We were reassured by the weight of his power. Who is there today with that strength?'

'Well-meaning idiots,' Misha said. 'People of the stamp of Lvov and Kerensky.'

'Kerensky's no idiot,' Lizochka said. 'Read his speeches.'

Glebov smiled brilliantly on her. 'A woman with a political opinion? One who reads speeches? First class. Our society must encourage women.'

'What society is that?' asked Misha.

'I meant our people as a whole.'

Nicholas continued, 'The terrorists must be smashed. But who's to do it? That's my point.'

'Everyone's a terrorist now authority's gone.' It was Misha again.

Nicholas said, 'Our armies, the naval forces, the railwaymen, the factory workers, they all want some impossible new disposition of authority. Everyone is to be equal. Capital is to be put on the same footing as labour, officers the same as their men. Thank God for our constitutional rights!'

I was getting restless. I couldn't abide the daintiness of Nicholas's approach or the pious shape of his lips. What I wanted was to crush Glebov and get out. No theorising, no wishy-washy stuff about rights. Just *crush* him. As in pulverise, as in shreds and atoms and an eggcup of dust.

Nicholas was talking – was still talking: 'There used to be one spoon in the soup. Today there are fifty and none of them clean. Lvov, Kerensky, Urusov, the deputies – who actually has the power? That's what we need to know.'

And now my bride. She was on the top of her form, having smoked a hashish pipe. In complete command, hand on her jutting hip, her silver-foxed elbow grazing the ear of Bobinski, who moved his chair a fraction and smiled fondly up at her.

'Whenever we think of an ideal ruler we use ourselves as the model. Thus we want someone who's sober, hard-working and concerned about our children. He should be afraid of God: this will show up in the humaneness of his policies. He must live decently, be tidy in his dress, have good manners, be affable to all classes of society – and yet be a man that our enemies fear.

274

Tsar Nicholas did not have that last quality. We need not mourn his going. But as my brother says, who next?'

I was so proud of her! I made a scene, moving about on my seat so that I could gloat at each of the other men in turn.

Nicholas said, 'The model for our new leader won't be a factory worker in Petrograd, that's one thing that's certain.'

Lizochka looked down like an angel at Glebov, who was on the other side of her. 'What's your contribution to the conversation? Who'd be the perfect ruler for you – a factory worker or a Robespierre?'

She glanced over at me, her eyes exultant.

'What makes you choose his name?' he said, blinking.

'A revolution is happening. Sixty years ago slavery was abolished in the Russian Empire. Now the Romanovs have abolished themselves. Everywhere the cry is "Down with Autocracy!" or "To Every Peasant His Vote!" Isn't that a revolution? There's always a Robespierre around at times like these, snatching at the hanks of power that have come loose. Don't you want to be him?'

She walked over to my side of the table – stood at an angle to me – looked back at Glebov in her severest intellectual manner. So strong! So beautiful! That nose! And her eyes so obviously brainy that I forgot for the moment that this was the woman who couldn't decide about America.

She went on: 'But I'd say you must hurry if you want the job. May there already be a Robespierre at work? Count Potocki was assassinated on the orders of someone. My maid was executed for it – but she was no Robespierre. Somewhere at the centre there is a dominant man.'

Bobinski said. 'I call that an excellent question. Answer her, Glebov. Every soldier has a bit of Robespierre within him – the desire to eliminate opposition. What's soldiering if not that?'

'If Glebov is a soldier,' I said.

'More than you, Mister Stay-at-home,' he said confidently. 'Your papers are worthless now he's gone. I could conscript you tomorrow.'

'So where were you soldiering last night?'

'It's a revolution, *madamochka* said so herself. A man's duty is no longer to the Tsar. It was for the State of Russia that I was working last night.'

'Humping for the common good,' squealed Bobinski with delight. 'Oh, the duties of a soldier, one after another.'

Glebov looked the tutor over scornfully. 'What's your purpose in life, old fellow? Amuse me. I've had a hard two days of it.'

'My purpose? You mean God's purpose as transmitted through me?'

'Don't be clever. Tell me what good you've done for the world.'

Bobinski rubbed his hands, blew on his fingertips. He beamed upon Glebov with ancient eyes and a mouth containing a few small teeth the colour of Sauternes.

Louis, speaking for the first time, 'Give him the short answer, Bobby.'

'I've taught three generations of Rykovs everything they know. I've emptied myself for them and on the strength of that the Rykovs have dealt charitably and honourably with the people of Popovka. That's the good I've done, and no more of your insolence, young man.'

Nicholas broke in: 'All I've ever sought from life is an honourable reputation. That's the highest rung on the ladder as far as I'm concerned.'

'A man who works and fights in his shirt. Count Rykov, a good honest farmer and that's all. Well, well.' Glebov tipped his chair back.

Bobinski wagged his finger at him. 'I said no more insolence. It's not fetching in a guest.'

'You trivialise humanity, old fellow. What of industry? What of the advancement of the sciences, of medicine, of engineering? Improve these and you improve conditions for everyone. Living becomes a pleasure. But charity and honour, if that's all that's come out of your teaching – pah! You're nothing more than a stupid old man. Is nothing political worth teaching?'

'Nothing.'

'Democracy – universal suffrage – nothing?'

'The trouble with democracy,' Misha said pontifically, 'is that it creates a vulgar middle class and contaminates the peasantry. All the proven balances in society are upset. Look around you. Read the better newspapers.'

'That's a typical attitude in your class,' Glebov said. 'It's liberals like you that are suffocating the country. You scoff at all forms of voting and of popular government.'

'The most votes are rarely the best votes,' Misha replied.

'Attention everyone! Merit in voting! Give every man's vote a mark between one and ten and add them all up at the end. That's the truest form of government, for then the wishes of the most intelligent citizens *must* prevail. Must – must – must.' Bobinski leaned towards Liza. 'Do you remember how often we discussed the system?'

'After the age of sixty, marks were to be deducted for senility,' she said with a smile at her old tutor.

He slapped his brow. 'Indeed they were. Dear me, dear me . . .'

And the dwarf, who'd all this time been covertly studying my bride and lapping up every detail of her scarlet shoes and her stole and the pearls and the slopes so easily imaginable beneath the cream pantaloons, said to her, 'So you've come awake, madame. I feared that the morality of politics was boring you.'

She said icily, 'Had you called me "*madamochka*" a second time I'd have slapped your face and had you leave this house. Why should I be treated as your inferior?'

He shrugged, no more than that.

She said, 'Very well. But I shall remember this exchange. Tell me, is the morality of terrorism included in the morality of politics or is it something quite apart – with different rules?'

'Terrorists can't afford morality. That's a luxury for the bourgeois.'

'Like Einem's chocolates,' Nicholas said, yawning. 'Enough, I say. My vote goes for a republic with a strong, sensitive tsar at its head.'

We smiled. It was a good way to signal a change of conversation was needed.

But for some reason Glebov coloured with anger. 'Attack me as much as you want. Do it while you have the chance. I've never had any desire to be loved. Other things have always been more important to me.'

'Ohhh . . .' I said, fixing him in the eye and drawing out the word to four syllables so that everyone was listening, 'is that so? What about "S"?'

He started in his seat. For a second I saw in behind his pupils, to his eye-grounds burning with a fierce red glow. Then everything snapped shut. I said to myself, I've got you, Glebov. He looked away, up the table to Misha. Tiny muscles were flickering along his jawline. 'What good have you done in the world, then?'

Sixty-two

'LISTS OF campaigns won, of government positions, medals, professorships, bridges constructed – the paper's blank. It's not the way I've lived. But I've done a few things I'm proud of, and since you asked, here they are.

'I've nursed my dying father and taken care of Lydia, my mother. Before her marriage she learned to play the piano to the very highest standard at the Conservatoire. Because I give her constant encouragement she's resumed her playing and now has a numerous and faithful public.

'I've bred the best cattle in the province, satisfied several women deeply, and made a home for my chickens. As a young man I trained some first-class dogs. I've given amusement to many. And since people remember a good joke or a happy event for months, sometimes for years, I think that should count double. My tailor is most grateful to me. I've never killed anyone, or had a man beaten. So mark me, Glebov. What would I score in your regime?'

'You are a superfluous man in any progressive society. That's what Stolz would have said.'

'Superfluous? If it weren't for Misha and myself and the work we provide, half the peasants in Popovka would have starved.' Nicholas rose angrily from his chair.

But Misha just lolled there, smiling at Glebov. 'Dogs, women, vodka, music, comfortable sofas – can the world possibly mean more? No one goes away empty-handed from Zhukovo. Vasili despairs of me. "What'll be left for my wages?" He must say that once a week. Because of this my cattle and hens live in the purple while I live in total disorder. My banker has insomnia over me. And if he knew the whole truth, about the tricks I've learned . . . Well, in fact I'm probably worth less than many peasants. I may be worth minus. So, Prokhor Fyodorovich, what are we to say of poverty in your society? Am I to be rescued?'

'Stolz would have said you'd brought it on yourself. Pleasure on your scale is impossible to excuse.'

'You're such an earnest young man. My behaviour is bound to be disgraceful if you adopt some inhuman standard of austerity. However – look at it another way. Should I not receive a civic honour from the shopkeepers of Smolensk for having kept them going? I'm serious. If the world were full of spend-nothings, how would anyone carry on a business? Trade would cease and money disappear. Life with it. Well, an enjoyable life anyway.'

'That's a good point,' Nicholas said, steepling his fingers.

'Crises rear up in my life every six months, with smoking breath like dragons. But as I said, I've grown clever. I soar above them like the lady who used to ride the trapeze when the circus came to Smolensk whose name was Topf, which she took from her husband, the clown. In the process I hurt no one except an occasional financier, and bring joy to many.

'I've harmed not one soul in my life except Maria Gorgulov whose hand I begged in marriage and was later obliged by my nerves to release. The meeting that ensued with her papa was a bloody occasion. I've been ashamed of myself ever since. I should have gone through with it and become reconciled to suffering. I say it again, forgive me, Maria Alexandrovna, though you may be dead . . . It was no fault of mine that the lady I did marry, died. Buying treatments for her in Germany was the cause of my first acquaintance with the Agricultural Mortgage Corporation.

'My conscience is clear. In fact – in fact, Prokhor Fyodorovich, I have benefited many. I suppose – you could say – an average guess would be one per week excluding the cattle and chickens. Three thousand total so far in my life. So how am I super-fluous?'

'Because you take resources from the general wealth and squander them on your own whims. You're a robber, stripping the country for your own inexcusable pleasures . . . These are the arguments and theories that were being bandied around in my regiment by Stolz. It was impossible not to hear them.'

'He means you don't work, that's the problem for Glebov,' said Nicholas loudly.

'Not for me, for the Stolzes,' he protested.

Misha said, 'Why should I? Did anyone in the Bible do proper work? Not one of them. They all dabbled at fishing and carpentry, amateurs like Nicholas here. If I worked my men wouldn't have jobs. I don't object to work in principle. But I've never tried it: everyone knows I'd lose money for them. Would that be in order for Stolz, to be industrious yet a bungler at the same time?'

'Attitude is the key to it all. One must kill desire. One must derive enjoyment only from work. This is the first stage on the road to perfection, they said. The state, our mother, cannot be responsible for loungers. Loungers are a negative influence.'

We stared at him. Nicholas leaning, one foot on the floor and the other tucked up behind him against the wall; Misha, caught in the act of raking through the nut bowl for a walnut; Bobinski, Lizochka and myself. We stared at him in disbelief – and began to laugh.

Misha wiped the tears from his eyes. 'That's me gone to Siberia.'

'What can you have been thinking of, Glebov, when you said that?' For the first time that evening Nicholas was at his ease.

Glebov had been picking mechanically at a wart on his thumb. Abruptly, with surprise, he looked up, at the circle of our laughing faces. His eyes narrowed. Then he relaxed and joined in. 'Those aren't my thoughts, Count, God forbid! It's what we heard from the agitators – the *bolsheviki*. One day the talk would be "The Crushing of Privilege", the next day "The Just Distribution of Wealth". Imagine! Now you know where Stolz and his sort got their ideas from.'

He seized the wine bottle and went round the table filling our glasses. 'To money! Enjoyment! To the selfish gratification of lusty pleasures!' His forehead was damp with sweat, likewise the shelf of his upper lip, which was composed of blue hairy fat.

Sixty-three

OUTSIDE OF Glebov we were friends and family gathered in an old mansion on the evening after the Tsar's abdication. The wine was circulating. Snow had started to fall again. The trees were humming in the blizzard, and spits were coming down the chimney and making the fire hiss.

I was showing off my wife. If you'd stuck a compass point in Smolensk and drawn a six-inch circle on the small map you wouldn't have found one comparable example of womanhood. Elizaveta Doig! Mine and mine alone! A rattling good mind and jiggling buttocks. Top woman – and in love with me.

I was too happy, too unconcerned. We all were. We were isolated from the war and politics, I suppose from mankind itself. We could afford to be theorists and to poke fun at Glebov.

'To money! To enjoyment!' we shouted, raising our glasses to him.

My Lizochka excused herself and went up to bed. Glebov's eyes followed her trembling pantaloons to the door.

Misha said, 'Apropos money, I was once asked what noise I thought best represented the concept of wealth. This man had read the phrase "a roar like a waterfall of kopecks" and wanted my opinion. No, I said, for me it's the sigh of a silk chemise descending to a lady's ankles. He was at first startled. Then he asked with a smile, "Rustle?" Too harsh, I said. It was a sigh, both of the chemise and of fate, who'd seen it all before. It transpired he was on his third wife. How foolish we are – one-horned beasts of really very limited intelligence.

'God, I get so drunk on these winter nights of ours . . .

'Maybe I am superfluous. What's the opposite, Prokhor

Fyodorovich? Perhaps I have a little bit of that too, just enough to redeem me. Let me think, what do I do that's vital . . . If I had my doves painted red, would that help when Stolz comes? Or my white shoes that I love so much . . . Oh yes, you shot him, so you did. Rat-a-tat-tat . . .

'Tell me what you'll do for old people when you're on the throne. Everyone should have a housekeeper and a Vasili, that's obvious. Make the bankers pay for them, that's my advice. Make them pay for free coal and firewood as well. Haul them in and shoot them if they don't hand over the money in those neatly tied boxes that haberdashers sell collars in. They're swine. You can never get the better of a banker. Take that fellow Kugel. He knows nothing whatsoever about my cattle, about how my bull mopes when he's left by himself – just stands there lashing his tail, his eyes *tiny* with resentment . . . But he knows their value as if they were in his own field. Charlie, I was being truthful when I said I was drunk. It's the relief at finding myself still alive . . . Superfluous, eh.' He looked around for somewhere to lie down.

Bobinski said to Glebov, 'One can understand the general desire of idealists to do good. But it would be a great mistake to abolish poverty. The sight of it disturbs the emotions of people who are rich. It's healthy that they be disturbed for it shows they're still sensitive.'

'A pin could do it as easily,' Glebov said.

'One could try to abolish it but one should fail,' Bobinski said. 'Poverty makes a good teacher, both for those going up and those coming down.'

'A teacher one could well do without,' sneered Glebov. 'My father was a poor man. My mother worked herself to death for us children. She became phthisic, started coughing her lungs up on the kitchen table, into the bacon rinds she was sending us to school with . . .'

I pushed one of the easy chairs from the hall into the room and positioned it near the fire for Misha. He fell into it with a wallop. 'My dear, pray cease your morbid tale. Your family does not have exclusive ownership of grief. Shall we move on? Let us consider agricultural matters, Prokhor Fyodorovich . . . Shall I tell you why I call my chickens the Hapsburgs? Because they're so inbred. Until ten years ago, no one in Popovka had bought a new cockerel for centuries. Then I did. You see, if they're less dotty they won't get their legs scythed off so frequently. Swish swish they'll hear and start hopping – leaping – skipping – flying perhaps. But even now they always hang around just too long. Like the Romanovs. Have the world perfected by the time I wake up. That's all.' He closed his eyes, snorting, and fondling his stomach.

Nicholas yawned. 'Let's speak freely with each other. What would you call yourself, Prokhor: utopianist – liberal reformer – Christian democrat?'

He never quite answered the question, this was another trick of Glebov's. He said, 'The principal question is whether great events descend on us according to some law of historical gravity or whether we can coerce them into happening. I belong to the party of coercion. I'm an optimist. I don't believe in fate, or God.'

He lit the stub of a *makhorka* like a common soldier and began to smoke it furiously, snatching staccato puffs. 'This sitting around and waiting isn't for me. One must propel history, kick it in front of one down the street. What matters are deeds. Rifles, horses, artillery, sacrifice' – his cigarette was burning its cardboard holder and making an unpleasant smell. He ground it into the carpet with his boot – 'so that everyone in our motherland who has suffered injustice can bathe in the sweetest champagne in the shop, which is revenge. The pink champagne of revenge, by which the mighty are lowered and society is reborn.'

He paused and looked at us. 'That's the typical speech of an agitator. I can reproduce their arguments word for word I heard them so often in my regiment.'

'Such realism is commendable,' Bobinski said acidly.

'The question you should have asked is how much history can be speeded up – the difference humans can make when they act as one,' Glebov said.

'That's what anarchists believe,' Bobinski said flatly. 'No discussions, no Duma, just guns and bombs and wholesale change. You're one of them.'

'I was repeating the arguments I heard from Stolz. They're not my beliefs, old fellow.'

'No. I've been watching you. Everything has been a pretence until your speech just now. It rang true. Your eyes gave you away. They were those of a believer. You're halfway to being a common terrorist. I can smell it.'

'Your own shite's what you're smelling. What would I be doing here if I were a bolshevik? Watch what you say, old Bobby fellow.'

'Revenge of some sort. Red champagne.'

'Live long enough, old Bobby, and you may find out.'

'Prokhor Fyodorovich Glebov, the eel beneath the rock,' Bobinski said quietly.

They stared at each other. Leaning forward I hissed into Glebov's ear, 'Revenge for your wife. For Sonja, whom they hanged. That's why you're here.'

His head whipped round like a snake's. Misha was snoring in his chair. Nicholas had gone to his office. Louis – somewhere. There were just the three of us.

Bobinski said to him, 'Go and convert someone else. You give my nerves goose pimples.'

Glebov eyed us in turn. He tilted his blue chin, he aimed his charred nostrils straight at me. 'I shall have left by breakfast. Revenge is as tasty as a good thigh of ham. It was a saying of Stolz. I remember it well.'

' You're a cocky little shit,' Bobinski said.

'Know many of them do you, old Bobby?'

Liza called for me down the stairs, worried.

Sixty-four

I WAS HOT with argument. To cool my head before going up to her, I fetched a tray from Louis's pantry and began to load it with glasses. Bobinski had the same idea. We'd had enough of Glebov.

He sat and watched me, smoking. It was his way of showing his superiority. He wanted to accrue advantages over me step by step, to belittle – to dominate – to thus arrive at a position where he could utterly conquer me. His sitting there so pat was a part of this.

I took the tray to the pantry.

Between the two rooms the corridor made an elbow. Because Nicholas was saving up to pay off Helene, there was only one candle to light the corridor. It was at the pantry end. The darkness of the elbow was made more so by the state of the panelling, which was stained to the colour of mahogany by soot and smoke.

I unloaded the tray and started back.

The darkness at the elbow was thicker than before. I saw it in an instant and knew it for Glebov. I had the candle at my back. He'd have got a clear image of me against the light. Smoothly I wheeled round as if I'd forgotten something, dumped the tray – and charged back down the corridor, head levelled, like a bison. I rammed him in the lard – got my forearm across his throat – prised him off the floor – whacked him up against the panelling. With my left hand I groped and caught him, root, balls and cords all in my strong fist.

'Look at my wife again like that and I'll pull it off.'

His teeth flashed below me. I was looking down onto his bald patch. 'You'll need a winch.'

I yanked him up by the root, onto his toes. Wisps of candle-light crept in between us. He balanced himself on tiptoe, arms limp, not attempting to struggle. Quite passive: it seemed to me smirking, even though I was squeezing him like a wet cloth. That was when I realised how confident he was.

More than ever I wanted to destroy him. I wished him to disappear from my life. He was hanging there, chin on my forearm, eyes glinting. I said, 'A rope'd stretch your spine. You'd gain inches. Become a big boy.'

Liza called again for me from the top of the stairs, an edge to her voice.

'Low-hanging fruit, ready for the basket . . .' he murmured.

Again she called, sounding to be on the verge of hysteria. 'Charlie, where are you?'

'Shall I come with you, Charlinka? She's the sort that needs two men.'

I brought my knee up. He'd been expecting it. As I whipped my hand away he clamped his thighs so that I scarcely shook him.

I shouted to her that I was coming. I pushed him away – sent him flying to the floor. He picked himself up and shrugged his coat straight. His face was gleaming with sweat. He made a cutting motion with scissored fingers. 'Snip, snip, what one does to ripe grapes.'

Halfway up the stairs I turned. He was in the vestibule, putting on his snow cape and boots. I ran back down, hope being the idiot that it is. In his slimy purring voice, 'No, it's tomorrow I leave. Now be obedient, Charlie. Take your little wand up to *madamochka*.'

She and I quarrelled. I said we must get out the next day. Pack a saddlebag each, sew the jewellery into our clothes – and escape. Glebov had chalked a cross on our gate.

'What harm have we ever done him?'

'Sonja. His wife.'

'You're guessing.'

'He admitted it.'

'She was a virgin. She hated men. We had no secrets.'

'You mean *you* didn't, not by the time she'd finished with you. She was a spy and a nymphomaniac.'

'They used torture on her.'

'That doesn't prevent her having been Glebov's wife. It's why he's here. To get the lot of us. Revenge. Loot. The abdication's like a starting pistol. Don't argue, woman, just begin packing.'

'Well then, how exactly are we to get out?' She went over and folded back the inside shutter. She held the candle against the window. 'Look at it. There'll be two feet of snow by the morning.'

We argued about the weather. I pointed out that it was actually freezing hard and below a certain temperature it became meteorologically impossible to snow. She said, What did an Englishman know about winter? We set about the virginity and character of Sonja, about Glebov, about the reason for her fits reappearing, about my giving her so little time to prepare for exile—

Exile! Again! Of course this animated a new and vigorous front. She'd been brooding. Americans were coarse – they were all Swedes or Poles. Americans were addicted to money, Americans were insincere, they fomented revolution – look at what they did in Cuba in '98 . . .

We were like two dogs contesting a shin bone to the death. Nothing of what we said was important and little of it true. But the words were ready and available to each of us and say them we did until we were shouting like the crashing sea and Bobby tapped on the floor above.

'I'd have been better off married to Andrej, a thousand times better,' she declared and climbed into our marriage bed, which was as welcoming as the tundra.

We occupied opposite sides, separated by a Gulf called Frigid that we were too proud to bridge. We lay there doggo, pretending to care so little that we'd fallen instantly asleep.

Sixty-five

THROUGH THE wool of my doped sleep it sounded like the weathervane – the dolphin twisting in the blizzard. It came again, directly above us – a shorter scream – abrupt – no tail, that part of it sliced off. Poor Bobby, some nightmare that.

A door slammed. I thought, That was no dream.

There were quick footsteps on the attic stairs. They crossed the landing outside our room – did they pause? I had my Luger from under the pillow and was out of the door. He ran down the main stairs into the hall. He looked back and up at me. He was fully dressed. I raised the pistol. He grinned – and pinched out the night candle with a butterfly pluck of his hairy fingers. His cavalry boots went thumping down the corridor towards the kitchen and the back door.

I raced upstairs to Bobby's room.

A meagre light was coming into the house off the snow. I put the time at around five o'clock. I tripped on the top step of the attic stairs and smacked into the pine-planked wall in front. It somehow bounced me back upright. I shouted to Kobi to wake up and pounded along the cold linoleum.

The candle was burning. But Bobby's book was tight shut and still on his table. It was Glebov who'd lit it. So that Bobby could see what was coming; would awake blinking and confused, look out from the shelter of his dreams and espy revenge leaning over him like a crimson blister, and the flickering steel of the descending bayonet, its blood-groove facing his bewildered eyes.

He'd plunged it vertically through the base of Bobby's throat, pinning him to the mattress. Bobby's thin blood had spurted a good yard, streaking the grey pillow. His eyes were staring at me, shocked by the betrayal.

I looked swiftly round. Nothing had been moved. Revenge for what? Which remark had so touched Glebov?

I pulled down the chicken skin of Bobby's eyelids. Kobi came into the room, glanced at him, took it all in.

There was no point in disturbing Misha.

'Go! Go immediately!' Nicholas said, rousing himself from sleep the moment I spoke his name. 'Take another of my rifles. Misha and I'll manage till you come back. There's Louis and the grooms as well. I'll have one of them go up to Popovka with the news and then on to Smolensk. Now go, Charlie, find Glebov and kill him. I want him dead and I want proof that he's dead.'

Liza reached up her long arms and bound me to her. I said nothing about Bobby or about going into the forest after Glebov. Only that Kobi had need of me and we'd be back by luncheon.

We kissed. I held her sweet face between my hands. She pulled the counterpane over our heads, shutting out the candlelight. We kissed savagely, mixing our foul night-breath. I stroked her belly, where Dan Doig was cooking.

'Kobi is waiting?'

I said yes. She pushed me away. I rose from her.

'Don't be late,' she whispered. Her hair and the hollows of her face were black as trumps against the pillow. 'Lilacs in May, that's all I ask of America. There's so little worth taking into exile when one thinks about it carefully.'

'We leave this afternoon.'

She nodded. 'I can hear Kobi outside with the horses. The snow sounds hard. You'll travel fast. Charlie?' She raised her arms and drew me down again. She rubbed her smooth, warm, sleepy cheek against my bristle. 'You are my life and my soul, wherever we go. I am yours unalterably, as you would ever have me be. Let me bless you.' She drew the sign of the Cross on my back, with her left hand. 'Now go, and leave me to our packing. It'll make me cry.'

Sixty-six

TEN MINUTES later Kobi and I were riding past the stables. I had the Mannlicher .256 with the vee sight and barleycorn across my back, and in my belt the Luger Kriegsmarine. Kobi had an old Nagant .300 that took five in the magazine.

The light was just sufficient. We picked up the track of Glebov's pony at the iron gates, at the bottom of the pleasure grounds, exactly where he and I had first met. Kobi grunted. It was also the same way he'd tailed him two days earlier.

Kobi led, sometimes halting to examine other hoof marks. Within the forest the snow was less but it still covered the ground. I said to him, Hurry, if we can see the marks they must have been made this morning, why stop? He pointed to fresh snow and he pointed to old snow which I'd taken for fresh. It's the way snow falls in a wood, patchily, because of the trees and the swirling quality of the wind. Kobi said, 'Men muffle their horses' hoofs to disguise the truth. To avoid mistakes I must go slowly. Do you want to be the first to get shot at, Doig, or will you ride behind me and be quiet?'

Thereafter we moved with care and skirted the clearings we came to. He could have been waiting for us to cross the open ground: two plump targets in the snowlight. Easy enough for stopping shots.

'Is he fleeing or leading us somewhere?' I asked.

'He's riding steadily, not in a panic. I'd say he's going to a rendezvous. His horse is carrying no extra weight. Someone else has the food. He's going to his soldiers, that's where he's going.'

Our horses moved crisply and silently through the trees. Mine was a bay, Kobi's the grey called Xylophone. There were no branches to snap underfoot so close to the village: they'd all been gathered for firewood.

Kobi stopped. Glebov had been joined by his soldiers. He supposed from the number of footprints and wandering hoof marks that they'd been a while waiting for him.

He said, 'It's them. No morning shit left around. Good discipline. What do you want to do, Doig?'

I couldn't see the tone of his eyes. It wasn't light enough for that yet. I said, 'You mean, how do we do it.' Glebov had wanted me to see him at the foot of the stairs. He'd waited for me to appear. He wished us to follow him. 'How far are they ahead?'

Kobi had at last found a knob of shit. 'Half an hour?'

'How well do you know this ground?'

'Very.'

'Can we get in front of them?'

'Yes. In about two miles there's a place they used to quarry stone. There's a way through their old workings, though we'd have to lead the horses. We come out on top of the track they're using. It's the best chance.'

'They may have thought of it too.'

'Of course.'

'So we'll decide when we get there. You lead.'

But we actually rode one on either side of the woodcutters' sledge track they were on, in case they played tricks on us and split up.

After half an hour we halted to confer. Nine ridden horses, he said, two packhorses. He could recognise Glebov's pony by the put-on of its near-front horseshoe. He was leading. But there was something funny going on. 'Maybe one of the men is wounded,' he said.

We rode slinking through the still wood, peering and stooping, for behind every tree there was a dark space.

Dawn came up – or rather, a lessening of night. The sky was sheeted with cloud – a continuous menacing roll, the roof of a prison. Our breath was like grey smoke. It was too cold for snow. A vast of cold, Bobby would have called it in his olden speech. God knows we didn't feel it but the air must have got warm enough to rouse the animal kingdom. Suddenly we began to hear the gloomy, raking calls of the eaters of carrion, the crows and the ravens.

To hurry along and fall upon Glebov and his men and rout them as they idled would have been perfect. I ached to do it: to gallop after him, shoot him dead and gallop home to Liza. *To make him disappear, become zero, vanish.* But always there was Kobi to check me. Riding on the other side of the track, slumped in his saddle and occasionally flicking a loop of the reins from one side of the horse's neck to the other and back again. Dozing, a fool might have said.

He rode over to my side of the track.

'Fifteen minutes, perhaps twenty in front. They're going slower now. Look,' and dismounting he pointed out how the grains of snow that had been disturbed by the horses' hoofs began to slide down the sides of the hoof print and after a certain time to smooth out the irregularities. The time depended on the temperature. 'The grains lose their grip,' he said. 'I expect if you sat and watched you'd see them do it. That's how I judge how far away they are.'

He got back on his horse. I thought it had been all he wanted to say. But now: 'There's a man riding always very tightly in the centre of them. It has been like this since they joined up with Glebov.'

'Tightly?'

'With someone close on either side of him. Almost knees touching.'

'He may be a prisoner,' I said.

'The hoofs are silent.'

This morning Kobi looked more like Genghiz Khan than I'd ever seen him. His face twitched with pleasure as he delivered the snub. He wanted only one thing: to kill these men and to kill Glebov last, to see the red froth billow from his gasping mouth. The identity of the ninth man was unimportant to him. If he was a prisoner then he was a chump. I knew Kobi's philosophy well.

A little farther on the ground began to angle upwards. The track skirted an enormous slab of rock resting, tilted, upon a boulder the size of a cottage – relics from before measured time. Around this outcrop no trees were growing.

Kobi carefully scouted the open ground. He returned to where he'd left me in the trees. 'If we go uphill here we come to the old quarry workings. The way through's in single file. Glebov's gone the long way round. They don't want to have to trail one behind the other. They could be ambushed themselves. There are other men out here who may be their enemies – we don't know. Also the prisoner would impede them.'

'The prisoner may not be a prisoner. It may be a woman companion. She may be common property. Glebov has vices.'

'My woman thinks bad ones – not polite, she says.'

'Sonja didn't think that.'

Scarcely a muscle moved in his face. 'Not ordinary screwing then, Sonja and Glebov . . . ? It was Count Nicholas who had Sonja executed. She wouldn't let him have her. That's what they say in Popovka . . . Anyway, it's not a woman – unless she's in child. The hoofs cut too deeply into the snow.' He thought it over. 'Their prisoner, perhaps their hostage.'

I said to him: 'How long did they stop back there?'

He clicked his tongue. 'You noticed?'

'There was horse piss in the snow. Two or three blocks of it, too much for a man. They're getting careless. Glebov never believed we'd come after him so fast.'

Kobi took the leather cap off the muzzle of his Nagant and slid the bolt out. He checked the barrel for snow, worked the foresight leaf a few times to prevent it freezing solid. 'But why did they stop at all? A horse can piss on the move.'

Sixty-seven

WE RODE up towards the saddle on the ridge, into an awkward jumble of boulders and spoil heaps, moss beneath snow, a difficult footing. The terrain changed its character, became more open, nearer to heathland with some birch and oak scrub.

The sky fell down another notch. It pressed on us, occasional boils and swirls of light grey amid reefs of black and purple. It spread itself over the land like the sac of an octopus. The cold was intense.

Out of the rocks and over the saddle we rode, fast, looking for a place we could spring the ambush. The track was below us. Glebov was still somewhere in the forest. But we didn't have much time. An advantage of minutes.

A knoll with hazels on it, two hollies growing entwined, and a solitary birch: dead bracken hummocked beneath the snow but here draped over the lowest branch of the birch. We tied our horses in the gully at the back of the knoll. We were in our snow capes.

Shrouded by the fronds of bracken, I knelt in the snap-shooter's position at the foot of the birch, the Mannlicher resting on that low branch. Kobi was a yard behind me and to one side. The bracken obscured us completely. To the woodcutters' track was a hundred and twenty yards. I was shooting over open sights. The ground was falling away gently: white with black tussocks and dark green clumps of rushes, quite clear of trees.

The time was about eleven o'clock. The light was good enough. I could pick out the gold bead of the barleycorn sight.

Kobi said, 'Keep your trigger glove on until the last minute – when you see him coming.'

We settled down to watch the edge of the fir trees. My heart-beat was steady. *Pray God I kill him.* So I thought and I repeated it often, moving my lips.

There was no preliminary noise or sighting. We knew nothing about it until we heard him cry out to his horse. He was already out of the trees and galloping down the hill at an angle away from us. A three-quarter shot. I could be certain only of the horse.

'Wait,' whispered Kobi.

I lined up the barleycorn on the hunched, plunging figure. The scarlet cockade on his *shapka* stood out like blood against the snow.

Kobi whispered, 'He's going down into the dip to cross the stream. The far bank's steep. The horse'll be puffed as it climbs it. It'll slow – or stop. Shoot him then.'

He came funnily out of the dip, not in the place or at the angle I'd expected.

The pony faltered, struggling to get its wind back. Glebov showed well in the sights, plump and black. *God go with that bullet.* I squeezed the trigger. It whipped him out of the saddle.

The shot faded into silence. Kobi let out his breath, placed his hand on my shoulder. 'You're the horse's cock, Doig.'

But I'd hit him low, I knew it as I fired.

Glebov's pony looked round, startled by the shot and by suddenly finding itself without a rider. It looked down at Glebov, who was on his knees and trying to haul himself up by a stirrup leather. It smelled the blood on him and bolted across the bleak landscape with the stirrups flapping against its ribs and wads of snow flying up from its hoofs.

Glebov, Glebov alone, wavering in my sights. He got himself upright, hands clamped round the hole in his belly. His *shapka* had come off. His head was bent over watching the blood ooze through his fingers. His bald patch was as pale as the bottom of a saucepan.

I shot him again. The force of the .256 bullet flung him into the air. It was as though he'd been asked to leap over an obstacle. Then he pitched to one side like a falling tree and rolled down the bank towards us, out of sight and into the stream.

Kobi grinned at me, just like a boy. We flattened ourselves into the bracken.

Its strong stems had made a tent when they folded under the snow. We lay in it like rodents. We couldn't have been better placed to command the track. An entire company of soldiers would have had a hard time of it against us.

The echoes faded, Glebov's horse vanished, and the boiling clouds got a little lighter as we approached the middle of the day. But no one came out of the trees.

Nothing stirred except the circling crows and buzzards.

The silence was thick with meaning. Glebov's men, scattered along the edge of the trees, were daring us to make the first move. We waited, fingers crooked round cold triggers, flexing them to keep their warmth.

Half an hour must have passed when Kobi nudged me. He flicked his eyes to the right.

God knows where he'd got the strength or blood from. The dwarf had inner reserves that I would never have dreamed existed. It must have been the memory of his tubercular mother spewing her lungs over the kitchen table that kept him going. Maybe that second shot hadn't been in the chest, but in the shoulder.

He'd climbed out of the stream, was teetering on the edge of the bank, one arm useless at his side and the other flailing the air. His cape clung blackly to his body and his face was streaked with dirt and blood. 'India rubber, as bad as Rasputin,' I whispered to Kobi and snuggled my cheek against the rifle stock.

'Don't – the noise. It'll give us away.'

Glebov fell to his knees. He looked down at the guts cradled in his good hand, inspected them. He may have spoken to them – he had that look about him. We were too far away for these details, which would have been interesting. His head dropped onto his chest. It sank lower and lower. He was bowing to his guts – had his nose in them – was saying goodbye. Then he toppled to one side, kicked as though kicking a boot off, and lay still.

Kobi nodded. 'Where we can see him. Not any more like Christ, body moving around.'

His death passed the time. We watched Glebov's corpse and waited for his men to make a showing. The clouds continued to grow lighter. Around midday an angry sun appeared fleetingly behind them. It was a distraction to wonder what it portended. Then we didn't see it for a while.

The minutes hobbled past. In due course I came to understand that we were the only watchers. With that advantage of numbers they'd have attempted some manoeuvre against us. Had Glebov been couped out of our sight? Sent out into the wilderness by his men – to be shot?

Cautiously at first we returned the way we'd come and made a cast through the wood to see what the horse marks told us. Back! It was back they'd gone.

'Back?' said Kobi, puzzled. We went a bit further, tallied the horses that were left. Everything was correct. Two packhorses, eight ridden horses, but not Glebov's.

'Going fast,' Kobi said. 'Fleeing.'

'Then we'll take a look at Glebov. He may have papers on him.'

'Money,' Kobi said.

We rode back along the track and out of the trees. Glebov was where he'd collapsed and died. Thank God! Ever since we'd been in the wood and out of sight of him I'd had a bad feeling. I'd hit him the second time – whump and he'd leapt, like a shot rabbit, and rolled down the bank for dead. Then twenty minutes later he'd reappeared staggering around in front of me holding his guts. Was he a magic man?

But there he was, heaped lifeless on the churned and bloody snow.

I could describe to you in much greater detail the emotional quality of this event – the killing of Glebov. It was of the same order as the naturalist's chase except that I was carrying not a butterfly net but a Mannlicher .256 and the quarry was not an insect but a terrorist. The differences are not worth talking about. Some hours before I'd found a harmless old man nailed to his mattress by sixteen inches of bayonet. God alone knew if Glebov had murdered before or how many he might murder in the future. I had to get him. The imperative was the same as for a rare beetle – a second Wiz. Kill that thing.

298

Purists will disagree, holding that human beings and insects are not identical.

The pursuit excited me. The possibility when we started in the half-light of dawn that there might have been a figure in the shadows hoping to shoot me made my blood stand on end: excitement has two parts and fear is one of them. At the other end of the scale was the moment when, as I flicked up the two-hundred-yard sight and waited for his panting horse to stand, I could be certain that I'd outwitted Glebov. My heart tingled as though someone was sandpapering its quimmy pink tip. My entire imagination was dwelling in advance on what would happen to his entrails as the steel bullet blasted through them. And when he died I was as elated as anyone would have been.

The elation was still there as Kobi and I rode along the track to the corpse. Within me an image was seething, of Liza packing our cases, of her indecision, of her flurries of despair, of her dark and determined beauty as she debated where to hide the pearls and awaited the tread of my horse. I glimpsed the train to Odessa – the voyage – docking in New York—

But elation is too mild: I was shaking with relief, and joy, and even more, a feeling that by killing Glebov I'd captured all of happiness for myself. I mean all of it that humans know to exist, the entire stock, the whole airy warehouse in which it was kept. I made Kobi ride in front so that he shouldn't see that I was trembling like a custard in the saddle.

All these I could draw out for you since they were my authentic feelings, and it was interesting to acknowledge them in myself during the process of hunting a man down in order to kill him.

But the exercise would have not the slightest value. I could see from twenty yards that the man I'd shot was not Glebov but a complete stranger.

He was lying half on his side – twisted at the waist. Middle-aged, an exhausted, decent, bourgeois face with a tuft of a beard below the centre of his lip. A government official or a lawyer. Mired and bloodied, lips snarling in his death agony.

Kobi moved the man's arm with his toe. 'Jew. Old dead Jew. The prisoner.'

He looked up at me. Our eyes locked like magnets. Glebov had known we'd be after him. He'd *wanted* us after him. He'd lured us up the forest track. Christ knows where the Jew had come from but the gang had had him ready, had given him a bald patch with horse clippers. Glebov had stuck him on his own horse, made him wear the *shapka* with the scarlet cockade and padded out his belly with a quilted jacket. 'You're free. Ride like hell, Jew, before we change our minds.' Then he'd whacked the horse on the croup and sent it galloping out of the forest.

Two hundred yards of freedom he'd had and then I'd shot him, clumsily. Having experienced nothing good for a while, he'd struggled even to die.

The rifle shots: Glebov would have heard them both. Known me for a dupe and wetted his fat lips. We'd lain low – more time wasted, the hour hand gone floppy. Even now, as we were standing over the Jew, Glebov and his gang were riding on the Pink House.

Sixty-eight

Y OU'LL HAVE heard of our saying, 'It would make a stone cry.' I never understood it until this day.

I was goring my horse, punching its ribs with my stubby spurs. If it went faster because I hurt it, that was fine. Animals were created to serve our purposes, not theirs. Pansies try to persuade them to do this voluntarily. But I've never believed in the carrot. Give me a stick and make it strong.

We were going back down that woodcutters' track. The reins were in my left hand. I had the horse tight on the bit. The sinews of my forearm were like strips of whalebone as I kept it balanced, steered it, and picked it up when it stumbled in the ruts. In my other hand I had a broken branch. Its side shoots had been snapped off leaving jags like teeth. I was without mercy. My bowels were boiling. The tears pouring from my eyes were as hot as a clear soup. My hand had acquired the notion that speed would save my Lizochka, and that speed was to be had by striking the horse with a ragged fir-tree branch and pummelling it with spurs. Which I did. I was capable of nothing else. The tears coursing down my cheeks, I thrashed and I thrashed that servant of man. I thrashed it like no one has ever thrashed a horse. With every blow I thought of her – sometimes Nicholas and Misha as well but always of her: upstairs in our room, humming as she packed and listened, already wearing her travelling clothes so as not to be caught napping when I bounded up the stairs and shouted 'Are you ready, then, woman?'

I was holding the horse in suspension, the proper distance from the ground, for to begin with it was a steep downhill and the animal had the momentum of three months of stable fatness behind it, and the firs were flying past. Also I had it in my over-wrought mind that because of the hill the creature's legs would go too quickly and run away with themselves; that unless I kept it upright it would gallop into the ground, up to the hocks and then up to the knees and so on until finally it would beach itself, on the keel of its breastbone, and be of no more use to me than a rocking horse.

So my hands were occupied and I had to shake my head to fling off the scalding tears of disaster. They went over my shoulder and every time I did this I glimpsed Kobi galloping at my heels, likewise keeping his horse off the floor with his left hand.

Under his long jerkin, tied at the waist, he was wearing a thick sheepskin waistcoat that we call a *dushegreika*, 'soul-warmer'. I remark on this because his chin was buried in the woolly tufts that straggled out round the neck and his head was between the horse's ears so that all I could see of his face were his slitted Asiatic eyes and his forehead, which was filthy with sparks of mud and snow.

'Old dead Jew. The prisoner.' Thus Kobi had summed up the abyss of our deception. Comprehension had come to us simul-taneously. I was in the saddle before my brain had stopped twitching.

And I was crying before my right foot was in the stirrup.

For Liza and the ease of the fraud. Had it in fact been Glebov who'd screamed as he slew Bobinski, in order to wake me up?

For my idiocy, therefore, for my utter simplicity.

I was crying out of frustration: at the impeding ruts in the track, at Nicholas's fat and wheezing carriage-horses, at the slight thickening of daylight that betokened night was closer than dawn.

I was crying because I could go no faster.

But most of all I was crying from the anger born of my powerlessness. What use was my fancy rifle or my physical strength or the name of Rykov? What use was Kobi? I could have had an army marching at my back and been incapable of changing anything. For the fact was that we were in one place and what mattered was in another. The anger boiled within me like magma; deep in the stomach, sharp and seething as if I was pregnant with a tureen of acid. Had I galloped round the corner and found Glebov and his men there, in my road, I'd have charged them, into the teeth of their bullets. Without a second thought I'd have done it, trusting in Right to see me through, like a warrior armed with a prayer banner. My anger was unconquerable. I raked that gasping elephant with my spurs and when I dropped the jagged branch I curled my hand into a block and fisted it in the neck and smashed at its ears. Every part of it I could reach I punched or kicked.

And all the time there were sudden spikes of bile jolting through my rage that I knew to be fear – fear for Liza. And a wider fear besides: that it was true, that our world was disintegrating.

For what purpose? Was a great lump of goodness lying unused out there that no one had ever stumbled across before? Justice for all? Some benevolent way of government that was infallible?

No, for the purpose of evil. The hoarse rasp of fear was insistent. It struck at me again and again, so that I pleaded with fate, 'Anything, but let us not be broken,' meaning Lizochka and myself.

The scene changed from Liza packing in our bedroom to the photo of her that Uncle Igor adored, taken on a Crimean beach when she was about fifteen. Long dark shorts that were almost bloomers and a white short-sleeved blouse. She was grasping with the sly grin of a veteran fisherman the wooden pole of one of the shovel-framed shrimping nets they use for small bay work along the coast. The fisherman himself was in the background in waders and a wide-brimmed straw hat, and behind him, in the very distance, could be glimpsed a striped bathing machine. Wearing her hair short was still to come. She was lithe and confident, one might have said boyish except that in the angle of her blouse I could make out the swell of one sweet breast.

Why that snap, unseen since I was last with Igor three years ago? It had occupied, by itself, a round occasional table in his favourite room, a sun-lounge in which he grew vines and semi-tropicals. In the due season it had rented out a space on the table to an orchid. A copy had been in his palace in Petrograd. How he'd doted on her – how I *worshipped* her –

I banged the stupid animal down the track. 'But let us not be broken . . .'

Flicking away the tears of rage and love and fear, I saw the blossoming stain of blood on the snow behind me. Kobi gestured to the flanks of my horse.

'Then halt, for God's sake,' I shouted. 'If that's what you want, halt.'

My wrecked horse dropped its head. Its ribs heaved with huge, shuddering breaths. The blood from my scourging dripped off its fur into the snow, also blood from its nostrils. I willed it not to collapse under me. Kobi's grey was little better. We could have cooked a meal on the steam coming off them.

The sun had reappeared, a brutish birthmark purple. It hung like a cheap lantern, half in and half out of the clouds so that it seemed to be squinting at us.

The corners of my mouth were crusty with dried foam and spittle. I spat into my palm and wetted all round my lips, cleaning them off on my sleeve. My breathing came back to normal. It was like regaining consciousness. The anger that had fired me had been drained by the insanity of our riding. We were back in the present tense.

I studied Kobi, as if for the first time. I looked round to see where we were.

About a mile away on our left, through the trees, was Popovka. The rusted old gates into the grounds of the Pink House were directly below us. Glebov's tracks ran straight for them.

Kobi was trying the air like a dog. 'They haven't burned the house.'

We stood at our horses' sunken heads. I said to him, 'The animals are finished. What else has Nicholas got? What's in Popovka?'

He said, 'I don't know, but I know who does. The man who was opposite you at your wedding feast.'

What we were both thinking: was Glebov still at the Pink House? We'd heard no shots. Had he ridden on? Would we or would we not need fresh horses?

I said, 'How far is he in front of us?'

'A long time. More than two hours.'

So he'd have done his purpose. I said, 'We'll ride down to the ford and see how many tracks are going up to Popovka. That's the way they'll have gone.'

This involved a detour and more time wasted. But it kept us under cover in case they'd left a man watching, and gave the horses a breather.

I said, 'You tell me why they haven't burned it.'

'Because the Count shot some of them. Then they ran.'

'And we didn't hear the shots?'

'We were a distance away. Galloping, with the noise of the horses in our ears.'

Having said that Kobi turned away and examined the powdery snow by the ford. 'Six men and one bleeding. Same horses as before.'

'Prisoners?'

'No. They're well spaced out, except for the horses being led. Riding hard.'

'Women?'

'No.'

Sixty-nine

THE PURPLE sun had slid down the clouds and taken up position on top of the stiff bare trees. There it was crouched, a vast battered eye half closed by the afternoon shadows. Beneath it, in total stillness, lay the rambling snow-covered bulk of the Pink House.

We tied the horses to the old iron railings. The brutes were scrap, good for nothing more than carrying our saddles around.

The gates had been torn off their hinges and thrown aside in the snow. But the ornamental ironwork arch had been beyond them so under the Rykov wolf we slunk amid a host of footprints, animal and human.

It was true we'd seen the tracks leading away from the house, towards Popovka. But I was afraid of surprises. Mines would have been too bulky, even the smallest, but explosive in the brick was light and easy to lay. To have booby-trapped the house instead of burning it would have struck Glebov as a pretty amusement. We moved slowly, scouting for Bickford cord, solitary footprints, the telltale smell of marzipan.

The monstrous sun studied me as I scanned the dark windows for life: a twitch of her scarf – or the swivel of a rifle barrel.

Was anyone watching us? I didn't get that feeling. I could sense no tunnels such as the human eye bores through the air as it stares out, waiting for something to move. The atmosphere was empty. The windows, overhung by ledges of snow like white eyebrows, stared blindly at me. There was no smoke from the chimneys, none from the conservatory furnace, no starlings on the ridge beams, no busy wrens insecting under the eaves. In the back courtyard the morning's washing hung as stiff as suits

306

of armour. A man's shirt was in two sections, sliced down the seam.

I'd agreed no formula for communicating with Nicholas. Neither of us could have expected this situation. When I said goodbye to him I'd been in a hurry. Bobinski was congealing upstairs. I was going to go out into the forest to kill Glebov: to do it and be home for luncheon.

'Don't be late,' my bride had said. We were departing for America.

So where was she?

We stole through the shrubs, trying not to dislodge their snow. Soon we'd be in open view from the house. I tied my handkerchief to the end of my rifle and pointed it to the sky. I pushed my breath to the bottom of my lungs and held it there. Then I stepped out onto the snow-covered lawn, at the end of the archery pitch.

'Nicholas!'

My stomach was flinching, as if it contained a fragile glass bowl. But nothing happened. I walked forward a few paces.

'Lizochka!'

The sun glowered at me with its great purple face. I hated its smugness, the ease of its lolling existence. 'Don't you ever have to struggle?' I shouted, shaking my rifle at it. Kobi, still in cover, hissed at me. I said to him over my shoulder, 'What's the matter? There's no one here to be quiet for.'

I stood on the archery lawn and I cursed the sun. I hated it for its pomposity. I hated it for its empty offer of warmth and happiness. 'Don't bother coming back,' I shouted, 'waste of time. This is the new Russia. They don't need old farts like you. Science will do everything. You're like Misha, superfluous.' It was a vain and bloated sun and I hated it for its snooping, sat up there in the trees, flaunting its roseate arse like an ape.

I hated it for not being Lizochka.

Kobi came out from the bushes and joined me: stood at my side nervously whisking his sidelong eyes. He was better when the enemy was unambiguous.

We were still wearing our long snow capes. They were cumbersome when the proceedings were on foot.

The o'clock was at that point in a winter's afternoon when

the true force of the gathering frost becomes perceptible. I could feel the bite of it on my cheek. The air had taken a glaze of light mauve from the sun – very light, the colour when winter glow is set in frost.

We were at the end of the archery lawn, walking up it towards the house and the tea-terrace, which was slowly disclosing itself to us. We could not have been more exposed. A machine-gunner up in the attic would have diced us for stew within seconds. Yet we halted. As one, without exchanging a word, we halted and stared at the section of the terrace that had just come into view.

There was the cannon, the greenish ceremonial *falconetto* that had been fired by Louis to celebrate the wedding of Lizochka and myself. And there was my godfather Mikhail Lvovich Baklushin, the ancientest friend of my family, the noblest man in the world.

Kobi, who saw it all first, looked away, looked down at his feet. Even Kobi did that. Then it was my turn. I couldn't hold my gaze. My blood went into reverse. Bending, I shot a tawny stream of vomit into the snow.

We have obligations of reticence to our especial friends: non-prying pacts. We succour them, apply comfort when they're distressed, and restore their self-confidence after humiliation. This general office we perform most willingly on account of friendship. We do it without poking around or spying. Between friends there is an easy privacy since so much has already been disclosed. In the same vein we are guilty of disrespect if, in describing the manner of their death, we show them as they would not have wished to be shown to strangers.

But there are times when we must say shit to our obligations simply because the civilisation to which they belong has ceased to exist. Also because it cannot be restored until the possibilities of barbarism have been displayed in their full bestiality.

The properties of revenge are as numerous and varied as those of love. Upon the terrace there was an exhibition of them.

Its mildest form was a pile of Misha's clothes. Its most extreme was Misha, naked except for his waistcoat. The Jew pushed out of the forest for me to kill had been practice, playing scales, call it what you will – perhaps even an act of clemency now that we were introduced to the full range of Glebov's filth; of his bitterness; of the prices on the board in Utopia.

Memory must be one's handmaiden, not an enemy. I write of the way in which we found them, both the dead and the single living person.

Seventy

ISHA HAD been stripped, or forced to undress himself,
stuffed back into his green and gold brocade waistcoat as
if he were an organ-grinder's monkey, and roped to the mouth of
his own cannon – navel to the hole, stretched down the barrel to
face his torturers. He would have had to take their jokes and taunts
and watch the soldiers having make-believe stabs of the lighted
match at the vent. Covering their ears, jumping at the imagined
roar of the cannon, shading their eyes to mark the fall of shot,
breaking their ribs with laughter. Words would have passed
between them as the metal grew ever colder against his flesh
and the soldiers cocked their heads and giggled into his terrified eyes, whispering, We'll soon warm you up, Excellency. I
hoped that he'd snarled at them and not known terror. But in
my heart I knew he was too human.

Then a signal was passed in secret, and the charge of horse
nails went whoosh through his lower belly.

His sagging corpse was the first we found. Misha, whose only
crime was to have enjoyed his life. I told Kobi to get sacking
from the gardeners' shed and cover him.

Now I realised why Glebov hadn't burned the Pink House.
He wanted me to appreciate the ingenuity and ostentation of
his slaughter. It was part of the contest. First he'd get the sitting
ducks and then he'd come after me.

We entered the house.

Louis and the cook had been shot in the mouth from in front.
They were in the kitchen. No sign of a fight – no upturned
chairs even.

In his office Nicholas had fought alone. A dead soldier was

in the doorway. Nicholas was lying beside his desk. I pulled his head up by the wheat-coloured hair. His eyes were quiet, thank God. The rifle press in the corner was open and the rest of the weapons gone. Huddled in the corner lay Styopka, the younger stable lad, killed I don't know how but bloodily.

I said to Kobi, 'Pashka,' referring to the stable lad whose grandfather had been swapped for a greyhound. A prearranged signal, an outside door carefully left unlocked, the scurry – the shooting. How else could it have been? I said Pashka because he wasn't among the dead and because of the greyhound. For what a Rykov did seventy-four years ago, five people died that afternoon in the Pink House.

Now I must tell you about the living person we found.

From room to room we hurried, calling for her everywhere. Echoing floorboards, tumbling half-pillaged cupboards, unmade hearths. Death had invaded the Pink House. The mean odour from its glands hung in every doorway. Cold was my bridal mansion, and desolate. Cold, cold, cold and already the cat's saucer of milk was frozen.

Two leather steamer trunks, a marriage gift from Nicholas, stood in our room with their lids thrown back. Full, but not to the very top, waiting for last thoughts – indulgences, luxuries, objects for the sake of their memories. Her empty cup of chocolate was on the mantelshelf. She'd spent the morning packing; fingering everything and wondering about the seasons in Chicago. She would have discussed her wardrobe with Louis. Nicholas wouldn't have told her about Bobinski. He'd have left the body up there until Kobi and I returned. He'd have tried to fob her off with an excuse for having the stable boys in the house. Maybe she'd swallowed it, being distracted by impending exile. Just said good morning to them and returned to her packing.

But where was she?

Kobi came jumping down the attic stairs. He'd been putting a few things in his knapsack. He had in his hand Glebov's bayonet, which he'd drawn out of Bobinski. He ran his thumb and forefinger down the runnel and flicked a clot of blood and tissue into the fireplace. I told him to leave it since it was awkward to carry. But he refused and stuck it through his belt, where it was sure to get in his way.

I stood there looking round the bedroom. Kobi, restless, was for instant action. But I sat down.

He was thinking, I could see it in his face, Why isn't Doig more energetic about her? Why doesn't he rush out and see if he can find her footprints in the snow: after all that stuff tracking horses he can't even do it for his woman – hey, Doig, what's hampering you? Make a stir – hustle – punish the day.

Yes, I was found wanting. I was irresolute in a tight corner and showed lack of experience. No one will ever understand how it was for me as we searched for Lizochka. *Never*. Whatever the imagination can grip is papier mâché compared with reality. We're speaking of the intransigence of fate, that's what everything comes down to in the end. Our individual helplessness, neither more nor less.

Kobi looked to me for orders. I'm not talking here of Kobi the policeman or Kobi the fireman or the janitor, the coast-guard, the postman or the nice next-door neighbour who's volunteered to lend a hand. He was a mercenary with a used bayonet stuck in his belt who expected me to know what had to be done at that very moment and not get it wrong. So we'd come out of it alive with Lizochka rescued.

But I was thinking of Misha's testicles blasted over the terrace: of my dead cousin Nicholas: of socialism, which cannot be among the dreams of reason, only the nightmares. I was thinking how to use the remaining daylight and where we'd go when we found her. I was thinking of the continent bristling with anarchy and me, Doig, standing against it. One mortal man versus millions.

Kobi bounced the knapsack on his shoulders. He fingered the bayonet. His look said, Come on, Doig, why are we waiting? Fighting, the best medicine on the market: no disease too complex.

But I did not know where Liza was. I could not even think where she might be. I was paralysed by the hugeness of Glebov's evil and by the chaos around me. Where should we start? How could the two of us accomplish anything against these forces?

The past being easier, I said to Kobi, 'We must bury the dead.'

'Why?'

'Because it's our custom.'

'What about your woman? Have you gone crazy?'

Kobi was right to pressure me, to try to jolt me out of my despair. For I was at the far end of hope, where there is no shelter.

His face was hard. Someone had pulled on a thread that drew in his cheeks and made them gaunt. I couldn't help but be conscious of the belligerence of this young, lean, impatient Asiatic.

'I don't have to stay with you. Times like these are good for my sort. Pay me out or make a move. Blood of Christ, Doig, what's happened to you?'

It was with a snarl that he spoke, following it with more harsh things, striking blows at my pessimism. He bundled me out of it. You could say it was Kobi who reminded me that the future has to be lived as well. He pushed me in front of him up the steep attic stairs and we began, ripping through the small brown-timbered rooms, through their wardrobes and the roof space, anywhere she might be hiding.

Seventy-one

WE FOUND nothing, despite searching that shameful house from top to bottom. 'Where next?' said Kobi. Then I thought: did she go to her scarlet room to smoke a pipe to settle her nerves, to assist her into exile? In this other smoke-wreathed world might she have glimpsed disaster riding in from the forest – started from her reverie – fled?

It took some time to narrow it down so that we knew what we were looking for. The imprint in the snow of her travelling brogues is what I'm talking about. She was ready for me, you see, ready and waiting. For *me*. But it was Glebov who turned up.

These shoes of hers: small, neat, tan-and-white. Unworn and so having an action that would have been a little stiff. That Andrej had bought for her trousseau and had since been lying tissue-papered in their pale pink box labelled Yteb, 14 rue Royale, VIIIe arr., Paris. And there the box and the strewn paper had been all the time I was sitting like a lummox in the bedroom chair. On the floor beside me, staring up into my stupid face.

A gritty sleet was blowing, scurrying over the hard snow in waves. I thought, But are those shoes too low? Will her feet get cold and damp?

This was as we followed her tracks from the front door and then squirrel-like through the bushes to the lane leading to the stables.

My love had run like a flying deer, in a cloak tossed over her shoulders that trailed as she ran, grazing the snow-dust with a fan-shaped ripple such as the wings of a crowing cockerel makes. Or any bird leaves in the snow when it stretches a wing to cleanse itself of its lice.

Here were her marks as boldly she went.

Boldness is the image I like, in her swishing cloak. Not sniggling timidly from corner to peeping corner but boldly, I repeat myself, boldly down the lane to the stable ran my bride, Dan Doig bumping in her belly.

To saddle a horse and ride for Popovka. To find me, who was late. To receive the protection that was her due.

Thus she ran to the stables, to the place where I was not.

They killed Nicholas and Louis and the cook. They bound Misha to his cannon and fired the cartridge of horse nails through him. When did she start running?

He saw her. Someone looking from a window saw her go a-leaping in her cloak and travelling brogues. If not Glebov then another, who shouted through the hollow house, 'There she goes, mine to have first.'

Whooping the pack had hunted her down. We saw where their huge leather-shod trotters overlay hers.

She heard the shout of discovery, flung a quick glance over her shoulder. What sort of fear did she experience? Did she call out for me? The sun knew. It would have been up there, its bloodshot eye clamped to the keyhole. Oh yes it knew, it knew well enough what was going on. Yet it had done nothing to help her, just sat on the top of the bare-branched trees and watched. I should have shot it down. I should have lifted up my Austrian rifle and shot its belly open as they did to Misha and brought it squealing to the ground and if it still lived, have kicked it to death in the stable yard and sliced up its tripes and fed them to the pigs. This is what I wanted to do to the sun as I ran down that snowy lane to the stables.

But she may not have called aloud for me. She had to get every inch of speed up that she could: there was her puff to think about. But in prayer form she would have called for a horse saddled and waiting, and she would have called for me, *wishing* me to gallop round the corner with the Cossacks and *wishing* to hear the sudden crack of my Mannlicher.

How far away were we when she called, I and that moronic carthorse?

We were running side by side. Kobi had the bayonet in his hand.

315

What else?

The sun in its purpletude, the snow-laden buildings before us, and the dancing sleet. The Tsar gone and Russia swaying. No woodsmoke curling from the tall iron pipe of the saddle-room chimney, no snickering of horses being groomed, no stable boys staggering beneath the yoke of wooden water buckets.

A scene deserted except for Elizaveta running, her heart like a stone, hope dead within her. Glebov and his venereal gang gaining on her with every stride, running at the crouch, panting, their red tongues like spears.

Seventy-two

THEY'D HAD her on the dung-riddled straw of the stable floor. Had her in chorus, then chucked her cloak over her. Of course they'd stripped her, what do you expect. Her neck and shoulders were bleeding from their mauling. Her hair was matted with straw and slobber. They'd probably quarrelled over who'd get her shoes. But not over who went first.

Sternly she lay there. Rigid, her unblinking eyes fastened on the cobwebbed window through which the sun was prying. A worm of blood was crawling from the corner of her mouth. I told Kobi to get out.

Kneeling I spat on my handkerchief and started to bathe her bruised face.

She turned it towards me – let it roll to my side. Her dark eyes examined mine incuriously. 'You're late. No America today.' Her voice was weak. More blood spilled from her mouth, which I wiped.

She said, 'You'll be alone.'

I did what I could. Calmly and steadily. There was no point in letting my feelings out. There was no point in having any. I had to deal with what was and consider what was possible. With small murmurs I cleaned her face and ears and wondered how her mind had been affected.

She kept her eyes on me like a dog, even when I moved her chin so that I could get behind her ears, where there was dried filth and blood.

But when I started to clean one shoulder she screamed. Horribly, gapingly she screamed and I saw they'd knocked her teeth about and that her mouth was swimming in raw blood. I tried to get her sitting up so I could drain it out. However, she screamed and fought me.

Kobi came back in, the callow mercenary attracted by human disaster. He stood there watching me grapple with her. Then saying nothing he tapped me on the arm and when I looked up with anger he pointed down, to the side of her shin, above the knob of the ankle bone. The cloak had slipped. As Liza fell back whimpering I raised its corner.

I'm a naturalist. My professional life has been spent killing insects, birds and a small number of mammals. I've prepared these specimens to museum standards and described them in my reports. I'm trained to tell of things as they are.

What Glebov had done: with his men holding her he'd cut with a razor a strip of skin about an inch wide from her ankle to the top of her thigh. He'd done it on both legs. Then he'd peeled the strips off.

You know why? To adorn his revenge for Sonja. To parody Andrej Potocki's regimental trousers, those of the Garde à Cheval: white with a blood-red stripe. That was his reason.

Her ribboned flesh was weeping. Straw was sticking to it. Quickly I covered her up. Kobi fetched a horse blanket and laid it over her cloak. By chance the initial 'R' and the golden Rykov wolf embroidered at the corner was next to her throat.

In English I said, 'Lord, save this woman, Elizaveta Doig.'

I sat back on my heels, holding her hand. I considered everything in the most rational manner that a husband is capable of. To be specific: the fact of night falling fast, her physical condition, the low outside temperature, the whereabouts of Glebov who was perhaps waiting to make a further attack, and the problem of getting her alive to Smolensk. What then? The hospital – a deathtrap. Corpses piled up on the lawn every morning like cordwood. I repeat, two strips of skin measuring one inch by thirty had been torn from her. Flayed – is that descriptive enough? I don't want to talk about the other thing. This woman – my wife of six days – naked under a horse blanket on the freezing stable floor – on the edge of insanity – in agony – with no drugs anywhere near – or telephone.

There are some sequences of action where one by one all the options are closed off except that which is the worst. Once this is accepted, the end has been reached. Nothing else is possible. No more can be said.

Kobi squatted beside me. 'It's a kindness to animals.'

I didn't respond.

He undid the holster flap at my belt. He handed me the Luger, butt first. Its long barrel was impossible to conceal. 'What's good for animals is good for us.'

Lizochka was watching. She looked from the revolver to my face. Her eyes were tranquil. Blood was coming from her mouth again. She said to me, 'Never be afraid of alone,' slurring the words.

She looked at Kobi, at me, at the world surrounding her. Maybe she was seeing the future as well. 'Charlie Doig, my own Charlinka. Let me go to your God and mine.'

Her lips moved but to me it seemed nothing moved except her soul, which I could see shining through her eyes. I mean from behind them, like a torch held at the back of a piece of soft brown velvet.

This smile, which came only from the eyes, was her legacy to me. It had such a luminous intensity that I knew she was lost. Well, I say lost because it's a placid little word that's not going to upset anyone, but stolen would be better and looted would be best. My wife was looted in the name of a socialist Utopia.

She smiled on me and thus said farewell. It was the smile of someone who has got to the far side of suffering and can make out a new shoreline.

This was the certainty that I drew from her smile.

'Don't be afraid,' she whispered. Her eyes took up the message, pleading with me.

'Elizaveta Rykov, Lizochka, Lizinka, love of my life – Mrs Doig . . .' I could say no more. She smiled on me again. She made as if to bring her hand up to stroke my cheek. I caught it, I kissed it, I kissed every inch of my bride's face.

I withdrew my hand – sat back – and she gave up. I saw the surrender take place. Her eyes, one moment as bright as street lamps, the next – gone. I'll tell you what I thought of: two ghost ships with full black sails glimpsed driving through the sea-fog very close to the rocks. The death of her soul, that's what I witnessed as I knelt beside her.

Seventy-three

WE BURIED them by candlelight, in the stable dung heap. It was the only place soft enough to dig. Kobi opened up the crust with the bayonet. We went down as far as the rot. Steam rose into our faces, and the tang of decomposing horse shit. Our breath, which seemed to be suspended in the frosty air like clouds of mould spores, hung around the yellow candle flame.

Misha was last since he was the heaviest. Kobi tied a rope to the wheel arch of the barrow and we trundled him off the terrace and down the rutted lane, pulling and pushing in tandem.

When death becomes a commonplace it ceases to terrify. I wish to declare that the physical act of burying these people was a method of obtaining some portion of freedom from them. I would point to the laying out of their limbs, straightening them up, folding their arms across the breast as befitted, and wedging the head so that the closed eyes looked in the direction of heaven. These contacts, the last, were most important and intimate to me.

I had never really touched Misha before, even though I loved him. Hugged him – yes, a thousand times. But I'd never been able to touch any part of him that I wished. And now I had to arrange his slack limbs I found myself doing so with the tenderness of a woman. I was grateful for the chance to help him in this service. Wasn't I alive and he not? I wept quietly as I prepared him – and over Nicholas also. Here was a man who'd tapped the rail of every hurdle erected for him by life. Yet in the manner of his death he'd achieved something given to few: death resisting injustice. As we dropped him in beside Louis, his hair flopping and obscuring his face, he ceased to be a failure. I saw that he was made for death. He excelled at it, reposing so nobly in the pit with the candle flame and our stooping shadows fluttering above him. I thought, Why did I always consider him such a hopeless oaf? I'd been mistaken, had used the wrong measure. Dropping to my knees I kissed my fingertips, reached down and laid them on the cold slab of his forehead. 'Forgive me, Nicholas.'

Speaking his name aroused in my mind an association with the Tsar. I bowed my head. Burying Nicholas was like burying the history of Russia. The whole cruel stupid magnificent parade was what I'd laid in the pit.

Then Kobi, with a tisk! of impatience, interrupted me by flinging horse blankets over the bodies. I went round straightening them. He began to spade in the spoil with short vigorous strokes.

My godfather, my cousin, Louis, my wife – I'd closed their eight eyes within the space of an hour.

Elizaveta: the light, furry consonants still tripped along my tongue as if nothing had happened, making me choke. My wife of just six days chased like an animal and raped in chorus by Glebov and his thugs to prove that the day of the common man had arrived. To inaugurate an era. Tortured and raped to death on behalf of a theory. Why not some worn and echoing harridan if that was the price fate wished to exact?

Kobi was spading lumps of dung onto them, and soon the thin red worms would be crawling down their throats, and this was being done on account of the possibility that rule by the common man would turn out to be more virtuous than rule by any other group of men. For this chance, which was no thicker than a cigarette paper, my Elizaveta had suffered a death as hideous as Christ's. For this she'd been compelled to die, for a whim, for nothing more substantial than the gossip of philosophers—

And it was I who'd done it. The slender nine-inch barrel – her braced jaw and tensing shoulders – then the spreading stain of ruby red. O my bold and bonny girl! She'd held steady for me, no jibbing, no last-minute change of mind. I believe it the greatest service I could have done her – that any man could do for his wife.

The rasp of Kobi's breathing, the flicker of the candle flame, the stillness of the frosty night, the thud of dung on my love's face and hands and on her cruelly mistreated body, of which our son, Dan Doig, was part—

I put back my head and howled. Grief poured out of me in bucketfuls. I buried my face in my hands, I shook both fists at my paltry God, I roared, I bellowed, I screamed her name and seizing a spade went snarling at the muck with teeth bared up to the gums, seeing Glebov's belly spread below me and clubbing it and carving at it with the side of the spade. I had thought before to say a prayer over them. But why should I have acted the saint? I didn't want to be a saint. I wanted to capture Glebov and slit him open and cut his balls off and crucify him. What else should I have wanted to do?

Wach auf! That's what Goetz would have shouted at me. Wake up! Stop prating and do something! I whacked her grave level with the back of the spade.

'May Christ have mercy on these men afterwards,' Kobi said, referring to what we'd do when we caught Glebov.

Seventy-four

I REPLENISHED THE Luger, taking the rounds back up to eight. Kobi wiped the bayonet on a scrap of hessian and stuck it in his belt. He wanted to talk about the question of our new horses while we stood beside the grave but I thought that to discuss departure was breaking faith with the deceased and took him to the shed where the sleighs were stored.

The moon was up. It was a risk I took, that Glebov might return to burn the house. But my greater opinion was that he and his men would be riding like hell to put miles beneath their belts. Strung out with a rolling rearguard, that was how I reckoned it, what I'd have done in his place. Avoiding habitation. Not stopping tonight. Pushing on, pushing on.

I wasn't in a hurry now. The longer we left them the less vigilant they'd be. By the second night they'd need sleep. That was when I planned to be on their tail. Tickling them, getting them worried.

They were eight, including Pashka. No one likes a traitor. He'd served his purpose. I couldn't see how he'd last long. Say seven, then, of whom one had been wounded.

We pulled the sleigh back to the Pink House. We found where Nicholas had cached his reserve supply of ammunition; loaded it on with food and quilts. Then we harnessed up and ran it through the bitter early night down past the old gates and up the track to Popovka.

The village was as silent as the grave. Not even the dogs were out. The windows of the small wooden houses were shuttered tight. The place stank of complicity. They knew what had been going on, probably in advance. Thick greedy peasant knowledge, as secret as incest. Already they'd be carving up Nicholas's fields, bidding out his threshing stacks, his cattle, his implements, carpets, furniture, saddlery, anything that was useful.

Luck was with us for the moon was still low and one side of the street was deep in shadow. Despite being greased, the sleigh runners made a gritty scraping noise on the ice. We unharnessed and left it for later. Like wraiths we stole through the ribbon of dark, past the hovels hushed in guilt.

We reached the church. There we ducked into the space behind the hanging post of the big wooden gates.

Opposite was the inn.

Not a glimmer, not a tallow rush of candlelight could I make out. But at the back a dog was kennelled. The second time it barked I caught a glimpse of a bundled figure sneaking in at the door beside the water butts. The third time I turned to Kobi.

He'd already gone, a ghost with flat eyes. I saw him flitting down the lane to the left of the inn so as to get up to the back of the water butts. Had there been a wind that night you'd have mistaken him for the shadow of a moving branch.

Then I lost him. I never saw him get into position. But the dog barked.

I levered a bullet up the spout. The bolt was smooth in my fingers, the action like butter. I took a deep breath. Then I pelted across the street and went up the two steps and shoulder first through the door.

But I'd been clumsy. They'd heard the rattle of my boots on the ice. Some of them were on their feet trying to get clear of the benches. All the men of the village must have been there, rows of beards and secrets. Candle stubs had been placed in the wall recesses and shielded by black card. There was a home-spun rostrum and a clerk with a ledger. The air was thick with tobacco smoke and sweat – fresh, rancid sweat. Fear too was in that smell, sweat and guilt and fear together.

The stench of all their shit smacked me across the face. It was good. It was justice that they knew shame. Traversing my rifle across them, I laughed terribly. The shaggy, veinous faces stared up at me, close-packed ranks of them.

I said, 'Count me in. I'll give a hundred roubles for the red carpet in his dining room.'

I said, ' I'm a cash buyer, boys, you can trust me.'

No one spoke. They didn't want my sarcasm. What they wanted was to hear the bare bright details of my business. So I said, 'Alright, cunts, tell me who's got the best horses in the village.'

Their beards curled with relief and their faces went lopsided and sly. They were thinking, Thank God, it's not about the killings, we can talk this one out. I saw the change. Cunning sprouted like mushrooms in the darkened cellars of their eyes. I began to hear movements among them, of their feet and clothing as they shifted their buttocks or uncrossed their ankles. They were relaxing. One of them even raised his drinking horn.

I recognised the man from our wedding feast. Fawning, he'd had Nicholas give him a tour of the Rykov family photographs. Later he'd sat opposite me and got drunk. It was he who'd told me that Sonja had been hanged.

Picking on him I said, 'Well, who? Give me the name.'

Of a sudden there was a displacement of bodies towards the back, a heaving of shoulders and elbows in the semi-darkness. The door slammed, the one that led out to the water butts.

'Pashka, your stable boy, Excellency,' called out a voice. 'He's been bad all day with the trots.'

'Silence!' I roared. I held up my hand. I didn't want them to miss it by their jabbering.

A man with concrete in his ears mightn't have heard his scream – no one else. It cut through the night like a hatchet. And when one breath had been exhausted, another started up, at a higher pitch.

I fixed that wedding guest in his shifty eye and pursued it everywhere as he tried to evade me. Having trapped it I grinned, wolfed, at him. 'Tell me your name. I want to think how your balls hang, how well you'd take the knife.'

The scream rose to a peak, turned into a whimper and finished, with a thud and a long gurgling sigh. Those wooden walls were thin and we could hear every bubble in his throat as the boy died beside the water butts. I was still grinning at the peasant. I waved the sights across his stomach.

'Was he a eunuch anyway? Then he'd scarcely have felt it. Still, not much fun when you've had the trots. Poor little Pashka.'

'Pashka was his son, Excellency,' called out a brave voice.

'Then you're Pappy Pashka and now there's only one set of balls left in the family. What a day you've all had.'

'Semyon Andreyevich,' the man said in a rush, half rising and trying to bow to me but getting tangled between the bench and the table, 'he always has the best riding horses, Excellency. He keeps them in the barn in the orchard on the left going to Zhukovo . . . Your worship, we had nothing to do with it. The creature Glebov and his speechifying—'

He was pulled down onto the bench. Other voices rushed up at me to say they'd been away the whole day – tending a sick cow, seeing relatives, gathering firewood.

I saw Lizochka before me, I saw her beauty and her agony, and I shot Pappy Pashka through the chest from five yards, the rifle resting on my hip. His head dropped instantly but he went on sitting there, wedged upright by his friends. The perfume of cordite – the inviting curve of the trigger – their treacherous cowering faces – I put a second and third shot into their yowling, nowhere in particular, browning the pack. I could have done with a machine gun, hosing them down from right to left and back again. You read about people being insane with grief. This I was not. They'd collaborated in the torture and violation of my wife. They should pay for it as brutally as was possible. Liza, an innocent, had paid one price. Why shouldn't the guilty pay a greater one?

What punishment would be crueller than her suffering? Could Kobi and I burn these people alive? I glared at them through the hanging gun-smoke. Was the timber dry enough? How would we manage to keep them enclosed?

A tiny sidling advancing movement took place in the corner of my eye. The shadows were creeping forward. They'd seen me work the bolt. They knew it wasn't a repeater. The animals were working up to rush me.

Spinning round I shot the nearest and leapt for the door. Kobi came running down the lane. He got off his magazine while I was reloading. Someone inside the inn slammed the door. I put a couple more shots through it for good measure. Then we went quickly up the moonlit road to the barn, walking side by side with our rifles at the ready.

The horses were as stated. Kobi saddled them while I stood guard. But I didn't think the peasants would try anything. That we departed taking our troubles with us would be the main thing. Good peasants, good cowards. I could never have handled them if they'd banded together at the start.

Kobi led out the horses, two to ride and one with a pack-saddle. They hadn't been out all winter and were bored and fresh. We curvetted down the main street like vaqueros and loaded our supplies off the sleigh. The villagers let out their curs to harrass us. Seeing us ride out down the Zhukovo road, they rushed barking and snapping at our horses' hoofs. Chuckling, Kobi shot a couple of the nearest, which did for that game as the others stopped to fight over which should eat them.

The largest of the dogs, a mastiff with cropped ears, seized a smaller one by the lappet of its under-throat and began dragging it out of the way, despite the latter's stiffened legs. The others were knotted snarling around the corpses, but these two were alone and silent. Seeing the technique of the mastiff made me understand why its ears had been cropped. The peasants also tethered their hot bitches overnight in the woods to have them covered by wolves.

I said to Kobi, 'We'll service Glebov with the bayonet. We'll do that first.'

'Like the stable boy,' he said with satisfaction. 'But that's not what killed him.'

We rode on, saying nothing but thinking about it.

The moon had painted the fields with an aluminium sheen. This was ground that had been awarded to my great-grandfather for having saved Russia. Now we ourselves were riding away to be saved not from the French but from our own people. In the atlas of my mind I laid out all the Russia I knew, its valleys, forests, plains, cities, villages. I was above it, looking over the edge of my cockpit like a fighter pilot. The cold may have had something to do with the intensity of this trance. It had frozen the muscles of my face so that my skin was a suit of armour in which only my eyes had life. Two worlds were operating for me simultaneously. In the existing one I was the passenger on a well-fed horse fiddling along an icy road: in my imagination I was hovering on the brink of the clouds.

I saw a myriad plumes of smoke and cinders from our manor houses. I saw the shots, the stabbings, the field executions, all the acts of revenge: the Pink House repeated five thousand times. I saw baby aristocrats having their brains dashed out, held like chickens by their podgy ankles. I saw the future. I saw bloody chaos. I saw it as clearly as any mad woman saw Christ chopping wood in heaven, for on my behalf it had been written across the sky in leaping flames. No one with a drop of Russian blood in their veins can be mistaken over a signal like that.

Kobi spoke to me. I awoke. And I found that what was left in my mind was one sole consideration: how do I get out of this with my skin in one piece. Liza wasn't there, nor my boy Dan Doig grown cold in her womb. I'd been instantly faithless. Already I'd forsaken the only woman God had made for me while she was still twitching in her putrid grave. I rode on through the pitiless moonlight.

Seventy-five

O NE LIVE hen was all that remained at Zhukovo. Feathers and carcasses were everywhere. Had they eaten them raw?

Misha's housekeeper was lying dead across the threshold. Vasili and his sons had been slain. Glebov's men had killed and skinned a bullock. Only the tail had been rejected. Every other part had been butchered and packed away on the horses. The trail of dripped blood was black in the moonlight. We followed it into the forest. Seven men mounted and four horses with the plunder.

The cold was at the outer extremity of the word. The air felt hollow – desiccated, its juices frozen out of it. When I dropped a riding gauntlet it fell as rapidly as if it had contained a five-pound weight or been made of iron. My cheeks and ears were paralysed, despite being scarved, and my lips were shapeless. I had to concentrate in order to form a word. Barrels of snot could have been running out of my nose and I'd never have known. The hairs up my nose were frozen, so that breathing was like inhaling red hot needles. My spit froze in mid-air and tinkled onto the ground like a piece of broken glass. Spurting blood would have been petrified into slabs in mid-air. Only the inside of my thighs, which were close to the vast furnace of my horse, were warm.

We slept for four hours in Misha's hay barn. His watchdogs woke us, fighting over the bullock skin, which one was hauling across the cattle yard. We saddled and mounted in darkness.

We rode roughly north and west. Kobi led. I had the pack-horse on a rein. The cold tickled the horses' noses as well as ours. It was good that Glebov wasn't hunting *us*. You can't stop a horse sneezing. Nor can the sound be disguised.

It is not the case that frost is silent. When as severe as it was now, it can freeze the sap in certain species of tree and thereby cause it to expand to the point of bursting the trees. The forest was alive with groans and sighs and the sudden splinter of falling boughs.

Dawn rose pink and smokey. For a while it became warm enough to snow. It fell meanly, in small hard pellets, and continued for a couple of hours, sufficient to coat everything with fresh tinsel.

Occasionally we came across a summer grazing meadow, a stretch of blistering whiteness that hurt our eyes. Find me the man who can say what lies beneath a surface of fresh snow and I'll kiss between each of his ten toes – the man who can say for sure, who'll put his neck at risk. I had no intention of chancing the horses on these innocent-looking plains. We kept well back among the trees.

I was right about his rolling rearguard. Usually one man but sometimes two, at intervals of about a mile. The history of these outposts was abundantly clear from the quantity of tobacco shreds and sunflower seed husks strewn upon the snow. Also from the piss-holes, which were not extensive, and tawny from insufficient nourishment.

We went slowly. Out of the night, out of nowhere I was going to take Glebov.

In the middle of the morning we found where they'd stopped. Why? No fire had been lit. A quarrel – to consult – had Glebov harangued them? There was no clue.

Here and there, in clearings, were the ruins of tiny snow-mantled farmhouses. A raven kept us company for a bit. Some tracks – iced-over lakes – woodmen's huts.

The forest stretched before us throughout that day. At some stage we'd meet either the Dniepr or the railway or the Moscow road. They were bunched together hereabouts. What worried me was if he got to the railway before us; walked his horse up the ramp of a military train and vanished.

I caught up with Kobi. 'We'll do it tonight.'

He stood up in the stirrups to ease his crotch. 'How?'

'He'll have to let them sleep. They're deserters, not after medals.'

'Three men sleeping, three as sentries, one wounded. How do we work that?'

A straight-line pursuit of the enemy offers only an approach up the arsehole, which is always nailed tight in these circumstances. It's from the side one must attack, or better still from in front. In that way one can assail the neck, the ribs, the armpit, the entire extent of the thorax, whatever has been left unguarded. To do this one must deviate. And to deviate successfully one must make the correct assumptions about the other man's speed and intended line of march, about how he thinks.

I was wary. He'd made a fool of me before. But either you have the nerve to play the king or you should watch from the stalls.

'Wait and see.' It was my father's well-worn phrase that I gave Kobi in reply. It was ages since I'd had Pushkin's likeness in my mind. I thought, I'll slice away Glebov's balls and nail him naked to a tree and his balls to another, and that'll even the balance between me and Russia, which has slain all whom I've loved.

I raised my gauntleted fist and smote the air. I spoke their names: George Doig, Elizaveta Doig, Nicholas Rykov, Mikhail Baklushin. I saluted them, my mother too.

Then I'd go to Chicago where I'd be freed from memory.

'Hurry,' I said to Kobi, 'or he'll get out on the railway.' Then we drew away to the south of Glebov's route so as to fetch a semicircle and grab him by the neck.

Seventy-six

NIGHT FELL and made no difference to us. Beneath a sheet of stars our horses strode implacably through the forest. A time came when I reckoned we'd gone far enough to the west. I made a sign to Kobi and we turned north on a course of convergence. This wasn't admiralty navigation but my instinct alone. When it felt right, we dismounted and went on foot.

Kobi scouted in front while I followed with the horses. If I was right we'd soon cross their line – or meet them head on. I didn't want that. I wanted to lie back a little and play on Glebov's nerves. But first we had to find them. We went very slowly. It would have been better on skis.

Now something good happened to us: our luck turned. Once it's on your side you can do no wrong. If that horse hadn't sneezed, we'd have walked right into them. But it did, on cue, and that's the difference luck makes.

It was down the slope, about four hundred yards away, where the forest was a bit thinner. I couldn't see the horse. The rapist was leaning, smoking, against a tree. It was all we could make of him. He was in a shadow of the moon, in a nicotine dream. Shall we leave him? Kobi's look asked me. I nodded. He handed me his rifle, hauled his *shapka* well down over his face – slipped away into the night. I bound the muzzles of our horses and waited.

When he returned we mounted and rode back to a dry hollow we'd passed earlier. We didn't unsaddle the horses but sat comfortably on the quilts and ate the slab of cold gruel we'd taken from Misha's porridge drawer and some wrinkled apples from his loft. I fired up Nicholas's little travelling stove and made tea.

I said to Kobi, 'So it's possible.'

His eyes gleamed. 'They're tired men.'

'Then yes?'

'Yes. But we need to come in from another angle.'

We took it in turns to doze.

By three the moon was well down the sky. The safest course was to take the horses with us in case we had to make a run for it. The easiest was to leave everything where it was and bet the bank on success. That's what I did. I could feel luck circling me – like a dove. Nevertheless I hobbled the horses and tied them to a tree. If they ran away you couldn't have snapped your fingers and got more from the shop, the forest wasn't that sort of place.

We came in at a slant, as Kobi directed. I was carrying our rifles wrapped in a quilt.

'Three sleeping, three as sentries,' he whispered.

In front was the ridge above Glebov's camp. To the left was the gully that Kobi had marked. He took the bayonet out of his belt. He kissed it. He gave me a quirky sardonic look. Within twenty paces he was invisible.

Pushing the rifles in front of me, I crawled to the ridge. The tip of a sentry's cigarette glowed. I could smell the coarse tobacco. The glow walked round for a bit. Sat down: disappeared.

Throughout the forest branches were groaning and cracking. The cold was unbelievable, even for Russia. I had my hands deep inside my coat, rammed into my armpits. They were under me as I lay there. It would have taken long seconds to get into a firing position. But I knew the sentry'd be no quicker.

He yawned, lengthily and gustily. These were common soldiers. They were having a good time: plunder, rape and killing. No one was in pursuit. Hadn't they been diligent with their precautions? So why shouldn't they get some sleep? It wasn't the army they were in now.

The moon found a chink among the trees.

He was seated broadside to me, clasping his knees beneath his chin and rocking gently. God I bet he was cold. I got my hands out of my coat and sighted the rifle on him. Easier to maim than kill in that position. He'd be slow to his feet if the balloon went up. He'd probably stand and listen – dither for a few seconds. Like the old Jew's horse. Then I'd shoot him at the sixth thoracic vertebra below the neck.

It was up to Kobi to squirm down that gully, do it and get out unseen. I wanted Glebov to know fear – the fear that turns guts green. Liza had known it as she ran; looked back over her shoulder when she heard the shout and felt its iron shaft. Glebov should know it also. I wanted him to brood upon the corpse he'd find beside him in the morning. His sentries – still in position. No noises, no alarms. But here was a dead man with sixteen inches of bayonet sticking out of his throat.

Then he'd know I was toying with him, that he could have been the body if I'd ordered it.

There's a point, reached very early by some people, at which hatred expressed in word and thought ceases to be a sufficient ointment for the soul. A curse goes only so far before it loses its sheen. Once the plaintiff recognises that the criminal is unmarked by his abuse and admits to wishing for a better result, he's more than halfway to revenge, which should be cruel, elaborate and humiliating in order to assuage at the highest emotional level. Refinements, that's what I'm leading up to. Stabbing Glebov as he slept would not have been revenge but a cheap form of murder. The pinnacle of revenge is to destroy a man before his own eyes.

This is what I was considering as I lay in the snow beneath the groaning trees and the milky arctic sky. I'd lost my wife, I was about to lose my country. I was owed revenge, principal and interest together.

I admired the waning moon. I targeted the sentry's head. I waited for Kobi's return.

If Glebov's camp suddenly exploded with gunfire and shouting, the game was up. I myself was as good as dead. But the alternative . . . Silence was success: silence was revenge slithering down a snow-filled gully. Would fifty years be long enough to dull my appetite for it? Perhaps everything would fade when I reached Chicago. I could find a new woman and grow faithful to the United States. Or the killing of Glebov might satiate me—

The tawny owl hooted to my left. Turning my head I saw Kobi approach like a shadow through the trees. I went backwards down the slope with the rifles. I could read nothing in his sunken eyes. For a moment I was gripped by the awfulness of failure. Then he turned into the moonlight and held out his hand. It was wet and shining, the most perfect blood I ever saw.

334

Seventy-seven

W E SLEPT a little but well. Around dawn we were back in the saddle.

For some time we had before us a defile between two low, wooded hills. It was the obvious route for Glebov. Being down to five fit men, he couldn't spare any to guard his flanks. So he'd rush it, come barrelling through in a bunch. If we had a good position we could take out a couple of them. Disabling the horses was one way. Ditto the men another. But all round dead was the best, apart from Glebov.

Beyond the hills I thought would be the railway. When we got there I found that first came the river, the huge sullen gunmetal grey of the Dniepr. How was Glebov going to do it? It was obvious that he regarded his escort as pawns and intended to finish up alone, on the train, with the entirety of the spoils. How was he going to get to the railway without being stripped and dumped by the ferryman?

What could be on his mind?

We tied the horses and found ourselves a handy place on the forward slope. There was only one decent track in the forest. We were on top of it where it left the trees. In front of us was a substantial boulder, bright with lichen. We fixed on it as a firing mark. The ground was open for another hundred yards beyond. We had ample room to follow through.

I said to Kobi, 'Does this remind you of anywhere?'

He smiled grimly.

We wiped our rifle barrels with leaf mould to prevent them glinting and settled behind the bank. Kobi lined up the path's debouchment from the trees. He grunted. 'If I was a man reaching that point, I'd pray for wings.'

I reminded him not to kill Glebov. We spoke no more.

A Zeppelin was strafing the main road to Moscow, Napoleon's road. What I'd taken in the distance to be brown ploughed fields was a continuous flow of retreating infantry and refugees. Or fleeing or deserting, however you want to express the fact of people having their lives destroyed. Slowly the Zeppelin cruised northwards, firing as it went. Packets of smoke from the few of our guns that still worked pursued it.

Did the airship have any metallic protection against our shells, or was its gas wrapped only in an onion skin? I pictured Glebov trapped in a stricken Zep: frying and screaming, the fat round his waist forming pustulous black bubbles like the pouches that despatch riders wear.

Ant-like soldiers scattered and regrouped as the bombs fell amongst them.

Glebov wouldn't want to be involved with that rabble. They'd have his plunder off him in seconds. Loot the looters! Indeed. Now the Zep was turning, like a plump, cumbersome louse—

The shot rang out. Close by, from within the forest.

It was exactly like the Jew whom I'd killed that this soldier bolted from the wood. Monstrous boots clubbing the laden horse in its ribs, hands pumping at the reins, a gasping mouth and a wild, scarlet, blown-out face.

The barrel of Kobi's rifle followed him. 'Wait!' I laid my hand on top of it so he couldn't see the foresight.

A second shot from within the wood threw the soldier against the horse's neck. He slithered sideways towards the ground. His feet got caught up in the stirrups. He hung there, pulling the saddle over, fingertips brushing the snow. Kobi, baulked and astonished, inched his head higher to see everything more fully.

Two more soldiers rode out of the forest, neither of them Glebov.

The leader flicked the used shell out of his rifle, which he kept at the ready. He had our bayonet slung by a cord across his back. He held the reins in both hands, above the pommel, riding-school style. Toeing the stirrups, heels well down. Talking out of the side of the mouth to the man behind, though with an eye always on the horse standing in the track in front of him. He had the jaunty air of a professional adventurer. But my private opinion was that not for all the undrunk vodka in the world would I have been him, riding in front of an armed man when the question so obviously concerned the spoils of war.

So maybe there was a war throughout Europe, and a civil war starting in Russia. Maybe the present sequence of history was unfavourable to me. Maybe I was witnessing the forging of a new hell. And maybe we should have shot both those soldiers as they rode before us.

But the fact remains that a man and his horse going in unison, stepping out as if in love with each other, is a spectacle so sweet that it has forever been gazed upon as if it were treasure. Which it is, for a woman and a horse are equal in the estimation of man and to witness either on their honeymoon with him is to truly understand the romance of history. He had this little bay mare gripped between his legs, the pair of them moving with a beautiful sense of balance. He was haranguing the man behind him, slicing the air with his gesticulations. His horse, listening to him and feeling his movements, was batting her silken ears in admiration. They were going at a small bouncing trot, snappily, in complete and trusting harmony.

He said over his shoulder in his rough voice, 'No, they're mine. We've talked about it enough. You agreed. I refuse to discuss the whole business again. Be content with the . . .'

My eyes were fixed on him. Should I have this fellow executed while he was riding so tenderly? The question engaged me. I wanted to hear what their quarrel concerned. But the best moments for killing him were going fast. I said to Kobi—

I said nothing to Kobi. As I opened my mouth the second soldier shot his friend. The bullet struck him in the base of the spine: the words ceased. Spasming he arched his back – clutched at his waist and stiffly, like a milk churn, toppled from the saddle. His *shapka* came off as he rolled down the slope. He had thick grey hair. He stopped himself, hands clutching at the snowy tussocks. Lips clenched, an expression on his face of manic hatred, he began to haul himself up on his elbows. His back was broken. He dug in his elbows one after the other, his useless splayed-out legs dragging through the snow. Another shot finished him off.

'No, let them do our work for us.' I kept my hand over the barrel of Kobi's rifle.

The second man went quickly through the other's pockets. He found what he was after, threw open his coat, jerkin and shirt, pulled up an undergarment and stowed the small package in a belt next to the skin. He tried on the man's greatcoat, glancing over his shoulder at its length behind him. He rolled up his own coat and rammed it into a saddle bag.

The man who'd been killed first had kicked off the stirrups in his death struggle and was on the ground. The soldier went through his pockets as well. He took both their rifles and ammunition and lashed the stirrups of the two captured horses over their saddles. Holding their reins he looked back into the forest. Then he rode past us and out of our sight as fast as he could. He'd have galloped if the track hadn't been so rough.

'We could have shot him and still got Glebov,' Kobi said.

'We might have scared him off.'

'He's not coming out this way. They've quarrelled. Shared the stuff and split up. Last night frightened them.'

'Anyway that's three more. Four including the man last night. Leaving two of them, one being Glebov, plus the wounded man.'

'Forget him. They'll have tapped him on the head. Just Glebov and a friend. But where, Doig?'

'Back.'

We rose stiffly to our feet. We checked our rifles for snow and dirt. Kobi said, 'I'm going down to get the bayonet back. I like having it.'

From behind us, up the hillside, there was a dry cough. Someone wanted to say something. I thought, That mother of all cunts has made a monkey of me again. He won't mess around this time. It'll be a bullet each.

We were standing there right out in the open. He had us covered whatever we did.

I tensed for the shot. I prayed to God it'd be Kobi he went for first. That way I'd have a chance. With lowered eyes I judged the best place to dive over the bank. Then very slowly I started to turn.

Seventy-eight

B UT IT was only a wolf staring down on us, whisking its brindled tail. It moved off into the trees, a glossy mature bitch with swinging dugs.

I couldn't bring myself to look at Kobi. Nor did he look at me. We acted as if we'd known all along it was a wolf.

Abruptly he seized me by the arm and exclaimed, 'The horses!'

It was like cats that we went up that hill. Any moment we expected to hear their scream of terror. They could break loose – disappear for good into the vastness of the forest. What then? What could we possibly accomplish on foot?

They'd scented the wolf and were twitchy as hell: stamping and rolling their eyes and rubbing their heads against their forelegs, trying to get their muzzles off. We croodled them and let them smell us all over. They quieted down. We gave them a nosebag with a little hay each. We had something to eat ourselves, some more of Misha's cold porridge. Then we mounted and began a back-cast to Glebov's camp.

I was quite clear about most of what had happened. The soldiers had pushed out shit when they awoke and discovered that someone had crawled through the sentries, bayonetted a sleeping man in their midst and crawled out again. A bayonet haft and a pool of ice-white blood are not cheering sights at dawn. So they'd divided the spoils and taken off into the forest. Every man for himself, true brotherhood.

But Glebov – had they deposed their fat little king? Slit his throat before I could?

There was a lesson in all this hide-and-seek with Glebov and

I'd learned it already: getting the answer wrong was a sentence of death.

We therefore circled the camp at a safe distance and examined spoor for half the day. At length Kobi was willing to swear that early in the morning five men had left on horseback with four packhorses and two on a loose rein. That left no horses for the last two men. One had been the man stabbed by Kobi. The other should be Glebov.

Not inevitably, not like night following day. But it was probable. I was willing to bet on it. We started to close in.

He was propped against a tree. Dead, I thought from a distance. Eyes shut, his head at an angle. But closer up I saw there was colour in his pig-bristled face, and when Kobi kicked the sole of his boot he screamed.

'They've broken his legs,' I said.

'Wait.' Very deliberately Kobi kicked each boot in turn. Again Glebov screamed. But Kobi shouted at him, 'Liar,' and seizing one boot by toe and heel twisted it back and forth to show me the leg was a good one. 'It would have been cheating,' Kobi said to me humorously.

'Why? What did you have?' Kobi kicking Glebov freely, 'What was it they wanted from you, scum?'

Glebov screamed terribly. He tossed his head and banged it against the tree. His pale eyes looked first at Kobi and then me. 'The pearls. The pearls that were bought with the blood of my countrymen and sported by the breeding sows of your family.'

I admired his spunk. For sure he knew what was coming to him. I told Kobi to get out our travelling stove and make tea. At last we'd got him, alone in the forest.

Glebov said, 'Are you going to cut me?'

'No fuck could be worth what I'm going to do to you.'

'I did it for the sake of history.'

'Of course.'

He lay slumped, watching me, blinking slowly.

'Which one took the pearls?' Kobi asked. 'The man with grey hair, who sat his horse well?'

Glebov nodded. 'Blyzov.'

'He's dead. He can't help you.'

I said to Glebov, 'There's no loophole.'

'Nor is there a God. So I shall suffer only once, here on earth, at your hands. God is tripe. Only mankind is worth suffering for.'

'What you did to my wife was an abomination both to mankind and to God. It'll take you a long time to die.'

'It was for the sake of Sonja, whose execution your class ordered, that I had your woman. It was for my country that I authorised that syphilitic rabble to go after me. Such white aristocratic skin, unblemished by want or hardship. Being used solely for fucking, thus to perpetuate your class. It was satisfying to destroy such perfection, especially to the soldier called Blyzov. It was he who killed Potocki, for having had him flogged for a crime he didn't commit. The regimental stripes on her legs – the final touch. It was Blyzov who thought of it. That was afterwards. But it was I who had her first—'

Kobi rained kicks on him. I thought he was going to pass out. Bending over Glebov I said, 'I know what you did to her, you don't need to tell me. But it wasn't you who killed her. I did that. I, Charlie Doig, her husband.'

He started up. Eyes suddenly hard, testing me for the truth.

'I shot her in the temple.' I took my Luger from the holster and jammed it into his head. 'There, at the nervous place.'

He said nothing: continued to stare up at me with shrinking pupils.

'So who was the coward and who was brave, Glebov? It was my Lizochka who had the courage. How many women would ask to be shot? Your Sonja bitch, she howled for her life. On her knees, all ugly and blotchy. I heard it from the police.'

His tongue, a thing of wet pink, dabbled round his lips.

'For Lizochka I fired from a distance so as not to mark her skin with the blast. But for you . . .'

'Do it, do it quickly,' he whispered.

'. . . for you there will be no shot.' I laughed. 'Why should I be merciful?'

I walked to the horses and got out my razor. Flicked open the blade and ran my thumb across it. I ordered Kobi to tie Glebov to the tree and to put a second rope under his chin.

He turned off the paraffin. Tea could wait.

'Strangle him a bit?' he said, tensioning the rope with a stick.

Glebov's head was against the tree, his jaw tilted and his throat taut. His eyes were closed.

I said, 'Praying?'

'There is no God.'

'You'll need one' – and I put my forefinger on the edge of his eyelid, where the lashes started.

He opened his other eye. 'What are you going to do?'

'Cut off your eyelids.' I pulled at the skin, drawing it out to consider the angles next to his nose.

'Blind me instead. Anything but piece by piece. Blind me, Doig, and then let us forgive each other. That's how true men should behave. It's not our fault we commit these crimes. We're driven to them. It's the fault of the times we live in.'

This was such typical Russian humbug from a man on the brink of the pit that I bent down with my hands on my knees and stuck my face into his. I laughed outright at him. 'Ha ha ha, no-God Glebov is now of a mind to seek forgiveness. Ha ha ha. The rapist repents. So how would that leave things between us? Should I expect my Lizochka to shout down from heaven: Prokhor Fyodorovich, because you repent I forgive you for what you did to me . . . in fact, you may do it again . . . do anything you want so long as you repent – is that how my wife should be thinking? Ought I to be kissing you and calling you brother, is that what you mean?'

'I never talked of repentance. That was your idea.'

'So what's forgiveness if it's not to involve repentance?'

'Quits, that's what forgiveness is. You blind me in one eye – quits.'

'One?'

'It was Blyzov who tortured her. Let him bear half the price.'

'You think one eye sufficient for what you did to my wife?'

'It happens to the women of Russia every day, especially in the cities. Women are weaker. No one can say that's untrue. However . . . in view of what Blyzov did . . . Come, Doig, you can see what my men have done to me. I'm helpless. Let's get on with it. I forgive you in advance.'

'Keep your tricky words for God, not me. Yes, God, whom you say is nowhere. See if He's around when you need him.' I'd started to shout. All his talk about forgiveness was revolting to me. I was shouting, and spitting into his face, which was blotchy and had hair coming up in clumps like a sprouting potato. 'If He's out then try the Devil. They're the same to you.'

He said, 'I won't recoil. I'll make it easy for you. If I could just have something to bite on . . .'

He was a cunning bastard. Bringing in the idea of forgiveness was his first ploy. It made me mad with rage – but it lodged the seed. It gained him a little tempo. It was like someone saying, Have another glass of tea. You know you don't want one but a few moments later you begin to think about it: perhaps I will, after all . . . You see his game? Anyway. Then saying he wouldn't flinch – that was his second trick. That this murderer and rapist could offer to be my assistant – I was astounded. He wouldn't recoil! I'd work my razor into the corner of his eye, just beside his nose, which is not easily done, slice the skin between the eyeball and the bone – and he wouldn't even twitch! Not a murmur! He'd probably expect me to say, Thank you so very much, Mister Glebov, you've been an ideal patient. He'd worked it so that in the end it was I who'd be in *his* debt . . . There he was half frozen to death, with a smashed leg, on the point of being condemned to continuous wakefulness until he grew new eyelids, if he ever would, and he came out with a remark like that. It took my breath away.

I straightened up. The razor was still open in my hand. I looked at it, I looked at Glebov. The image reached me of his two pallid triangles of skin lying on the flat of my palm. I could see them, the lashes still trembling. Were they trying to do something, get rid of a loose hair or a spit of melting snowflake? At what stage would life depart completely? Would they attempt a final blink? Would I go on feeling this tiny fumbling on my skin, as of two white grubs, for the remainder of my life?

That was the idea I had as I stood over him. It defeated me. I stayed my hand.

Kobi was disgusted. It was the *duty* of the weaker man to provide a spectacle. They'd been invented for the purpose. 'What makes you so soft, Doig?' he yelled, kicking Glebov on the point of his hip. 'This is the second time. Remember in the house, when we were looking for your woman?'

I snapped my razor shut. 'Not in cold blood.'

Kobi said petulantly, 'It doesn't have to be his eyelids.' In his annoyance he slashed in half the rope holding Glebov, so ruining it.

'He'd only have fainted,' I said. 'So why do it?'

'It'd have been good to watch. Then I'd have shown him his face in a mirror.'

'Why?'

'Show him what a woman would see.'

I looked at Glebov stretching and manoeuvring his neck. His blue eyes regarded me superciliously: I'd proved weak. But he said nothing, which was wise.

He passed out as we settled him on the packhorse – we had to rope his broken leg to his good one beneath the animal's belly. But Kobi brought him round.

In the afternoon we reached the Dniepr. It still had a good flood from the earlier thaw and was free of ice. The ferry wasn't much more than a floating platform with a wooden rail round it. I suppose it had a vague bow and stern. Four men with sweeps operated it – a family arrangement. We could have hidden nothing from eyes like theirs. Seeing the direction of their thoughts I pointed at Glebov's legs: 'He tried something on us.' Then they became respectful. Their head man struck up a conversation and named to me the regiments whose retreat was thronging the highway: 102nd Vyatski, Krasnostavski and so on. Their tribe occupied an entire village that he pointed out to us, on a promontory a little way above the landing place. Because of their monopoly over the ferry, the menfolk were able to select whatever woman they fancied from the surrounding villages.

We chose not to dismount and were shipped across sitting like conquistadores. It took forty minutes. We paid with Glebov's money from out of his boot – fifty roubles for us all: they were in a position to squeeze the traffic.

The railway line was about a mile to the west of the river. We camped near it. I wanted to get an idea of the trains that were moving.

Another mile over was the Moscow road. It was clogged with peasants pushing handcarts or tugging at their ruined cattle, with deserting soldiers, with dingy canvas two-wheeled hospital wagons, with curs, thieves, children and shuffling old babushkas.

344

Every age, nationality and degree of wretchedness was on display. The noise they made from afar was a sullen, shapeless roar, the noise of thousands of frightened people on the move. But when I went closer I couldn't understand where it was coming from since no one was speaking, except to curse. They were too exhausted, too demoralised, too near the point of giving up and dying. It must have been the sound of their movement along the road, of wooden wheels churning through mud, of despair and their inner lamentations.

On my return to camp I said to Glebov, 'That's where you should be, in a Red Cross *dvukolka*,' referring to the hospital wagons. 'I'll find one for officers tomorrow. They'll straighten out your leg for you.'

Seventy-nine

H E SURVIVED the night. One could say no more. We took him to the highway where we stood back among trees so as not to draw attention to our horses, which were still in good fettle. (Animals such as ours were the equivalent of ready money.) Soon a convoy of ten Red Cross carts came along. Beside the first one a giant of a man in a greatcoat and officer's cap was levering himself along on crutches at a good rate. When his coat flopped back I saw he'd had his left leg amputated halfway up his thigh.

We dragged Glebov over to the giant, his legs trailing. At first he tried to scumble along on his good leg but Kobi kicked it away every time. I asked the giant if it was an officers' wagon. He said they all were. These days officers had to stick together. I showed him my Tsarist travelling papers – holding them privily between us. I rolled my eyes towards Glebov. 'It's not a hotel,' the giant said.

He hopped round to the back with me. We rolled up the canvas and looked in. It was like a mass grave, all the bent, dishevelled, torn limbs. The smell of shit and rotting flesh was indescribable. But eyes were glinting in the grey light and after a bit I saw there was an order to the bodies.

'Room for another, boys?' my friend asked.

The grumbles being subdued, Kobi and I each took an end of Glebov and swung him over the backboard.

Kobi flipped down the canvas and addressed the ties. I said to the giant, 'He's a bolshevik.'

'Tickle him up, then?'

'Slowly.'

He put his head through the gap between the canvas and its supporting pole and spoke into the hellhole. Turning to me with a grin, 'They say they'll need to interrogate him before they feel entitled to take any further steps.'

Swinging himself round the cart to his old position beside the driver's seat, he pointed to our horses with his crutch: 'Those yours? Must be. You're too clean to have come here on foot.'

Kobi went to fetch them. There was only Glebov to keep us there.

The man opened a conversation. 'Bravo your catching that fellow! The fate they dish out to us officers,' – he ringed his lips and puffed out a cloud of hatred – 'it doesn't bear thinking about. I suppose I've been lucky – sliced in two for a noble purpose, that of helping our country. I'm a big man . . . What's your name? Doig, that's a funny one. Thought there was something in your accent . . . The nurse told me afterwards about getting my leg to the dump. It kept slipping off her shoulder. She felt like a butcher carrying a side of pig. In the end she had to call a friend. They bent my leg at the knee, tied it up with string and wheeled it away in a barrow. Life's droll! None of us expect to end up where we do. Your fellow – you yourself – your man here – and look at me! Consider my life for a moment, sir . . . Do you have the time? I won't be technical. It was like this. Floor by floor, room by room, my widowed father came down in the world until he had to sell the house of his parents, its garden and its orchard. At that time I was halfway between boy and man. He took me to live in an old summerhouse down by the river. It was only one floor and we thought we could go no lower. But the mists got into his bones. He fell gravely ill. To pay the doctor he had to surrender one of his cow meadows. All he had grass left for was one milking cow with a tousled topknot between its horns that he'd named Brisket.

'She was his mistress. That's not a lie, sir, Brisket was by then the only woman in his life. She was warm and large and indolent and her milk bubbled like champagne. She loved him as he loved her, and would produce cavernous gurgles from her stomach and flash her eyes and toss mouthfuls of grass in the air when she saw him coming. Then she died of bloat. It was the truest form of tragedy for my father. Without Brisket he couldn't afford to keep me. He sent me off to be a sailor. The only book he ever read to me was about the sea, and I loved it, that was how that happened.

'Imagine it, I was once a sailor! And now I'm a one-legged soldier – a cripple, to be sure. By the end of the week I may be dead. Who knows except for Him, and He's busy these days. Back into the pack I'll go for shuffling . . . I tell you, Doig, the whole business is a drollery. It's the only way to consider it unless you want to live like a vegetable or in a shoebox . . . Hey, there's your fellow starting to sing . . . Go and have a peek – I'll hold your horses for you.'

We went to the back of the wagon. I wanted to be sure that Glebov was paying his dues. I wanted to see him *properly* suffering and for him to see me watching, so that he understood all the connections.

The officers had him naked on the straw-covered bed of the cart. Which was just, for they had him like he'd had my wife. Sprawled round him with their slings and splints, picking and prodding at him, all in this thick sweet gangrenous fug, they were discussing what to stick up him – castration of course – fingernails – humiliation and pain – his grating leg bone – the order of proceeding – how to make it last – how to prevent him becoming unconscious.

'What's the best stimulant in your opinion?' an officer asked me.

I smiled on him, and on Glebov, to whom I said, 'You should have settled for eyelids.'

'Eyelids!' exclaimed that officer as if making a medical discovery.

Glebov was perfectly aware what was going on. He rolled his eyes towards me, then the whole of his face, pallid and hairy. Straw got shucked up beneath his cheek.

I said, 'You'll remember Elizaveta Doig.'

'My cause will give me strength.' Even then there was pride in those fanatical blue eyes.

'Anything else to say?'

'You tell them.'

I waved on the officers to get busy. A second one, a fellow with a bandaged skull, called out to me hoarsely, 'Bring us another fifty like this one, friend.' I said for them to shout to me when Glebov began to beg.

Kobi said to them, Did they need any help with Glebov, odd jobs and the like – and climbed in before anyone could refuse. I went back to see my friend the giant.

But one horse only was there – our packhorse. And one man, the carter, with his puckered drooling idiot's grin.

'What have you done with them, shitsucker?' I shouted.

He pointed up the road with his stubby whip, direction Moscow, which is where the column was heading.

Together we stared along that dull, drab coil of humanity. Then he turned his head towards me to gauge my harshness and simultaneously to stroke me, so to say, in order to lessen the blow.

Spittle was running from the corners of his mouth down into his beard. I could see the droplets creeping around in it like lice. 'Most sweetly he spoke, your honour . . . most *handsomely* considering his shortened leg – "Shall I go to my grave like a prince or like an earthworm?" I said, "Like a prince, of course, Excellency." He said, "Cup your hands under my last good leg, then, and let the glory belong to the swift." What else could I do, your honour? A poet!'

'What do you mean, *do*,' I shouted. 'You could have told him to go to hell. A man with one leg – a *cripple* – you let him ride off?'

'But we must honour our poets, your honour. It's the only school learning I ever had.'

'What's wrong with shouting? Screaming?'

'Whatever would I have shouted . . . ? Two good horses as well,' he said reflectively.

'It's late to be saying that,' said Kobi at my side. The three of us gazed up the column of refugees.

Already my friend was a quarter of mile away, lopsided in the saddle but riding furiously, with Kobi's horse tagging on at the end of a rein. The scarlet band of his officer's cap stood out boldly. I wondered how he hadn't been pulled to the ground and knifed. He seemed oblivious to the danger. I could see him hustling his animals along. (The animals of a man in Popovka, then mine and now the giant's.) I could hear him shouting to people to clear a way for him. The god that protects lunatics and drunkards had him under his wing. What a din he was making! Ordering them about as if he was a general! Yet they willingly let him through. They could see he was one-legged, that his balance on the horse was precarious. They must have sensed his adventure and smelt the fire in his soul.

'*Zhivo*! Look lively now!' a woman screeched. 'To the Kremlin, then, *golubchik*!' meaning 'my precious dove'.

These wretched people were honouring him. Out of nowhere he'd appeared, this huge lurching figure. They were showering him with the tatters of their hopes and their dreams – he'd become their child, their errant son off to conquer the capital. To ride one-legged into Moscow! Such a thing!

He was at an angle, his cap was at an angle, his whole world was at an angle of his own making.

The highway turned – and dipped. He disappeared, and our horses also.

Eighty

I SAID TO Kobi, who didn't understand my moderation, 'Look at the robber go. We had two good horses and now we're on foot. But that man is riding to victory. He was right. Life's droll, and there's the proof for you.'

And to prove it a second time, in his haste to go tilting the fellow had left us the packhorse on which was all that was valuable: rifles, ammunition, bedding and food.

Glebov was squealing away. I thought of looking in on him – but then Kobi was beside me, sulky and complaining because he could no longer hold sway from the back of a horse, which is indeed a veritable dominion when everyone else is on the ground. He was stepping disdainfully through the slubby ochreous mud, like a cat.

I said, 'Then leave me. Take one-tenth of my money and quit. You've served me well. Give someone else a chance.'

He would have if he'd still had a horse to ride. But being at the same level as that tide of desperates had unnerved him. He was a man of the steppes, uncomfortable here, and it was obvious. People were eyeing him in a speculative way, asking themselves how an advantage might be had from him.

He glowered and looking down said they'd been his best riding boots ever. But he kept walking with me. He was leading the packhorse.

And suddenly I got nervous. Our best horses had been stolen. What was to stop these vagrants rushing us and having our packhorse, with all our working capital on it? I bet we looked juicy, and our horse would make many meals. So we acted ostentatiously with our rifles, spoke loudly about the rest of our troop, and began to inch our way out of the scum. We'd return to our last camping place. There I'd leave Kobi to guard the horse. I'd come back on foot to enjoy Glebov.

This was a wise decision – related to luck – for we'd only just got into camp when a couple of Zeps returned and leisurely bombed their way up the entire column. I don't expect the Red Cross signs swayed them a bit. They did as they pleased, unchallenged, for the remainder of the day. It was only when they'd cleared off that I could set out to run Glebov to ground.

But everything was in total confusion, and people were crying out like sheep for their lost ones. There were broken corpses strewn along the highway and folded into the ditches, wounded of all ages crawling through the churned-up mud to keep going from the Germans, a shattered cow being bled at the throat, wrecked carts, abandoned old women – chaos. Over the entirety of this desolate and Napoleonic scene hung the usual mauve veil of cold.

No one recognised my description of Glebov's carter. Weren't they all dottled old fools?

At last I espied a tall straight man, transparently honest, walking alone. No sooner did I ask him where the hospital wagons had got to than he pulled a revolver on me. Looking into his eyes I saw they were hollow. 'Are you mad or blind?' I asked, at which he aimed his weapon at somewhere near my liver and pressed the trigger three times – viciously, grimacing at the clicks. There was a cry from behind us. A girl, his daughter maybe, on all fours, dragging a mangled foot through the mud. Red cheeks, flaxen hair, a big blubbery mouth. 'Keep them for us, one each. Keep them, idiot.'

I said to him, 'Goes better when loaded.' He hid the revolver from me like a child, behind his back. I left them to it and fiddled my way up the column, trusting in none but my eyes as witnesses.

Night began to fall. Hundreds of small bobbing lanterns sprang up. I could find no trace of the hospital wagons. The village of Chernukh came in sight, where there was a railway halt. Having a fresh idea, I went back to fetch Kobi.

He said, 'Glebov's dead by now, must be, Doig. Let's sleep.'

It wasn't enough. I wanted to hear Glebov beg for his life, I wanted to be called in as arbiter by those officers, to look in the eye the destroyer of my happiness – and shake my head. Perhaps I'd dither a bit, spin it out. But in the end he would die, and I would watch him die. It was to be the certificate of completion, as close to quits as I could get it, remembering always that the other party had been my wife.

'Killed and thrown out of the wagon like a dog,' Kobi said.

'Maybe,' and I told him to repack the horse so the two of us could ride it to Chernukh, Kobi going pillion. We'd board the next horse train so that by dawn we'd be well ahead of the column. Then we'd ride back down it until we found Glebov. One way or another we'd get him.

I thought about the one-legged giant. Wherever one looked there was misery. A rational human would have rated the chance of a decent life as nil. Yet here was an amputated fellow who'd thought well enough of the future to steal our horses and engage life head-on. Even now he was riding on Moscow. He'd have met others of a like mind. From hand to hand the torch would have been passed until the night sky was brilliant. *Na Moskvu*! To Moscow! Freedom from Tyranny!

Was everything really so uncomplicated? Should I say of Elizaveta and thus Glebov – gone? Draw a line beneath their names and start up again?

'They broke his other leg, for the sake of symmetry,' Kobi said behind me. He was annoying as a pillion rider, always fidgeting around to get his balls comfortable.

'What with?' I wanted a dispute.

'The carter's lump hammer. He fainted. In my opinion he's certain to be dead.'

Nothing more was said until we arrived in Chernukh. A lantern was hanging in the station porch. By its light we saw them, the ten hospital wagons, all open at the back and all of them empty. Just pissed-on straw and bloody rags. I woke up the stationmaster. He thought we were bolsheviks. I said we had a mind to be unless he told us where the wounded officers had been taken. He said St Petersburg – 'I mean Petrograd, your honour. When they get better they're to join the Tsar's new army. That's what I heard them being told.'

'What about a one-legged giant riding two good horses?' I asked.

'I couldn't say, I see so much madness every day.'

Eighty-one

I T WAS three days later, at dawn, that we reached Petrograd. We went to the hospitals in turn. Through every ward for officers and every bed in them. The nurses didn't like it until I told them everything about Glebov. Then one of them gave me a list of private houses that were still taking officers.

We took a trolley along Nevsky Prospekt to the stop at Kazan Cathedral. From there it was only a short distance to Uncle Igor's palace. I'd no idea what had happened to it since he'd been blown up. If Joseph was still there I was going to ask him about protocol at these other houses where Glebov might be: introductions, passwords and the like.

Its huge grimy façade was bright with clothes hanging from the windows. Within the courtyard was an encampment of families waiting to claim a room. Children were playing with snowballs. A milking goat with tight yellowish udders like parsnips was eating from a nosebag. From the neck of the emperor Tiberius radiated a network of washing lines to the naked marble catamites that Igor had positioned round him.

Here and there sprigs of Igor's box parterres could be seen, each wearing a bonnet of snow. I was surprised the goat hadn't eaten them. The long stone benches were level with snow between the armrests.

I was told that Joseph had been allocated a room at the back. Kobi and I went in. The stuffed lion in the hall had gone. So too had the wooden panelling and the splendid sequence of stateroom doors.

Joseph hurried forward, arranging himself. He'd put on for me his old shiny frock coat with satin lapels. We embraced and patted each other. He'd done his best after the other servants had left. Igor's steward had urged him to save himself. He'd refused. 'I am my father's son. Why should I run away?' One morning the steward himself failed to arrive. A little later soldiers came and ordered him to take in common people. Having given up all hope of seeing the family again, he conceded.

He brushed away the citizens gathered to eavesdrop and led us to his room, well out of the way, at the end of a quiet corridor. We could scarcely get in at the door for all the furniture he'd rescued. Piled-up tables and chairs filtered the light from the window, which was crusted with cobwebs. He himself had a cot to sleep in. Beside it was a French drum from the 1812 campaign. On it was a seven-branch candelabra, one of five that used to be on the dining table. He lit a candle from the little fire.

'I spend much of the day sleeping,' he said.

'Think of the flies here in summer,' Kobi said. Then he left us, saying he was going to find Glebov.

I told Joseph about the information I was after. He knew nothing about any such houses: no one dared shelter officers any more. Not openly, anyway.

He wanted to hear about Lizochka. I told him she was dead, at the hands of terrorists. He cried out and fell back into the hideous American chair made of chrome in which Igor had been accustomed to drink martinis. He waved his hands at me. 'Brutes, brutes, the worst sort of our people. String them up. Or shoot them. Nothing has ever been as bad as this in our country.'

His ikon lamps were in the central pigeonhole of a nice French bureau. He bowed to them. Then he sat on the edge of his cot, his frock coat all rucked up. He crossed himself in advance of the story about Liza's death. But I refused him, saying I wanted to talk about good things only. 'For a start,' I said, 'your employer, by whom I mean Count Igor, saw fit to bequeath all his possessions to Liza. You know what that means by our law.'

It was as if a spring had gone off inside him. He jumped up and hugged me. 'And thus to you, Doig, to you! These are all yours! My humble backside – I was only warming it for you, Excellency, knowing that no Russian aristocrat enjoys placing his behind in a cold chair – please, Excellency, I implore you,

355

sit in it, it's yours . . . oh, this day has not been in vain! How have I deserved such fortune? Well, no matter how it was done, what's important—' His voice dropped. He toed a Rykov coal scuttle significantly. It was red-lacquered, with our wolf, now sadly bruised, on both side panels. He winked horribly. 'I've still got some of his gin. English, the best, like oil, never freezes. I beg your pardon, Excellency, *your* gin. Count me as your gin creditor, Doig.'

I said, 'Joseph, are you drunk already?'

'Excellency, I am always drunk. It's the only consolation available in the city.'

'She was a goddess,' I said.

'She was more than that. She was from the Bible. Excuse me,' and he disappeared to wash the dust off an antique *lampachka* so that we might drink with old-fashioned graciousness.

It was some time later that he produced the photographs, slyly: three albums on brown cartridge paper and a collection of frames.

There were ten of her. Some as a dark, gangling, bob-haired child; one miracle of her skating, so clear that I could see the fanning spray of ice chips as she cornered, a look of mathematical concentration on her face, showing the tip of her tongue, fur-muffed wrists wrapped across her chest; and the stunner I was after, taken at close range as she stepped off the running board of the Astro-Daimler, her face filling the loom of the picture: the black beret, curlicue on top like the tail of a miniature pig, the surprised grin, the first-class teeth, the Saracen nose, and the deep truffling eyes, so full of shyness, in each of which was centred a pinpoint of silver light.

'Ah, Elizaveta.' Slowly Joseph pronounced the letters, pinching his forefinger against his thumb as he rang each chime. 'Elizaveta, Madame Doig.'

I wrapped the photos in tissue. Joseph cut two slices of cardboard and taped the photos between them.

'Now we shall drink to her properly,' he said.

We finished off the coal scuttle. He said he knew where there was more. He had hidey-holes everywhere in the palace. All servants did. It was so dull waiting for a man to finish writing a letter or having a nap. He'd often longed to march in and say,

356

'That's enough of that, Excellency. You should have heard their rudeness about you when they were leaving *your* house.'

In his many hours of leisure Joseph had perfected a thank-you letter for uncle Igor. 'My dear Alexander Alexandrovich and esteemed lady, the food and your company last night were from God. I was unworthy of your wines. This morning it is snowing. My steward says there are more riots to come. I shall stay inside with my cat. Heartfelt salutations from . . .'

'He was lonely. There was no one good enough for him except Elizaveta . . . Gone! Both gone! Leaving us with the barbarians. With the rubbish, Doig! With the country's absolute shit, *pardonnez-moi, excusez-moi cinq mille fois, monsieur le Duc.* That was a saying of your uncle's that became a joke among us servants.'

I said I'd never heard it on his lips. Joseph said he couldn't have picked it up anywhere else.

After a while I said to him, 'Joseph, tell me this: can a woman be one's sole reason for living?'

He debated with himself, quite visibly. In the end, 'Yes, if the man is weak or stupid.'

'I'm neither. I've got no enemies in Chicago. That's where I'm going.'

'Why not? Go to Nicholas Station and ask for a ticket to Vladivostok. Then take a boat. There'll be nothing to cry for when you leave, except your lady.'

We drank, we wept, we drank.

I gave Joseph the palace, but he refused it. Offered no reason, merely ignored what I said.

Later I gave him all the statues and pictures and books and folios of botanical illustrations, and the silver and towels, and everything within and without the room where we sat in the great warmth of gin and latterly vodka. I pressed these important arte-facts on him so amiably that I could see his refusal was insincere and done from embarrassment only. So I wrote the gift out on a scrap of paper and tucked it into the top pocket of his coat. He bowed to me and taking his coat off, hung it up so that, as he said, the valuables would be 'out of harm's way'.

Much of the day passed doing suchlike things in that strange candelabra'd den. Then Kobi came to remove me.

'What about Glebov?'

'Disappeared. Dead, alive, I don't care any more. I've been to all the houses. The last soldiers in them were made to leave two weeks ago. If you want to see Glebov stiff in his grave, find him yourself.'

I stuck up my hand. He heaved me out of Igor's chrome chair. Joseph, lying supine on his cot, murmured, 'The Tsar, has he risen?' Bending, I kissed him farewell.

I was in a dangerous condition. Kobi was right to take my rifle away. The rabble in the courtyard might have suffered, or their goat, or the snow-capped head of Tiberius. Anything could have happened the way I was.

Kobi said, 'Glebov's lying dead with the rest of them. Bombed by the Zep or broken up by the officers. Anyway in pieces. Dead, Doig, *dead*.'

'Does he have to be?'

'Yes.'

We walked past the gatekeeper's lodge and out into Nevsky. Her photographs were strapped to my chest, inside my shirt. Turning I flung kisses at the festooned windows. 'Keep the palace! Money will be useful when paying the coal bills. Best of all would be a bank. Enjoy it! Don't let your children mark the floors.'

I stood to attention and sang a verse of the Marseillaise in its striking Russian version. I saluted the flag. I lowered it for the last time, the slinking Rykov wolf. It was so obviously a failure. An old babushka was stood watching me. Seeing the rapid, nautical movement of my hands and my upturned stare, she asked me what I was doing. I told her. 'It's been there since 1813. You're not worthy to look upon it any longer. I shall have it made into a pair of trousers and fart out of its mouth.'

She gaped into the grey sky, seeing nothing. She looked at me cunningly and nudged her companion. I said, 'Do you suppose that I'm mad? Is that what your potato brain has indicated?' Kobi came forward to restrain me.

But like a gazelle I sprang from his grasp and ran out into the middle of Nevsky Prospekt. I stood astraddle with my hands on my hips and looked down the long, straight, noble view towards Znamenskaya, where Nicholas Station is. It was sensational in the blond light of March. Here, captured in a glance, were the last two hundred years of our fraught and horrible history. And the next two hundred? Tears came into my eyes. The horse-cabbies swerved around me. Complicated abuse issued from their mouths, its intensity blowing aside the curtains of their black, sucked whiskers. More punctually than usual, my darling tripped daintily from the palace (*her* palace: I hoped Joseph wouldn't be offended that I had to take the gift back) wearing her scarlet dancing shoes. Hearing a noise, I looked up and saw that the Rykov wolf was again snapping in the wind.

I bowed to my bride, bowed low. She laughed, and curtsied in return.

'Shall we . . . ?' My hand went round her slender cream-taffeta'd waist. To save arguing later, I said, 'Will those shoes do for a mazurka?' She laid her hand on my shoulder. 'Long-step, my soul?' 'Long-step,' I said, hunched over her, the tip of my nose in line with the tip of my boots. She raised a pinch of her dress and looked into my heart and then my face. Black eyes, white teeth, that sharpish nose – my love forever and ever, amen.

We clasped hands and cocked them at the ready. Sunshine was suddenly around us.

'*Paidyom,* then let's go,' I shouted.

But she held me back. 'Gradualness, Charlinka, remember what your mother told you . . . to Nicholas Station – and then?'

'To Moscow, Vladivostok and Chicago,' I roared. 'To paradise, my angel.'

'Then, two – three – to paradise, oh yes!' and away we swirled down Nevsky.

A policeman stayed us with an out- thrust baton and said, 'Where are you going, comrades?'

'Dancing to Moscow,' I replied, and he stood back.

My breath was coming in lumps and the blood was strong in my cheeks, suffusing them with happiness. I kissed her, I cradled her, I had her recline against my arm so I could kiss her the better, and together we fell among the heaps of rusty Tsarist snow that had been shovelled into the centre of the street. A pedestrian ran out to help us up. He said, 'I shall remember this day until I die,' which was similar to what Joseph had said. I gave him the change in my pocket. He brushed the snow off my greatcoat. With the back of his forefinger he flicked more off my eyebrows. 'Like a prince,' he said, straightening my lapels with fatherly solicitude, as Pushkin would have done for me had he lived. But I wouldn't let him touch Lizochka, though he obviously wished to. I gathered her up and on we went, east along Nevsky, towards Znamenskaya and thus Vladivostok. Now I gave her only little dabbing kisses and held her tighter so we didn't fall over again. Her eyes gleamed like coal. I laughed into them, I kissed the pointy tip of her nose and I glissaded my palm over her rump, which was tight and corky from our dancing.

Nothing could stop us. I had borrowed the god of good fortune from the giant one-legged robber. Even the militia cheered us. 'Bravo, bravo Natalie,' one shouted, clapping his gloved hands above his head, applauding Liza with the stage name of the immortal Goncharova, for whom three ballets altogether were written.

Down Nevsky we spun, her scarlet lace-up dancing shoes flicking through the corners of my vision like fireflies. Past the Gostiny Dvor, from which a shop assistant in a long black skirt ran out to gawk at us, still holding a silvered cake stand and a pair of pastry tongs. Past the Public Library and over the Fontanka. The entire street came to a halt. Cars pulled into the side, the cathedral bells stopped in mid-chime, horses ceased their shitting. A platoon of soldiers presented arms to us. A newspaper vendor started to cry 'Miracle on Nevsky! Miracle on Nevsky!' Otherwise, because we were dancing for the Orlov gold medal, we danced through silence except for the whiffle of my darling's red shoes across the dirty snow and the thunder of my boots.

We reached Znamenskaya. The horse-cabbies stared at us. I held her at arm's length.

'Oh, Charlinka, what you do to me . . . my poor heart, it's out of practice, there's so much it still has to learn.'

'Then it must learn quickly.'

'*Zhivo*, heart, *zhivo*. Get on with it down there.' That was what she said, giving her breast a couple of taps with her light fist.

I never was so satisfied with a woman, I mean from a practical sense, quite apart from all the crashings of our love. Smiling, we gazed upon each other.

Then Kobi called out to me.

A locomotive howled.

She was gone.

I looked down at my trembling fingers. I spread them before my eyes. Empty! No one! I threw back my head. Goodbye love! Goodbye sorrow! Goodbye Russia!